'ZOO EVENT ... imaginative plot ... There are enough gory shocks to keep the die-hard horror aficionados happy' *Samhain*

'The pacing of this novel is some of the best I've read in a long time. Beginning with a bout of suicides and seemingly isolated murders, Douglas weaves his own tapestry of Hell until the central characters are literally clawing their way through streets filled with corpses and characters that seem to have fallen out of a George A. Romero movie . . . so vividly descriptive as to give the reader an almost cinematic trip through his nightmare . . . it's that total immersion that gives Douglas's work the edge and kept me gripped throughout' *Moonlit Fables*

About the author

John Douglas was born in 1955. He graduated from Oxford University in 1976, since when he has worked on the creative side for various advertising agencies. His first three novels were published in hardcover by Hodder and Stoughton and in paperback by New English Library. He lives in Manchester with his wife and son.

Zoo Event

John Douglas

NEW ENGLISH LIBRARY
Hodder and Stoughton

Copyright © 1996 by John Douglas

First published in 1996 by Hodder and Stoughton

First published in paperback in 1997 by Hodder and Stoughton
A division of Hodder Headline PLC

A New English Library paperback

The right of John Douglas to be identified as the Author of
the Work has been asserted by him in accordance with the
Copyright, Designs and Patents Act 1988.

10 9 8 7 6 5 4 3 2 1

A CIP catalogue record for this book is available from the British Library

ISBN 0 340 66053 7

Printed and bound in Great Britain by
Cox & Wyman Ltd, Reading, Berkshire

Hodder and Stoughton
A division of Hodder Headline PLC
338 Euston Road
London NW1 3BH

**To everyone I know in the zoo event
that is Manchester advertising**

Time flies, death urges, knells call,
heaven invites, Hell threatens.

Edward Young, *Night Thoughts*

Part One

THE DARKENING

And when night
Darkens the streets, then wander forth the sons
Of Belial, flown with insolence and wine.

John Milton, *Paradise Lost*

1

MR FARMER

Mr Farmer had been annoying women. It was one of his less harmful hobbies. He had been sitting in a bus shelter outside Blair Town Hall, enjoying the heavy afternoon rain, Marmite sandwiches on his lap, bottle of banana milkshake by his side. Whenever an attractive woman came by he would leer at her and if she showed any reaction – a speeding up, a nervous glance – he would take it as his cue to speak. He tended to run to observations such as 'Nice tits' or 'Show us your knickers'. Sometimes the women would stand up for themselves, but as often as not they would simply walk on, their faces pictures of disgust. It was usually left to men to turf him out of his seat, often with threats of violence even though size was definitely on Mr Farmer's side, he being more than twice the weight of the average man. Whenever there was violence, Mr Farmer would simply smile and let them do as they wanted. After all, touching was what it was all about. Eventually, however, some uptight citizen had called the police and a constable arrived.

As the young policeman approached, Mr Farmer deposited the remains of his food in the litter bin next to his bench. He didn't know the policeman, and PC Bates 233 hadn't heard of Mr Farmer and his habits so he was placatory. But his patience was soon tested, not least because their dispute was drawing a crowd, mostly red-faced women anxious to see the fat man get his comeuppance. So, inevitably, the policeman ended up manhandling Mr Farmer to his patrol car.

And no easy task was it, getting the man's bulk into the confined space of the Rover Metro. But amid giggles from onlookers, the quart eventually filled the pint pot, the policeman got in and they set off for the police station.

'What will the charge be?' asked Mr Farmer.

'Disturbing the peace,' said the constable. 'You done this before?'

'Too often,' said Mr Farmer.

'Why, then?'

'When you get to my age, there's little left that amuses.'

'You think it's funny scaring women?'

'Constable, what on earth do those women think I could be capable of? They were insulted, not scared.'

'So why insult people you don't know?'

'You wouldn't understand.'

The policeman didn't pursue the conversation so they drove on in silence.

A couple of minutes later a message came through on the radio about a disturbance at Horton House: a man threatening to jump. PC Bates took the call, saying he was a minute from the scene.

'What about me?' said Mr Farmer as the car pulled into the kerb on High Street across the road from Horton House. The policeman wasn't sure what to do. Mr Farmer helped him.

'Look, young man,' said Mr Farmer, squashing his face up against the car's side window in order to see what people were looking at. 'What's happening here looks a lot more important than my misdemeanours. You have my address; your colleagues know me. When all this is over, simply come and pick me up. Better still, I'll report to the station myself. Save on transport.'

The young constable scratched his head, but renewed shouting from the foyer of the building distracted him.

'Okay,' he said. 'But if you land me in it . . .'

'No, not me,' said Mr Farmer. 'Help me out, will you?'

The policeman helped haul the sweating fat man out of the back of his Metro, the suspension rising in relief.

'Thank you,' said Mr Farmer, clasping the policeman's hand firmly. 'I shall report your sensible behaviour—'

'Don't bother,' said PC Bates, locking the car. Then he ran across the road between the slowing traffic to the crowd gathered on the steps of the office block.

Mr Farmer walked across the pavement and looked around. Soon there would be chaos, and he wanted a grandstand seat, but where?

He spotted a tea room on the first floor of Bentall's Department Store. Perfect.

By the time he had settled into a window seat with his coffee and éclair, the diners were just beginning to realize that something was amiss outside.

Traffic had ground to a halt, there was the sound of sirens and, despite the persistent rain, a growing crowd was milling about on the pavement, spilling out into the street and causing cars to honk their horns. Oblivious, all the pedestrians' heads were craned up to peer at the fifteenth floor of Horton House, the tallest office block in Blair.

Looking up, Mr Farmer could see a man silhouetted on the narrow ledge outside an office window one hundred and fifty feet directly above the entrance to the building, his feet dangling over the edge. There were several people in the office behind him.

Mr Farmer blew on his frothy coffee and took a careful sip. He hated burning his tongue. *Hmm, still too warm*. Instead he picked up his giant éclair and bit into it. The chocolate was crunchy rather than gooey and the choux pastry too rubbery but beggars couldn't be choosers. It was the view he was after, not the refreshments.

He settled back, savouring the cream – at least they didn't stint on that – and watched the figure on the ledge shuffle further away from the open window as, yes, the young policeman arrived to do his bit.

Mr Farmer edged his chair towards the window, the legs scraping on the tiling, and cast a frown at a woman trying to edge into his line of sight. She decided it wasn't worth arguing about and retreated elsewhere, no doubt to ruin someone else's view.

Several minutes passed as the policeman leaned out of the window and talked to the man on the ledge. Police cars, fire engines and ambulances had all arrived but were of little use. Either the man would be talked inside or he would take flight, and Mr Farmer had already made a bet with himself as to the outcome. And, sure enough, two minutes later, to gasps and screams that came from inside and outside the tea room, the sitting figure pushed himself into space and plunged to the street below, landing on an empty circle of pavement with a thud that could be felt even through the plate glass.

Bits of the man exploded on impact, spraying several bystanders with gore. The shrieking, not surprisingly, intensified, most of it led by women, but the hysteria wasn't confined to one sex. A man in a brown suit walked into the road and collapsed on his knees, hands clasped in prayer, wailing like a baby.

Mr Farmer smiled and sipped his coffee. Much cooler now. Perfect. The mayhem that erupted in the street was mirrored by the mania in the tea room, people shrieking and burbling and begging to God as they tried to appreciate that a fellow human being had taken, literally, the final plunge to end his existence – an act and a consequence impossible to comprehend unless you have ever touched the depths of despair that could prompt such an irrevocable decision. Women with children were particularly upset, shielding their babes' eyes as if there was about to be an action replay. If only they knew what Mr Farmer knew.

He looked up at the ledge. He could see the lone figure of young PC Bates by the window, the crowd in the room lined up slightly away from him, as if he had said something that had sent the man to his death. Which, of course, he had.

Mr Farmer drained his coffee cup and dabbed at flecks of pastry and cream on his plate with his forefinger and licked them off. Any moment now . . .

Screams and cries receded as people looked back up at the office block and saw another figure – the policeman – clamber over the low window ledge and stand upright looking down at them.

A hush suddenly descended on the crowd as effectively as if the volume had been turned down on a sound effects record. Mr Farmer smiled, chasing a piece of pastry around his teeth with his tongue.

And then the constable who, barely ten minutes before had arrested Mr Farmer, let himself fall forward and, in a slow arc, turned through 270° and landed with a crump that echoed around the packed but silent street. There was a long-drawn-out pause, as if what the crowd had just seen hadn't quite registered with them, and then bedlam.

Mr Farmer edged his bulky frame away from his table and pushed his way through the eager hypocrites who continued to stare at the gruesome sight across the street whilst simultaneously expressing their horror and outrage. *Ghouls*, thought Mr Farmer. *Gawping, ghastly ghouls*. He loved them.

There was little point in his remaining. He had started the chain and wouldn't be able to see it through to its conclusion. But no doubt he would be able to read about it in the newspaper tomorrow, for the policeman's self-destruction was not going to be the last inexplicable death in Blair that night.

2

MARK DAWSON

'What's the hold-up?' demanded Mark Dawson, storming into the Creative Department.

Everyone – two art directors, one visualizer and an Applemac operator – was at the window staring the ten floors down to the melee in High Street.

'Somebody jumped. *Two* people jumped,' said Annie the visualizer tearfully.

'What? Suicides?' said Mark.

'Well, they weren't taking flying lessons,' said Stan, one of the art directors.

'Very funny. So, what's the hold-up?'

'Hey, Mark, two people just died out there,' said Stan.

'Oh, they died out *there*. Sorry. I thought you meant they'd died on your prod lay so George couldn't work it up on the Mac.'

'You callous fucker,' said George.

'The presentation is tomorrow at 9 a.m. If you want to work into the small hours, feel free. But I don't! I'm sick of hanging around waiting for you tossers to finish. Now get to it.'

No one moved.

'Please,' said Mark. It was a standing joke. Since Mark had set up his own advertising agency he had been working on a nervous breakdown, his manners a dim memory.

Slowly they went back to their desks and resumed work, while Mark guiltily edged his way to the rain-spotted window to look down. True enough, there were two bodies on the pavement surrounded by police and ambulance personnel. *Bloody hell.* He wondered who it was but realized he didn't know anyone else in the building. Dawson Creative Associates had only been renting its half floor of offices for four months. He wouldn't even recognise the doorman.

He caught sight of his reflection in the window. His face was white, and it wasn't shock. God, he felt tired. Then he saw the others' reflections, everyone looking at him. He spun round but suddenly they were all looking down at their work.

'Sorry,' he mumbled walking out.

He caught sight of Annie making to rise but thinking better of it. He knew she had a crush on him but he had no intention of taking advantage of it, despite his problems at home. And those problems were, at that moment, nothing compared to his problems with the fledgling DCA. Not least their promotional campaign for Eclipse Petroleum.

Three hundred sites throughout the North, a need to increase forecourt sales by four per cent over the next year, and ideas wanted for goodies to give away and, just as important, advertising that would attract motorists. It didn't help that they'd had their first lot of work rejected; that the client had an aversion to green – this despite his corporate colours being green and red – and that it was all speculative: they only got paid if they won the account. It was a three-way pitch and the rumour was that it was all an exercise to put the wind up their existing agency. So far the creative costs were approaching eight thousand pounds and rising – a hefty whack when DCA's current billing was only nudging half a million, and two-thirds of that was the Kleenspray account. Mark sometimes wondered why he had ever taken the plunge and set up on his own: he'd not only dropped himself, his wife and his colleagues in at the deep end but, as he was coming to realize, none of them were very good at swimming. Still, if it all panned out, he might be out of hock to the bank in five years. So the intrusion of someone else's business problems and their drastic remedy was a distraction, nothing more. Besides, he pondered as he fixed himself his eighth black coffee of the day, the attraction of taking the quickest way to the basement car park was fast becoming too appealing.

He slammed the door of his office and plonked himself behind his word processor and carried on with his report. One of his economies had been to dispense with a typist; stupid move. Not having Spellcheck was another. They were going to be at it most

of the night. He amended *committment* for the fifth time and
laser-printed what he had managed to complete so far.

After half an hour there was a knock on the door and Stan poked
his head round the door. He looked thinner than ever, his straggly
beard an object of neglect. It wasn't fair for Mark to pick on them
the way he did but if they didn't deliver they would all be signing
on the dole.

'Yes?' said Mark, running his hands through his hair. It was
greasy. He would have to remember to wash it tonight, and dig
out his suit for the presentation.

'Problem,' said Stan.

Oh shit. When Stan said there was a problem, he meant just that.
The man had survived car crashes, muggings and pneumonia and
come into work without letting on, but if he said something was
up, it was time to take a deep breath.

'Tell me the worst,' said Mark, swinging his chair round to look
out at the rain-lashed Blair skyline, the blue of police lights flashing
like lightning on glass across the street.

'The trannies for the presentation. They're downstairs.'

'The courier's finally got here?'

'Sort of.'

'Sort of what?'

'One of the blokes who went out the window sort of landed
on them.'

'Sort of?'

'The courier dropped the package when the police moved him
out of the way and before he could pick them up . . .'

'So they're . . .?'

'Covered in blood and stuff . . . and the police won't let him
have them back. Evidence, apparently.'

'Evidence? It's our fucking futures. There's no chance they can
be persuaded?'

'Tried. No go. As this copper told me, one of their boys is dead
so they're not going to give a toss about some poxy ads.'

'A cop? Shit. What about the negs?'

'With them. Remember, you told the studio to send them—'

'— because we didn't want them impounded until we paid them.
Anything on disc?'

'No. We haven't got the shots so we haven't been able to scan
them yet.'

'Obviously. Any chance of shooting—'

'Paul's off to the Lakes for a truck shoot. Client wanted the product back straight away.'

'And they've got it.'

'Yes. We could always go back to visuals . . .'

Mark didn't bother to explain that the client had demanded photographs in the layouts and expected an agency to deliver what was promised without any cock-ups or excuses. He stood up, leaned his head against the cold window and looked down at the lucky bastards splattered on the pavement, police photographing them while an ambulance edged through the crowd.

'How do you open these bloody windows?' he said.

Stan didn't laugh.

'It's a joke, Stan,' he finally explained.

'Not funny.'

'For me or those two?'

Stan didn't answer.

'Give us five minutes. I'll call Marchant.'

Stan went to break the bad news.

Mr Marchant, marketing manager of Eclipse Petroleum was, of course, as sarcastic as ever. Even when Mark explained the unusual circumstances, the man sighed like a school-teacher hearing a third former's excuse for being late.

'If we could just have the gear back, take the shots again . . .' Mark gave up. He had never liked Marchant and a little voice inside his head couldn't help cheering at the prospect of not having to meet the jumped-up rep again.

'Mr Dawson, when you asked to pitch for—'

'Fuck it.'

'Pardon?'

'Fuck it,' said Mark. 'You weren't going to give us the account anyway and if it takes two suicides to stop us presenting the best work we've ever done – work that you're just going to dismiss with snide remarks about the size of the tits on the girl we use on the poster – then I give up.'

They slammed their phones down together. *Sod it*.

Mark marched into the Creative Department, broke the bad news and apologized.

'Let's call it a day. Go home, get pissed, pray. I'll see you tomorrow.'

'You sure we can't . . .' asked Annie.

'No, love,' he said. 'Those two downstairs have more chance of picking up this account than us. Sorry.'

But this time they laughed. They had to: unemployment beckoned. There was a limit to how long they could survive on half-salary and the odd freelance job. There would come a day when they would have to tell Mark to forget his job – and Mark knew it, and suspected he might beat them to it.

He went back to his office, grabbed the Haig from his top drawer and swigged a hearty gulp, then put it away. It was as much a punishment as an escape, the hot liquid making him feel even sicker than he was. *What a fucking business*. The shame of it was, he loved it.

3

DR WESLEY LAMBERT

Dr Wesley Lambert woke with a start. There was a noise, outside the window. He forced himself to roll over. Yes, there was definitely a figure outside his bedroom window. He reached over to the bedside table, picked up a book and hurled it at the shape.

The book buried itself in the heavy floral curtains, but maintained sufficient momentum to bang against the glass. There was a cry of surprise and then a metallic clatter and an oath. A bucket? The window cleaner!

Lambert smiled. He looked at his clock. 4:15. Must be afternoon. Late-night reading was screwing up his timing. He threw back the covers and checked his catheter. His night legbag was full to bursting; he'd better get to the loo. He had also leaked from his arse. Mrs Dibbs would have to deal with the soiled bedding.

He hauled his spindly legs over the side of the bed then, hanging onto the rail, edged his motorized wheelchair into position, shuffled his bottom onto the plastic-covered seat and hefted his legs into their stirrups. He flicked the motor on and headed for the bathroom.

Fifteen minutes later he had changed his bag and washed away the shit from his backside and legs with the high-powered shower head. He would let Mrs Dibbs put his nappy on when she turned up. He cleaned his teeth but didn't shave; he had never been very hirsute so his beard looked half-finished. A bit like his body, he reflected bitterly.

He drove out onto the landing, slotted the chair into the electric stair traveller and waited as it slowly carried him downstairs. Living on the ground floor might have been easier – he had more than enough money to pay for any necessary conversions – but as long as life was a struggle, it meant he was still alive. Driving off the platform he went into the kitchen and made some coffee. He debated whether to have some cereal but, following his life-long maxim – *If in doubt, don't* – he decided he could do without it.

While the kettle boiled he collected his post and newspapers from the doormat using the hand-operated mechanical grab strapped to the side of his wheelchair.

Nothing of consequence, other than an invitation, complete with air tickets, to attend one of Max's conferences in Denver. It was a month away. That would make it a week before his fifty-third birthday. A treat or a chore? He'd had twenty years to get used to the problems of international travel in a wheelchair, but half the fun of conferences was what you did outside the hall. All that ever seemed to happen to him was an endless succession of dinner parties where he was expected to hold forth on his subjects – and strapped to a bloody wheelchair he wasn't exactly equipped for a rapid escape. Getting a hooker could also be awkward, especially as organizers almost always insisted he stay with them rather than in some hotel and the wives would follow him round as if he were some straggling duckling. He knew from experience it was as much out of pity as a desire to get closer to him – in all senses of the word. And some wives were very tempting in their veiled hints, but again, escape would have been impossible; it simply wasn't worth the risk. He had long gone through his drunken bitter stage – some friendships hadn't survived that era – but now he just wanted peace. So, Denver? Beautiful Colorado scenery but a long flight. Interesting company but a boring host. He'd have to think about it, though he did have that publishing deadline. No, he would probably have to send the tickets back. Now, if it had been Vegas . . .

Coffee made, he scanned the *Daily Telegraph*. The usual load of bollocks. One war ends, another breaks out. Government going back on promises; opposition going back on policy; a film star dead of a drug overdose; a plane crash on a Belgian housing estate kills a hundred. He looked at the ads; they said more about his fellow humans than the events they conspired to call news. The only interesting one was for a limited edition Astra. His Nissan Sunny was a couple of years old now and he fancied a new model. Should get a good trade-in – he'd only driven about four thousand miles, after all, but the colour was getting on his nerves. Ah, the indulgence a steady income allows. There was a time he would have been disgusted with himself for thinking in such a way but where had being right ever got him? Well, in a wheelchair with pork scratchings for legs for a start.

He stared down at the thin members hiding under his towel. Maybe Mr Carter was right; having them amputated would make things easier. Cut off just above the knees he would be much more mobile; the number of times they had caught on something and forced him to fall. There was that time one of them had got wrapped up in bed and the only way he was able to get out was to cut the bloody sheet with some clippers. But, then again, they were there, they were him; checking into a hospital room in the knowledge that they were going to be hacked off like some unwanted cuts of meat . . . that was a hell of a step – no pun intended, he thought – whatever the eventual advantages.

He binned the *Telegraph* and picked up the *Daily Express*. He liked to get a balanced view of the news – as long as it was a balance provided by the Tory press. Same stories, only shorter. He switched on the radio and let himself drift with the classical music, only to have his pleasure interrupted by the news. He was about to switch it off when he heard that a millionaire called Eldred Horton had committed suicide in Blair. Something about the story intrigued him but he wasn't sure. Did he know a Horton?

As he whirred through the hallway Mrs Dibbs came in, slamming the door behind as she always did. As Lambert always did, he asked her if she had to slam it every time and she, as ever, said at least they both knew it was shut and then he would say yes and so does the whole street and she would say good they know you're not out frightening the children. He would then laugh and they would discuss local gossip. There were days when he would sit behind the net curtains just staring at the comings and goings on the street and he liked to know everything about everybody. He called them his human days; otherwise he was locked in his study most of his working hours, or up at the University library researching. There was no woman in Lambert's life. He hated fuss, and any woman who would put up with him was bound to fuss, so he contented himself with the company of his colleagues outside his home and, when the mood took him, the company of a professional young lady called Catherine and her specialist 'massage' skills.

After Mrs Dibbs – a barrel of a woman in her fifties with the

face of a footballer, so no temptation there – had cleaned him up
again, dried him, talced him, put on his nappy and helped ease
on his Manchester City shellsuit bottom, she had adjourned to the
kitchen to do his laundry, He whirred his wheelchair into his study
and switched on his Compaq. He was still curious about the story
on the radio, but decided to let it ferment in the back of his mind
while he completed his short article for *Fortean Times*.

The connection between UFO abduction stories and suddenly
remembered details of suppressed childhood abuse was so obvious
he wondered how he could write it without his scorn coming
through. However, despite his professed contempt for most things
occult, he did believe in the inexplicable nature of certain events.
Had he known just how close he was to encountering one himself,
he might have wished his interests lay in more mundane topics,
such as baking or embroidery.

4

MR FARMER AT HOME

Mr Farmer settled himself at his kitchen table, scissors and paste to hand. The lift hadn't been working and it had been an effort to walk the four flights down to the newsagent on the corner, particularly as the little urchins were there to insult him. Sad how standards had declined over the years but what did he care if the little beggars grew up unemployed and disaffected? More grist to his mill, wasn't it? Indeed, some of the little tykes who called him Mr Elephant could well be doing him some favour five years from now. Then they would regret their insults. Besides, he couldn't help having a glandular problem.

He opened his second can of rice pudding and wolfed it down. Just a snack before dinner. He checked the greasy clock above the cooker. 5:45pm. *Long* time to dinner. Good thing he'd got a loaf as well.

He had bought the evening paper, and several magazines, much to the delight of Mr Patel who could do with the business. They'd had quite a pleasant chat, Mr Patel bemoaning the appalling weather, the lack of respect youngsters had for all elders and the racial harassment he had to endure after some lout had called him a 'Paki cunt' to his face and run off without paying for his Sherbet Dab. Mr Farmer had agreed that things were not as they had been and that what was needed was a sense of discipline. Mr Patel was so pleased to find a kindred spirit in the moral wasteland that was the Catchmount Estate that he insisted on shaking Mr Farmer's hand and giving him a free bar of chocolate. Mr Farmer wished the newsagent hadn't shaken his hand – as Mr Patel probably would too at some point in the not-too-distant future – but he was grateful for the Twix. They really were kindred spirits, he thought as he walked back through the rain. Both outcasts, victimized and taunted and both simply wanting to get on with their lives. At least Mr Farmer had an edge; poor Mr Patel could only look to a future where everything would get worse.

The evening newspaper covered the suicide of Mr Horton and the 'sad' death of the policeman but hadn't had time to go into detail. Didn't matter anyway – their puny minds would be unable to comprehend what had really happened – and for that he had to admit he was grateful because, if they ever did, the fun would end.

He snipped the story out and pasted it into his scrapbook. Volume three now. A good few tales it would tell, though he would never share his story with anyone. Pity that, but everybody has to make sacrifices. He closed the scrapbook and pulled open the thick-slice Mother's Pride. *Hmmm, toast.* While it was grilling, he went into his lounge and looked outside.

It was still raining, another miserable day. Lovely. He looked at the people scampering out of the drizzle in the bleak streets. Mothers with prams, layabouts sheltering in shop doorways, the drug dealers chatting to youngsters on mountain bikes. What a pathetic advertisement for humanity – he'd buy it!

Mr Farmer smelled burning and waddled back to his toast. As he slapped on the Lurpak he wondered if he should go to the police station or let them come for him. Chances were they wouldn't bother, not with PC 233 Bates all over the pavement. No, leave it. If they did turn up sometime, he'd just say he'd been ill. They might sneer at his build but they'd accept his excuse. Besides, bad language isn't exactly a capital offence. Two rounds downed, he grilled two more slices and boiled some milk for a hot chocolate. So, what would he do tonight?

Truth of it was, today's event had tired Mr Farmer out. The policeman had been a fit young man, few problems, high hopes, a rewarding career ahead of him. Planting the seed of doubt had taken its toll. More toast and a cursory glance in the fridge. Ham? Chicken? Cheese? Sod it, he'd have all three. The big question was, of course, what to do next? He hadn't really planned today but it was satisfying for all that and he wanted to build on it. Spread a little terror. It gave him a warm feeling inside to know that people he passed in the streets were hurrying home because of something

he might have done. To hear the women gossiping in the bakers, in
the Co-op, on the bus . . . he could feel their fear despite their tough
words. There had been a time when he had believed naively that
what he did would actually liven up their grey existences; that a little
unfathomable fear would put a spark into their daily round of fatty
foods, fags and cheap booze. But life was so tough for them, and
their vision so stunted by the daily grind, that the fates he inflicted
on their weaker compatriots, instead of offering some amusement,
had them huddling by the school gates. He considered what he saw
every morning and afternoon at St Gabriel's School gates.

Normally one in ten children had been met by a parent. Now it
was over half. The cynic in him had decided that most of the parents
weren't so much worried about the security of their children as about
the reaction of others to their lack of concern should they not collect
them. Still, fear was fear. He could smell it in the air like the scent
of rotten fruit. Delicious. How he loved to see his people squirm.

He settled in his Parker Knoll armchair by the window – his only
luxury – toasted sandwiches to hand, and popped the top on a can
of Diet Coke. See, he drank diet drinks, took no sugar in his tea,
so how could he be fat? Glands, he was cursed with glands.

There was a screech of tyres in the street and he leaned forward
to look. A boy had been hit by a car, his bike a tangle in the middle
of the road. Mr Farmer opened his window to catch the screams, but
the boy was standing up holding his scraped knee. Damn, nothing
serious, but the boy's mother was giving the driver some grief, her
shock translated into basest Anglo-Saxon which he could discern
even above the rain. Disappointed, he closed the window and sat
back, allowing his belly to subside, and stared at the stormy sky.

For some reason Mr Farmer couldn't understand he suddenly
felt very happy; even happier than today's little adventure should
have allowed. Over the years his twisting had become increasingly
sophisticated, opening up whole new areas of despair but, really, it
was all much of a muchness. Like sex, he supposed, though that
particular activity had never held much interest for him. However
often and however many different ways one copulated, at the end
it all came down to that brief ejaculation, the pricking of the bubble
and the calm after the storm. For all the wild abandon of the vinegar
strokes, it always felt the same, did it not? The same old ins and
outs? Boring. But like sex, that old urge would eventually well up
and have to be satisfied, and so he would venture into the world

outside and touch some innocent's heart – and some not so innocent, thank heaven. And, again like sex, the difference between the two was as wide as that between a virgin and an experienced harlot. So why the excitement? Today had been little different, but there was an undeniable undercurrent of warmth. Odd.

He looked out at the clouds scudding across above the tower blocks. What was it? The weather? The recession? The misery that rose up around him, apartment upon apartment, block-high and family-wide? No, they were always there, nothing had changed, so what? Something was coming, wasn't it? That was it: something terrible was reaching out for Blair. Something dreadful. Mr Farmer shivered at the thought and found he had an erection. Long time since that had happened; maybe something beautifully evil *was* coming but, even if it wasn't, he could dream, couldn't he?

5

MARK DAWSON AT HOME

Getting out of Horton House proved frustrating for Mark. No one was allowed out through the lobby, yet it contained the only entrance within the building to the basement car park. Mark had to leave by the rear exit, then walk round the building through the crowds and down the ramp to the car park, explaining not to one, not to two but to *four* different policemen what he was doing. By the last policeman Mark's temper exploded and he very nearly got himself arrested. But, aware that his anger was not really aimed at the policemen and their duty but at his own business problems, he calmed down and apologized and was allowed to collect his BMW 320i and drive home.

Home. Interesting word. It was supposed to conjure up cosy images of a dog yapping a friendly hallo; kids watching TV as they scoffed sandwiches; someone there to greet you with a peck on the cheek and a smile. What home wasn't, however, was Mark's flat.

The gas central heating had broken down and his wife had been away for two days. Not her fault, it was her job, but her absence and his late working and the bare state of their abode – they'd moved in six months before and still hadn't unpacked anything other than essentials – made it less welcoming than a motel room.

He dumped his artbag on the sofa and checked the fridge. As empty as ever. Neither of them were particularly domesticated: children of the Eighties – and about time they grew up. He'd have to dial up another pizza. He picked up an old Gino's Pizza box from the swingbin for the number, but decided a wash took priority. He stripped off and ran a shower, the only warm place in the apartment, and stood soaking in the hot rain for five minutes, letting his mind settle.

Going into business for himself had always been his dream, ever since he started copywriting eleven years before. His father's death and the money he had left, together with the money Mark and Karen had raised selling their house in Manchester, had given Mark the chance to set up his own agency in Blair, near to the one account he could count on taking with him, Kleenspray. Karen had been happy to make the move, pleased for his ambition and hopeful he would make a go of it. As a commercial artist she wasn't tied to any locale and they were only an hour from her main contacts in Manchester. She had recently moved into book illustration so there was even less need for her to be based in the city. However, this illustrating did at present take her away every other week for a couple of days as she was working with a children's writer in Bristol. She would do her drawings, take them down by train for approval and then make amendments there and then. It was an arrangement that worked well, but it did put a strain on their relationship when combined with Mark's habitual late-night working. Karen was due back the next day, but then she had to go on to Manchester to an agency, which would involve making an evening of it – her contact was an old agency colleague and girls would be girls.

He towelled off, wrapped himself in both of their dressing gowns and sat down in front of the TV, gin and tonic in one hand, pizza menu in the other.

Oh, fuck it, Mark thought as Des O'Connor came on. Instead he got dressed, downed the drink, then walked to the local wine bar. He didn't like getting drunk on his own, but then he didn't like blowing out an account either. Pretty soon he might not be able to afford the price of a pint, let alone a decent bottle of Niersteiner, so he might as well indulge while he could.

He had been in Cobblers for half an hour – an old shop tarted up with brown brick, barrels and Edwardian bric-à-brac and boasting an atmosphere every bit as authentic – and had almost downed a full bottle, when a woman walked in. She was over forty, ten years older than Mark, and attractive in a big-boned way, her hair too red to be natural but still stylish. She was dressed in a tight burgundy suit that emphasized her curves and an expensive-looking black over-coat. She went up to the bar and ordered a half-bottle of house red. She then turned and looked for somewhere to sit, aware that most men were watching her – and not a few women. She spotted Mr Misery on his own by the yuccas and nodded a query. Mark nodded back. If he was to have company, better an attractive woman than a half-cut salesman with a thing for Vauxhall Vectras.

Exactly eighty-five minutes later the woman was leaning over his kitchen table, her dress rucked up to her waist, her panties and tights around her ankles, her generous buttocks quivering as he pumped his erection between her shaven labia. She had told him she liked angry sex and, despite the alcohol, Mark was in a very obliging mood.

He leaned over her, his hands squeezing her breasts underneath her bra, his mouth offering her glowing ears a stream of obscenities detailing what he was doing and what he was going to do after he had come in her. Only when she shuddered her orgasm did he let himself go and, holding hard to her hips, fill her.

As he slowly pulled out, the air in the kitchen plumed with their rapid breathing, she turned and kissed him, her lipstick smeared across her cheek, her hair lank with sweat, and forced his hand to her cunt to feel what he had left in her. As he caressed her dampness, he kissed her again and again, telling her how much he loved her.

'And there I was wondering if you ever really missed me,' said Karen, his wife.

Settled after their unusually desperate bout of intercourse – it had been six days since the last time – they retired to the snuggly comfort of their bed.

'I've screwed up the Eclipse account,' he said. 'Told Marchant to go fuck himself.' He explained what had happened.

Karen didn't know what to say. She had met Marchant once and had disliked him on sight, but she knew Mark had to put up with people like him if he wanted their business. After all, as they had tried to convince each other over the years when they'd had to deal with some pig-ignorant client: it's the product you're working for, not the marketing manager. One day he'll go, but the product will still be there and still need good advertising.

'So what's the *bad* news?' she finally said, nuzzling into his shoulder.

'I've heard a rumour Pete's thinking of moving.'

'Oh shit, I was joking,' she said.

Mark smiled and hugged her. Pete Dimbleby was the marketing man at Kleenspray, the reason they kept the account. Yes, the work they did was good and sales were steady, even for a recession, but it was the way of marketing that people had their favourites. Whilst it was possible a new man would stick by Dawson Creative Associates, there was every chance he would bring in his own agency. And while Pete might be able to give Mark his new account, there were no cast-iron guarantees.

'What does Pete say?'

'He's in London. Out of reach.'

'So what would that leave?'

'The receivers. We've got maybe fifty grand's worth of business, most of it paid up. I'd have to let the office go, most of the team . . . we'd be seriously fucked. So, how's your day been?'

'Good. I finished *The Fish that Could Fly*; now Marjorie wants me to do *The Cat that Could Cook* and the *The Dog that Could Drive*.'

'That's great! When do you get to do *The Aardvark That Could Advertise*?'

'Funny. No, those two, plus some other work Susan promised me – some children's guide to animals – and I should be busy for the next six months; no need to take any ad work.'

'Good. I'm glad.'

'We'll survive.'

He caressed her nipple, ducking occasionally to tease it with his tongue. 'I know we could survive on your money and I don't feel guilty at all about sponging off my older, wealthier wife, but if the agency goes, there's Stan and the others to—'

'They knew what they were getting into, Mark. They were all freelance, they can always go back to it.'

'You're all heart.'

She grabbed his balls. 'They're in it because they hoped there'd be money in it. You're the one who put up the cash, not them; they just changed their employer. You've done your best, so no guilt.'

'Yes, dear,' he agreed keenly. 'Whatever you say, dear.'

She let go and he bit her breast. 'Rent's due in a month on the office. If I quit next week I don't have to pay it; but then there's the suppliers, rented gear, the acountants. We owe a good twenty-five grand, to say nothing of getting another job.'

'We can cover it if we have to. And getting a job's no problem.'

'By spending all our savings? I really like that idea. Besides, I don't want to go back to shovelling shit for others.'

'Well, look where shovelling your own's got you, dearest. Come on, you gave it a go, don't feel so guilty.'

'You're taking this rather easy, aren't you?'

'Post-orgasmic bliss, sweetie.' She ruffled his hair. 'Look, it's just you've always said the business wasn't worth losing sleep over. "It's a job, not a way of life," you said. "Leave that to the creative tossers in the hot shops", you said.'

'You never thought I'd make it did you?'

'Uh-oh, here we go.' She got up and walked to the door, her white flesh goose-pimpled by the cold.

'Don't go, Karen! I didn't mean—'

'I need a pee, don't panic.'

He slumped back and stared at the ceiling. It needed decorating. He heard her long stream splashing in the toilet bowl. If it had been warmer he might have got up to have a look . . . She came back and slipped in beside him, her coldness making him shiver.

'What I said – as you bloody well know – was you had to do it otherwise you'd always regret not trying,' she said. 'And you had to do it before you were too old not to be able to afford to screw it up – which is what you seem to be doing. Is it your fault Pete's got a career? No. Is it your fault some suicide jumped on your shots? No. Is it your fault Marchant is a total arsehole?'

'No,' he said in his small boy voice. He was feeling pathetic and horny and, if he played his cards right, he would be able to make capital out of both.

He slowly slipped down into the bed until his head was level with Karen's lolling breast. The funny thing was, now that unemployment and disaster seemed virtually inevitable, it didn't seem a problem. He knew full well he could get a job tomorrow in any one of half-a-dozen agencies in Manchester or Leeds. He knew the debts that would accrue from DCA going down were ultimately manageable and that most people would accept his failure for the bad luck it was and not incompetence. Yes, they'd survive; he'd given it a go and that was what counted. He edged towards her nipple, his tongue running over the roughness of her dusky areola. What it all came down to, really, was that he didn't have the gut fortitude of a fighter, or a true businessman.

Instead of going down with all guns blazing, he was just going to shut up shop, tell everyone he was sorry, and look on it as an idea that hadn't come off. He'd still do good work, still earn a decent whack; it just wouldn't be him signing the cheques. Did it really matter that much when, whatever he did at work and for whoever he did it, all he wanted was to come home, get under the covers, and hold his precious wife?

He took her teat gently into his mouth and began to nibble, pleased that she didn't stop him. Indeed, she held her breast out to him with one hand and felt for his already rising cock with her other. Sex and love: they always put things into perspective. Of course, he wouldn't feel the same tomorrow; that's when the shit would hit the fan and the metaphors would really start flying, but until then, he had warmth and flesh and desire and love and his gorgeous wife. And those nipples . . .

6

MR FARMER AND THE SOLDIER

Mr Farmer had ventured to the local pub, the Lamb and Flag. He disliked alcohol – it fuzzed his mind and his mind was where he lived – but he knew he had to be there. Over the last couple of days a feeling of inexplicable joy had been growing in him, a warmth that coursed through his body as surely as if his central heating had been turned up. And then, this evening, dozing after sending the policeman to his death, he had woken up with an image in his mind of a young man standing at a bar ordering a drink, his life an empty hollow waiting to be filled with purpose. A purpose Mr Farmer could deliver with a look, a word, a touch.

So sure was he that what he had seen was not a dream or a wish but a premonition that he had resolved to visit the pub that very evening.

It was a little after nine o'clock that he walked through the door to the usual sniggers and looks. The Lamb and Flag was a modern open-plan pub, little more than a room for inebriates – and all newcomers entered in plain view. He was aware his weight caused amusement but he had long got used to it. Besides, words meant nothing, as some had found to their cost in the past. He reached the bar and ordered a Diet Pepsi. The landlord struggled to avoid making a comment and instead tilled Mr Farmer's seventy pence and returned to his *Sun*.

Keeping his back to the other drinkers Mr Farmer supped his drink and waited, soaking in the smoke-laden atmosphere and the smell of beer. A jukebox played a muffled tune in the corner, no one listening. It was a place for the depressed and dispossessed to

try and forget why they were in there in the first place. It was sad –
and as pleasurable to Mr Farmer as the fug of a warm kitchen with
its smell of sauces and frying food. If only they would leave him
be he would spend more time imbibing its delicious atmosphere of
decay, but there was always some failure seeking an outlet for his
inarticulate rage and the fat man in the second-hand clothes was
an obvious target. Too many times he'd had to endure abuse, and
too often the threat of violence had hovered in the air like the smoke
from the cheap cigarettes that seemed compulsory for all customers
of such public houses. Nonetheless, Mr Farmer felt light-headed,
as if he had indeed ordered alcohol. Joy pulsed in his veins like
adrenalin at a cock-fight rushing through a spectator's system. Soon,
so soon, the boy would come in and they would connect and . . .

He was there! On the other side of the bar, drinking cider. Twenty
or so, short dark hair, a bland tight face, tall. A soldier, had to be.
He was dressed in a black sweatshirt and jeans, his eyes downcast,
avoiding everyone. Mr Farmer could *smell* his contempt. The boy
hated everyone, even people he hadn't met. Chances were he would
hate him even more, his fatness, his sweat, his clothes . . . Mr
Farmer found he was hard again, just thinking of the scabrous
pit that had become the boy's mind. Oh, how he would wallow
in it . . .

He finished his own drink and worked his way round the bar until
he stood next to the lad. The young man had a tattoo on his wrist, a
regimental badge of some sort. Army.

'Want another drink?' said Mr Farmer, aware that the landlord
was watching him, the smallest of smiles playing on his lips. Mine
host was expecting trouble and was going to enjoy watching the
lad's reaction to what he clearly thought was a gay fat man trying
to pick up a bit of rough.

The soldier turned to look at his inquisitor, his face falling from
blank indifference to utter disgust in one smooth movement. Mr
Farmer was beside himself with anticipation.

'What the fuck did you say, you fat wanker?'

Mr Farmer edged his hand onto the counter. 'I offered you a
drink. Cider, is it?'

The bar was silent. Mr Farmer was acutely aware of his slight lisp.
He could see the boy's bottom lip quivering with suppressed range.
Oh God, his cock felt *so* hard. The boy was a positive *volcano* of
suppressed anger.

'I said, do you want another pint?' he repeated.

The boy let go his glass, clenched his fist and slammed it on the bar top. 'Fuck off, fatso!'

All drinking stopped, only the jukebox making any noise. Mr Farmer reached out and touched the soldier's rough knuckles. He actually felt a jolt as the boy's rage electrified his senses. Mr Farmer could see his other fist rising to strike him, and heard a collective intake of breath from the half-dozen drinkers behind him. He looked into the boy's eyes and squeezed his hand and as he ejaculated for the first time in weeks, his jowls betraying his pleasure, the boy stopped as if frozen, staring back, letting the man invade his thoughts. Then he slowly lowered his fist and nodded.

Mr Farmer didn't need to say any more. He let go of the boy's hand and turned to walk out, but a punk kicked a chair into his path.

'Where you girls going, then? Bog's out back.'

Mr Farmer smiled and shook his head and walked on.

The purple-haired punk stood up, his eyes glazed from drink and drugs, his breath oniony. 'You ain't going anywhere, you tub of—'

He was on the floor, his nose broken, blood smeared across his face before his sentence was finished. Mr Farmer smiled indulgently at the soldier . . . told him to put the bottle down. They left in stunned silence.

Ten minutes later they were in Mr Farmer's bedroom, the boy naked and humping a pillow as Mr Farmer sat in the corner, fully clothed, telling him what he was going to do. The boy's mind was so fertile Mr Farmer had only to point him in the right direction and he was as primed and ready for action as the rifle he said he had back in his bedsit.

Later, when Mr Farmer was sure the twisting was ingrained in the boy's mind, he let him indulge his physical needs, despite the pain. If the boy held true to his desires, then it was a more than just trade. Because the pleasure his final actions would bring Mr Farmer was *so* much greater than the boy's pathetic need to abuse another man's body.

7

LAMBERT'S ZOO EVENT

Sitting bathed in the blue glow from his computer screen, Wesley Lambert felt calm and relaxed despite having spent most of the last two hours answering correspondence. He was growing tired of indulging every crackpot who considered him a kindred spirit. The last straw tonight had been a letter from a man in Aberdeen who claimed that his recent confinement in a wheelchair was not caused by the multiple sclerosis diagnosed by his doctors, but was due to repeated visits by aliens who were 'sapping my strength limb by limb'. Lambert had every sympathy for people faced with crippling diseases going through denial – hadn't he done enough of that himself in the late Seventies? – but he had little time for lunacy. If only they would channel their minds into making the most of what they had rather than finding someone or something to blame, they would be so much more at peace.

He leaned back and rubbed his eyes. Enough was enough; time to get back to the real work. He switched out of his LETTER file and pondered whether to complete his article for *Fortean Times* or review his latest batch of newspaper and magazine clippings. The clippings won, and the very first one set his mind wandering. It was about car crashes. Lambert's interest in the oddities of the natural world had started with the car crash that had killed his wife and made him a paraplegic.

It had been a bright autumn afternoon in 1976, the weather was fine, cloud cover altostratus, a light breeze, the road dry. He was travelling through Cheshire to visit an old college friend who was celebrating a posting to an American college. He was driving his

Vauxhall Cresta at forty-five miles an hour, the radio-cassette playing Johnny Mathis – his wife's choice – and they were discussing what to do at Christmas. He was happy in his job as a statistician attached to the University, as was his wife in hers – she was an accountant – and they were even thinking of having their long-delayed family, both of them in their mid-thirties and, until then, more interested in careers than caring for children.

And then the three-hundred-pound block of ice fell out of the sky three metres in front of their car, exploding on impact with the force of a small bomb, shattering the windscreen and causing Lambert to slam on the brakes. But hitting the smashed ice spun the car across the road where it hit the verge, bounced off and slammed sideways into a farm gatepost on his wife's side of the car, killing her instantly, then whipping round until it dived nose-first into a ditch by the road, throwing him through the windscreen.

Things were vague after that, until the day almost a week later when he came out of his coma to be informed that he had lost the use of his legs and his wife had died. (In his bitter moments, he had always wondered how they had decided on the order in which to break that double whammy.)

A savage self-imposed course of physiotherapy led to his leaving hospital two months later to embark on an obsessive investigation into the source of the ice – for which there was no evidence other than a small dent in the tarmac.

Lambert pursued airports, airlines and the RAF in an attempt to find out if anything had been flying overhead at the time, determined to discover if it was simply ice dislodged from an aircraft wing or fuselage, or if it had been the contents of an aircraft's toilet. But nothing came of it.

Accident and insurance policies on both him and his wife left Lambert relatively well off but obviously money was not the issue. His insistence on the ice-block being the cause of the accident – rather than his falling asleep or swerving to avoid an animal – was seen as a desperate need for denial of culpability, and the hostility it aroused made him even more bitter about his wife's death and his own paralysis. He was prepared to accept that what had happened was a fluke: all he wanted was acknowledgement of the facts. But he could never prove his case.

The final straw came when a letter in a local newspaper complained about the amount of space given to his insistence on the 'giant ice cube mystery'. Lambert had wheeled himself around to the letter writer's home in the early hours and, armed with a bag of marbles, had smashed as many of the man's windows as he could before being forcibly stopped. The court case and subsequent publicity did him no good and he was asked to give up his academic post.

However, he had always been astute at the politics required in university life and had used his inside knowledge – the vice-chancellor's vices, a personal tutor's personal habits – to ensure that he was allowed continued and unrestricted access to university libraries and computer facilities in perpetuity. This, and a private income that would support his limited lifestyle, allowed Lambert to dedicate himself to investigating the provenance of all manner of 'zoo events': natural phenomena for which there are, as yet, no proven scientific explanations.

Early ambitions to prove disputed theories in all fields from ESP to UFOs, from poltergeists to parapsychology, from witchcraft to wild cats, were soon destroyed by the sheer volume of data that was available. Lambert therefore began spending most of his time devising programmes for the collation and cross-referencing of material rather than attempting actually to solve any of the mysteries. As the years passed and he was forgotten by the scientific community at large, he became a regular fixture on the occult circuit, often as a debunker of popular myths. His nicknames included Dr Scorn, The Lambaster and, his favourite, Dr Strangelove – after the Peter Sellers character in the wheelchair. (For those he held in especial contempt, such as trepanners, alien abductees and mediums, he used to dress up in black and wear a single black leather glove. He would even adopt a cod-German accent when attacking more insane theories.) As a result he was a popular figure on the scene, even to the extent of having his own television series on Channel Four where he spent half an hour each week examining the evidence for famous mysteries, and effectively demolishing the validity of all of them except fire-walking.

And yet, for all his apparent success, Lambert was at heart intensely frustrated. Like a serious composer who makes a living doing TV jingles, he felt his deeply ingrained belief in the need to understand the occult – in its widest definition as 'the unknown' – was not being satisfied.

As a result, over the last five years, he had developed a particular interest in the idea that places have in-built histories that influence the present inhabitants. Inspired by the idea of hauntings, the recurrence of UFO sightings in certain locations and the theory that certain sites are so holy that different religions adopt them as places of worship, he had attempted to translate this into a meaningful concept for the twentieth century. His basic thesis was simple – if a place wasn't right, avoid it. On the most obvious level, if there was excessive incidence of cancer, there should be a check for old landfills, chemical works, or upwind or upstream nuclear installations.

On a more mundane level, Lambert had successfully correlated freak falls of fish and coloured rain with local weather anomalies, on one notorious occasion actually predicting a yellow rain in London twelve hours before the windblown Saharan sand in the upper atmosphere was brought to earth by heavy precipitation. His aim, however, was not so much to arrive at a solution or even a prediction, but rather to provide the groundwork for more intensive and dedicated research by others.

Lambert's biggest problem was that he got bored easily. The prospect of spending the rest of his working life probing into whether electromagnetic disturbance from transformers and over-head powerlines causes childhood diseases or if underground nuclear tests precipitate earthquakes was, however worthy, anathema to him. His interest could only be held over short periods – three to six months, perhaps – rather than spread over five years. He wasn't interested in the credit, only the chase. Like the ice block that fell on his car, he wasn't seeking to apportion blame, simply to discover the truth; it was for others to deal with the problem.

His thoughts about the car crash had been aroused by a report his clipping service had sent to him about a spate of car crashes in the northern town of Blair. Every night, for a fortnight, a different stolen car had been crashed into various church doors, the culprits either just running away or sometimes torching the cars before making off. Damage was already running into thousands of pounds and the police hadn't the manpower to stake out each church in the town. As a result religious vigilante groups had been set up, producing the prospect of mob rule by Christians. That in itself was interesting, but Blair had already been cropping up regularly for the last three months. Taken individually the events were nothing more than odd, but taken together Blair was beginning to look like a suburb of hell.

Curious, Lambert typed a string of commands into his computer, then printed out the results. He employed a full-time secretary who worked at home transcribing clippings onto her own computer then sending the data by modem to his machine. The print-out made for fascinating reading. So fascinating that he switched off his computer and motored into the kitchen to make himself a drink. It was 3:30 a.m. and he was still well awake. Then, settled in the lounge, the radio on softly in the background, he ran through the unusual events that had been plaguing Blair.

There was a serial rapist on the loose, said to have attacked at least three women. A poltergeist at work in a council house. A phantom knickers stealer, ripping off women's underwear from clotheslines, launderettes and shops: a total of ninety-five reported cases! Three multiple family murders: mother, father and sister knifed by a son; a family of three's suicide by carbon monoxide; a father shooting his two children, critically injuring his wife and killing himself. Two suicides by car crash. Three joyrider deaths and two pedestrian deaths by joyrider. Three suicides from a bridge over a canal – a site never used for suicide before. Two families raided and their eight children removed by social workers following allegations of ritual abuse – 'More arrests expected'. Two vicars arrested in a public toilet. A rash of amateurish bank robberies, all petty, all unconnected, leading to six arrests. Eleven drug user overdoses – three times the annual average. The firebombing of a Social Security office. A fourfold increase in reported sex crimes, none the work of a repeat offender, and with no link to the activities of the serial rapist, which meant headlines like 'What turns men into monsters?' Gang warfare between teenagers on neighbouring estates with guns brandished and several youngsters knifed. The sudden disappearance of dozens of pet cats and dogs without a plausible explanation. A strike at a local textile factory which had led to 'unprecedented violence' with several hospitalizations and rancour between people ostensibly on the same side. And now he could add the church car crashes and the odd deaths of a millionaire and a cop he had heard about on the radio earlier.

Now, in a major city like Liverpool or Manchester, these events might be regarded as statistical anomalies – over the year they would average out and clearly there was no connection between sex crimes and armed robberies, or hauntings and drug abuse, but the population of Blair was – and he checked the figure from the

1991 census – 44,508, an eighth of that of Greater Manchester. It had an above average level of services such as police, hospitals and local radio because of its relative isolation – in winter it could be cut off by snow for a couple of days. Some newspaper reports were calling it a 'Town in Torment', or the 'Unluckiest Town in Britain' but hadn't really pursued the matter. One local clergyman had pontificated that modern morality had caused a general lapse in standards. Ironically he was arrested a week later charged with the buggery of minors.

Checking his dates Lambert found that most of his clippings were at least two weeks out of date. He wanted to see if anything more had happened since, so he faxed his various contacts to source a street map of the town, and for more information on each of the stories he was interested in.

For the first time in several months his interest was piqued – and he knew from experience that whenever that happened there was usually good reason. Lambert only hoped that the rapid beating in his chest was caused by excitement and not, as he suspected, by fear.

8

IZOTTA TONISKI

Their lovemaking had provided no pleasure for Izotta Toniski, and even the joy she usually experienced hearing the little gasps Gordon made as he pumped roughly into her failed to excite. She had simply lain there, legs open, and let him use her: a fitting end to yet another doomed relationship.

He rolled off her and reached for his cigarettes, a movement so predictable and clichéd that she almost laughed, but she knew the effect that would have on him. Men had such fragile egos when it came to sex: one wrong word and they could become as deflated as their flaccid members.

She watched the light from his match flare and ignite the end of his cigarette, smelled the burning tobacco as the smoke drifted around the bed. They used to share the old joke about smoking after intercourse but not any more.

Izotta got out of bed, wiped between her legs and stepped into the bathroom. She wondered why they had done it. Both knew it was goodbye; one last fuck wasn't going to heal the rift or let them part in a blaze of erotic glory. Gordon was married, he was not going to get divorced nor split up his family. Yes, he had said it all along, but a girl was entitled to her fantasies.

She stared at the bite marks on her breast. There had been a time when she had carried them like trophies, once even showing them at the badminton club in the shower, ensuring Gordon's wife saw them. God, if only Izotta could have told her then that it was her devoted husband who, only a couple of hours before, had been biting them in rhythm to his ejaculation . . .

She touched the marks and winced. Not so much passion this time as anger. Yes, she knew the split had been coming and she should be all grown up about it, but Christ, she was thirty and she'd played out this scene, what, seven times now. What did she see in married men anyway? Probably just what she was complaining about: lack of commitment. There was never any real danger of the passion of an illicit affair becoming routine or a matter of habit. Whenever they fucked, they did it because they needed to; when they enjoyed a secret rendezvous, they did it with that delightful tinge of fear that comes with guilt. That and the theft: stealing another woman's man was *very* satisfying; to know that he was willing to jeopardize his home, his happiness and, in Gordon's case, his career, just to get her out of her underwear.

But now Izotta felt like the used tissue she was flushing down the toilet. There would be days of misery, a couple of panic attacks as her hand would hover over the phone, and then she'd throw herself into her work and go with the flow, no doubt letting herself be fucked by the first good-looker who made a pass. (Whatever her heart felt, her hormones could not be denied and she had never found masturbation a satisfactory alternative to the real thing.) It was all a matter of smell and sweat and words and presence . . . and whatever she thought of Gordon, he had all those and more. *If I didn't know better*, thought Izotta as she splashed water on her face, *I'd say you were in love.*

She towelled her face dry, flicked her bobbed black hair back out of her eyes, and went back into the bedroom. Gordon was sitting up, pulling on his socks. He hadn't been kidding about his 8 a.m. appointment.

'So that's it?' she asked.

'Yes, Iz. You know it is. And I don't want any—'

'Crap?'

'—arguments. Dorothy's going through a bad patch—'

'Spare me the CV. Just promise me one thing: you'll still give me the stories.'

He had stood up, naked apart from his black socks. Men and socks, not sexy. 'You mean that, don't you?'

She sat down and took a drag on his cigarette from the ashtray, even though she had given up months before. 'Yes.'

'You're one hard—'

'Says the dutiful husband and careerist!'

'Hey, you knew what this—'

'Skip it, Gordon. We've had this talk too many times already. We shouldn't have done this now. Get dressed, go, but let me keep in touch. You owe me that.'

'Owe?' he said, standing up, his muscular, grey-haired body sheathed in sweat, his whiteness contrasting with her own coffee colour. 'Let's not forget who got who into bed at Harrogate. Who kept up the—'

She flicked the cigarette at him and he danced out of the way, his large penis slapping his thigh.

'Bitch!'

'Bastard.'

She lay back, her arms over her eyes as he got dressed. Eventually, she heard him open the door, then speak:

'Iz, I'm sorry it's had to end. I enjoyed our time together.'

She looked over at him. God, but he was attractive – and she'd always had a thing about uniforms.

'Get back to your duties, Gordon. They're finished here.'

He was going to say something else but thought better of it and left the room.

Izotta stretched and tried to cry – the situation demanded it – but couldn't. Truth was, Gordon had been too preoccupied the last few weeks to be good company, never mind a good lay. She touched the bite marks again; the bugger had drawn blood. It probably was for the best. He'd become a stranger, his lovemaking more urgent and selfish, verging on rape the last couple of times – and no longer any apologies. There had been a time when she liked a bit of roughness, but this had been more than over-enthusiasm; this time she could have sworn there had been disgust, almost a hatred in his eyes, as he had pumped his seed into her. She rolled over and hugged the pillow. Where had it gone wrong?

That morning they had met in her car outside the Little Chef at 6:30 a.m. as usual, both aware their affair was set to end, but reluctant to admit it. Instead, she had asked him about work. After all, she was a reporter, and Gordon Dougan was a policeman who could give her the inside track on news stories worth investigating. He had been strict about how much he let her know, avoiding anything that could be traced back to him, but had also been helpful and even when they had decided to become unprofessional in their relationship, he had remained a steady source.

'Is this off the record?' she had asked sipping on a paper cup of tea.

'It's so off the record it's still in the sleeve, okay?' said Gordon.

'Right,' Izotta agreed.

They were sitting in her red Ford Capri, parked facing the main road, the steady rain effectively screening them from anyone who passed. Izotta worked for the *Sentinel*, a large-circulation evening paper covering the north-west of England. She was based in Blair and wanted to discuss the deaths at Horton House and the story that had run in that morning's *Daily Mail*. She had filed an early report with some background on Horton, but nothing as sensational as the *Mail*'s overnight concoction.

Gordon supped his coffee and cursed. 'You sure this is coffee? So, it was nothing to do with you?'

'That *Mail* story? No, I don't string for them, only the Sundays. Besides, if it was good enough to get up your nose I'd keep it for the *Sentinel*, wouldn't I? I've just followed up the Horton angle. They dug up their own story. Sounds good but it's bullshit.'

'Is it?'

Izotta was intrigued. One thing she had come to appreciate about Gordon was that the man didn't lie. He either said it like it was or he shut up.

Pleased to have got her attention, Gordon continued: 'I'm telling you this so you don't include anything you shouldn't. Horton's business is in the red and there's a DTI investigation. He also dabbled in kiddie porn. The only surprise is that he hadn't jumped before now. Anyway, a call went out for assistance when he was reported as trying to jump. First unit on the scene was a PC Blake. Been on duty six weeks. Good lad but inexperienced. They should have let someone else handle it but they were tied up with that siege out at Dintree. So Blake is first on the scene, so keen he let a prisoner go.'

'Important?' said Izotta, taking notes.

'No, a flasher. Blake gets up there, witnesses say he was scared shitless and I don't blame him. He leaned out of the window and spoke to Horton. No one remembers what he said, even though he must have been shouting to be heard. They talked for about four minutes, then Horton takes the quick way down. Obviously the boy's distraught, blames himself and so on, but rather than coming in and having his breakdown, he climbs out onto the ledge and does his own swan-dive.'

'Some guilt.'

'I've checked his psychological evaluations, right from day one. He wasn't the sort to do that. Okay, all of us have a turn now and again, takes different people in different ways. Me, it's faces.'

'Faces? You've never said.'

'Man, woman, child, dead, injured, I can handle it, but if someone's face has been really badly damaged by a windscreen, beer glass, explosion, whatever, I usually throw up. One of the sergeants, he can't take drownings because his mother drowned when he was a kid. Another guy, a traffic PC I think, can't cope with needles. He'll shovel up dead babies on the motorway, but if he catches sight of just one needle, he's out like a light.'

'But PC Blake went overboard. Literally.'

'Yes. I don't know how we're going to sell it. Try and pass it off as a tragic error. You know, he slipped.'

'What if someone doesn't buy it?' She scanned the *Daily Mail* on her lap. 'The *Mail*, for one. They've got the cop climbing out after Horton's jumped. Can't cover that up.'

'I know, but where's the dirt? The poor sod died. Try and kill it in your paper, okay?'

'OK, but I'm not the editor. And what about the rest?' She summarized the other points in the *Daily Mail*'s so-called 'BIZARRE CHAIN OF DEATH'.

'All this is strictly off the record,' he said. 'There's enough shit going down in Blair . . . On the way to the morgue with the two bodies, the ambulance driver, Barry Townsend, drove into a tree.'

'Drove?'

'Yes. There was no other traffic, he was within the speed limit – his patients were dead, after all – and the conditions were dry and clear. There were no mechanical defects, no steering or brake failures: he just drove into the tree. Went straight through the windscreen, died instantly.'

'No seat belt?'

'Townsend was the union rep and a fanatic about procedure. He always did his belt up. *Always.*'

'Meaning?'

The policeman shrugged and drained his coffee. 'Meaning he didn't have it done up when he drove into the tree.'

Izota didn't need him to say the word 'suicide' for his meaning to be clear.

'What happened then?'

'Local guy driving behind, he pulled up. Found Barry dead. Got into the back of the ambulance, pulled someone clear. It was the young cop, Bates. He freaked, the kid had lost most of his head. Someone else pulled out the other crewman. He's in hospital with a broken arm and leg.'

Izotta looked again at the *Daily Mail*. 'This guy who freaked: he was Walsh? Hadleigh Walsh?'

'Yes. Lives over near the golf course. He was treated on the spot for shock but refused hospital treatment. Drove himself home. What happened there we don't know, but about eight o'clock we got a call from the next-door neighbour. They reported gunshots. Tactical were sent, waited an hour, then broke in. The wife was in the bath, her head blown off, Walsh in the kitchen, most of his chest over the wall. He'd left a note.' He pulled out his notebook and flipped through it. 'The *Mail* don't know this, and neither do you, okay?'

Izotta nodded. There seemed to be a story here all right, but what she couldn't fathom yet.

'It said "I've seen the darkness coming and I'm going to spare us both. Tell Petula it's for the best." Petula's their twenty-year-old daughter, away at university.'

'"The darkness coming"? Did he have any problems?'

'They're checking that today but his GP says not. His boss was also happy with him. He was a rep for a cardboard box company. Their best.'

'So you've got . . . what about Townsend in the ambulance?'

'His biggest problem was how County were doing. Mr Normal. I met him at a charity barbecue once. Nice guy. Straight down the line. Married, no kids, lots of cats.'

'So why have you told me all this?'

'You can work that out.'

'Horton, the cop, Townsend, Walsh – all suicides, and only one of them predictable.'

'Exactly.'

Izotta was unimpressed. 'So they weren't as level-headed as people thought. We've all got our little secrets.' She gave him a look, which he avoided.

'Very funny. And what they saw pushed them over the edge, is that what you reckon?'

'Off the top of my head, yes,' she said.

'There's more,' he sighed.

'Suicides?'

'Some. But that's not all.'

Izotta scrunched up her coffee cup and tossed it onto the back seat with the other accumulated rubbish, indicating that Gordon should do the same with his empty cup. He did so. 'Before you go on, why are you telling me this?' she said.

'Two reasons. One, I need your help on it. I daren't put any of my suspicions in writing. I'm up for promotion and I don't want to spoil my chances. Second, I haven't got the access you have to investigate it anyway. I have to do it officially, you can do it your way. I'll give it you exclusive as long as you keep it quiet till I say so.'

'No bullshit?'

'No bullshit.' Dougan stretched and loosened his tie.

The car had steamed up now and they were in a little world of their own. Izotta couldn't help thinking of other times the car had been steamed up.

'I think evil is loose in Blair.'

'What?' The one thing Izotta had come to respect about Gordon was that he wasn't melodramatic.

'There's something terribly wrong in this town,' he said.

'Oh, come on, Gordon, that's a bit much from you.'

'Is it?' he said, his eyes flaring. 'I've been a copper for seventeen years, eight of them in Blair, and I've never seen the like of what's happening now.'

'Like what? I don't see—'

'Exactly. Nobody does, but I do.'

'You're sounding a bit omniscient—'

He grabbed her hand and squeezed hard enough for it to hurt. 'I'm not joking, and I'm not having a religious conversion.'

'All right, Gordon, I believe you! Just don't break my hand.'

He looked down at her scrunched fingers, muttered an apology and let go.

'I know there's been some bad stuff lately,' she offered. 'But nothing really out of the ordinary, surely.'

He wasn't listening. 'I have a map on the wall in my office. It shows the town and its geographical boundaries. A month ago, I decided to keep track of every crime committed within the town using coloured pins for each type of crime. Red for murder, pink for assaults, blue for burglary . . . Now there's this near-perfect circle exactly two miles across, containing ninety-four per cent of all recorded crime in the area.'

'So it's a coincidence.'

'It is not a coincidence, Iz, it's a sign. The town is under siege. Every category of crime is up.' He reeled off the figures. 'Rape a hundred and eleven per cent, muggings a hundred and five per cent, assaults eighty per cent, vandalism two hundred and twenty per cent, even suicide is three times the norm . . . the list goes on. It's like there's something in the air, or in the water, polluting people.'

'That doesn't make sense. The weather's been lousy, maybe it puts people in a mood. The recession, there's bound to—'

'Yes, yes, yes, yes, I know all that. So I asked for a check on everyone charged in the last two months to see how many had previous convictions. And do you know what?'

She shook her head, worried about him. He was staring at the windscreen, his face tight, teeth biting his lower lip.

'More than half of them had no previous convictions.'

'Which means?'

'Obvious as it may sound, most crime is committed by criminals: over two-thirds of people arrested have had previous convictions. Our figures are almost exactly reversed. People in Blair are *becoming* criminals.'

'Oh, that's nonsense.'

He slammed the dashboard with his palm. 'It is not nonsense, Izzy, it's fact. *Fact!* We're undermanned, what few men we do have are pulling overtime the force can't pay just to keep things at a relatively safe level but if it gets any worse, we'll be in deep shit. And the word is they will. There's trouble brewing on three estates which could go up at any time.'

'Surely it's—'

'*Wake up, Iz!* This town is in the toilet and it's about to get flushed. I've already sent Dorothy to stay with her mother in Ipswich. She's taken the kids with her.'

This threw Izotta: she knew how serious Gordon was about his children's education; the last thing he would do was take them away during term time.

'So what are you telling me . . .?'

'To go too. There's no story here anyone would print, but I truly believe something dreadful is going to happen and I don't want you around when it does. Especially with your penchant for trying to get in on the action.'

He rubbed the back of her head, feeling the scar made by the brick the time she had covered a police raid.

'Can't you give me anything more specific? I mean, if you're sure something's wrong, there *is* a story in it. The *Sentinel* would carry it, no problem.'

'I know, but what would it achieve? Every official would deny it, especially with the town negotiating for that Japanese factory. Those who were scared already would just get hysterical. And those bastards out there causing all the trouble would get publicity – and go all out for even more! The town would become a bloody media circus. Everything from bloody Kilroy to "Twenty Things You Didn't Know About Barmy Blair" in the *Sun*. This is serious, Iz. I'm . . . I'm scared. And you know how hard that is for me to say.'

She looked at him, trying to read anything other than the truth in his eyes but he kept avoiding her gaze. She cupped his chin and turned his head towards her. Still he looked at her lap.

'You're really that worried?'

'I've been in raids, car chases, crashes, been stabbed, shot at, fallen off that roof . . . but I've never felt so . . . so *frightened*. And so *sure*. It's squatting there in my stomach, like waiting for someone to pull a trigger or drop a clutch. I can't sleep – and that's after double shifts! And no one will listen. I've mentioned it to everyone I can, shown them the statistics, the map . . . they're not interested.'

'But why?'

He took a while to consider his answer as the rain drummed relentlessly on the car roof. 'Because they know there's nothing they can do.'

This last statement was delivered in a quiet cracked voice that was so unusual that it had more effect on Izotta than his actual fears.

In the seven months they had been intimate, Gordon had always given the impression of being a real man's man, both in and out of bed – fearless, strong, driven – but now he was like a frightened rookie. She stroked his face and leaned forward to kiss him. He didn't respond, his lips chapped and cold.

'Come to bed,' she said.

'I've got an eight o'clock meeting. And we agreed to stop. Dorothy—'

'Dorothy's in Ipswich. We—'

'For her safety, not so we can go to bed! I'm sorry, sorry. It's just I'm on edge about all this. Worried . . .'

'All the more reason; you know how it helps . . .'

She remembered a couple of occasions when she had let him do what he wanted to get the aggression out of his system. One time it had been unbelievably enjoyable, the other uncomfortable, but whatever they had decided about their relationship, she still felt for him.

'Come on, Gordon. Use me, let me help you . . .'

He smiled weakly, the temptation obvious. She checked her watch. 6:50 a.m. 'Plenty of time. Come on, you know you want to. No strings, just this last time. You deserve it.'

He nodded. 'But do you?' he said ominously.

She thought it was a slur on her, but once they got into bed, she realized what he really meant. He was going to take it out on her body and, that early in the day, she wasn't up to it. So she let him do as he wanted, hoping that his roughness wasn't a true reflection of his worry about the town because, if it was, Blair was in bad trouble.

After he had gone Izotta dressed, careful with her bra. He had never been that possessed. Perhaps it was for the best. The more she thought about Gordon's paranoia about Blair, the more she thought the problem lay with him and not the crime rate. He had always been paranoid about their being discovered; maybe his fears had developed into an all-pervading psychosis. Sending his wife and children away when he was trying to avoid arousing suspicion either spelled genuine worry or imminent madness. If it were the latter, it would be just as well they had split. If, however, it was the former, then she could be sitting on a major story.

She locked her flat and walked down to her Capri. She decided to check the newspaper files for recent stories about Blair, to see if any of it tallied with Gordon's fears, then she would take it from there. But first, the Horton suicide – now there *was* a story and she had been assigned to it. Did the cop fall or did he jump? And if he did jump, why? For that she needed to know his state of mind prior to stepping out on that ledge. So who were the last people to see him?

9

LAMBERT'S SUSPICIONS

The smell of urine was all-pervading but Wesley Lambert was ignoring it. His day bag was overflowing, and although he couldn't feel it, he certainly could smell it. He really should change it, get himself cleaned up, but what he was seeing was just too amazing for him to worry about something as petty as a leaky pissbag.

He tapped the mouse and scrolled the graphs. He had logged into the Meteorological Office database – the university paid – and was studying data from field stations in and around Blair. They had one on the tallest building and one outside town. At first the data had been flagged with a warning that it might be in error, but it had been double-checked at his request and the figures were true.

It had been raining in Blair for four days, the total rainfall equivalent to three months' precipitation. Yet the rainfall three miles away was exactly as per the norm. He had spoken to a couple of meteorologists and both had explained it away as a microclimate. Blair's position at the head of a valley ensured a localized wind pattern that could 'capture' rainfall from surrounding hill areas. Add to this the fact that the hills to the town's west were three hundred feet lower than those to its east, and it was bound to experience heavier rainfall as rain-laden clouds rose as they moved eastward. When pressed, however, they both admitted it wasn't really an explanation and the truth was probably that it was an anomaly. That word again . . . Lambert knew better.

Taking his recent press clippings as his cue, he scoured data banks for any reference to Blair. Crime statistics, accident reports, house sales, redundancies, unemployment, even obscure facts such as football match and cinema attendances – down by a third and a half respectively while the national average showed a slight rise in both areas. Unemployment in the town was running at fifteen per cent, well above the national average, but nothing inner cities across the country couldn't match. However, redundancies, receiverships and business failures were more than double the national average, and three-quarters of those had been in the last three months. In other words, the town's unemployment levels had doubled in twelve weeks.

House sales had plummeted – no one wanted to move into the town – yet there had been a net population decrease. In the first six months of the year the town had seen over two thousand people leave. The average figure should have been closer to five hundred.

Truancy rates, published by the government, placed Blair in the top ten – again no mean feat when compared to inner-city schools – with examination pass rates the worst in the region, and the statistics went on and on, painting a gloomier and gloomier picture. TV licence dodgers, pedestrian injuries, fires – in the home and on business premises – cancer rates, all were higher than the national average. Admittedly some features, such as the TB cases, involved just a couple of people, but in no single area of analysis which reflected the quality of life did Blair come out as anything other than below average. Statistically speaking, the place was falling apart. Even the worst inner-city areas can sometimes boast some good news. Traffic accidents can be low in bad areas (fewer cars); high redundancies can lead to greater business start-up successes. But Blair was just bad news all down the line.

The smell was getting worse now, and not just the smell of urine. Lambert decided to take a break, so he switched on the screen saver and, leaving the cats to chase the butterfly, motored through to his ground-floor bathroom, stripped off his soggy clothes and nappy and edged himself onto the seat in the shower. There he unstrapped his bag and poured the contents down the drain, then switched on the shower and soaped himself all over. He was surprised at how pleasant it felt, then remembered that he had been sitting in front of his VDU screen for almost eleven hours.

Towelling himself dry, Lambert edged himself onto the bidet and, reaching between his legs, put on a fresh disposable nappy. Then he wrapped himself up in a towelling robe and shifted himself back into his wheelchair. It was tiring work and it took a minute for his upper arms to stop shaking – longer than usual, he noted. Then he ferreted out another urine bag from the cupboard, connected it to his catheter, drove into the kitchen and made himself a pot of coffee, poured it into a vacuum flask, and drove back into his study. He looked at the clock. 2:15 a.m. How time flew.

He switched his screen back on and checked the progress of his Plunder Programme, designed to extract information from any data bank he entered by using key words or phrases. This time it was simply the name 'Blair'. He wanted all and any data on the town in forty-five categories – crime, unemployment, social indicators, health, business, weather, road accidents and so on – and had then asked for any town or city where four or more indicators were ten per cent above average.

As expected, virtually every inner-city area and various single-industry towns came out badly. Steel manufacturing and coal mining towns or areas of major single employers meant a lot of redundancies and unemployment and a knock-on effect on house sales, local shops and crime rates. But by eliminating those where there was an obvious cause, he was quickly reduced to half-a-dozen towns, Blair included. But Blair was far and away the worst affected. The nearest any other town came was Garlang, a Scottish town with an abnormally high crime rate and level of unemployment. But its figures had been skewed by a plane crash which had precipitated looting and a follow-up police operation which had uncovered a major drug ring supplying the west of the country, as well as significant stolen car and burglary operations. Blair, however, was the clear winner. Or should that be loser?

Lambert stared at the statistics on the screen. He was grateful he didn't live there. In time, the parlous state of the town would have come to the notice of the Press – its crime rate was already earning it the nickname of 'Town in Torment' – but when all the other factors were taken into consideration, the town was actually dying.

He supped his coffee, pleased with his deductions. The problem now was: what did it all mean?

He decided to let his computer do the thinking for him. Using his modem, he plugged into the database on unusual material he had assembled at the university. That Blair was disintegrating was interesting but, ultimately, of no value. Towns die, it happens. Five years from now it wouldn't matter: the damage would have been done, people would have left, the town would exist on welfare, like a hundred other ex-mining communities. True, it was bigger than most such communities, but look at the Tyne, the Mersey, the Clyde – and the contrast between what they used to be like when their ships were wanted the world over and their present selves. What Lambert needed to know was if there was anything more sinister at work. The odd weather in particular had been nagging at him most of the night. That towns decline and become trapped in a vicious circle where unemployment depresses the local economy and people turn to crime and so deter investment was a fact. But even then, murder rates do not rise significantly, the weather does not change, accidents in the home are not significantly more frequent. But it was the damn weather he kept coming back to. He had asked for enhanced satellite photographs of the area for the last three months to be couriered to him as soon as possible. The weather . . .

His screen suddenly flashed into life as it began to communicate with his computer at the university. Cross-referencing would normally take several hours, but he had devised a short cut to memory retrieval and, logging in the relevant programme, he was confident of suitable answers within half an hour.

Twenty-four minutes later the computer announced it had completed its task, having delved into almost eighty-three thousand events from the last eighty years, incidents where something inexplicable had happened. These 'zoo events' couldn't be explained by current scientific thinking, though they might turn out to have a perfectly rational explanation. His ambition was to get to a level of sophistication in his analysis where, as soon as an event could be deciphered and a reason attached to it, he would be able to eliminate the puzzle from a whole stack of other events. Prove that ghosts were the result of electromagnetic disturbance affecting the senses of victims – and he could explain hundreds of hauntings. Show that Spontaneous Human Combustion existed in one case – and dozens of other deaths could be understood.

Lambert punched PRINT and let the Canon printer chatter away. To his surprise it only ran for a few seconds, then shut down. He ripped off the paper and saw that it contained two names, both followed by a sequence of reference numbers which he knew to be file titles.

He stared at the names and couldn't help smiling, despite the images those names conjured up. His suspicions had been

confirmed. He rang several numbers immediately. The invariable
response, not surprising at 3:20 a.m., was anger and abuse. But,
as soon as he mentioned Blair and the two other names in the
same context, these same people suddenly woke up and by 6 a.m.
a meeting had been arranged at Lambert's house for the following
afternoon.

Calls completed, Lambert sat back and stretched. He really
needed to grab some sleep but he also needed to prepare for the
meeting. It would be his one shot at convincing them of his belief
and of the need for his involvement. He looked at the printout
again, heavy black rings round the names from his doodling while
he'd been speaking to sleepy officials. Pleased as he was at his
conclusion, he felt like a doctor who had successfully diagnosed a
rare illness only to find it was incurable and the patient was already
slipping away. He prayed he was wrong but, with the arrogance that
comes with experience, he feared the worst.

The names were innocent enough in themselves – Roswiay and
Warforn Peck – but they could also spell the end of Blair and all
its inhabitants.

10

IZOTTA AND HER EDITOR

Izotta Toniski grimaced as she sipped her frothy coffee. She had forgotten how bad milky coffee could be in a greasy spoon, but she'd needed to sit down and have a think and the bus station cafeteria had been the nearest. Parting from Gordon, however, wasn't what was playing on her mind.

After all, she'd split with men before, and there were plenty of husbands out there keen to sample something on the side, not least if that something was attractive and, what was the word? Exotic? No, before Gordon there had been Brian and before Brian, Mal. Or was it Fisher? Didn't matter. There would be plenty of Brians and Mals to come. No, it wasn't losing Gordon that was bothering her; it was the way he had been, and his fears about Blair.

Izotta knew she wasn't the most astute of reporters and had probably missed a lot of what had been going on. But now she took the time to look around her, there was something in the air – and it wasn't just the smell of frying bacon. The rain didn't help – she couldn't remember the last time it had rained so much for so long – and she had to admit she felt more vulnerable than usual at night on the streets. But she had put it down to a general decline in standards and not something specific to Blair. Still, just walking here from the multi-storey car park she had seen three separate kids begging in the street, a couple of drunks and two lads being chased by police – and it was only nine-thirty. It may have been the bad end of town, but that was still pretty heavy. Even sitting in the fuggy confines of the café she felt an edge, as if something was simmering, waiting to explode. She looked around warily.

A couple of teenagers were eyeing her but she could tell their stares were sexual, not violent. She smiled at them; she would have devoured the little toads whole if they'd got her into bed. There was also a scruffy man in the corner nursing a sausage roll and soup. She would have to be careful about him. Now she thought about it, Blair *was* in a definite decline. So why hadn't she noticed it before?

Well, she knew the answer to that. Sex. The fact that she was content to stay in Blair rather than chance her luck in bigger cities proved the point. Izotta liked to turn heads and in Blair she was guaranteed to do that almost anywhere she went, but in Manchester or London there would be too much competition. No, better to be the bright jewel on the dungheap than a rhinestone on the ballroom gown. *God, what a metaphor*, she thought, jumbled though it was. She'd have to keep that one for the novel. Ah, the novel, another of her excuses: she 'was only working as a reporter until she could sell her novel'. But six novels on and she still hadn't cracked it. She'd be thirty next birthday and it was time to face up to some home truths.

Her looks and her figure wouldn't hold out forever and she was still single. Likewise her career, such as it was, didn't hold out any glittering goals. It was about time she found someone to settle down with. No kids, of course. (God forbid she'd have to cart some creature around in her belly for the best part of a year then let it split her in two just so it could ruin her life for a couple of decades and her looks forever.) No, the problem was, as ever, between her legs. She loved sex but it was always best with married men. Yet, despite the fun, it hadn't got her anything but loneliness – and now Gordon had done a bunk like all the rest.

So maybe there was a story here about the rising crime rate, the falling standards – but how to follow it up without betraying Gordon? Izotta checked in her notebook, aware of the tramp in the corner eyeing her handbag. She purposely pulled out a large metal nail file, ran it over her fingers, then held it up so he could see its long point. He quickly looked away.

She decided that after she had followed up on the Horton suicide story for the *Sentinel* she would spend the rest of the week checking on Gordon's theory and, if it came to anything, she could . . . *could what*? It was only then she realized the position Gordon had put her in: she'd promised to keep anything she found out quiet! So what he had *really* wanted was to use her as a confessional to whom he

could pour out his fears – and *then* she'd let him fuck her as well!
Bastard!

Annoyed at her gullibility she got up and left, ignoring the crude
remarks from the boys by the door. But the more she thought about
Gordon's theory, the more she realized something *had* changed.
There was a time when she would have happily swapped insults
with the youngsters, but she was acutely aware that nowadays
banter could just as easily lead to battery. She shivered as she
remembered more 'innocent' times like the day in 1984 when
she had been chatted up by three young lads on a bus and had
ended up taking them back to her flat. That afternoon had proved
her theory that while youthful enthusiasm was no substitute for
mature experience, there was definitely something to be said for
quantity over quality. Now the thought of the risk that would be
attached to a similar encounter today actually made her shiver.

Checking that the lads hadn't followed her, she walked out of
the bus station towards the newspaper office on Egerton Street, rain
dogging her every step.

The Blair office of the *Northern Sentinel* was also home to the
Blair Advertiser, the local weekly newspaper. The *Sentinel* owned
the *Advertiser* and Izotta was their local correspondent, supplying
half-a-dozen stories a week from Blair for the *Sentinel* and a few
lesser ones for the *Advertiser*. It kept her busy and it kept her in
Blair and she was happy with both situations: she had always
preferred to be a big fish in a small pond rather than a small
fish in a big pond.

The office was little more than a shop – the printing was done
at the *Sentinel* plant in Stockport. She shook her umbrella, entered,
said hallo to the temp on reception, then went upstairs to see George
Fife, the *Advertiser*'s editor.

He was asleep, his fat face slumped back against the back of
his aged leather chair, snores like machine gun fire filling the
cramped office. He was a drunk and only a year from retirement
so the *Sentinel* tolerated him. He was one of the old school and
when it came down to the wire, the paper always came out on
time. (He had also hinted of knowing dark secrets about his
seniors at the *Sentinel* and that they didn't dare fire him. It
seemed to work.) Nonetheless, 8:40 a.m. and she could smell
his breath a desk away. Izotta liked him not least because, for
all his faults, George Fife was the most honest man she had ever

met. She sat down in the chair opposite him and kicked the table to wake him.

He sat upright, seemingly alert, another of his tricks. 'Good morning, Izzie, and how are we?'

'Fine, George.' Neither of them wasted time with small talk; there was no point. 'I need to find out about that copper last night who was killed with Horton. The *Mail* have made something of it already, so I need to dig deep fast. PC Bates had been called to deal with a pest at the town hall. I can track down other witnesses to the suicide, but how do I identify the guy outside the town hall?'

'Police won't say?'

'He never called a name in.'

'Go down to the town hall, same time, ask around. He might be a regular, especially as the cop let him go – unknown quantities you tend to hang on to.' His gruff Edinburgh accent was a pleasure to listen to, as if all the alcohol had helped burnish it to perfection.

'Fine,' she said.

George knew her well enough that when she didn't leave she wanted to talk. He waited, blinking the sleep out of his eyes and searching for a cigarette.

'What do you think of Blair?' she said.

'Dump.'

'No, I mean the atmosphere, over the last few weeks.'

'You're not talking carbon monoxide, are you? Well, it's rained a lot. Set a record, actually, putting it on the front page. This is officially the wettest summer ever in Blair, and getting damn close to the British record. But you don't mean that either, do you?' He fished in his drawer and pulled out a typed sheet. 'I wrote this a week ago, didn't have the nerve to run it. Might next week . . .'

She read it. It was an editorial about falling moral standards and rising crime. It didn't mention Blair specifically, but as it was meant for Blair residents the implication was clear.

'This town is slowly going mad,' he said. 'You and I know that what makes good news is bad news, but the last three weeks I've spiked more than half the stories I've had. Our readers would crap themselves if they knew what a cesspit the place has become. I remember a detective explaining to a WI audience once that there was on average one mugging every other day in Blair. That meant a one in eighty thousand chance of getting mugged. In other words, the average person never would. Now . . . only eight people work here, yet, in the last couple of weeks, two have been mugged, one burgled, one hit by a joyrider. Go figure those odds. If they knew I'd covered it up at head office they'd kill me, but I've a responsibility to our readers here. Locally they don't want grief; they want adverts, jumble sales and clever pets. It's what they pay for. But I think you'd better spot it, love – you're their man on the spot, so to speak, and bad news is what big papers peddle. Something's rotten in the state of Denmark and it ain't the cheese.'

He dipped into a drawer, pulled out a half-bottle of Scotch and took a draw. Izotta knew he was a lush, but he had never been so blatant. No doubt his cups of tea always contained more spirit than beverage but at least a semblance of dignity was maintained; now he was downing whisky before breakfast and didn't care who saw it. As he had said, she was head office's man and if she reported his problems . . . but she'd never do that: she loved the old sot.

'Gordon was telling me he thought the place was about to boil over,' she said.

George nodded and took another long sup. She knew he didn't approve of her love life but, as with his boozing, it was left unspoken.

'Too damn right. I've never known anything like it; it's as if people have caught a disease and they have to take it out on their neighbours.'

'You don't seem too bothered.'

He shook his head. 'I don't care any more. Doctors told me I have to quit drinking now or my body'll quit on me inside a year. As you can see, I have paid heed.'

He took another draught, the bottle almost emptying.

She grabbed his wrist and squeezed it. 'George, why don't you do what they say? Just give up this job and get that bungalow in Whitby you've always promised yourself and get some peace.'

'Too late. Don't you feel it?' he said.

'Feel what?'

'The darkness approaching. Like night's going to come early one day and not go away.'

'It's just your old bones,' she said. But that phrase, 'the darkness': where had she heard it before?

'Hey, the stuff I pack away, all my old bones ever feel is warm. No, something's terribly wrong. I just don't know what to do. What *should* I do?'

'You're the newspaper man, what do you think you should do?'

He smiled, bent under his desk and pulled out a front page dummy of the *Advertiser*. The headline typeface was so large there wasn't any room left for copy.

Izotta couldn't help laughing and George joined in.

'You're not serious?' she said.

''Course not. Just covering my back in case our good and gracious employers start throwing their weight around – but even they wouldn't run this.'

Izotta stood up and walked to the door. 'Would you stop drinking if I begged you?'

'You're a lovely lass, Iz, despite your boyfriends, but I can't. No more than you could give up sex.'

'That bad?' she said.

He nodded and dropped his headline on the floor. 'I don't know if it's my place to say so but I've been hearing stories about your Gordon Dougan.'

'Like?'

'Like . . . he's losing it. There've been outbursts at Police Authority meetings; a punch-up with one of his boys at a retirement do.'

'I know. It wasn't his—'

'Says he. Picture I get is, well, he's heading for a breakdown. And you're not helping.'

'Tosh. I listen to—'

'That's his *wife's* job – and you know how much he . . . look, the man's got to stop treading on toes or they'll stamp on him. And I tell you this as a friend, not a marriage counsellor.'

Izotta was about to lose her temper – the interfering old drunkard, what right did he have to lecture her? – but she realized he wasn't being censorious, and that his concern was with Gordon, not her.

'He's under a lot of . . . It's over, actually,' she said. 'This morning. He's got this thing about Blair being swamped by crime and he's . . . he's even sent his wife and kids away. And I'm not taking advantage.'

'His wife away? God, he must be scared.'

Izotta nodded. That was the word all right. Not 'over-worked' or 'pressurized' but *scared*.

'And you be careful,' he said. 'Blair's gone rotten.'

There was an awkward moment. Then she picked up her bag and

left, sad to see George reaching for the bottle even before the door
had closed. She liked him, he was like a father to her, except they
had no secrets. She knew about his drinking and the problems he
used to have with his late wife; he knew about her early trouble with
drugs and her ongoing bad choice in lovers. She'd hate to see the
old buzzard go, but he was right: he had as much chance of going
on the wagon as she had of becoming a nun.

George drained the half-bottle, then stood up and fumbled in the
filing cabinet for more scotch. Sat next to the Famous Grouse he
saw again the one secret Izotta didn't know about: his old service
revolver, loaded, a bullet in the chamber. He stroked the cold metal
and smiled. Damned if he would rot to death – and damned if he'd
let the darkness that was coming take him, too. No, his lethal little
friend would end all his problems just as soon as he knew it was
too late. He only wished he could explain to Izotta how he felt.

His headline had been the best he could manage but he couldn't
explain it. Intuition? A gut feeling? He didn't know, didn't care.
He was *tired*. He looked at the unrelenting rain, then stared at the
headline on the floor under his desk. Perhaps he should have pulled
the revolver on Izotta and forced her to comply with the message,
but she'd only have tried to sell it on to the *Northern Sentinel*.
Whatever her faults, she was a good reporter. The headline read:
GET OUT OF BLAIR BEFORE IT'S TOO LATE.

11

MR FARMER AND JAMIE

Mr Farmer woke up first and saw the soldier curled up in the corner asleep, dressed only in a T-shirt. He waddled over to him and touched him on the shoulder as he headed for the bathroom.

By the time he had finished peeing and had washed his chubby face, the soldier was dressed and ready to leave.

'Happy now?' asked Mr Farmer.

The soldier stared at him, his face a blank, and nodded vaguely.

'And you'll be ready this afternoon?'

Again the sleepy nod. Mr Farmer smiled and grasped the man's shoulder. The soldier jolted, as if touched by a live wire. His eyes opened wide but his pupils remained large and unresponsive. *You can see the darkness approaching*, thought Mr Farmer, wishing he could enjoy the same clarity of vision. But soon, soon . . . Mr Farmer opened the front door of his flat and let the soldier walk out. As he watched him head for the stairwell he couldn't avoid an involuntary shudder of anticipation.

For some months now he had felt some huge horror was going to happen but he hadn't expected it so soon. Then again, he'd been waiting for over thirty years, patiently watching as the world around him deteriorated. Law and order breaking down as children grew up without guidance or fear of punishment; sexual morality discarded like an ill-fitting condom; personal responsibility a nebulous concept bandied about in DSS pamphlets. Gone were the times when certain people and places were sacred: priests, nurses, doctors, pensioners, the disabled, children, hospitals, schools, churches, graveyards . . . now all were fair game, everyone

a target for any mindless thug or twisted psyche; everyone on the
street – and even in their homes – just so much meat waiting to be
butchered. Mr Farmer leaned back against the door jamb, his eyes
fluttering with the exquisite pictures his mind was conjuring up of
a society on the very brink of chaos. Poverty, pain, crime, terror: the
new Four Horsemen of the Apocalypse, stalking their prey without
fear of retribution. And now his soldier boy would set the seal on
all his work, the purity of the young man's rage transformed into
an epochal event that would shake the nation and summon up the
true darkness he had striven to ferment over the years. He wondered
if there was any more he could do to make the day truly memorable,
to turn the name Blair into a new by-word for horror. And that was
when he heard the crying.

He walked across the landing and looked out onto the balcony
that offered its dismal view of blustery rain and slate-grey sky.
There he saw, huddled up in a ball, a young boy, no more than
ten or eleven, his dirty jeans and ripped dark blue anorak damp,
his short hair wet.

Mr Farmer walked up to him and touched him lightly on the head.
At first the boy didn't notice the man's podgy fingers caressing his
hair, which gave Mr Farmer more than enough time to achieve
satisfaction. But then the boy gave a start and cowered back, his
face streaked in tears, his nose caked in dried blood.

'Some boys give you a rough time?' Mr Farmer said kindly, slow
to remove his hand. 'Or was it your dad?'

'Brother. Wanted me money.'

'And he got it?'

'Yeah,' the lad sniffed. He seemed to be relaxing but then he
realized he was alone with a huge adult and he'd seen too much
to feel safe with the situation. He tried to edge away but he had
nowhere to go, Mr Farmer's bulk blocking all escape routes.

Mr Farmer understood the boy's panic and stepped back, but
then crouched down as best as his belly would let him, the rolls of
fatty abdominal flesh pressed against his chest by his thighs making
breathing an effort. 'I'm no weirdo. People round here call me Mr
Blobby. Can't think why.'

The boy managed a smile, but it was obvious he didn't get much
practice.

'Look, you may think I'm a fat perv but I'm not. Now you can
come in my flat and have a hot drink and a chat, or . . .' He fished in

his pocket and found a five pound note. 'Or take this, buy yourself something nice to eat and find somewhere warm—'

The boy snatched the fiver before Mr Farmer could finish his sentence and scampered off down the hallway. Mr Farmer smiled and rose slowly, out of breath simply from squatting.

From the stairwell he heard an echoing 'Thank you, mister' and the sound of running feet. Mr Farmer was pleased he had made the boy happy. Pleased because the lad would have a few minutes of relative pleasure before the seed he had planted would begin to blossom and, if he had understood the boy correctly, it would be trained like a climbing rose on a trellis to reach exactly where Mr Farmer wanted it to. Except, of course, instead of growing towards the light, it would head inexorably for the dark.

He went back into his flat. Time for breakfast – black pudding, fried eggs, curried beans, French toast – and to make sure the radio was tuned in to a local station so that he could enjoy the panic as the news began to filter in. Of course, he still didn't know exactly where or when his soldier would let the world know of his troubles, but it was certain to be today: his mind was primed and could never be defused. And, as an added bonus, there was also the boy. How would his immature mind react to having the fetters removed from his battered conscience?

Oh yes, today was going to be a special day. A very special day.

12

MARK DAWSON'S TRIP TO WORK

The windscreen wipers on Mark's BMW were playing up, smearing his field of vision and making an irritating screaking sound. Worse, it was drizzling rather than raining, so the wipers didn't have much to work with. Add his headache, the fact that he had woken up late and was faced with the prospect of informing his staff, some of whom had been friends for ten years, that it was all over and they'd better get out their folios and CVs, and it was clear that Wednesday had started out bad. His only consolation was that it couldn't get worse.

Karen squeezed his thigh and told him to calm down. He gave her one of his patented fixed grins and stabbed at the radio. Some prattling moron was running a competition to guess Boyzone's combined inside leg measurement. He punched it off and peered through the blurry windscreen.

Traffic was slow – as if rain was some kind of impediment to urban traffic that only ever crawled at the best of times – and there was still a mile to the office. His plan of action was to break the bad news as one would explain a bereavement at a family gathering. Karen was to be there as moral and visible support – everyone liked her – while he explained that they were all in it together and it was better to give it up while there was an element of choice, rather than wait for the men in suits with their notebooks and padlocks to come in and start sizing up their meagre assets.

For his own part, Mark was already resigned to personal financial disaster and so was more concerned about the effect his decision would have on his team. Most of them would be OK, but some, like Annie, would find it difficult to find another decent job with the industry in the shape it was. Visualizers were two a penny, even good ones, and talented kids fresh out of college made a very tempting target for agencies as they were dirt cheap and could be expected to work all hours without complaint. Even Mark, with his experience, could look forward to being ripped off. People he would talk to about work, even old colleagues, would know he was desperate and so screw him, but then so would he in their position: that was business.

They reached a set of traffic lights and Mark saw the one thing he could *really* have done without that morning: car washers. He started begging the lights to change as he watched the scruffy youths attack the next car but one in front, one waving a rag over the window, a second slopping filthy water onto the bonnet, the third thrusting his hand into the car to demand payment. Karen saw what was happening and knew how Mark would react.

'Give them a pound, Mark. Just give them the money. No hassle. Please.'

Mark was speechless. He was all for charity and helping down-and-outs, but these thugs were simply demanding money with menaces. He knew if he didn't give them any cash the least they would do was spit on the car, but equally they might drag a key or coin along the paintwork, kick in a tail light, dent the boot or even smash a window. What did they care?

He cursed the traffic lights for not changing, cringing as he saw the three lads move on to the Cavalier in front. The lone woman driver, plainly intimidated, handed the skinhead with the bucket loose change before a drop of water had hit the car. And, of course, having got the cash, no water did. Instead they moved on to Mark's BMW, the skinhead in a Cure sweatshirt beaming as he saw the car.

Mark's life was teetering on the brink of chaos, his energy at a year-long low, his temper a thing with a life of its own. He usually found release in drink or a game of squash but right now, when he was at bursting point, the one thing he didn't need was to be harried by some yob on the lookout for easy pickings. If he gave in, he would be pissed off even more; if he argued he'd probably lose his temper and God knows where that would lead. He looked up at the lights. The hand tapped on the window, the threatening smile cracked open.

Amber-green!

Luckily the woman in front was as anxious as Mark to move off and Mark was able to accelerate away, his smirk barely concealed.

He looked in the rearview mirror at the lout waving his fist, his face twisted in anger. *Little bastard*, thought Mark. Just then Karen shouted and Mark looked back at the road and slammed on his brakes: the junction box was blocked, he was trapped. Oh shit . . .

He looked in the mirror again. The yob had spotted the delay and was marching back towards him, the other two concentrating on the grey Escort van behind. Mark edged forward a couple more feet as the yob kicked at the BMW's boot. The little fucker.

Karen begged Mark not to react, to just concentrate on getting across the junction and away. To be honest, angry as he was, he didn't fancy his chances with the skinhead. God, but he hated being intimidated . . .

He edged forward another short foot, the skinhead's boot making solid contact with his rear aerofoil. One more time and Mark would have to do something.

Just then he saw the Escort van behind move forward. Good. Maybe that would distract the trio, but then the van didn't stop. Instead it speeded up, closing the gap between itself and the rear of Mark's BMW in a blink. Before Mark could react, the Escort slammed into the back of his car, crushing the skinhead's legs between the two vehicles and making him shriek horribly. Screams from Karen and women pedestrians quickly added to the sudden furore.

Mark edged the BMW far enough forward for the skinhead to collapse out of sight. Then, putting on his hazard flashers – amazingly enough, the rear lights were still working – he stopped dead centre of the junction and got out, ignoring a fusillade of horns from all directions.

The skinhead was writhing on the floor, his twisted legs already bleeding. The driver of the van stepped out – a middle-aged Pakistani in a brown work coat – and stood, hands on hips, surveying his handiwork with evident satisfaction.

''Bout time someone dealt with their sort,' he said.

The other two louts rushed over to their screaming friend, then turned on the man. He stood his ground as they advanced on him like stalking pitbulls. The one in the sweatshirt grabbed his collar, but the man produced a large breadknife from behind his back and sliced at the boy's exposed wrist. There was a shocked pause, then blood and screams poured from the boy. As he staggered back, shrieking every bit as loudly as his injured friend, the man turned to the third yob, a lanky teenager in a scruffy leather jacket, and waved the knife tauntingly. He ran. The man then pocketed the knife and got back into his van with PATEL'S NEWSAGENT stencilled on the door and sat listening to the radio.

Mark didn't know what to do, so he stooped into his car and tried to calm Karen by urging her to call for help. But she was still too shocked, her hands gripping the hem of her jacket, so Mark picked up the mobile phone himself and called for an ambulance and the police.

As he finished his call, someone with medical training attended to the two youths, both of whom were hysterical. The pink-faced, middle-aged woman administered a resounding slap to both their faces as an introduction and they shut up, too wrapped up in their own misery to react to the applause that greeted their castigation.

'Keep quiet, keep still and shut up,' she said, folding her *Sun* to provide a compression pad for the boy's slashed wrist. 'No one here cares. Just wait for the ambulance.'

Mark stood watching, unable to formulate a response. Shock, horror, amazement, even grim satisfaction, all offered themselves for use. Instead he just joined in the general hubbub of surprise and condemnation and then, remembering Karen, helped her out of the car to the roadside. She was shaking but not crying and he comforted her, surveying the damage to his car as he did so.

As for the man in the Escort, he just sat listening to Radio Four, for all the world as if he was in an ordinary traffic jam and not one of his own making.

The bizarre accident delayed Mark for over two hours. First there were the police who had to take statements from Karen and himself, then move the cars. Karen was upset, but refused the offer of a check-up at the hospital. Instead Mark drove his battered BMW to a local garage and booked it in for a repair estimate. He then took Karen to a nearby café and they spent half an hour calming down – she over the violence, he over the damage. From what the police told him, the other driver had just blown a fuse and let rip – and was actually apologizing for the trouble he had caused to Mark.

He had been arrested and would be charged and, no doubt, at some point Mark would be embroiled in a court case, to say nothing of a heavy insurance wrangle. Only when Karen had convinced him that she was feeling better did he call a cab to take them both on to his agency.

However, as soon as they got in to Dawson Creative Associates their depression was augmented by a general aura of gloom already enveloping the office.

DCA was as quiet as a tomb, the dull weather giving the brightly lit office a grey north wall onto the world. Mark looked around and couldn't help being reminded of those shops that spring up for a month or two in empty retail units selling cheap crap, then disappear before the VAT man can trace them. Yes, he'd got in potted plants but they were rented, as was all the furniture, and whilst there were posters dotted about to offer a little colour – The Chase, Gask and Hawley, Letraset – they all came with the job, they weren't personal choices. None of them had managed to make the office seem anything other than a temporary arrangement and it was an omen that was soon going to be fulfilled. Yet, despite the bad news he had, he didn't think everyone would suspect that he was going to close down so quickly. There had to be another reason for the lack of enthusiasm.

'What is it?' Mark said to everyone huddled around Stan's desk.

'It's Annie. She's been attacked,' said Stan.

'What?' said Karen.

'Last night on her way home from a pub,' said George. 'A couple of guys grabbed her and they were going to . . . well, anyway, they were disturbed and instead they knocked her about before running off.'

'How is she? Is she in hospital?' said Mark.

'She's OK. A bit sore is all, but she's also frightened so her mother's taken her back to Manchester for a while.'

'How long's a while?' said Mark, knowing the answer.

'For good,' said George. 'You know her mother never wanted her to come with us.'

'Oh, and I suppose it's my fault?' said Mark, the anger he had suppressed over the accident about to burst forth.

'Well, you did encourage her.'

'I did not. In fact, I told her not to bloody come! I laid out all the problems – the money, the accommodation, the risk – but she managed to find an old schoolfriend to stay with. I wasn't about to deny her her gumption or the chance to use her talent.'

'Well, whatever, she's packed it in now.'

Mark sat down at Annie's desk and ran his hands over her layout pad. He looked to Karen for support but she just arched her eyebrows and went off to make coffee.

'Oh, great,' he said.

Karen had always had a thing about Annie. She knew the girl had a crush on Mark and had followed him like an obedient puppy from Manchester when they had moved. Mark had tried to play it down, not least because he had gone through a similar stage with Karen at his first agency when she was an art director. But the girl had also had real talent, and she was a sight more tuned into what was happening with fashion than the rest of them.

'Did they get the bastards?'

'No.'

'What is it with this bloody town? Me and Karen just got rammed by some nutter trying to kill a kid.'

He explained to the shocked group what had happened, everyone shaking their heads in disbelief. Stan then told a story about the women in the flats he lived in being scared to go out because of a gang of teenage muggers.

'The story goes that they not only rob but leave their mark on their victims' faces. Cut them with Stanley knives, like a branding. Although no one can name anyone they know who's been attacked, they're scared all the same. Made me kind of jumpy too, to be honest, though the area does seem to have gone down the nick the last few weeks.'

George shook his head. 'Of such authenticity are urban myths created. I was in the pub last night, mentioned those two that jumped. A guy told me the cop *pushed* the other one then jumped himself. Bizarre.'

Mark sat back his hands rubbing his eyes. 'Look, while we're all in such a good mood, I may as well come clean and tell you I'm going to shut up shop.'

Silence reigned. Mark noticed the radio wasn't on. He looked around, everyone's eyes on him, their faces blank.

'Eclipse?' said George.

'Forget it. And Kleenspray's more than likely had it. Plus there's nothing in the pipeline.'

'Told you we should have brought in an account handler.'

'Shut up, Stan. You saw the sums. Bring in a suit and two of you wouldn't be here. Look, we gave it a go. I'll pay you up till the end of the month plus a bit extra, but that's it.'

Mark expected bitter recriminations but they didn't come. 'Hasn't anyone got anything to say?'

'I was going to leave anyway,' said George. 'Studio in Leeds wants me to run the place. It's all about money, I'm afraid.'

'I've had an offer,' said Ron, the younger art director. 'Doug wants me back. He's thrown in a Calibra.'

'Hey, no excuses. At least I wasn't wrong about your talent. What about you, Stan?'

'I'll go freelance. Tout myself around Manchester. Still got the contacts.'

Mark let out a deep breath. 'So what you're saying, you bastards, is you're not only happy to leave the sinking ship, but you've already booked your passage on the next one that's passing.'

'First class,' said Stan.

'Port side,' said George, joining in the joke.

'With a porthole,' added Ron.

Karen walked into general laughter, a tray of steaming mugs in front of her. Mark explained that the only person in the room without job prospects was himself and Karen immediately proposed a toast to justice. Then she hugged him and everyone offered their advice.

The relief Mark felt at having finally divested himself of the burden of agency ownership far outweighed the worries he would have about the cost. Add to that the fact that everyone seemed relatively happy with their fate and the day wasn't entirely as black as it might have been, despite the accident. He supped his coffee, listened to the others cheering each other up and suddenly realized, as always, that everyone was sitting around Karen and he was out on an island of his own. It always happened, Karen the Mother Hen.

She was one of those women people gravitate to, not just because she was attractive but because she was in control. She was safe, reliable. Mark wondered, as he often did when he screwed up, what she had ever seen in him. OK, he was reasonably good looking, trim, fit and had a healthy – and occasionally unhealthy – sexual appetite that she was more than willing to accommodate (and embellish on at times, such as their pick-up scenario in bars), but there was more to a relationship than hot sex and mutual attraction. There was love, and he loved Karen and knew she loved him, despite her anxiety about her age tempting him to look at younger women, and his worry that her age would at some point lead her to find him too young. They made a paranoid couple but they had survived eight years of marriage, as well as Karen's inability to have children. Mark would have been happy to be a father, but paternity was not high on his agenda. He had enough trauma in his working life without adding lack of parenthood to the list.

A call came through after ten minutes. Mark took it in his office. It was his friend Peter Dimbleby at Kleenspray confirming the rumours of his imminent departure. Mark offered him his heartiest congratulations and explained about DCA's closure. Peter offered his heartfelt commiserations and both agreed to get heartily rat-arsed at the earliest opportunity.

Putting the telephone down was like the full stop at the end of a chapter in his career. That was it: he'd made his bid for freedom but had barely scaled the perimeter fence. Now to take his punishment.

He walked back into the Creative Department, told everyone about the call and, checking his watch, invited everyone down to the pub for an early lunch.

'It'll have to be a quick one,' said Karen, tapping her own watch. 'Train leaves at one.'

Damn, he'd forgotten. Karen was going to Manchester. He thought of asking her to cancel – he needed all the support he could get – but knew it would be both impractical and short-sighted. Karen was going to be the breadwinner for the next few weeks; no point upsetting her clients.

'OK,' he said. 'Then I'll run you to the station.'

'What with?'

'Oh shit, the car.'

'You sure it wasn't just the car got thumped in the crash?'

'What about the work for Farrells?' asked George, tapping his computer mouse and activating a packaging layout on the monitor.

'Fuck them. They haven't paid us in nine weeks.'

'You sure?' asked Stan.

'No, but fuck it anyway.' He led the way to the exit. 'Oh, and remind me to send some flowers to Annie – and her mother.'

Karen gave him an approving nod. He might not be the world's greatest businessman, but Mark had heart and he was honest and what more could you ask of a husband? Except a steady income, perhaps.

No one was really in the mood for alcohol so it was two rounds of orange juice, Perrier, Coke and glum faces. When a company goes bust, however small or young, it's still a blow to everyone who has invested time and effort in its creation. Mark wouldn't have gone it alone if he hadn't had Stan, George, Ron and Annie with him – and now they would all have to go their own ways, most of them back to Manchester. Only Stan and Mark had actually upped sticks, the rest commuting or staying with friends, but it meant settling in, getting used to new routines, new accounts, new coffee machines. Where did it come on the list of life's horrors? After bereavement, divorce and moving house? But, in some ways, it was all three, wasn't it? Whatever they might say now, Mark knew the people sitting with him would again be reduced to freelance favours, crossed paths at Creative Circle do's and Christmas cards. Good thing they weren't drinking alcohol, after all: they were depressed enough as it was.

Conversation was sparse and rambling and the wake dragged on until 12:30 when Mark nudged Karen and got up to call a taxi to the station.

He returned to the table to find everyone on their feet and making to leave. Stan spoke for them all.

'We'll go and finish up what's left, Mark. See you back there. It's OK if we make a few phone calls?'

''Course, you daft sod. I'm sorry . . .'

'We know, Mark. Stop apologizing.'

'Sorry.'

'Stop it.'

'Sorry.'

'Mark!'

'*Sorry*.'

Stan made to thump him and they laughed. Mark escorted Karen outside to wait for the cab, the rest following behind. He waved them back to the office and hugged Karen.

'That went well, I don't think,' he said.

'Could have been worse.'

'I could still fight the good fight.'

Karen shook her head. 'Leave it, Mark. You've made the break, stick to it. I'll try and get back tonight but if I can't, we'll sit down and go through all the figures tomorrow, see where we stand.'

Mark looked down and stepped into the gutter. 'A practical demonstration, madam.'

She punched him in the shoulder then pulled him out of the way of the approaching cab. He kissed her, handed over her portfolio and watched her get in.

'Good luck, love,' he said. 'Give us a ring to let us know if you're coming back. And don't get a train after seven, OK?'

She sighed at his familiar warning. 'OK. And don't get too depressed. It could have been worse, you know.'

'Oh, how?'

'*I* could be working for you.'

He gave her a sick grin and waved as the cab drove off, then turned back to the Red Lion. He could do with a real drink. He decided to order a double. Or two.

13

JAMIE'S REVENGE

The fat man's fiver had bought Jamie a chips and curry sauce and a Fanta and he'd scoffed the lot sitting in a bus shelter on Gibb Street. He knew he had to get back at his brother, teach him a lesson for thumping him, but the problem was how? How could a short-arse kid like him get even with a twenty-year-old thug of a brother without signing his own death warrant? Wayne had already done time for GBH and the drugs he took were making him steadily worse. He'd also hit mum a couple of times and dad was too scared – or pissed – to stop him now. One day he'd go too far and all they could hope was that it would be with someone outside the family. So it had to be something that wouldn't get back to him, something – what was that word? – *amominuss*.

He had walked the entire length of Gibb Street in the rain. It was on the corner where they were demolishing the old bus depot that the idea popped into his head as clearly as if someone had taken him into a shop doorway and shown him a full-colour plan, complete with working lights and little figures and sound effects. It was so simple, and so obvious, he wondered why he hadn't thought of it before. Of course, he wasn't to know the fat man's part in making it happen. Besides, the fat man was forgotten, the four quid in his pocket notwithstanding; revenge on his brother was everything now.

Wayne had a job – a rarity on their estate – in a scrapyard down by the railway. He drove an ancient mobile crane that carried the old wrecked cars about the place. Before the speed turned him on his own family, he used to take Jamie down there and let him sit

in the cab while he worked – a couple of times he had shown him
how to work it – and what had interested Jamie was that, apart from
the mechanical grab controls, it worked like any stolen car he had
managed to drive over the last few months. He was a crap driver
but would never admit it, and·was far happier to be a passenger
as someone else tear-arsed around the estate in a nicked 205 or
XR2. Nonetheless, his rudimentary driving experience should prove
very useful.

He began to run, partly because it was beginning to rain even
more heavily and partly because he was excited by his idea. If he
timed it right, Wayne would be having his lunch, and he could do
his stuff and no one would know he'd done it.

Sneaking into the yard was easy – the fence was broken down in
several places and as there was nothing worth nicking, they didn't
bother too much about repairing it. Jamie then slipped between the
tall towers of piled-up cars, rust-coloured puddles dogging his every
step. Maybe six people worked here and he was well into the site
before he caught sight of anyone and, what do you know, it was
Wayne. He was walking towards the hut in the middle of the yard,
pulling his jacket round his shoulders, obviously having been sitting
in the cab of his crane in the dry.

Jamie ducked down and watched his bastard of a brother pass.
There had been a time when they'd been good mates, Wayne acting
like a big brother should do, but now he was just another thug out for
himself, even if it meant stealing from his own kid brother. Satisfied
he was out of sight, Jamie edged between two rows of crushed cars
until he saw the object of his journey: a mobile crane, its four large
tyres planted firmly in the mud, the large grab swinging lightly
in the rain like the jaws of a dozing dinosaur. Jamie covered the
twenty yards to it in an instant and jumped onto the step leading
into the cab.

Pulling the door open he sat in the warm seat and slammed the
door after him. The cab was still steamed up from Wayne's morning
spent sitting in it and it smelled of cigarettes, the floor covered in a
film of ash-smattered phlegm. Revolting.

He looked for the key and found it where he knew it would be,
stashed under the seat. Good old Wayne, the dozy twat. Without
wasting any time – he knew what he was going to do as if his entire
life had been leading to this one action; it was the justification for
all the misery and cold-heartedness and neglect he'd had to endure

– he inserted the key, turned on the ignition, then reached down and pushed in the starter. The engine kicked into life immediately – it was still warm – and, stretching to depress the clutch, Jamie selected first gear and released the brakes.

Slowly the crane chugged into life and advanced inch by inch across the open space to an alley on the right between two rows of wrecks. Once Jamie was confident of his steering, he changed into second gear and accelerated, feeling the pronounced unevenness of the ground as he was gently rocked from side to side, and watched the closed fist of the grab swing back and forth like a giant conker on a string.

He reached the end of the alley and found himself on open ground, the grass waist-high with no definable track.

But he knew which way he was heading and he accelerated even more, being rewarded with a backfire and a surge of power as the crane coursed through the grass, the unrutted ground making for a smoother passage.

Up ahead he could see the wall made up of railway sleepers topped by barbed wire. At the speed he was going he would reach it in twenty seconds. He floored the accelerator, ignoring the whining from the engine as it demanded third gear. He relaxed his pressure momentarily as he wondered if he could wedge the accelerator and watch as it crashed through the wall, but decided he didn't have the time: it was a noisy machine and someone was bound to be wondering why it was working if Wayne was sitting with them having a cup of tea. Jamie would have to jump instead.

The wall came closer and closer, the grab swinging more wildly as the ground broke up. It was threatening to topple the crane, the grab's weight not perfectly balanced. Only thirty yards to go.

Jamie grabbed at the door handle and tugged it down. It spun uselessly out of his grasp. What? The door wasn't working? Twenty yards.

He took his foot off the accelerator, for the first time a flaw in his plan apparent, and kicked frantically at the door. It opened! He pressed the accelerator one last time, then turned to face out of the door.

The ground was whizzing past at some speed and for a moment he didn't want to chance jumping. But a glance through the rain-streaked windscreen at the fast-approaching obstruction and he had no option.

He leapt for his life an instant before the grab smashed into the top of the eight-feet-high wall. The bang coincided with Jamie's landing, his legs slipping away from him as he began to tumble and bounce in the wet grass.

In front of him the cab smashed into the wooden wall. Despite its momentum, it didn't break the sleepers. Instead a retaining concrete post snapped and the crane and a dozen of the sleepers tumbled out of sight down the embankment on the other side.

Even as he rolled to a halt, pain in his wrist and stomach, Jamie could hear grinding and smashing as the cab and crane somersaulted in an avalanche of heavy wood until it landed with a ground-juddering thud at the bottom of the steep embankment. Then there was silence.

Jamie rolled himself over and sat upright, dizziness slowing his rise to his feet. He looked back at the scrapyard and saw that nobody had appeared yet; maybe he had time to see the damage he had done.

He hobbled over to the gaping hole in the wall, the rain suddenly slicing down like cold steel and driving the breath from him. He stumbled and fell to his knees and decided it would be easier to crawl the last few feet. Slowly he approached the edge of the drop and looked down.

Yes! Thirty feet down, amid railway sleepers seemingly tossed about as easily as a handful of pencils, was Wayne's crane. The cab was smashed flat, the four wheels turned to face the sky, the grab splayed across the other track. Jamie whooped with delight and punched his fists in the air. *Way to go! Suck on that, Wayne, you wanker!* Then, for some reason, he remembered a fat man's smile . . . He looked at the grab. The other *track*?

There was a familiar sound, a two-tone horn blaring to his right and then, before he could even begin to comprehend the enormity of what he had done, a three-carriage train doing forty miles per hour and with no chance of stopping came round the lazy bend on the main line that led from Blair Station and ploughed into the wreckage.

The first carriage continued on its straight course, but its front third was crushed into mangled metal. The second carriage fell sideways off the rail and crashed into the grab, the impact slowing it enough that the third carriage had nowhere to go but over it, taking to the air at an angle of thirty degrees until almost its entire length was above the second carriage. Then it crashed down and rolled over against the other embankment. Smashing glass, splintering wood and rending metalwork filled the afternoon with a cacophony of death and destruction. It was almost a minute until the last wheel had stopped spinning and the last shriek of torn metal had died away. And then, in the silence, came the screams and cries.

But then there was another horn, and the sound of screeching brakes as metal wheels failed to stop on metal track and a second train slammed into the stranded carcass of the wreckage, stilling some screams, but replacing them with even more.

Before the horrendous noise had subsided a second time, Jamie had started to walk away from the scene, his face white, his numbed mind already trying to convince him that what he had seen hadn't happened.

14

MR FARMER'S VISITOR

Mr Farmer stretched his arms above his head and let out a long fart. He was lying on his kitchen floor, his whole body alive with anticipation. He was breathing heavily and he tried to concentrate on getting his respiration down, but every time he thought of what the boy was going to do, his heart raced and he began to pulse sweat anew. Even his penis was erect, despite having disgorged the contents of his testicles some ten minutes before. It was a delicious ache but one he had no intention of touching. He couldn't remember the last time he had touched his penis sexually – or seen it, come to that, his belly conspiring to hide everything, including his feet – but if he could ejaculate spontaneously because his mind could see things that excited him, then so be it.

He glanced up at the kitchen clock. 12:55 p.m. Plenty of time for his boy to do his best – and then there would be his soldier. The expectation was almost impossible to bear. He looked across at the scudding clouds, an endless panoply of grey misery that roiled over Blair like an inverted bubbling pot, quenching the light of the day and providing a perfect backdrop for the woe about to swamp the town.

Just then he heard a sound. The doorbell. At this time? The last time anyone had rung his bell, apart from the postman, had been at least six months ago, and then it was someone coming to a wrong address. He decided to ignore it and instead concentrate on the boy, but the bell rang again. And again. Then there was a noise and a voice: someone was speaking through the letterbox.

'Mr Farmer, you there?' It was a woman. 'I know you're there.

I can hear the radio. Would you answer the door, please? It's important.'

He debated whether to answer but finally rolled himself over and forced himself to his feet off the kitchen floor, disgusted at the grime that attached itself to his sweat. He grabbed his dressing gown, hauled it on and walked into the lounge.

'Who is it? What do you want?' he asked, his voice still breathless.

'My name's Toniski, Izotta Toniski,' came the voice, friendly and female. 'I work for the *Northern Sentinel*. I want to ask you about the policeman who arrested you the other day. You know, the one who—'

'I know what he did. Why?'

'Look, I'm not interested in you or why he arrested you, I just want to find out how he was. You were one of the last to talk to him. I want to find out why he jumped.'

'How can I—'

'Look, it's rather uncomfortable shouting into your letterbox. If you could let me in . . .'

He turned off the radio. He didn't want to be distracted while the woman was with him. He'd just have to hurry her on her way. 'All right, give me a moment.'

He looked around the room and decided it was too untidy to even attempt to clean up; he'd just be rearranging the mess, so he walked down the short hall to the door and opened it.

His visitor turned out to be an attractive half-caste woman in her thirties, dressed in a fashionable beige knee-length raincoat, the shoulders stained with rain, and a less than fashionable plastic rain hat. Her ankles were splattered with mud, her shoes obviously water-logged.

'Come in,' he said. 'If you feel you'll be safe.'

'I know your record, Mr Farmer. I'm not worried.'

Izotta squeezed past him and walked into the lounge. The room was as odd as the man.

Mr Farmer was well known to the staff of the town hall and had been arrested in the vicinity half a dozen times. They had described him as being huge; they were not exaggerating. The man must have weighed at least thirty stone. At five feet six he was as tall as Izotta but three times as wide. He had small dark eyes, a small nose and a mean little mouth, all dwarfed by a big fat head that looked like a balloon, his white crew-cut hair doing nothing to dispel the notion. His arms and legs were wobbly with fat, and his fingers so podgy as to be almost impractical. He was wearing a navy blue towelling robe that was threadbare and held up by a pink cord. He was flushed and sweaty, which was odd as his flat was cold. Cold and bare. Worn brown carpets throughout and only the most basic furniture present. There were no cabinets, no ornaments, no pictures on the wall, no lamps. The main light was a bare bulb, probably no more than 60 watts. There weren't even curtains, and the walls were covered in a dated blue pattern almost bound to have been put up by a previous tenant. The only sign of habitation was a congregation of empty food tins – dozens of them – and old newspapers.

Izotta sat herself in one of the two grey corduroy-covered easy chairs. A leather Parker Knoll recliner was pointed at the window. As there seemed to be no TV, that would be his only viewing pleasure, except today the picture was grey and streaked with rain that rattled the window panes like a hundred fingers trying to attract attention.

'Tea?' he asked, shutting the door.

'Prefer coffee. Black, two sugars. Thanks.'

Feeling like a waiter in his own home Mr Farmer went into the kitchen and switched on the kettle. The boy hadn't reached his goal yet so there was still time.

As he made the drinks, Izotta studied the room. Her first impression was confirmed: it was the room of someone who didn't care about living in it. It was functional: seats for sitting; a fire for heat – and sadly not on as she shivered in her damp clothes; and windows to look out onto a world as drab as the flat itself. If ever a home belonged to a creep this was it, and she had seen enough like it in her time.

Mr Farmer returned, a mug in each hand and, settling in the other chair which creaked ominously, proceeded to hold court like a pink Buddha, telling her what had happened the previous afternoon after the policeman stopped his fun.

Izotta took copious notes but Mr Farmer knew she was getting nothing useful about the man's state of mind. Until Mr Farmer had planted the seed, PC Bates had been as normal as she. He wondered if he might touch her and see what hid behind her elegance and determination.

'So when he went into the building, he was just doing his duty. He wasn't scared or upset?' she said.

'He seemed more worried about letting me go than what he had to do once he got up to the poor man on the ledge.'

'That's what I expected.'

'You've spoken to—?'

'Most of the people he met on his way up to the ledge and the people up there. Nothing out of the ordinary.'

'How did you find me? I don't believe he checked my name.'

'I asked around the town hall. You should change your haunts.'

Mr Farmer smiled. Half the fun was watching the reaction of women when they saw him *again*.

'I could do *you* a favour,' he offered.

She leaned forward, pointing her pen at him. 'And I could do you a mischief.'

Touché. He liked her. Much as he enjoyed the fear that flitted behind the average woman's eyes, he had admiration for those who could step outside the stereotypical behaviour of their sex and show a little fortitude. And he could sense she meant it. It might even be fun to see what she would do. The pain wouldn't matter and he was still feeling hot . . . but no, best not, especially with his boy ready to perform. Last thing he needed was to be in the company of others when that delight happened.

'Miss, I think I've told you all I know and I am tired, so if you—'

'No problem,' she stood up. 'To be honest, you haven't been much help, Mr Farmer, but that's not your fault. Looks like it will have to stay a mystery.'

'Seems that way,' he said, struggling to extract his bulk from the steep sides of the easy chair. He finally succeeded and offered her his hand, but couldn't stop it trembling – *oh, the temptation to delve into her secrets* – and she caught the movement and the look in his eyes.

What a slime, she thought, shying back from him and taking a circuitous route to the hall. She may have misread it, but his intentions were every bit as unpleasant as she suspected. Probing her mind would have been no different from probing her body.

He watched her go, but just as she reached the door, the ecstasy began. His boy had done it.

With a whimper he shuddered and blushed and fell to his knees with a loud thud, his dressing gown bursting open under the strain, exposing his sweating flab to her, his erection barely visible under the bloated sack of his stomach. She saw him and tutted her disgust – noting that his body was entirely hairless – but then he flopped forward on his stomach, his open mouth crashing onto the carpet, his body jerking in his pleasure.

Izotta hesitated again, but then she saw the blood on his face as he rolled his head from side to side, moans escaping like breaths from an exhausted swimmer. *Oh no*, she thought, *the bastard's having a heart attack*!

As the passengers died, so Mr Farmer's pleasure grew, as if the extinguishing of their existence lit a candle in his mind until his head was ablaze with light that coursed through every fibre in his body, causing him to twist and sweat, his rancid odour a cloud covering him. Then he lost control of his bladder and his bowels, voiding himself, oblivious to all except the utter pleasure the deaths he had helped to cause provided him.

Seeing the fat man having a seizure, Izotta feared the worst and, discarding her notebook and handbag, she ran back to help him.

With difficulty she rolled him over on his side, images of elephant seals springing to mind, her hands sliding on slick blubbery flesh the texture and colour of skinned chicken, searching in his bloodied mouth to see if he had swallowed his tongue, but the pink slug was safely visible.

He was shivering, his eyes rolling, his throat trying to spit out words but failing. He was *there* on the train, by the tracks with the boy, the destruction and terror as real to him as the hands of the woman seeking to right him.

She tried to lift him up but he was too heavy – bigger than Sumo wrestlers she had seen on TV – and instead she looked around for a telephone but, just as she realized there wasn't one, she felt his hand gripping her own, hot and wet. He was burning and she could feel spasms surging through him, like an animal convulsing in its sleep. His grip tightened and the pain began. She tried freeing herself but couldn't and then his face suddenly rushed up to meet hers, his eyes wide, the pupils impossibly large, his bloodied mouth wide in a silent scream.

His face stopped inches from hers, twisting slightly one way then the other, deep sighs shuddering his flesh, his jowls taking on a life of their own.

'Please, Mr Farmer, let go, you're hurting me.'

Her left hand fought to free her other hand but his grip was too tight. He pulled her within inches of his hot face, then laughed and stared her in the eye and spoke, his voice frighteningly calm, like a badly dubbed foreign film.

'Are you afraid of the dark?'

15

JAMIE'S HIDEOUT

Jamie didn't know what to do as he wandered back from the train crash. All he had wanted was to get back at his rotten brother and here he'd killed people and wrecked trains and . . . He walked zombie-like towards the piles of scrapped cars, sleeting rain drifting across the open ground in waves like net curtains being opened and closed. And then he saw Wayne and other men running towards him, shouting and waving their arms.

Jamie looked behind him in the vain hope that he had imagined the whole incident, but there was a cloud of dust rising despite the rain – and he thought he could hear screams. The men reached him, Wayne grabbing him by the upper arm and yanking him off the ground.

'What you doing here? What you done? What's happened?'

Jamie couldn't speak; all he could see were the trains crashing in Wayne's eyes like his bastard brother was giving him a private action replay.

One of the men came up to them. 'God, the crane, the damn crane! You left the fucking brake off!'

Wayne exploded. 'Oh, I left the brake off and it ran uphill? That fucking thing was off and parked back there!'

Never the quickest of minds, Wayne suddenly looked down at his brother. 'It was you!' he shouted, spit joining the rain on his brother's white face.

He started to shake him. Jamie's vision blurred, his head beginning to hurt. Suddenly Wayne stopped and Jamie saw one of the older men slap him across the face and he dropped Jamie to his knees where he stayed like a scolded puppy. The man, his face red with shock, thin white hair plastered over his forehead leaned down to him and asked: 'Did you drive Wayne's crane?'

Wayne's crane? Wayne's crane? That sounded funny, thought Jamie, *like Fred's Bed or Bill's Pill or . . . or Dave's Grave*. His blank expression seemed answer enough.

'Kid's out of it,' said the man. 'Let's see what happened.'

The men ran on, Wayne dawdling long enough to grab Jamie by the collar and yell into his face.

'If you've done this, kid, you're dead! You're fucking *dead*!' And he threw him onto the ground and ran on, his first step splashing Jamie's legs with mud.

Jamie sat on the wet grass in the pouring rain and watched his brother run towards the broken hole in the fence. Of course, Jamie knew he deserved to die. He'd killed people. He hadn't meant to, he'd only wanted to . . . he *hadn't* meant to, had he? All he'd wanted to do was wreck the crane, not drive it onto the railway and cause . . .

The men had reached the fence and two of them immediately fell to their knees, the others standing and staring. Then Wayne reached them and he too just stood and stared, then slowly turned to look back at his brother, and even from fifty yards in the grey light and pouring rain, the hatred in his eyes blazed at his younger brother, searching across the grass and mud like twin laser beams. Jamie could almost feel their heat, and he could certainly feel the pain they promised.

Wayne was about to run back to him when the big guy caught hold of his arm and shouted at him. Wayne pointed at Jamie, then nodded and all the men started off down the slope towards the wreck.

Safe for the moment, Jamie stood up and tried to think what he could do next. Help? No. Run? Yes, but where to? Confess? Yes, confess. Go to the police and tell them what he'd done? Yes, tell them he hadn't meant to, hadn't wanted to hurt anyone. It was just a prank, a way of getting back at his bastard brother. All Wayne's fault really, if he hadn't taken his money, if he hadn't . . . He remembered the money in his pocket. He still had four quid left. He *could* get away. It was enough to get him to Manchester or Derby by train. He could go to the station . . .

And then it hit him again and he threw up. He'd wrecked the trains, there was no escape, he was a murderer. *He was a killer*!

Once he had finished regurgitating his lunch onto the grass he stood up and, on shaking legs, loped across the rest of the field to the hulking piles of dead cars and walked through their ranks towards the exit onto Gibb Street. They'd lock him up, wouldn't they? He'd seen newspaper stories about youngsters who had committed crimes: burglars, joyriders, murderers . . . everyone hated them; he'd seen the people outside the courts screaming for blood. You could tell they'd kill the kids if they could. Kill kids . . . Well, he *was* a killer, he *should* die.

He walked on, grim satisfaction gained from his deadly equation, but soon realized he was lost. The weather had rendered everything grey and rusted so all the cars looked the same. It was like a metal maze. How long he walked he didn't know, and cared less. He was cold and wet and he was a killer; it was the least he deserved. Suddenly he found himself outside the hut where Wayne had been taking his break. It looked bright and cosy; maybe if he got out of the rain he might be able to think better.

He opened the door and walked in. It was warm and smelled of tea and farts and cigarettes: it was like coming home. He rushed to the stand-alone stove and stood in front of it, shivering as he warmed his hands and face and backside, then he looked around.

The hut was small and cramped, containing only a table with steaming mugs and sandwiches, chairs, the stove, a wall-mounted metal cabinet with a padlock, a small filthy sink and a battered electric kettle. But there were the pictures all over the walls. *Hundreds* of naked women, more than Jamie could have imagined, all of them with their tits out, showing their hairy cunts. He'd seen plenty before – didn't he keep track of Wayne's hidden horde of porn under his bed when he knew he was out? – but he'd never seen so many naked females together. Three of the four walls were just *flesh*, and many of the women were fat. Most of them, in fact. He had little time for girls yet, but even he knew fat was ugly, yet here there was row after row of fat women with big tits hanging out and fat bellies and arses and thighs so chubby sometimes he couldn't see their privates . . . He was mesmerized. It was like seeing his mum and his aunts all together in a changing room. Gross.

Suddenly there was a noise and fearing it was Wayne coming back, Jamie clambered out through the hut window, fell into mud, then ran off into the rain without looking back. He heard voices and ducked into the first car he could find.

Huddled down inside the back of an old Ford Granada that rested under other wrecks, he found an old blanket that was still dry and wrapped himself in it and tried to stop his teeth chattering.

The crash kept running through his mind, and what he could have done to avoid it. Steered the crane another way? Not got into it? Not gone to the bloody scrapyard at all? If he'd gone to school he would have been all right, wouldn't he? Right now he could be in lessons and the trains wouldn't have crashed. OK, he'd be bored, but was it his fault he found school too easy?

English, maths, history: he could do them real quick but then all the teachers would do was tell him off for being untidy and then spend all their time with the thickies who couldn't keep up with him. So he skipped lessons. Teachers obviously didn't know what to do with him, his parents didn't care and, if Wayne ever caught him with a book, he'd call him queer and rip it up! It had got to the point where he would secretly read books under his bedcovers by torchlight and wake up so knackered he'd avoid school for fear of falling asleep in classes and getting into even more trouble! He knew other kids read comics or porno mags on the quiet; he preferred to read fantasy like David Gemmel and Terry Pratchett but all that would be gone now. He was a killer, and killers went to prison, and prison was *full* of Waynes . . .

Over and over, as the tears coursed down his face, he tried to find an excuse, an explanation for what had happened, but for some reason the only image that kept coming to mind was the hut's amazing walls of fat, naked women. Ugly, horrible fat. Then he remembered the fat man he'd met that morning and, as lightning suddenly flashed overhead and thunder cracked loudly enough to shake the cars he was hiding under, Jamie realized the fat man was the cause of his troubles.

He had wanted to get back at Wayne, true, but he'd been thinking of letting his pigeons go or putting sugar in his petrol tank. He hadn't thought of anything so drastic as the crane; it was too big a thing to do, and the trouble it caused would be worse than anything Wayne had ever done. No, he hadn't thought of the crane until he met that fat man . . . Another lightning stroke illuminated Jamie's metal world and the puddles outside lit up like neon.

Suddenly the fat man's face leapt at him from the darkness, jibing at him, ordering him what to do, then laughing like those clowns at Blackpool, rolling back and forth, eyes wide, yellow teeth bared, jowls livid red. Yes, the fat man. He'd given him money, touched him. He remembered his fingers like fat worms, cold and sweaty, running through his hair. Jamie's scalp felt itchy where the man had touched him and the thought made him shiver. And he could hear the man's voice in his head, long after he had gone, taunting him about Wayne, telling him he deserved to be punished, to be put in his place like all bad brothers should be. The fat man. Jamie hadn't wanted to do anything until he met him. He was used to it, being bullied and picked on and wanting to get his own back, but . . . but it was the fat man who had made him come out here and get in the crane and . . .

Another lightning flash, deafening thunder and then the sound of police sirens. Jamie huddled out of sight as cars and people began to fill the scrapyard, the easiest route to the crash. Guilt and fear kept him in his hiding place as people milled around. Too frightened to move he sat in a puddle of urine, crying until his eyes were sore, his only hope of salvation a confession from a fat man he'd only met once and who *had been in his mind*.

Yeah, and like Wayne was wonderful and pigs could fly and everyone would forgive him for his prank. Outside the rain lashed down and the rescue continued but inside the crushed Ford, Jamie kept out of sight, tears his only friends and even they ran away.

16

WESLEY'S LECTURE

'Gentlemen, thank you for coming. To be honest I didn't expect your response to be so prompt – which leads me to believe that there is indeed something wrong in the town of Blair.'

The audience assembled in Lambert's darkened lounge didn't react. There were eight people there: General Stanley Roberts, in charge of Army–Civil Liaison; Squadron Leader Wilson Carter, supervisor of the RAF's Red Light programme; two senior civil servants, one from the Home Office, the other from Defence; Doctors Horrigan and Hatfield, both attached to Department O in Llanfestri; and a Ministry secretary, a bulldog of a woman called Mrs Ellis, who had the fastest shorthand he had ever seen. He had met all but the Ministry people before and had become used to his meetings being treated as little more than comic diversions. However, their prompt attendance gave him hope that, for once, sense would prevail.

'No doubt you will leave the meeting as unenthusiastic about my ideas as you have been in the past. However, I would remind you that I have also been *right* in the past.'

Lambert chose not to embarrass any members present who had poo-pooed his warnings about Red Light's over-enthusiastic debunking of UFO sightings – a national newspaper had faked several reports to see how the government reacted and had subsequently made their spokesmen look complete fools as they stated quite categorically that what had been a dinner plate was a weather balloon, thus proving they *were* paranoid about *something*.

'I will not prattle, simply state facts.' He switched on a slide

projector and a black-and-white shot of a fishing village came
on screen.

'Roswiay, north-east Scotland, 1908. Small fishing village,
population 126, the vast majority dependent on that fishing. A very
close-knit community, thirteen miles from the nearest settlement.
Snow in winter and high seas often led to it being cut off from the
outside world for weeks at a time. There was one public house, the
Gannet, one shop, which included the baker, butcher and post office,
and a school for the village's eleven children. In 1908 they ranged
from six to fifteen, with five other children below school age. There
was also a Presbyterian chapel, which contained all the records of
the village's births, deaths and marriages. My information is based
on contemporary accounts, local newspaper reports, interviews with
people who left the village prior to 1908 and to the one survivor,
a boy of eleven, Euan MacIntry.

'Euan fled the village in October 1908 after a series of rapes and
murders. By definition they must have been committed by villagers
and an atmosphere of recrimination and distrust swiftly blew up
into a lynching of the local shopkeeper. An attempt by the priest
to intervene led to his being attacked and his legs being broken.
As the highest moral authority in the village, his confinement did
nothing to improve the climate of fear and hate and, despite pleas
for the villagers to call in the police, they became obsessed with
solving their own problems. Eventually Euan ran away, afraid of
his father's behaviour towards him and his sister.

'He had never been out of the village, the weather was atrocious
– records show it to have been the worst gale in ten years – and,
although he followed the road, he got lost. It was two days before
he was found, and a further two days before he was able to tell the
doctor caring for him where he was from or why he was there: he'd
had to have several toes amputated due to frostbite.

'The local police called in the army and they set out for
Roswiay, arriving mid-afternoon, six days after Euan left, on
October 29th 1908.'

Here he paused, sensing the impatience of his audience. He
switched the slide to show another black-and-white shot, this time
of wave-lashed rocks.

'Roswiay had disappeared. Twenty-one houses, a main street,
four fishing boats, a church-cum-school, a shop, an inn, a meeting
hall, all completely vanished. And before you say they slipped into

the sea, the coastline there is granite, the hardest rock to erode, and subsequent underwater examination of the area the following summer revealed not one single brick within half a mile of the shore. No artefacts, no evidence whatsoever that there had ever been a community there. No bodies were ever found around the village and none were ever washed up. Furthermore, no relative of any of the inhabitants was ever contacted by anyone in the village. The village simply disappeared in the six days that Euan was away.'

The civil servants and military men shrugged their shoulders, but he could see the scientists were intrigued. They knew him well.

As Lambert continued, he showed a succession of slides of official reports, newspaper articles and ships' logs. 'I have collated as much information as I can. There were reports of unusual weather in the area, specifically an extremely low cloud base causing, in the words of one captain on a passing cargo vessel: "to black out that part of the peninsula as if night had settled there for good." Weather records, such as they were, showed an exceptionally high level of rainfall and high winds, strong even for that time of year, and odder still, westerly winds blowing offland rather than the usual Northerlies. But the key element is how Euan described the atmosphere in the village prior to his running away.

'Decent God-fearing folk simply lost control and became suspicious, twisted people, looking for any excuse to attack others. Violence and sexual deviation became a horrifying reality almost overnight, and all of it to a backdrop of weather fouler than any could remember, so bad it kept their boats in the harbour for two weeks. Now frustration is bound to build up in any group of people forced together, particularly fishermen used to being out at sea, but occasions like this must occur every year, yet nothing had ever come of them before. The degeneration witnessed by young Euan was out of all proportion. They were used to pulling together – but they stopped, surrendering to their baser instincts.'

'This Euan, what happened to him?' asked Dr Horrigan.

'He became more and more withdrawn and eventually had to be institutionalized in a clinic near Dundee. He became completely catatonic – lying in bed, staring at the ceiling – in the 1930s. He actually lived to be sixty-three but for fifty of those years he ceased to function. Before he lapsed completely, his only words about what happened whenever asked were "The Darkness". Oh, and one other thing: he always had to have the light on. Whenever it was switched off he would begin screaming hysterically – even at sixty years of age.'

There was a long pause, and then one of the civil servants spoke up. 'Well, that's all very interesting, but I fail to see—'

'You're here because I mentioned Blair. Please let me finish. If you can't see the connection, you may as well leave.'

No one moved and he couldn't help smiling. It looked as if he was right. He turned his wheelchair back to face the screen and clicked on the next slide, this time showing a hand-tinted photograph of a pretty English country village.

'Warforn Peck, Suffolk. A village of about five hundred people, mostly agricultural workers, but during World War Two a good number found employment at a US air base, Hambleton Ferry, about five miles away. Like Roswiay, Warforn Peck was isolated, but a pleasant place to live. In the winter of 1942, there were a series of rapes in the village, both of women *and* men, the latter almost unheard of in those days. The local police were useless and called in Scotland Yard. The attacks continued, culminating in three murders, two schoolgirls and a man, all of whom had been sexually assaulted prior to being stabbed. As it was wartime and bad for morale, news of the crimes was never released to the public. Fifty or so residents chose to move out, but the others remained, confident that the presence of two dozen policemen and a detachment of military police, twenty strong, would stop the carnage.

'On February 8th 1942, Warforn Peck disappeared, together with its remaining three hundred and eighty-four residents, ten policemen and nineteen military personnel.'

'I've never heard of that,' said General Roberts.

'You won't have. It was covered up with an efficiency every bit as watertight as the date of the Normandy landings. Officially, nothing happened. Unofficially, and given out to those who needed to know – relatives, the military, the police – there had been a terrible accident involving a bomber crashing while carrying a toxic gas bomb stolen from the Germans and being transported to a research centre in Wiltshire. It caused instant death and all the dead were removed and their bodies cremated for fear they might carry some contaminant.'

'And people bought that?'

'Most, surprisingly. Those that didn't were leaned on. Some, I suspect, though I can't prove it, were silenced.'

'Killed?'

'We'll never know and, without being callous, it doesn't matter now. The exigencies of war allow much that would normally be avoided. However, the important point is not the cover-up, but the real cause and *why* there was a cover-up. The abnormal and snowballing crime rate, despite the heavy police concentration, was odd enough, but combined with the cover-up and the weather conditions, well . . . The weather at the time was so bad that bombing raids from the nearby base were suspended, even though other bases were unaffected. On the last day of the village's existence, the local newspaper reported what it called "the shortest day of the year" around the village as darkness, caused by the exceptionally low cloud, made day night.' He showed a slide of a newspaper headline.

'One other thing, gentlemen, and I'm hoping that certain of you will be able to confirm this: in the two weeks following the village's disappearance, regular convoys of army lorries were seen *entering* the so-called "forbidden zone" around Warforn Peck carrying debris – bricks, broken wood, concrete. When the village was finally opened for access, all that was left was rubble, a total of one hundred and eight buildings flattened as effectively as if by a nuclear explosion. Indeed, at the end of the war, as atomic tests became more common knowledge, rumours of a dreadful accident at Warforn Peck were circulated – and not really discouraged – to the effect that perhaps there had been a "premature" experiment.'

'I don't see the point of all this—' said one of the civil servants impatiently.

'The point is, I have sworn statements from three of those drivers that when they first entered the village there was nothing. Not one piece of debris, not a single structure, road sign, shed, nothing, just blackened earth. Even the roads had disappeared. Their task was to dump rubble and bomb-damaged material from the East End into a pattern approximating the old layout of the village.'

It was General Roberts's turn to speak again. 'That, if you don't mind me saying so, is a load of poppycock—'

Lambert flicked on another slide.

'I have obtained German reconnaissance shots taken over Suffolk for the period of February 2nd to March 4th 1942. The Germans flew sorties as often as they could spare the aircraft – the casualty rate was, as you could imagine, quite high – to determine the strength of bomber forces on the ground. Often they would tail bombing raids back from Germany and pose as straggling aircraft, photographing at will, then head back to Germany eluding any fighters. These shots are in sequential order, taken from a height of ten thousand feet. I have numbered them one to ten and circled an area of one mile across, which contains the village of Warforn Peck at its centre.'

He flashed the slides one after the other and let them tell their own story. The first three showed the clear layout of a village set around a crooked crossroads. The next two showed what could only be described as a black spot. The sixth showed a grey spot. The next two showed the same grey spot but with flecks within it, one with a long column leading to the south. The remaining two shots showed the pattern of the town from the first three slides repeated but poorly delineated.

Lambert then ran through the slides again showing that a normal Suffolk village had been covered by an extremely dense and unnatural dark cloud and that, once it had cleared, the town had completely disappeared. There was then an investigation by army personnel, including tanks and armoured vehicles, followed by a process of dumping material to recreate the layout of the village, the long column proving, once enlarged, to be trucks full of rubble.

'You know and I know that whatever secrets the war held, it does not include anything that could destroy a town as completely as that, either by design or by accident. The subsequent cover-up underlines just how frightened the authorities were of something amiss being discovered, *even to the extent of inventing a military accident* – something that even today all efforts are made to avoid.'

There was silence again, Lambert certain he had made his point but, to ram it home, he flashed up another slide.

'Gentlemen, this is an aerial shot of Blair, taken less than three months ago. As you can see, it's a moderately large industrial town in Derbyshire, somewhat isolated because of its valley position. And this . . . is an aerial shot of Blair taken twenty-four hours ago.'

There was an audible gasp.

'You see, in Blair it will look like bad weather. Approaching from any road or rail link and it will look odd, but just a fluke, but from above . . . Blair is entirely enveloped by a rain cloud of ferocious density that extends in all directions for almost a mile and a half from the centre of the town. Your presence here has confirmed my worries about the state of the town as shown by a wide diversity of perverse and abnormal behaviour, much of it criminal in nature, as reported in the Press and media, as well as by indicators of economic and social deterioration – all of them showing a rate of coincidence far beyond any possible statistical anomaly. And this photograph shows the physical evidence. Blair is being consumed by something and, just as happened with Roswiay and Warforn Peck, I believe it will disappear off the face of the earth within the next few days.'

17

MARK DAWSON'S NIGHTMARE

Mark had his mobile phone and although the Red Lion wasn't the friendliest of public houses, no one hassled him when he kept having to answer its insistent beeping. He had five calls in less than an hour, each putting a further nail into the coffin of Dawson Creative Associates.

There was confirmation from Marchant that Eclipse wouldn't touch DCA if Mark *paid* to handle the account; a friendly warning from Peter Dimbleby that his successor would not be retaining DCA's services – Mark congratulated him and ordered another double; the other calls were from suppliers harrying him to pay bills. Instead he paid for more scotch until, by 1:30 p.m., he was pretty much sozzled and finally switched his phone off.

He ventured out of the pub into the rain, unsure of where he was going. He knew he should get back to the agency to check on the progress of what little work they were handling but found he couldn't give a toss. So instead he decided to walk off what he now realized was too much booze. His lunchtime limit was usually four measures and he'd had, he thought, six doubles, so he was well gone. And, as he trudged through the lunchtime crowds in the rain, he had to acknowledge that alcohol's reputation as a depressant was well-founded.

Even a cavalcade of screaming police cars and ambulances failed to interest him. Indeed, he wondered what lucky bastard had been given a way out of his particular mess by some lucky accident. He walked into W H Smith and, out of habit, bought a couple of magazines, asking the girl for a receipt but then realized he wouldn't be able to claim it back as he didn't have a bloody company any more, so he dropped the receipt back on the desk and walked out.

Deciding he preferred the real weather to the artificial climate of the shopping centre, he pulled up his collar and walked wherever his feet took him.

At a little after 2:15 he was wobbling while he waited at a pelican crossing when he heard a woman swear behind him. He turned to see her pointing at a window. Soon a crowd of pedestrians had gathered to view whatever had upset the woman. Curious, he pushed his bleary way to the front of the growing crowd to get a view, and heard several other oaths and exclamations of horror and, suddenly, several people were running away, shouting. What the hell?

Finally he could see. A dozen television screens showed a newsreader sitting at a desk, talking. What was the fuss? His haircut wasn't that bad, Mark smiled drunkenly. Then the picture cut to a split screen with the picture of a reporter on a telephone and, on the left, a simple map, showing a line leading to a blob captioned Blair and an arrow pointing to a red star labelled 'SITE OF COLLISION'.

One of the sets suddenly changed to Ceefax and page 150 flashed up over the picture: **SERIOUS TRAIN CRASH NEAR BLAIR, DERBYS. SEVERAL FATALITIES, RESCUE WORKERS AT SCENE**.

Drunk as he was, Mark knew enough about Blair Station to realize that it had at most two trains an hour during the day. Any recent crash could have involved the train Karen had caught. He pushed his way through the crowd. A man remonstrated with him and he pushed him aside, frantically working his way through the packed crowd until he stumbled onto the road and fell onto the bonnet of a car that was screeching to a halt.

The driver wound down his window and swore at him, but Mark ignored him. All his mind could comprehend was that his wife, his lover, *his life* might have been in that train crash and he wanted to get there to find her and see she was all right. But even as he ran on through the rain dodging in and out of the slowing traffic, the 'might' became a positive belief that Karen *had* been on the train that had crashed and, though he fought the notion that was jabbing at his mind as insistently as the car horns that punctuated his desperate race along the street, he began to fear that she had been hurt, might even be . . .

'*Karen!*' he screamed and charged on.

He ran, ignoring the pain in his lungs and his side, his vision blurred by wind and rain and tears. More than once he bumped into a car and felt the solid sting of its metalwork as it brushed his thigh. As he reached the end of the road he found the intersection jammed with traffic, no clear passage visible, but he would not be denied. The railway station lay due north and he saw no reason to take any diversion.

He leapt up onto a bonnet and bounded across four others, drivers screaming abuse at him and stabbing at their horns. One tried to grab his ankle as he flew past and Mark missed his footing and fell on his backside, denting the car's bonnet.

The burly driver immediately got out and started shouting at him. Reorientating himself, Mark slid off the wing and stood upright, holding his back. The guy pushed him in the chest, his face red and twisted in fury. Mark was in no mood for delay and tried to brush past him, but the man grabbed his shoulder and screamed obscenities at him. Mark wasn't really hearing; the only sound he could hear were the screams of terror as the train crashed, and the cries of pain from those still left alive. His Karen could be hurt or worse . . . he had to get to her, *had to*.

The guy pushed him again. Mark swung his fist round and caught him on the side of his face. It was a poor punch but the guy took it as the first of many and backed away screaming to others nearby that he was being attacked. Seeing the look on Mark's face, no one wanted to intervene.

Mark ran on, his gait made stiff by the pain in his lower back. He judged he was halfway to the station but everywhere traffic had come to a halt, flashing blue lights and emergency sirens urging movement but failing to get any response and, looking down the long sweep of Turner Street, he saw traffic bumper-to-bumper in all four lanes with several vehicles on the pavement and central reservation. It was utter chaos, the dark afternoon lit spasmodically by blue lights, with a chorus of sirens and horns sounding like the very cars themselves were screaming in frustration – and more and more people were milling about, some abandoning their cars altogether as they dashed to the station.

Mark decided to cut through the municipal gardens that ran down the slope from the road. Others had the same idea and he joined several dozen people of all ages as they swept down the slippery grass and sodden gravel paths, several losing their footing, but no one stopping to help. Each had their own agenda and nothing was going to distract them from their goal.

Mark found himself on a path that ran diagonally across the grass towards the station. He had perhaps two hundred yards left to cover and then he would be there, but even through the inordinate gloom and driving rain he could see a thronging crowd outside the entrance to the railway station, police struggling to keep them back and open a path for emergency vehicles to get onto the concourse and down the long slope to the platforms. The road was jammed with cars, people clambering over them with, here and there, fist fights breaking out as tempers flared.

As he closed the distance, Mark was debating his best course of action. If he joined the crowd he would be just one in a hundred, and would have to fight his way to the front and then battle the police to get into the station. Better that he find a way to get onto the tracks so he could make his way along to the site of the crash and help that way. Karen *needed* him and he wasn't going to let her down the way he seemed to have let her down in every other part of their life.

He skidded to a halt, a man behind him cursing as he swerved and fell over on his backside. Mark ignored him and took the time, despite his panic, to check his route. And there he saw it: a street running parallel with the railway tracks that led from Blair station. On the station side there was a high brick wall, on the opposite side a long row of terraced houses.

Mark cut across the grass, his slippery route made all the more hazardous as it crossed the paths of others running down towards the station. He threw caution to the wind and, despite the pain in his chest, ran as fast as he could, uncaring of who he inconvenienced. By a miracle no one collided with him and he reached the jammed street that ran to the station.

Like a scene in a horror movie where everyone is running from some approaching monster, waves of people were converging on the station and it was inevitable some would be crushed, so wild-eyed and desperate were they to get to their loved ones.

Mark wove his way between the cars, careful to avoid the people running from the right, then dashed down the terraced

street, surprised to find it empty. *I'm coming, Karen! I'm coming!*
He wondered why no one else had had the same idea, but didn't
care as all he was concerned about was getting to Karen and saving
her. He stopped and jumped up to grab the top of the wall and
looked over.

Jesus! There was a sheer drop of forty feet down to the tracks.
No way he could get down that. He looked further up the street.
Shit, the high wall continued all the way along the cutting as far
as he could see. He ran another fifty yards and leapt up to grab the
top of the wall and look further down the track. The wall ended and
a grassy embankment came down to within ten feet of the railway.
He could cope with that. Just before he dropped back down, he
glanced back at the station. *God* . . .

People were streaming up the track, men, women and children,
shrieking and shouting, policemen and railway staff batted aside
if they tried to intervene. At first there were only a dozen frantic
figures, but soon it became a human tide, a hundred or more strong,
all of them stumbling along the twin tracks in the pouring rain. If
someone slipped, the others just ran over them. It was hysteria
beyond all reason but the sight that most shocked Mark was that of
a young girl being dragged on her bleeding knees by her possessed
mother along the sleepers and then, when she slipped out of her
mother's grasp and fell on her face, the mother *didn't even pause*,
just charged on, oblivious of everything but her need . . . her need
to what?

As Mark fought to get back his breath, an element of sanity crept
into his befuddled mind. He believed his own desperate reaction was
a natural consequence of his concern for Karen, but he knew the
train she caught. It was usually less than half empty, maybe thirty
passengers at most. So far he had seen at least five hundred people
trying to get into the station. Not all of them could know someone
on the train, and even if they did, not everyone runs pell-mell to the
scene of a disaster. Most ring emergency numbers or call hospitals,
then sit and wait and pray. They wouldn't go to the scene, so why
this bedlam?

Mark's arms ached from holding himself up so he let go and fell
the three feet back onto the pavement, pain blasting up his legs.
He fell back against the wall and doubled up in agony. But even
through the pain he could tell something was very wrong.

The sound of sirens and screaming was all but drowned out in

the street by the brick corridor created by the high wall behind
him and houses opposite. And this temporary disconnection from
the hysteria behind him gave him the space he needed to think
straight.

How many times had there been disasters on TV and how many
times had mobs descended on the scene? Never. Yes, there were
those who came out of fear and there were always gawpers and
creeps who had to see. Christ, if a plane had come down, the
temptation to visit the scene, even if it was a couple of days
afterwards, was obvious – after all, how often do you get to see
a plane crash? – but this . . . this was madness. He hauled himself
up to the top of the wall again and looked down.

The initial rush had died to a trickle – someone must have shut
a gate – but down there on the railway lay a dozen bodies, some
twisted and still, others shaking. It was unbelievable. What was
happening?

His arms protested again and this time he slowly lowered himself
to the street then loped along until the wall ended and he found
himself by a high fence guarding a steep grassy embankment. He
began to scale it, but found it harder than expected and had to
pause at the top. He took the time to look up the railway cutting
and saw the mob still running and, about a quarter of a mile
ahead around the bend, a smoking tangled heap of metal with
yellow ants crawling around and over it. Seeing the crash, and
the emergency crews toiling to do everything they could, brought
him to his senses.

If Karen was in the train, she would be brought out sooner or
later without his help; in fact he would only hinder the work being
done to save those still trapped. He would be better off heading for
the hospital and nagging staff until they could tell him the truth. Or
he could get to a telephone, call the agency in Manchester and see
if Karen had actually arrived.

The one o'clock train would have got in just before 1:45 p.m.
and the taxi ride was five minutes. She would have arrived by 2:00
p.m. at the latest. He looked at his watch. 2:40 p.m. For all he knew
she could be sitting in a meeting with Janey, oblivious of this horror,
discussing an illustration for a children's cakebox or nappy label.
Yes, phone Manchester, check the obvious first. He took one last
look at the wreck. God, please let her not have been on . . . *what
the fuck*?

The first members of the mob had now reached the scene, some beginning to climb the wreckage, firemen and police trying to stop them. Then one of them *hit* a fireman, and another joined in. Seconds later there was a brawl as the emergency crews were punched and kicked by the growing band of onlookers. Another minute and he could see several firemen on the ground being kicked mercilessly by the mob.

'No! *No!*' he shouted. *What were they doing?*

He looked around, his mind a blur. There were people in the crash who needed help and these bastards were fighting the emergency crews? For God sake's why? *Why?*

He began to climb down but his jeans caught on a wire and as he tried to tug them free he lost his balance. With a yell he fell forward over the fence and, landing on his back on the grass, he tumbled down the embankment.

Suddenly he was airborne and then, just as suddenly, his head hit something hard as his body landed in something soft and cold and everything went black.

18

MENAGERIE A TROIS

Izotta woke up to find herself where Mr Farmer had thrown her; slumped across the bottom of the lounge wall next to the open kitchen door, surrounded by empty tin cans, the remains of their long-consumed contents rife with mould and stinking of rot, the stench strong enough to breach the barrier of dried blood in her nostrils. She tried to sit up but her limbs refused to co-operate and all she could do was roll over, cans digging into her side, and look across the room at her assailant.

The room was dim, the light from the naked light bulb too weak to fight the oppressive greyness that hovered outside the flat's windows. But there in the gloom, on the floor, like a living pyramid sat the form of Mr Farmer, luminously naked, his white flesh glistening in what little light there was. He was facing the window, his little piggy face perched on his body like an afterthought, rocking back and forth like a contented baby, cooing to himself. Around him were vomit and urine and faeces and semen, each adding their own distinctive odour to that of the rotted food surrounding Izotta.

She tried to judge the time, but the day was so dark it offered no clue. It could have been any time after 1:30 p.m. She craned her head round and looked into the kitchen. On the wall she saw a clock and, straining to focus, finally deciphered the time as 4:20. She'd been unconscious for three hours. But had she?

She remembered Mr Farmer's fit, her trying to help, then his exploding into life to throw her around the room, ranting about the darkness and promising her sights she had never dreamed of, but then he had tired and cuffed her into a daze against the wall. She had succumbed to the pain, and had . . . had what? Slept? Dreamed? No, she had seen – she had *watched* – blood and pain and fear, seen people tortured, heard children shrieking their last, witnessed bodies being dismembered even as their horrified owners stared at the slicing of their flesh. What had happened? And then, for some reason, she remembered that, just as she had slipped away, Mr Farmer had held her head and stroked it, almost lovingly, promising her pleasure and . . .

She shivered and dislodged some cans. Mr Farmer cocked an ear towards her, his reverie interrupted, and slowly turned to look at her, his face blank, his eyes unreadable in the gloom.

'He's ready,' he said quietly, then took a huge breath which he released in short bursts as if afraid to let himself go. 'My soldier is ready, and once he starts, nothing will stop it.'

The soldier had experienced no problems checking into Blair's Grand Hotel. Knowing better than to attract attention, he had dressed smartly and broken his equipment down to fit into his Head bag and suitcase. Booking in with a promise of staying for two days, he had insisted on Room 100 but, when told it was unavailable, had settled for any overlooking the Precinct. (He didn't know why the number hundred was so important but he felt it had a part to play in what he had planned to do.) The receptionist was happy to oblige, especially when she saw the credit cards in his wallet. Little was she to know they were his father's, were diligently settled every month and only boasted £500 limits.

Tipping the bellboy a pound, he had locked the door to room 109 and immediately stripped off – how he hated suits – and went into the bathroom. There he ran a hot shower and, using shaving foam and razors, shaved his entire body. It took longer than expected but finally he had shaved his face, head, arms, legs, chest, stomach and pubic area of all hair and, turning the shower to *Cold*, suppressed a shriek as the water pricked his body in ten thousand new places. Clean, he had to do the job clean. He stepped out and towelled himself dry. He felt good, *alive*.

Walking back into the bedroom he unzipped his bags, took out his gear and set to work. His time in the army had stood him in good stead and he knew he could have done it in the dark if he'd had to. Finished, he went to the window and surveyed the view outside.

The Grand Hotel took up the top four floors of an office building overlooking the Peak Precinct, a two-hundred-yard-long open square with shops on either side, two floors high on the right with an underground piazza and, on the left, a department store and offices rising to four storeys. The north-west corner opened out onto a car park and the main road leading into the town centre. The precinct was modern, unattractive and open to the elements. A perfect shooting gallery.

The soldier checked the time. 4:25. Still on schedule. One thing he had learned in the army was routine; if you had a plan and stuck to it, you knew where you were. He'd been thinking of doing something for a while, but only since he had met that fat man had it all seemed to come together. The time, the place, the method. And the hundred. A hundred what? He sat down puzzled and studied his hands. Long thin fingers with nary a tremble. God, he was in *control*. He thought about what had led to this.

The fight, the discharge, the disgrace. His father's taunts, his mother's wringing hands. Thirty years, his father had reminded him: thirty years *he* had served Queen and country with not a blot on his record. But his son, just three months in Ulster and *he*'s up on charges and thrown out. His father had contacts and knew all about the boy losing an eye. Not a Provo, just a fucking joyrider driving the wrong way. Well, he wouldn't be doing any more driving, would he? The army had hushed it up – delicate period, negotations in hand – and he'd been lucky just to have been cashiered. Borderline mental, they'd said. His son! Unstable. Bad material. Well, he hadn't got it from his father, no. Thirty years he'd—

Thirty fucking years and what had it got him? thought the soldier. A mouse of a wife, a failure for a son and a council house in fucking Blair. Oh, and another uniform, earning two quid an hour guarding fucking toys in a store. Thirty years of real achievement. Well fucking done, dad. But he'd show them now, show his dad and his mum and the fucking army and every fucker in a uniform . . . *everyone*. No one he knew had ever done anything with their lives except follow fucking orders, his dad following his officers', his mum following dad, and he himself following every fucker else – including his dad into the fucking army. Well, after today, everyone would sit up and listen *to him*. They'd not forget his name or his achievements, oh no. He'd be the one in charge today.

And last night, somehow, it had all become clear. That fat queer, he'd had something to do with it. Fat fucking queer bastard. Well, he'd shown him last night, made the fucker bleed, made him hurt and now he was going to make the whole fucking *world* sore, make every fucker he could find *bleed*.

He looked at himself in the wardrobe door mirror. Tall, thin, muscled, erect. He remembered his mother and the look on her face that morning when she'd seen him like that. And his dad, eyes open, brain dead, watching as he did it. And then the blood. He'd had to shower then, looking down and watching as the pink water turned clear while his mother burbled her life away in the bedroom. No more orders, no more disappointment, no more fucking nothing. He looked out of the window again, idly stroking his cock, then put his watch on the windowsill. Timing was important. Vital. He had an objective and he had a schedule.

The precinct was surprisingly busy, the wet weather little deterrent to people armed with plastic. Plenty of fodder. He checked his watch again. 4:30. Feeding time.

Despite her pain, Izotta caught the significance of the fat man's last word. Whatever 'his soldier' was going to start, he had said it was an 'it' that wouldn't be stopped, not a 'him'.

'What do you mean?' she croaked, her cut lip stinging.

He leaned down to the radio on the floor and switched it on. There was a live news report about a train crash. As she listened she realized it had happened in Blair. There was something about the rescue being hampered by sightseers and how the police were having to control violent crowds and that ambulances couldn't get away from the scene. The male reporter was almost in tears.

Mr Farmer switched it off. 'Nothing. That's nothing compared to what's coming.'

Izotta saw him quiver with delight, then turn back to the window where the rain slashed across the glass and the clouds boiled madly as if reflecting the madman's mind. She tried again to move but hadn't the strength. Instead she slumped back down, her face in a sour pool of creamed rice.

Lightning suddenly seared across the sky, lighting up the fat man's profile like a neon sculpture. Then he started to laugh, his frame shaking like a giant blancmange, and Izotta knew the unimaginable was about to begin.

*   *   *

The soldier, naked and erect, picked up his Kalashnikov AK-47 and, pointing it out of the window facing onto the Peak Precinct, took aim at a group of pensioners leaving the Museum of Industry and started firing, one shot after another, regular as clockwork, used cartridges winging past his head like miniature empty coffins.

When the oldsters had scattered arthritically, not a one of them understanding why their friends were jittering and bleeding about them, he spun round to his left, took aim at the Elevenses Café on the first floor of the Allcock Brothers store and brought down nine diners before swinging back to the crowd cowering around the fourteen dead and dying senior citizens on the wet concrete of the Precinct. He killed another nine people – mostly head shots – then changed clips.

Up at the far end of the precinct a passing police car had mounted the pedestrian area and was screaming towards the bloody chaos in the square, scattering shoppers and water in equal proportions. Darryl shot the driver but didn't even bother to watch as the car ploughed through a gaggle of people sheltering under the awning of a record shop.

Instead he swung the gun to the right and stared through the telescopic sight at the piazza. Even with the lightning flashing and rain blustering across the precinct, he could hear the panic of people jammed on the open air escalators. He bided his time, pumping shots into victim after victim, their twisted contortions echoed in his smiling lips. This was *good*.

A siren. He ignored it. Time was short. He also ignored the discomfort of the myriad hot cartridges under his bare feet as he swung the weapon down and aimed directly into the street below. A bus had stopped but the driver was refusing to let the frantic queue of people get on board. He took them out one at a time, like an eagle picking up mice. One, two, three, four, five . . . down they fell, some dropping without a sound or a notion of their demise, while others danced spastically as if their brains were struggling to escape the confines of their dying bodies. Some succeeded, their heads exploding like overripe tomatoes.

A police car pulled up behind the bus. A policeman got out but, on seeing the massacre, he got back in and reversed down the street. The soldier checked his watch. 4:35. Not much time. He popped off shots at the retreating police car but only hit its bonnet. *Fuck it*. Wasted bullets, wasted time. Once they knew where he was he would have lost control. He only had minutes.

Another clip. The crashed police car outside the record shop on the north-east of the precinct: people were crouching down on all sides of it, unsure where the gunfire had come from. He let them know. Eight more died.

He drew a bead on the office windows that looked down on to the precinct. People, stupid people, were looking out to see what was happening. He shot five, one after the other in a row, like shooting ducks at a funfair, all of them ricocheting back into their offices, pin-wheeling over desks and VDUs. Then he swung back and aimed down at the police cars again. Another had arrived, as had an ambulance. He trained the sight on them with extra care. They were beginning to realize where he was and would soon get out of range. He bloodied four uniforms before the rest scattered for cover.

Not long now, he thought. The train crash was occupying a lot of cops, but when they heard what was going down, they'd get here as fast as their cars could carry them. He lowered the rifle and, wiping the sweat from his eyes, looked around the Plaza and found the group trapped by the Museum. Someone must have fallen over on the steps and a huddle of people were desperately clawing and screaming to get out of sight behind the suddenly very thin stone columns at its entrance. There must have been twenty or more of them, many of them women with children. Bye bye.

A minute later there wasn't any movement from the bloody pile. He edged his sight back towards the escalators and emptied the remainder of the clip into anyone who moved. Replaced it. Continued to fire. Laughing as he saw the heads erupt and the limbs dance and the blood spurt into the wet afternoon, red against grey. Then, at last, police cars, and flashing blue lights. So pretty, really, more colour to add to the red he'd created. He also noticed the precinct wasn't being cleared. People were too frightened to break for cover and the police didn't seem keen to cross his field of fire. So, what now? He dropped the spent clip onto the floor, then sat back against the wall to get his breath back, running through what he had done, each action etched in his mind like acid on crystal.

Seventy hits, maybe forty-five dead. Numbers were important. Shit, they'd remember that OK. God, better than he had dreamed. And he felt so fucking *high*. But what about sixty dead, eighty . . .

a *hundred*. The magic century. *That* was what the hundred meant.
It was a target! No way would they *ever* forget a hundred dead!

Do it.

He slapped another clip home, took a deep breath and took aim
at the car park to the north-west of the Precinct. He started picking
off women and children crouching behind cars. The day might be
gloomy, the light fading fast, but the white street lighting gave him
all the help he needed. A couple of policemen and – what a tosser
– a traffic warden dashed to their aid and he picked each of them
off, even as they sprinted and zigzagged the fifty open yards, good
sports every one. After he had emptied the clip, he leaned back,
reloaded and, spinning through ninety degrees, started firing into
shop doorways, certain to hit someone with virtually every shot,
the sound of exploding glass drowning out the screams.

A dozen shots later and he looked down at the oldies again in
the middle of the Precinct. Poor fuckers. He picked off anyone
moving.

Clip empty, he pulled back from the open window and rested
against the wall, surrounded by a carnival of spent and smoking
cartridges, the room hazy like a friendly bar. He took a long drag
on the gunsmoke. Mmmm, better than dope.

Now what? He must have hit the magic hundred mark. Time
to pack it in? He reached for a clip, slipped it home and stood
ready to swing into open view. Suddenly there was a crack, then
another, then the window to his left imploded. Gunfire! Armed
police, at last. Good. He would go out shooting, take a couple
more of the bastards with him. But then he realized that if he
let them shoot him, some fucker would get to be the hero for
popping him. Well, screw that! No fucking cop was going to
get the credit for bringing him down. This was his show from
beginning to end. He was the one giving the orders for once –
and for all. He turned the rifle upside down and slipped the hot
barrel into his mouth.

Shit! It burnt his lips and inhaling the cordite made him gag. He
leaned forward coughing and hacking, the gun limp by his side.
Stupid arsehole. He grabbed the Kalashnikov again and pointed it
at his heart.

Just then he heard noises outside the bedroom door. Police. They
must have sussed which room he was in. He debated whether to
have a go at them but there was every chance they were armed

and, again, they'd get the credit for killing him. No, he'd started it, he'd finish it.

He pulled the trigger.

Izotta huddled against the wall, unable to tear her eyes away from the sights before her. She had long given up trying to understand how she was able to see what was happening a mile away in the Peak Precinct. All she knew was that she was there, with the mad soldier, watching him kill and kill again, no person, no age safe; anyone that came within the cross hairs of his telescopic sight dying with a squeeze of his trigger and a smile of satisfaction.

She had screamed and begged for him – and it – to stop; had vomited, peed and pulled out her hair in her desperation to switch off the images, but all Mr Farmer had done was sit and smile and let her share his vision. There was no flat, no grey window, no furniture, just a grandstand view of carnage. Turning her gaze away made no difference: everywhere she looked the view was the same, like being trapped in a room with a hundred video screens. Even closing her eyes, the images remained, playing on the inside of her eyelids, a virtual reality display from hell. And then it stopped, the killing ended and rain began washing away the blood.

Breathless and weak, Izotta slumped back against the wall, her limbs as numbed with exhaustion as her mind was with horrors. She looked at Mr Farmer and saw he had changed. He was still his fat bloated self, but his features had blurred, and he was vibrating, his skin rippling with little waves as if something stirred inside him. His arms and legs were also losing their definition, the skin beginning to glow and distend like heated plastic. He turned to look at her, his eyes wide and black like snooker balls, his mouth a perfect 'O', his face quivering. Then he started moaning, his voice buried somewhere within the amorphous mass of his body.

'So much more than I expected, so much more. He held the key and now the darkness is unlocked, here for us all. At long last.'

He tried to rise to his feet but his legs couldn't take his weight and he fell, burying them beneath the bulk of his torso, his pyramid shape even more apparent. Then he started to *slide* towards her, his distended belly edging forward on the floor like a giant slug, giving him the movement denied by his legs.

As the mound of flesh that had been Mr Farmer came within three feet of her she caught his stink, saw lighting flash over skin the texture of stretched rubber, heard the rumblings and burbling from within its insides – and knew he meant to absorb her, to devour her. He would slowly crawl over her and . . .

The big window suddenly exploded inwards, showering the two of them with glass and rain. The lightbulb exploded as cold water dashed its hot surface and the room was plunged into darkness, the only light provided by lightning strokes that whitened the room for a millisecond at a time, each flash revealing Mr Farmer to be another inch closer, his black eyes fixed on her face, his mouth open in hunger, his tongue running greedily around his lips.

Izotta's screams were soon devoured by thunder that bellowed around the room like all the gods of hellfire shouting their encouragement.

19

PLAGUE

Gordon Dougan had had enough. The train crash, the massacre in the square and now these bastards rioting for no reason other than that they were bored.

He looked up the street at the burning barricades, the buildings on fire, the kids, some as young as eight, running around smashing anything breakable, throwing bricks and tiles at anyone older than themselves, especially those in uniform. He had been pelted with bricks himself, had seen ambulancemen and firemen assaulted, one even set alight with a petrol bomb. Madness reigned, the eyes of the youths lit by flame and bloodlust. Those they had managed to capture had been like wild animals, oblivious of anything other than the need to maim or kill. And killing there had been.

At least one officer had died, as had two women whose car had been commandeered and set on fire before they could escape. It was as if the horror of the last few days had opened up a floodgate of hatred into the streets as though releasing a sea of vomit, with society's unwanteds making themselves known, determined to revenge themselves on everything they considered played a part in their suppression.

There was a time when he'd had some sympathy for teenagers from broken homes on bad estates who could see their bleak futures mirrored in their drunken parents. A petty pointless existence, with drink, drugs and sex the only relief, financed by the dole or crime. But here there was no sense, no logic, no limit. It was a *zoo*. And so he had decided order needed to be restored. He had seen the darkness coming and was going to let in some light – and the only action that would stop the mayhem was for the mob to see what would happen if they didn't.

He chose his moment with great care, sure that both sides would see him. He edged his way through the police barricade, most of the men brought in from surrounding forces, Blair's own force still dealing with the aftermath of the massacre and other minor events around the town. He had the rank so no one argued with him and he slowly walked into the rain-sodden, brick-strewn No Man's Land between the two sides.

For a moment there was a lull – as if neither side could understand what he was doing. He stood his ground, the hundred-strong mob barely fifty yards away, waiting, the driving rain the only thing the two sides had in common. If he was any judge of what was left of humanity in the baying horde, one would soon come out to challenge him to prove his manhood. And sure enough, a cocky teenager, sixteen at most, a red bandanna round his mouth, baseball bat in hand, swaggered towards him. He clearly intended getting as close as he could before lashing out then running before the police dashed forward to grab him. It was a deadly game of tag, but what the youth didn't know was that, despite his bravado and his bat, the odds were stacked against him.

He stopped three paces from Dougan and jeered at him, his eyes wide with hatred. Dougan smiled, pulled out his .38 revolver and shot him between the eyes.

The youth fell like a stone, dead before he hit the ground. Silence descended like a curtain, the only sound remaining the crackle from the fires and the heavy drumming of the rain. Before anyone else could react, Dougan took aim and shot dead a ten-year-old white boy, a twenty-year-old black and three others. The murderous intent of the crowd turned to terror and they began running. Dougan fired after them through the rain, pleased to see several fall.

As the street cleared he heard his fellow officers rushing to surround him, more than one screaming at him to drop his weapon. He slowly turned to face them, blinking away the rain in his eyes, and saw strangers in familiar uniforms. He licked his lips, tasting the cold water that streamed down his face, then pointed the gun at his head.

'That should make them think twice.' And he pulled the trigger.

The hammer clicked but there was no discharge. He pulled the trigger again and again, but it was empty.

He dropped his arm to his side and let the gun clatter onto the tarmac. There was a long pause and then, through his tears, he said: 'It's been one of those days.'

Chief Superintendent Dougan's fellow officers swiftly kicked him to death, then charged after the mob.

'There, there, love, soon be over.'

Dr Carter patted the old lady's hand as he watched the poison seep into her system. Another minute and she'd drift off, her aches and pains gone for good.

He watched her eyes flicker and close, felt her respiration grow shallow, her pulse weaken, then stop. Satisfied she was dead, he moved on to the next room. It was for the best. Life couldn't be much fun when you found it difficult to walk, someone had to wipe away your drool or change a colostomy bag, and taking a bath was as much an exercise in avoiding a broken limb as keeping clean.

The next room contained Mrs Collier. Eighty-two, blind and almost deaf. What kind of existence must she have? Two minutes, a kind word and her struggle was over.

Next room Mr Fraser. Incontinent, only one leg and too weak now to support himself when walking. He had been a war hero but now his only battle was with his own lungs. An injection, and death claimed another quick victory.

He reached the top of the stairs. The third floor was now silent, eighteen miserable existences terminated. So much better for them all. He really was a saviour. Besides, that now freed up their beds for other aged casualties, the duration of their lives to be determined by him. After all, he was the doctor, the professional: he knew what was best. He stretched – the infernal wet weather was bad for his shoulder – and looked out onto the street. Through the pouring rain there was a flickering glow on the horizon. A fire? He'd check the radio when he finished his work.

As he walked down the stairs he wondered why he hadn't done this before. In the past he had helped one or two suffering souls to eternal peace and had felt guilt at his action but now, for some reason, there was no such moral dilemma. He felt light-headed, as if each death infused him with righteousness, making him a better person.

Turning the corner into the quiet carpeted corridor, rain drumming against the windows that looked out onto the courtyard, he bumped into Nurse Dart. She stepped back, her face downcast, embarrassed as ever to be in his presence. He had been aware for some time that the girl had feelings for him; indeed the older staff teased them both about it mercilessly, but he had never been interested in the girl. But now, here, flushed with the life he seemed to have absorbed from the many deaths on the floor above, he saw the girl in a new light.

'Nurse, what are you doing?'

He then realized that her red face and nervous demeanour was more than her usual shyness. Was she feeling guilty about something? He grabbed the hand she was hiding behind her back and pulled it clear. A syringe fell noiselessly to the floor. She looked up at him, her wide eyes frightened. He pulled her roughly into the first bedroom where Mr Campbell lay, his bare chest stilled.

'Did you do this?' he demanded, checking for a pulse.

'Yes,' she said quietly, tears forming in her eyes.

He sat on the bed in front of her and held her hand. 'Why?' he asked gently.

She was reluctant to answer, but he placed his other hand on hers. How small it was.

'Because they deserve peace. Good people shouldn't have to suffer for so long. It's . . . right.'

He patted her hand. 'And how many, my dear?'

'Mr Campbell was the . . . sixth.'

'And how many were you intending to . . .?'

'As many as needed my help.'

He nodded and squeezed her hand. It was hot.

He pulled out his own syringe and smiled and she slowly realized that he had been doing the same work.

'You too?' she said, her eyes wide with astonishment.

'Yes, my dear, you're right. There's too much suffering. My job is to help end it.'

'Yes!' she agreed, her eyes sparking with enthusiasm.

Dr Carter nodded with her. Then he stabbed the syringe hard into her left eye until his knuckles filled her eye socket. She crashed to the ground as if she was a marionette with its strings cut.

He let go the syringe and stepped over her body. At the door he paused and looked down at the dead girl, her limbs splayed unnaturally, the white plunger of the syringe afloat in a growing pool of blood that was dribbling across her slack face.

'Remember, Nurse Dart, *I* am the doctor. *I* decide the medical needs of our clients, not you.'

And with that he walked off to the dispensary to find another syringe, rain thrashing at the darkened corridor windows like a drum roll.

Dinner was ready. Dan Foster had been in charge of evening meals ever since he had been made redundant and his wife had been working full-time at Braddocks. He didn't resent his new househusband role – indeed, he was proud of how clean the house was and how the quality of the cooking had improved – because it gave him something practical to do and he had made as good a job of it as he had at his lathe. What did peeve him, though, was his son. The girls, Zoë, eight, and Carrie, six, he could excuse, but David, their fifteen-year-old, was another matter.

Sullen, unhelpful and given to treating the house as a hotel rather than a home, he had become a real thorn in Dan's side. It wasn't as if the boy had any excuses. Dan was his natural father, their home was warm and cosy, he and Meg were supportive parents and as generous as their limited budget would allow, and there was no drunkenness or neglect. No, the fault lay with the boy, or with the yobs he had chosen to hang around with. He had been set for a promising academic career, probably ending up at university where he would have earned the right to be sullen and to determine his own future, but as a fourth former, GCSEs on the agenda, he was still dependent on his family for everything. All they asked was a little respect and for him to do his best at school, but David was just downright unpleasant most of the time. Bad language – especially irritating when the girls were present – was the least of his bad habits. They knew he smoked but figured it was just a phase and as far as they could tell he wasn't involved with drugs. But his room was a tip, his awful music either too loud or piped into his ears via a Walkman that ended all hope of communication – and now his school was complaining about absenteeism. Dan was almost grateful when the boy wasn't around – but then he would worry about what he was up to. Well, he had decided to call a halt. They had enough worries on their plate without him upsetting the delicate cocoon they had created to protect their daughters from the humiliation and privation his enforced unemployment had produced.

The last straw had been the argument the night before when David had come in drunk and soaked to the skin. Dan's mild rebuke that Blair wasn't the best place to be out in at night – or during the day, unfortunately, if local radio was to be believed – had been met with a ferocious attack on his right to tell the boy anything when he couldn't even hold down a 'fucking manual job'. Only the intervention of his wife and the crying of the girls had stopped Dan giving the boy the hiding he so richly deserved.

All night he had tossed and turned, fretting about how to deal with the problem, but then, in the early light, as he listened to the fifth siren of the night screaming past the end of the street, he'd had the answer.

'This roast is delicious,' said Meg that evening. 'But how could we afford it?'

'Yeah, it's really yummy, dad,' said Zoë.

Carrie would have agreed but her mouth was full and she knew her manners.

'Oh, a bit of ingenuity,' he said, tapping his nose. 'Remember, I'm in charge of the housekeeping secrets.'

He glanced over at the door leading to the garage wherein sat the chest freezer and its new cuts of meat.

'Pity David isn't here,' said Meg. 'He'd have liked this.'

Carving her another generous slice of the well-done meat, Dan said, 'I'm sure he'll be all cut up about it.'

Meg took the meat with a resigned sigh then, unwittingly, continued eating her eldest child.

Sam O'Shay closed the door of the neat lounge and walked over to Mrs Bartlett, brushing the rain from the sleeve of his coat. A large, attractive woman in her early fifties, Mrs Bartlett had clearly been broken by recent events and looked ten years older and shrunken within her dark blue skirt and blouse. He settled himself on the sofa beside her and patted her shaking hand as it clung to her knee.

'Mrs Bartlett . . . Rhonda, can I call you Rhonda? I know this is going to be very painful for you, so soon after your husband's death and all, but remember you rang the radio station and said you wanted to say words of comfort for those parents who lost their children in the crash?'

'I know, I know,' she whispered. 'Those poor children. How many was it?'

'Eighteen now, two more passed away this evening.'

The woman shook her head, her eyes moist. She fumbled for a handkerchief and dabbed at her nose.

'I think it would be easiest if you began to say whatever came into your mind,' he continued. 'I'll set the recorder running and if I want you to clarify anything I'll ask you, but feel free to shut me up. OK, love?'

He offered her one of his sincere smiles and she responded. He wasn't nicknamed Sympathetic Sam in the business for nothing. He patted her hand again and gave it a little squeeze. She was cold.

He switched on the recorder, checked for level, then adjusted the microphone, listening in the headphones if the squalling rain outside could be heard. Satisfied everything was as it should be, he slid off the sofa and sat down in the easy chair opposite, a kindly look on his face. He desperately wanted a cigarette but the lack of ashtrays ruled it out. He slyly checked his watch. If he could wrap this up in half an hour, he could get back to the station and edit it in time to offer it to Independent Radio News for national airing.

Jack Bartlett had been the driver of the second train in the Blair rail disaster, killed instantly when his passenger train hit the wrecked 1 p.m. sprinter to Manchester. More than fifty people had died, with twice as many seriously injured, including a party of schoolchildren on their way to a matinée theatre performance. Ironically, they were from the very school for which the Bartletts regularly organized fund-raising events, and his widow was now desperate to help alleviate the suffering of the parents – and Sam knew a good story when he heard one.

The house was a modest suburban semi, full of cups and trophies for ballroom dancing. A wealth of photographs and framed newspaper clippings gave evidence of Mrs Bartlett's youthful beauty, and Sam was willing to admit that she was still attractive. But should he be thinking such a thing, or surreptitiously peering between her legs as she tried to put into words her unimaginable grief? Fuck, a woman's a woman, doesn't matter if she's a widow or a whore. They've all got cunts and they all need to put out sooner or later.

'Jack was such a kind man,' she was saying. 'We met—'

He let the woman ramble, let her get it out. He wondered how long ago she and her Jack had fucked and when she would do it again, if ever.

'He used to come into the school and tell them about rail safety. Nothing to do with British Rail . . .'

Sam wondered whether, if he went upstairs – he could tell her he was going to the loo – he could slip into her bedroom, look in a drawer, find a bra, look at the tag. Forty inches, he guessed. 40B's or 40C's? He sure wished he could see them for real . . .

'The children liked him. One young girl asked if girls could be engine drivers and he—'

God, won't the bitch shut up? He checked his watch. Ten minutes she'd been rambling now and still no message to the parents. He wondered if he should prod her in the right direction but decided to let her carry on. He was enjoying the view, after all. Time for a closer look?

He stood up. She stopped talking.

'Sorry, need to stretch my legs,' he smiled. 'Just carry on, love, you're doing fine.'

She took a moment to find her thread but then continued to talk about the Easter Fair Jack had helped organize. Sam slowly walked around the room until he was standing behind her – and able to look down her cleavage.

He could see the fine wrinkles at the top of the divide, and a sprinkling of freckles on the stretched white flesh like an old faded tan. He felt himself hardening. *Naughty, Sam.* But then there was nothing like a bit of experienced female flesh, was there? Much as he enjoyed fucking the bimbos who thought he was something special, he always preferred older women. *They know what they want and how to get it.* He wondered what Mrs Bartlett liked. Did she let 'her Jack' suck those tits till they hurt? Did he give it her up the arse?

He walked back to his seat and sat down, clipboard covering his crotch and smiling indulgently as she waffled. He wondered what she would look like in black. Would her widow's weeds cling to her body? Would she wear tights or stockings? Would her knickers be black? And her bra. Her bra? He wondered again about his trip upstairs.

'I only hope they can come to terms with such a tragic loss. At least my Jack had a good life, saw something of the world—'

Well, he would wouldn't he, being a fucking train driver, thought Sam.

'—but when I think of all those . . .'

Yes, that's what he'd do. Go upstairs, try her bedroom, maybe even check the laundry basket, sniff something . . .

He held up his hand. 'I'm sorry to interrupt, Rhonda, but I need to go to the loo. Is that OK?'

She looked slightly lost for a moment, then nodded.

'Won't be long. I'll leave the tape running if there's anything else you feel the need to say.'

He took one last look at her thighs – she really should wear longer skirts at her age – and walked to the door. As he reached for the handle he paused to look back at the grieving woman.

Fuck it, he thought, walking towards her and unzipping his fly. Good thing he had left the recorder running: he'd enjoy listening to this later.

The priest had his churchwardens lock the temporary doors – they had been rammed by a stolen car a week before – and stand guard against anyone leaving, but Father Donnel knew none of his flock would. Wednesday evening Mass he could count on perhaps a dozen stalwarts. Tonight there were nearer forty, some faces he only saw on Sundays, cowering in St Cuthbert's on a stormy night to pray to their God for help and guidance while their home town tore itself apart.

One poor dear at the back was nursing a grazed cheek where some thug had tried to snatch her handbag, only for him to be beaten senseless by two passing cab drivers.

He had debated whether to conduct the full service but had decided to offer an abbreviated version. This produced some concern but he allayed their fears by promising extra blessings and a special event that would more than make up for their worries about diverting from the path of true worship. The last organ chord died away and people re-seated themselves and sat back expectantly.

'My dear friends, we are gathered here because we wish to worship Our Lord the Father and thank Him for the many blessings we enjoy. We may be here to pray for loved or lost ones, particularly in light of the tragic events of the past few days. As you are only too well aware, our fair town seems to have lost its senses and madness and savagery roam the streets as if it were a medieval town under seige. Incidentally, the minibus will be available for any of you who wish to be escorted home.'

This elicited a ripple of appreciation. Father Donnel smiled and continued.

'I have thought long and hard – and prayed long and hard – for guidance as to what these portents mean. Has Blair as a community incurred the wrath of the Lord? Or is the Devil, as a roaring lion, walking about, seeking whom he may devour? To be truthful, I don't know. All I can do is pray and beseech the Lord to look kindly upon His faithful and spare us from the horrors. And that He make those who are committing these heinous acts look into their hearts and reconsider their ways before it is too late.'

The congregation could only mutter their agreement.

Father Donnel then nodded to his two wardens, who walked down the aisle and across to the vestry. After a moment of puzzled silence, they returned, a hooded figure held up between them. They brought the person to the front step of the altar and forced him to kneel facing the muttering congregation.

Father Donnel whipped off the hood covering the boy's face to reveal a short-haired lout, his face streaked in dried blood, one eye bruised. He had been crying and was plainly terrified. He wore a soaking wet dirty orange T-shirt, grey jeans and trainers. His hands were tied behind his back.

'This is Greg, presumably short for Gregory. He was found in the apse earlier this evening urinating. When challenged by myself and Mr Potts he put up a struggle and after we had subdued him we found he had stolen the cash from the poor box. Four pounds and eight pence, to be precise. That he would deny the poor of our parish even this small amount is despicable enough, but that he then chose to desecrate holy ground is even worse.

'We considered calling in the police but decided it was time the Holy Church and its true believers stood up for themselves. As some of you know, St Cuthbert's has been robbed no fewer than four times in the last few months. Well, enough is enough. I intend that young Gregory here should be an emissary and take our message of strength and resolution into the world and let everyone know that the Lord's people have had enough.'

There was a scattering of applause but the majority remained silent, unsure as to what was going to happen.

At a nod from Father Donnel, the wardens untied the boy's hands and laid him down on his back on the wooden floor fronting the altar. For his part, Father Donnel stepped behind the altar, then walked back to the prostrate youth as the wardens pulled his arms out straight from his body and laid their weight on his legs. The boy complied, clearly too weak to protest.

The church was hushed, the only sound the howling of the wind high in the bell tower and rain rattling the mesh that covered the stained glass windows.

'Forgive him, Father, for he knows not what he has done,' said Father Donnel as he positioned a six-inch nail above the boy's wrist and aimed the lump hammer.

The boy's screams echoed around the church as metal was forced through flesh into wood. Some of the congregation fainted or cried out in surprise or horror, but most slowly edged from their pews as the hammering continued, and walked down the aisle to stand and watch as the boy was pinned to the church floor by his wrists and ankles. Finally the pounding and the screaming stopped as the boy fainted and the wardens were able to stand back and admire their priest's handiwork.

Father Donnel wiped the sweat from his brow and offered the hammer to one of the wardens. He accepted it with a nod and raised it above the boy's head then, careful to cross himself – an action imitated by all watching – he brought the hammer down with all the force he could muster into the boy's face.

It would be half an hour before all who wanted to vent their righteous anger had finished with the long-dead youth. And then it was the turn of the nine people cowering at the back of the church, banging on the locked doors, pleading for help or to be allowed to leave.

Father Donnel led the procession from the blood-spattered altar to the back of the church. 'In the name of the Lord, I urge you to do all that is necessary to persuade these unfaithful ones to see the error of their ways.'

Mary Coningsby wondered how the Pollock twins had found out where she lived. They had rung her bell a little after 8 p.m., all giggles and red faces, asking if she could help them with their homework. Even here, on the outskirts of town, she could hear the sirens in the distance and see the warehouse fire near the town centre. She looked up and down the rain-lashed street for their parents' car but couldn't see any that didn't usually park there.

'How did you get here?' she asked, concern making her frown.

'Walked,' said one.

'But you live over the other side of town, don't you?'

'It's OK, miss, we got permission,' said the other.

Seeing how drenched they were, she hurried them in and steered them in front of the fire. It didn't matter whether they had permission or not; the weather alone was reason enough not to let youngsters out on the streets, but with the riots and the fires . . .

She made them hot chocolate and biscuits and gave them towels to dry their hair, determined to ring their parents as soon as she could.

Neil and Nicholas Pollock, eleven, bright and inseparable, were tall and gangly for their age and among her favourites in Form Seven. She turned down the volume of the television and was glad to see they didn't object. She should really watch less herself but since her boyfriend had left she didn't have much company and, wallpaper though it was, TV did at least provide friendly voices and faces.

'So, boys, what homework was it you were particularly interested in?' She was doubly puzzled because she hadn't actually set them any work to do.

'Biology, Miss,' said Nicholas, only distinguishable from his brother by the length of his ginger hair.

'Biology?' she asked.

'Yes,' said his brother. 'Repropruck . . . repostuck . . . remprobduck . . .'

'Reproduction?' she said.

'Yes, spazzhead,' sneered Nicholas to Neil.

'What do you mean, exactly?'

'Babies.'

Uh-oh. Mary felt herself beginning to blush. Usually she left this kind of thing to the specialist videos designed for pupils of their age.

'I don't really think—'

The doorbell rang again. Who now?

'Wait here, boys. I'll see who it is,' she said, walking out to the hall and opening the door. *Good God*.

There were a dozen or more young boys and girls, the dim porch light revealing that most of them were fellow members of Form Seven.

'What . . . what are you lot doing here?' She looked over their heads for a car, but again the street was empty.

A voice behind her piped up. 'It's all right, Miss, they're here to talk about babies too.'

Mary turned and saw the twins standing in the lounge door holding a knife apiece. Suddenly she felt herself being pushed into the hall as the children outside surged forward. Neil then came up to her as she felt little hands grab the hem of her skirt and haul on her woollen jumper.

'You're going to show us where babies come from, Miss,' he said.

'And how they're made,' said a girl's voice.

Mary started to scream but someone kicked her in the shin and she fell forward, soon to be covered in a tentacular mass of enquiring hands that poked, pulled and prodded at every part of her body.

As she fought to regain her balance and failed, she caught a glimpse of Nicholas smiling at her, his knife glinting in the hall light.

'And we want to see where the little egg comes from too,' he said.

George Fife stared out of his window into the back yard of the *Advertiser* offices. There was a body of a young girl lying beside the wheelie bin. He hadn't seen her die but he had heard her screams as he had cowered under his desk. He had wanted to help, to go to the window and blast away with his revolver at her attackers, but he only had the one bullet and he wasn't going to waste that on someone else. No, that little cordite-powered bolt from the blue was destined for the inside of his own head. But as he had cowered there, awash in scotch, his vision blurred, his thoughts a mangled void, and listened to the town he had called home for the best part of thirty years eat itself like a crazed cannibal, he had managed one conclusion: he deserved to be punished before he died.

So he had listened to the smashing, the sirens and the screams, and watched with bleary fascination as the flickering flames reflected on his office walls gave sick life to the ageing yellow newspapers stacked on the shelves. Time splintered as he mulled over his fate and slowly came to realize that all the dreams he'd had starting out on the *Evening News* in Edinburgh, and during his time in Fleet Street and abroad – Aden, Vietnam, Nigeria – had all been pickled in alcohol and pissed away. And that all the little problems he had blamed over the years for his slow and steady descent to the editorship of a backwater weekly paper were of his own making: *he* had ruined his life, not his unstable wife; *he* had made the wrong decisions, not his employers; *he* had supped the booze, not his fellow journos.

He heard the sound of crashing glass downstairs, followed by evil laughter. Kids. They would wreck the place, then probably work their way up to his inner sanctum where they would descend on him like a pack of dogs. Good. He deserved it. For, at that moment, he hated himself more than he could hate the mindless cretins wreaking havoc below him. After all, hadn't he foreseen all this and hadn't he had the power to warn people? Yes, there would have been an outcry but what was the worst that could have happened? He was going to die within the year anyway! He could have run his editorial, his spike articles, his banner headlines, and given everyone in the town an idea of the powder keg they were sitting on and, if only one person had paid heed and left, then he would have saved that person's life. But he hadn't; coward to the end, he had avoided controversy. And now look . . .

He turned away from the window and sat down at his desk, took a reflex swig from his long-empty tumbler, then placed the revolver in his drawer and waited for the baying madmen to mount the stairs and deal out their punishment. Soon all would be over, but until that last desperate bloody gasp, there would be the pain he had earned and well-deserved retribution.

The pattern of madness was repeated throughout Blair. The criminal, the embittered, the insane, the brooding and the bored as one went on a mindless rampage, raping, looting and killing at will. Those citizens that didn't take to the streets cowered in their homes, terror their only companion, prayer their only rescue. Or they indulged in private insanities, executing family and friends, torturing their children, burning their neighbours' homes, savaging anyone it pleased them to as their vilest desires welled to the fore, destroying reason and morality, each taking their lead from the darkness that had descended on the town like a giant hand intent on stealing their very souls.

At 1:11 p.m. all electrical power died, plunging the cloud-covered town into an inky darkness relieved only by the flames of burning buildings, most of which were quickly dampened by a monsoonal rain so strong it shattered windows and forced those in the street to their knees. Even the hardiest of psychopaths was driven indoors, there to continue their evil work on those who, only minutes before, had considered them to be allies. The strong destroyed and the weak perished as Blair was consumed with evil.

20

KIDNAPPED

They came for Wesley Lambert when he was asleep. Although it was 5:18 a.m., Lambert had only been asleep for an hour. They picked the lock on his front door, circumvented the burglar alarm and made their way up to his bedroom.

He was shaken awake, a hand over his mouth, two figures wearing black balaclavas demanding to know if there was anyone else in the house. Lambert shook his head, convinced he was about to be killed when he saw that both were carrying pistols.

One of them pulled back the bedclothes, disconnected his night bag with an audible groan of disgust, then replaced it with another bag. The other man then pulled him out of bed and helped him dress, ignoring the shit covering his thighs and backside. No one spoke throughout the kidnap.

One of the men then carried him downstairs over his shoulder while the other reversed an unmarked dark blue Bedford van up to the front door. Then, checking that no one was about, they bundled him into the back where they laid him out on a stretcher and instructed him to stay quiet. One of them then went back into the house, re-set the burglar alarm, locked the door and joined the other man in the front of the van.

As they set off, Lambert sat up and dragged himself to the end of the stretcher and tried the back door, but there was no handle on the inside. He also found all the windows had been painted over, the only illumination provided by a single bulb in the ceiling.

He crawled back to the other end of the bed and hammered on the partition behind his head to get attention, shouting until he was hoarse, but it did nothing to slow the van, so he gave up, his arms sore. He lay back down and tried to calm himself, but it was almost impossible.

Whilst fear may inspire action, it does nothing to help thought processes: all he could think of was how easily they had got into his house and the fact that they were armed. Where were they taking him, and why, and what would they do once they were there? He was nothing if not a realist and accepted that there was nothing he could do, whatever it turned out to be that they had in mind for him. Even if he had been fully mobile he would stand little chance against armed professionals. He wasn't in any doubt as to why they had kidnapped him – his threats about Blair – which at least gave him the satisfaction of knowing he was right and something *was* happening, but he wondered who had ordered it. Who had he pushed too far? And would they kill him? Of course they would, if it suited them. Anyone could be killed. No doubt they were planning to pump him for more information, and then dispose of him. Why had he put himself in this mess?

He pulled himself upright and leaned against the cold metal of the van's wall. It was then he noticed the bag on the floor. Oh God, what was *that*?

It took him fully five minutes to pluck up the courage to unzip the bag and discover its contents. It wasn't a bomb or a gas capsule – though the initial sight of the contents made his heart miss a beat, so perfectly did it resemble an artillery shell – but when he unscrewed the cap of the vacuum flask and found piping hot coffee he couldn't help laughing, hollow though it was. And wrapped up next to it in greaseproof paper were cold bacon sandwiches. He debated whether they might be poisoned but couldn't fathom the kind of mind that would pass up any one of a hundred ways of killing him simply to poison him in the back of a van.

The coffee and the sandwiches were delicious and he managed to relax a little, reflecting bitterly on the ultimatum that had brought him here.

At the end of the meeting where he had disclosed his fears for Blair, he had forestalled attempts to have him excluded from any team that might be sent to investigate events in the town.

'I am to form a part of the team. There will be no debate. All the material I have shown you, together with additional research, has been downloaded onto computer disks and sent to ten contacts worldwide, with instructions that should anything happen to myself or the town of Blair then they should be opened and the material made immediately available to any newspaper or TV station of their choosing. I have no interest in personal publicity; I am simply curious. I would like to study the problem and try and understand it. You must realize that should Blair succumb to whatever destroyed Roswiay or Warforn Peck, the government will be faced with a disaster of unimaginable proportions.

'Never mind the physical cost of the destruction of an entire town, or the impact that forty thousand innocent lives being lost will make. Just imagine the effect on the government's authority when it shows it just isn't up to the task of dealing with the problem but worse, neither understands it nor has a solution to prevent a repetition! And, if after all that, it's then revealed that the government suspected something was going to happen and did nothing . . .'

'So what would you do?'

'Evacuate, cordon off and monitor. I would not leave anyone within the area but I would install as much equipment as possible. If you accept what is going to happen you have a chance of minimizing the tragedy. It will still be a disaster, but lives needn't be lost if you act. Delay, and the consequences could be fatal.'

'You realize what you're asking?' said Horrigan.

'With the will, you could empty that town inside twenty-four hours by creating a fictitious disaster, instituting martial law and forcibly evacuating every living soul.'

'And what if nothing then happens?'

'You'll lose your jobs.'

Lambert couldn't help smiling at the memory of their faces. For him it was one of the greatest possible zoo events which, handled properly, could cost little in lives. For those in the room, however, it could be a career-destroying decision. His current predicament only served to underline his growing fear that they had decided to sit and wait, and wanted his silence – but at what price?

After an hour the van bumped over a section of rough ground. He spilled the remainder of the coffee over his shirt and banged his head against the side of the van. As it came to a halt and he was dabbing his shirt with a tissue from his trouser pocket, the doors of the van swung open and a man dressed in black carrying a sub-machine gun levelled his weapon at

him and ordered him out. Wesley shook his head and pointed
at his legs.

Someone pulled the armed man aside and climbed up into the
van. 'Hallo, Wesley. Glad you could join us.'

'I didn't have much choice, did I, Horrigan?'

'Well, that'll teach you,' said the scientist in a white lab coat.
'You didn't give us much choice either.'

They both laughed and Lambert was helped out of the van.
Horrigan, a big ruddy fellow Lambert's age, not unreminiscent of
James Robertson Justice, clipped an ID badge with his photograph
onto his lapel. Then he helped him into a motorized wheelchair
and guided him across a flat but muddy farmyard to an old
weather-beaten barn.

Armed soldiers let them through and Lambert found himself in a
darkened room crammed with electronic equipment, red and yellow
and green lights winking like a Christmas display. A dozen or more
operators sat at keyboards and VDUs and several others walked
about consulting a number of illuminated glass boards covered in
maps. It didn't take Lambert long to realize what the purpose of
the room was, or how seriously the situation was being treated.

'How's the town looking?' he asked Horrigan.

The scientist turned and leaned forward, his hands on the arms
of the wheelchair. 'We were too late.'

A helicopter flew low overhead, drowning out Lambert's
response. Once quiet returned he reiterated his question.

'What do you mean, too late?'

Horrigan pointed at a video screen. It showed a green valley
stretching away for several miles, a grey sky above. In the middle
was a dark shape, like a giant black dome. Judging by the scale
of its surroundings it must have been about two miles across and
a couple of thousand feet high at its crown.

'Jesus Christ . . .' said Lambert.

Horrigan shook his head. 'Blair disappeared at 1:11 a.m. We had
delayed the evacuation for twelve hours to allow time for a realistic
cover story to be put in place, but two hours before we were due
to move in, *that* appeared. Blair's gone.'

Lambert stared dumbfounded at the screen. His insane theory had
proven correct and the evidence was right there before him – and it
had cost the lives of forty thousand people.

Part Two

PANDEMONIUM

Farewell, happy fields,
Where joy for ever dwells! Hail, horrors! hail.

John Milton, *Paradise Lost*

21

LAMBERT AND THE DOME

Funny how things spring into your mind, thought Lambert as he stared up at the giant black dome a hundred yards in front of him. In moments of extreme stress the human body is wont to void itself: pissing, shitting, vomiting, they can all happen spontaneously. He remembered occasions before his accident when he had lost control of his bowels. The time someone told him his mother had been burned to death on holiday; and once when he was a student and had been beaten up by some teddy boys. But now, here, in the presence of the one thing certain to make any intelligent man lose control of his bodily functions, he didn't know whether he had or not. Being numb from the waist down wasn't only inconvenient and awkward, it was now preventing him from responding fully to the creation he was confronting. After all, words were pointless and, as they had all discovered, scientific analysis even more so.

Dr Horrigan walked up and grasped Lambert's shoulder. 'Something else, isn't it?' he asked, rather uninventively.

Lambert forgave the man his banality: it was too cold, and the situation too grave, to be picky. Besides, the man was draping a blanket over Lambert's chilled shoulders. They were standing about one hundred paces from a near-perfect hemisphere of deepest, darkest black. It towered above them and filled their horizon, only the barest curvature visible upwards or sideways at such close proximity. It wasn't shiny or smoky or matte; it was almost like looking at the night itself, so dark and infinite did it seem. If someone had held up a large photograph of a Pennine valley, then ripped a semicircular hole in its centre and pasted the shot to a blackboard, it would have looked exactly the same – and that was what made it all the more unnerving.

Never mind the sheer scale and illogicality of the event, or the unimaginability of what it must be like *inside* the dome, it was the dome's intangibility that made it all the more awe-inspiring. It was there, as plain as night, but by all and every scientific reading they had succeeded in making, it might as well not have been.

So far, with the limited resources they had ferried in over the last eighteen hours, the assembled scientists and so-called experts had discovered that it gave off no radiation and was impenetrable to light in all spectra. Even infra-red satellite scans had recorded neither heat nor warmth, whilst ultra-violet light just disappeared. White light seemed to be absorbed as the dome had no measurable albedo, and laser light entered but did not reflect back from anything it might have hit inside.

It also gave off no radio waves at any frequency, nor did it offer up any abnormal electromagnetic measurement. And seismic surveys using test bores and controlled explosions had only shown that it seemed to be ovoid in shape, buried in the ground along its mid-line, and two miles in diameter and half a mile high.

It wasn't solid, however. Objects could enter as easily as slipping into fog. But they did not return. Probes, booms, rocket-propelled grappling hooks, microphones, film cameras, video cameras, fibre optics, transmitters, distress beacons, radios, Geiger counters, thermographic cameras, cameras fitted with image intensifiers, all had been lowered by helicopter or driven in on remote control units, but all contact with the items had been lost within seconds of their entering the darkness. Any attempt to retrieve them, whether by remote command or the simple expedient of tugging on a rope, had always met with failure. By all measurable data, the thing did not exist. It should not, *could* not be there. And yet, plainly, defiantly, it was.

Lambert closed his eyes and let out a long sigh. He had been stuck out in the cold surveying the dome for three hours and needed food, but couldn't bring himself to ask for any as it would disturb his study. What he was achieving by staring at the darkness he didn't know. All he *did* know was that for the rest of his life he would never be this close to anything so important. He was witness to a unique event – an event he had predicted – and it would be gone in a matter of days, judging by the events at Warforn Peck. He couldn't tell if the length of its appearance related to its size or not, but he was certain of that one thing: it would go, and with it would go his life.

Oh, he could mull over the data and talk it through with endless committees of enquiry – secret or otherwise – that no doubt were already being set up by bureaucrats who could see new careers being spawned by the tragedy at Blair. None of them would discover the cause of the disaster but without experiencing firsthand what was going on inside, all would be speculation anyway. Science fiction of the biggest magnitude. That an entire town could disappear was horrific enough, but for it to vanish in a way that could neither be understood nor explained left the obvious fear that it could happen again.

'Want some food?' said Horrigan, leaning into Lambert's line of sight.

The sudden intrusion startled him. 'Oh . . . oh, yes. OK. If you can—'

'Bring it here? No problem. Get this down you.'

He handed Lambert a ham sandwich and started pouring tomato soup from a vacuum flask.

'How's the world coping with this?' asked Lambert, the food helping him to come to his senses.

'They don't know,' said Horrigan crouching down beside Lambert's wheelchair.

'Surely even a "D" notice can't cover this up.'

'"D" notice? No, this has got a "J" notice.'

'"J"?'

'National Jeopardy. Beyond national security; published information wouldn't just help or succour the enemy, it could bring down the government and provoke civil unrest. All journalists in any media, all publishers, all broadcasters, have been served a "J" notice, and the heads of governments with any journalists in this country have been informed of the seriousness of the crisis and, in return for full access to any data, have served similar notice on their own people. If any of this leaks out before the government authorizes it, those responsible face instant imprisonment under martial law. We're officially in a war zone; anyone breaks the rules, *anyone*, and they're likely to disappear. Plus we're allowing access by scientists from the US, Japan, Europe, Russia, even China. Not so much out of a spirit of comradeship as desperation – we haven't a clue what this bloody thing is and we need all the help we can get.'

Lambert was impressed. It wasn't like the British government – or any government, come to that – to let others help solve their problems. Horrigan must have been throwing his weight around the last few hours.

As for news coverage, Lambert didn't care about the freedom of the Press; most journalists' jobs were simply to entertain their readers. An MP dying is information; an MP dying in women's underwear, that's showbiz and it doesn't matter whether it's the *Sun* or the *Guardian*. What had happened to Blair was a tragedy, a nightmare, but it needed to be studied and understood in order to save other places from the same fate. Any interference in that process would be unhelpful and possibly harmful. With the globe visible for miles, it would become a world media event, with live TV coverage and endless debate by ill-informed 'experts', to say nothing of the religious implications for countless tubthumpers. And when it was gone, and the town's population with it, what price news control then? Not least because, for the forty thousand people inside the darkness, there would have to be ten times as many people outside who had a friend or relative in Blair. It would fast become a circus the like of which had never been seen in Britain before – or anywhere else, come to that.

'What about the world media? Helicopters, zoom lenses?'

'Air exclusion zone, perimeters one, three and five miles radius. Anyone caught within the five-mile zone will be incarcerated. Anyone in the three-mile zone will be fired upon. Within the one-mile zone, shot on sight, no excuses. By tonight we'll have twelve thousand troops stationed around the town, with a couple of dozen aircraft in the air at all times. We're putting nearby towns under curfew, clearing all habitations within sight of the dome, and restricting traffic movements throughout the North. They're redirecting civilian aircraft as well.'

'What's the cover story?'

'Toxic gas. Accident at a storage depot; the valley position of the town and the recent rain conspiring to keep it trapped in the town. But I've advised the government to come clean as soon as the dome has gone and we find everyone inside has died. They might not want to cause panic or be seen as not being in control, but they equally don't want to be seen as the cause or to raise doubts with a cover-up. Someone suggested there might be mileage in the train crash and massacre that happened in the town yesterday being the work of terrorists – you know, they blew something up they shouldn't have – but I think that's pushing it.'

'All pretty extreme.'

'Pretty necessary, though.'

Lambert nodded.

'And speaking of necessary,' said Horrigan. 'You're getting a mite whiffy, Wes.'

Lambert nodded again, only half aware of what the man meant. 'Get someone to fix me.'

'Out here?'

He looked around. They were in the middle of a field, military vehicles and men dotted about, two dozen scientists reading instruments, double that number of troops. Lambert would be in plain sight of perhaps a hundred people.

Lambert followed Horrigan's train of thought. And smiled. 'Do you really think, with that *there*, anyone's going to be looking at me and my shitty nappy *here*?'

Horrigan gazed up at the seemingly endless wall of blackness. 'When you put it that way . . .'

Horrigan walked off to the helicopter to call up a nurse. Lambert finished his ham sandwich and supped on his soup. As always, he burned his mouth but the pain meant nothing. Nothing did any more. He couldn't help thinking of the dome caused by the initial blast of an atomic bomb before it explodes outwards and up into its familiar mushroom cloud. This dome looked like a negative of that image of unimaginable energy and release. He wondered what kind of energy could have created this – and why the word 'evil' kept reoccurring. But, after all, his prediction was based on what had happened in Roswiay and Warforn Peck – and the mass insanity that preceded it. And the idea, however nebulous, made him shiver more than the early-morning temperature could have done.

22

JAMIE AND THE CORPSES

It was the cold, Jamie decided; that was what was making him sleep so much. The rain wasn't stopping and, dry though the back of the crushed Ford Granada was, he was already soaking wet and the rain dripping round the car in a dozen places had turned it into a refrigerator. Besides, what else could it be?

The noise in the junkyard was enough to keep anyone awake. Police cars, ambulances, fire engines and hundreds of people all running and shouting, most towards the scene of the crash, but others seemed to be totally off their heads.

So Jamie had drifted in and out of sleep, always to be jolted awake by some loud noise nearby. One time it was to find the cars above his Ford shifting as some maniac was chased up the pile by a screaming policeman. He saw the two of them fall off and land in a puddle and neither of them get up. Some men came and dragged the policeman away but left the other man on the floor, his eyes open and staring in at Jamie, unblinking in the heavy rain. His head was at a weird angle and Jamie guessed he had broken his neck, so he had hunkered down even further and tried to hug himself warm but it was pointless. Sleep was the only way he could find the comfort he wanted and even then there were dreams of trains and mad people.

All was confusion and terror until the time he woke up and found the rain had stopped. It was also quiet. No loud thrumming on the car bodies from the heavy rain, no people running about like lunatics, no shouting, no sirens. Scarcely able to believe they had gone at last, Jamie edged himself out from inside the car, making sure he kept out of the way of the dead guy who was still staring at him. His whole body ached and his head roared but he was prepared to put up with that if it meant he was alone again. And he was. True, there were still emergency vehicles about, their blue lights stilled, but there were no policemen, no paramedics, no one at all: they had all gone.

Jamie walked away from the dead man on the ground and through the abandoned vehicles, for abandoned was what they were: several had their doors open. He counted two fire engines, two ambulances, a fire chief's car, two police cars and one with a green light he knew would belong to a doctor.

He looked inside every vehicle but could find no one, except in the back of one of the ambulances where there were two bodies: a boy about Jamie's age whose legs had been ripped off, blood everywhere, and a middle-aged man whose head was covered in blood and who seemed to have lost his eyes.

Standing beside the empty ambulance, catching his breath, Jamie looked around and began to notice other bodies, some almost submerged in mud, one hidden under a police car, and a couple hanging from wrecked cars, one twenty feet in the air. They looked like litter tossed about by a giant. He cocked his ear but still couldn't hear anything. He often stayed up late on the streets – it was better than being in at home when his dad was drunk or Wayne was in one of his moods – and one thing he had always noticed wherever he hid at night (he wasn't stupid enough to walk the streets on his own) was noise. Whether it was distant traffic, people shouting in nearby houses, loud music, even trains and aeroplanes, Blair never slept. There was a hum, even at 4 a.m. But now, whatever time it was (and it was dark, so it must be night) there was no sound at all. He held his breath and strained to hear any noise but all he could discern was a rushing sound, like water undergound, and it took him a panicky minute to realize it was simply the sound of blood pumping in his ears. *Dickhead*, he scolded himself. Relieved and worried in equal measure, he decided to see if he could find the small hut with the fat women on the wall. If it was empty he might be able to get warm by the stove.

After five minutes of aimless wandering he found it, the door ajar. Carefully he approached, then ducked down and peered through the crack. But it was too dark to see, so he edged into the doorway and looked inside. Even in the dull light he could tell that going inside would have been a bad move.

There were more bodies there, and from what he could tell, most of them were naked women, blood covering them like tattered sheets. He lost count – and his cool – after eight corpses, and ran away to the shelter of a car and threw up.

Retching finished, he fell back on his knees and lifted his shaking head up to the sky. And that was when he noticed something else. The sky had gone.

He knew the idea was rubbish even as he thought it but it was the only way he could explain what he saw. There were no stars or clouds or moon; for all intents and purposes it was a moonless night, but the sky was a sort of grey, like a thunderstorm cloud, the dark colour completely uniform, almost flat. Maybe it *was* a giant cloud; he didn't know, didn't care, all he did know was that it gave him enough light to see by.

He walked out into the open again and looked around. What was it? A flat grey light, like an early winter morning, but it was June. And if it was dark there should be streetlights. One thing he had always remembered from when he was younger was looking down on Blair from the hills and seeing an orange glow. But now it was all grey. Maybe there had been a power failure. Yeah, that was it. Black-out. Except . . . except it was a *grey*-out. So maybe it was early morning and he'd slept through the whole night. Fuck, what would his mum say? And then he remembered the crash and Wayne's threat and what he had done *and the bodies*. He began to run, horror overwhelming him once again.

He ran pell-mell through puddles, dancing over debris, unsure of his destination but certain of his journey. Something terrible – perhaps even more terrible than what he had caused on the railway – had happened in the junkyard. He needed to get away from it and see if it had happened anywhere else.

He soon found himself running through long grass that reached up to his waist, the long wet stalks slapping at his legs and soaking him anew, but he found the feeling pleasing. If nothing else, it proved he was alive. The grass was grey rather than green and now he noticed that, in the odd light, *everything* had turned grey, like those old films he sometimes saw on TV. It was really weird. So weird, in fact, that he stopped and looked down at himself. Grey. His shirt and jeans were grey, his hands were grey. He looked like a black and white photograph!

Jamie stumbled on, his mind struggling to keep him from stepping over that final drop into insanity. Maybe that's why everyone had run away or died; they couldn't stand what had happened. And what about Wayne? *What about fucking Wayne*? It was that thick bastard who had got him into this fix. Let him rot, wherever he was.

Suddenly he bumped into a chain-link fence and bounced off it with a rattle. He cursed, the first time he had spoken aloud, his voice sounding pathetically inadequate in a world of silence and about as much use as a pen-torch would be trying to brighten the all-pervading gloom. He picked himself up and felt at his bleeding lip as he looked over the new obstacle. He could climb it, no sweat, but he would have to be careful with the barbed wire that ran along its top.

Checking there was no one around (he had a growing feeling that somewhere someone was watching him), he clambered up the fence, grateful for once that he had small feet – Wayne called them his 'girly feet' – but he was able to put his toe into the diamond-shaped links and make easy progress.

Soon he was at the top and able to see where he was. *Oh no* . . . he was by the railway. He forced himself to look both ways and there, sure enough, to his left just at the range of his vision, was the train wreck. There too were emergency vehicles and, it seemed, a lot of bodies, but no movement. He wavered, unsure whether walking along the track into town was such a good idea, but the alternative was to walk back through the maze of wrecks in the yard and brave whoever might be lurking there. Looking back he decided he preferred the open highway of the railway to the back alleys provided by the junked cars.

He pulled his wet sleeve over his hand to help him grip the barbed wire, then lifted his leg over until he was straddling the three strands of the rusted stuff. So far so good. However, as he tried to lift his other leg over, he slipped and, in his panic, grabbed at the barbed wire with his other bare hand. As a tine pierced the flesh of his palm he screamed, his other foot lost its hold and he began to fall head first towards the railway embankment. He had no choice. He grabbed harder to stop his fall, but his weight was too great and the wire had sliced across the palm of his hand before he could complete his fall.

He hit the ground screaming and, as he kneeled up to clasp his torn hand, the slick grass gave way and he slid down on his front the twenty feet to the face-raking stones beside the railway tracks.

He rolled over, pain tearing at his senses, his face and hand hot
spots of agony.

It took him fully five minutes to stop crying and dare to look at
the damage to his hand. It was every bit as bad as it felt and the
blackness of his blood in the strange grey light only made his horror
all the more complete. There looked to be a deep slash four inches
long right across his palm. He found holding his palm half-closed
helped staunch the flow of blood but it did nothing to alleviate the
incredible pain.

He decided he had better wrap it or he might bleed to death before
he got to a doctor, so he checked what he could use. Nothing, no
handkerchief, no tissues but then, sudden inspiration. Carefully
sitting himself down on the cold steel rail, he took off one of his
trainers, then removed the sock with his good hand. Squeezing out
the excess water, he wrapped it around his hand. It was crude and
it hurt like hell, but it could be called a bandage and that's what
he thought he needed. Getting his soggy trainer back on, however,
took a long time because he had to do it one-handed and the wet
laces wouldn't budge for him to pull out the tongue. But eventually
he managed it, though he couldn't tie a knot. His face felt hot and
as he wiped away sweat he saw blood on his other hand. He felt
his face and found the blackness there and a couple of cuts on his
right cheek. He needed a doctor, all right.

He walked along the edge of the track, noting that even here
there were dead bodies. A couple of women, three men, a boy, all
of them bloody, their bodies lying across the tracks, but they all
seemed intact, so they hadn't been run over by a train. So what,
or who, had killed them? And why?

He was within sight of the station, the train wreck now out of
sight round the bend behind him, gone like a nagging aunt, when
he saw a group of bodies spread across the track in front of him.
All four were facing him, arms outstretched as if they had fallen
while dashing to catch the 8:15. Or, he thought with a wince, as
if they were pointing accusing fingers at The Train Wrecker.

Jamie turned sharp left and crossed both tracks to the other side
of the cutting, aware that the only sound in the world was the
crunching of grey pebbles under his grey trainers. But even that
sound was muted, as if the greyness infected sound as well. He
suddenly felt the sock fall off his hand, the friction over his wound
making him cry out in pain again and, looking down, he saw it fall

in an oily puddle between two sleepers. It was too much, just too much. He fell to his knees sobbing.

The pain, all this darkness, the dead people, the crash he'd caused and, up ahead, where he thought he might at last find someone to help him, he could already see more and more bodies dotting both platforms of Blair Station. Dozens of them, scattered about like the victims of an explosion. He would have to walk through them, maybe even climb *over* them. Him, touching bodies. Dead people. He knew he was to blame for the train crash – although he still remembered something about a fat man – but this was different. It was strange and terrible. Unnatural. And, for all he knew, some of them could still be alive, could be the murderer, for none of the people he had seen had died quietly. Extreme violence had ended their lives – and someone must have caused it . . .

He sat down on his backside, laid his damaged hand on his lap and started rocking back and forth like a baby. Useless as she was, he wanted his mummy. Wanted her to take the pain away like she used to a long, long time ago, when dad had a job and Wayne was like a big brother should be; he wanted his mummy to put on the light and kiss his bad dream away and let him find out all this wasn't true, that it was just some stupid—

Suddenly a hand grabbed him by the waist and pulled him back down into the ditch beside the track.

23

LAMBERT'S OFFER

Lambert and Horrigan were sitting in one of the bedrooms of the farmhouse, downing scotch and staring out at the black on black of the dome that covered Blair. Sitting far enough back from the window, they could have been staring out at a cloudless night, the only evidence of the dome's unnaturalness the lack of stars within its shape. Yet, despite the best part of a half-bottle of Bell's having been consumed, both men were very sober and very awake – and it wasn't the constant hubbub from downstairs or the continuous chopping sound of passing helicopters that was keeping them alert.

'Remember the moon landings?' said Horrigan, staring up at the white orb to the west, its light bright enough to make the contents of the room visible.

'I watched them while I was in bed with Hilary. Good sex, great science.'

Horrigan laughed. 'I watched them with the Prime Minister, did you know that? Me and Harold Wilson and a dozen or so other bigwigs from the Department of Science. They still had dreams in those days, despite TR2 and Blue Streak. "The white heat of technology". What a joke.'

Now it was Lambert's turn to laugh. 'Ah, the follies of youth. But you didn't pack it in, did you?'

'And you did. I didn't see you staying true to the school after your crash. Sorry, didn't mean it to sound—'

'Forget it. Subtlety never was your strong point. After the crash it all seemed so . . . well, look at me. I'm a bag of shit on wheels. Whatever I eat or drink, some poor sod has to empty me out. Piss

I can cope with – it's delivered in bags – but the nappies . . . If I'm not sitting in shit I'm stinking of it. And no matter how much I joke about it or try to put my carers at ease, it's not funny. There's nothing remotely amusing or dignified about a middle-aged man having the shit scraped off his arse twice a day, then being washed, disinfected, talced and wrapped up like a fucking baby. God knows what'll happen when my mind or the rest of my body goes.'

'What do you mean?' said Horrigan, pouring another measure of scotch for them both.

'My father died of Alzheimer's when he was sixty-five, and it can run in families. So far, physically, my upper body has compensated. Weights, fitness routines, they've built up my strength, but now I'm losing it. Used to be able to pull myself off the floor and hang for a minute at a time. Proud of it. Now it's just seconds, my muscles ache, my arms shake . . . Some time I'll start finding it difficult just shifting this useless carcass about a bed. Right now I'm half-human. If I lose any more I don't know . . .'

'You're wallowing, Wes. You didn't used to feel sorry for yourself.'

'My point exactly, Horry. While I have my work, my interests, I can put up with it. Hell, I even put up with a sex life that consists of letting some tart use my face as a seat for half an hour. Developed strong jaw muscles, too,' he laughed, but not for long. 'I still enjoy what could loosely be called sex, and eating, even if half of me couldn't care less what comes down the tubes, but . . . *look at that fucking thing*. Forget the moon landings, cancer research, AIDS, genetics, virtual reality, nuclear fusion . . . this is bigger than all those because we don't know what it is. It's a blank page. No data, no theories, nothing.'

He wheeled himself in his chair over to the window and tried to remind himself of the sheer size of the phenomenon in front of them, but it was simply too big. Half a mile high, four times as wide, it was as mountainous as it was monstrous.

'And you think you'll make your name with it.'

Lambert shook his head and threw an ice cube at Horrigan.

'Since when have I cared about my good name? Christ, you don't write articles on ghosts and corn circles for the *News of the World* if you're interested in your reputation! All I want is to *know*. You used to be a scientist once; you must remember how that felt?'

'Hey, that's a bit steep . . .'

'You know what I mean. You spend all your time arguing on bloody committees. When was the last time you sat down with some raw data and tried to come up with some answers? Was a time people became doctors because they wanted to cure people; now they spend more time pushing pens than they do pushing pills. And it used to be the same with us. Remember that first term at Oxford? When we not only found ourselves in the same room with guys who'd formulated theories we took as gospel, but were actually arguing with them? Didn't matter we were wrong; it was the thrill of the chase. And that first time when you proved someone else wrong and you were right? I never had the dedication to follow it through, but you went the whole hog, doctorates up your arse, and then . . . well, you got sucked in.'

'Don't start . . .'

'I know, I know, this country's a joke when it comes to scientific research and you thought fighting from the inside could get us more than fighting from the outside. But admit it, whatever you've achieved, it's nothing compared to how you would have felt if you were still pumping out papers.'

Horrigan's downcast eyes and steadfast silence told Lambert all he needed to know. He decided to press home his point; always kick a man when he's down, especially if it's to your advantage.

'I've got no wife, no kids, no relatives who visit. My career's going nowhere, I've got no axes to grind, no ego to massage, just that little spark left that made us all want to know more about the world around us. And I want it to glow and flare one last time before I give up the ghost.'

'What do you want, Wes?' said Horrigan, idly chinking the ice in his newly empty tumbler.

Lambert nodded out of the window 'I want to go into that.'

The chinking stopped. *'You're joking!* This isn't a bloody Quatermass film you know, where we order a few squaddies in and see how many come out screaming. No equipment that's gone in there has come out – and no *person*'s going in there and that's final.'

'I don't care about coming out.'

'What?'

'I need to know. Listen to me, please, Horry.' He leaned forward and clasped the man's hand. 'The life expectancy of a paraplegic is less than the average person's. I might have inherited my father's

Alzheimer's. Ten years from now I'll probably be happy watching my drool fall into my lap, or I could well be dead. What's kept me going all these years is curiosity, and creating data programmes to help others' curiosity; that "need to know" we were talking about – and you agreed with me. As soon as I find myself going downhill that'll be it, there'll be no point in hanging around. But while I've still got that "need to know", I want to use it. I want to go into that thing and even if it kills me, at least I'll have had the satisfaction of knowing I did it. Even if only for a millisecond, if I can formulate some answer, or gain some inkling of understanding, that'll be enough.'

'That's bullshit, Wes! It's like needing to know the make of truck that's going to run you over. You'll still be dead, it doesn't matter.'

'Yes, but if you're going to die, it's better than absolutely nothing.'

'*But you're not dying*! And don't give me that little-by-little crap. You've got years left, useful years, and when this thing's gone you'll be making a valuable contribution.'

'Contributing what? I *may* have predicted it and we *may* be able to guess where it'll happen again but that's all it is: guesswork. But if I go in I might find out more – *and* I might come out.'

'And you might not.'

'Well, are you sending anyone else in?'

'No! And I'm not asking for volunteers either.'

'Too late. You've already got one.'

Three hours later, the two men were sitting in a car in a lane to the north of Blair, the curtain of blackness stretching across the green fields on either side of them like a work of art by a demonic Cristo. It was 6:15 a.m., just over twenty-nine hours after the darkness had engulfed Blair.

Two armoured personnel carriers and a Land Rover shielded the white Ford Escort from view further up the lane where several camera crews had been ordered to shut down their equipment and moved out of sight. Soldiers dotted the lane and the landscape, weaponry cocked, eyes alert, some nervous about their nearness to the dome, others bored by what they saw as little more than glorified guard duty.

Lambert was sitting in the driver's seat of the automatic Ford

Escort, accelerator and brake handles attached to the steering
column. It had been commandeered from a local JP who was
only too pleased to 'Help out someone from the government'. The
door had been removed and Lambert's electric wheelchair clamped
to a frame hanging from the roof rack, the idea being that when he
stopped the car he would be able to ease himself out onto the chair
and become relatively mobile.

'Someone should go with you,' said Horrigan, solemnly handing
over a pack of food, neither of them acknowledging that the last
thing Lambert would be worrying about would be sandwiches.
'Someone able-bodied; to help you out. Change your . . . stuff.'
He nodded at the bundle of nappies and cleaning gear in the back
wedged between the jumble of equipment.

'I bet every one of these lads here would be only too pleased to
join me.' Lambert smiled at the nearest man – a sergeant in full
battle fatigues and camouflage make-up – who didn't react, even
though Lambert was certain he would have heard him. He turned
back to Horrigan.

'Look, you know and I know I'm not likely to come back –
whether I'm in a wheelchair or wearing a bloody jetpack – so let's
keep the toll down to one.'

Suddenly there was a shot somewhere behind them and several
soldiers ran up the hill, but then there was a shout and they returned
to their posts.

'What was that?' said Lambert, squinting into his mirrors.

'It'll be a dog, maybe a cat.'

'What?'

'For some reason there are dozens of dogs and cats roaming the
countryside, presumably from Blair, some instinct making them
leave before the dome appeared. Any they find they trap or shoot
to dissect later.'

'Dissect? What the hell for?'

'Keeps the pathologists busy. Don't knock it: the biochemists
are examining their urine!'

Lambert shook his head. No wonder he couldn't cope with
specialization – all this and the bloody biochemists are checking
out dog piss.

'There *are* volunteers for going in, you know,' said Horrigan,
resuming their conversation. 'All with relatives in Blair, which
makes them ineligible. But I could come.'

'Horry, we're looking for cause, not cure. Whatever's happened here, we're not going to be able to stop it. It's not a bomb we can go in and defuse. Sometime soon the whole bloody thing's going to vanish into thin air and there'll be a couple of square miles of earth left for you and your lot to sift through. And that's when you'll be needed, not me. If I come back, I'll tell you all about it. Promise. But if I don't, well, it's been good to know you.'

'You don't have to—'

Lambert started the car, afraid that if he left it longer he would start listening to reason. He tried justifying his action one last time, as much to himself as his friend.

'Horry, when Hilary died I should have died with her, but I survived – or at least half of me survived – and since then have I really done anything to justify God's intervention? I think not. Now's the time to pay back. Whatever faults I have as a scientist, they're my faults. I could have stuck at one area of research and maybe have achieved some good; instead I flitted about like some bored schoolboy.' He looked at the black swathe that cut off their view from the world beyond. 'Well, no more. Now I'm going to take a wholly dedicated interest in one thing and one thing only: *that*. Now, before we both start blubbing, step back and let me do some motoring.'

Horrigan offered him his hand and Lambert shook it firmly.

'I'll be back,' he said in a mock-Austrian accent. 'My nappy needs changing.'

Horrigan stepped out of the car, closed his door, then ordered the soldiers to move the barbed-wire barricade aside and let Lambert proceed the quarter-mile down the country lane to the giant black wall surrounding Blair.

Lambert drove at a steady twenty miles an hour. There were eight cameras fitted to the car as well as numerous measuring devices for light, heat, sound, radiation and electromagnetism, all of them feeding information back to the central command post in the farm a mile away. He also had earphones and a microphone strapped to his head through which he could hear Horrigan telling him to tell them everything he could see. Lambert gave a final wave to the camera pointed directly at him from the bonnet of the car, switched on the headlights, then readied himself for the impact with the wall.

He had always wondered what his last thoughts would be if he found himself facing death but now, maybe a breath away from

oblivion, all he could think of was Alice stepping through the
looking glass and finding another, odder world. For a brief second
he wondered if he might just be passing through a curtain, to find
Blair on the other side, but as the darkness swallowed the car, such
thoughts evaporated.

Lambert found it difficult to talk. 'I'm about to enter it. Everything's turning black, like night. The headlights aren't showing—'

There was no resistance as the Escort touched the blackness, no
discernible effect at all. The car, and the panting Lambert, slid
smoothly into the blackness as easily as if the car had entered a
shadow.

All contact and telemetry with the car was lost within three
seconds, but not before the microphone clamped to Lambert's face
carried his final utterance to the scientists listening intently in the
farmhouse.

It was a scream of terror.

24

MAKING TRACKS

Jamie didn't have time to scream before the hand had clamped itself over his mouth and he had fallen back into muddy water. His hand took the brunt of his landing and he began to thrash about in agony and terror, certain he was about to be murdered.

He found himself being rolled onto his back and a figure pressing down on him, its eyes bright even in the dull grey light. The figure sat astride his chest, his knees pressing on Jamie's upper arms, a hand over his mouth to stifle his shrieks.

Finally Jamie exhausted himself and as he stopped screaming and struggling, the figure slowly released the clamp over his mouth. Jamie saw his chance and bit into the flesh of the hand – and was rewarded with a scream and a slap across the face followed, oddly, by a stream of apologies.

'Hey, I'm sorry kid. Sorry. Didn't mean to do that. I know I must have . . . Sorry, sorry, I just didn't want to attract . . . sorry.'

The man held his hands up as if in surrender and slowly rose off Jamie's body and stumbled back.

Jamie didn't know what to do and convinced himself it was just a trick, but the man hobbled even further away.

'Last thing I want to do is hurt you,' he said. 'If you want to run, go.'

Jamie stood up, the pain in his hand almost beyond endurance, and shook his head. Truth was, he didn't have the strength to get out of the ditch, let alone run away. Instead he stepped against its side – it was about three feet deep with six inches of water in the

bottom – and eased his sore hand onto the muddy platform of its
edge so that it had some support.

The man looked at Jamie's hand. 'Did I do that?'

Jamie shook his head. 'Barb wire, back there. Climbing over.'

'Sorry I can't do anything about it, but I don't have a first aid
kit.' For some reason the man thought this funny and laughed, but
he soon started to wheeze so he stopped. 'My name's Mark, what's
yours?' he said, offering his hand.

Jamie said nothing; instead he gazed at the dishevelled grey
man before him, with skin the colour of his shirt. He had just
remembered the zombie videos Wayne had let him watch a few
years back. Movies where the dead came back to attack the living,
drawn by their warmth or their blood or something. He looked down
at his hand, black blood lacing the knuckles. He glanced back at the
man and caught him looking at the hand.

'That looks really nasty, I thought my knee was bad . . .' He
pointed at his ripped jeans and the bloody mess where his knee
should have been. 'But that needs seeing to. Stitches probably.'

Before he could stop himself, Jamie burst out: 'You're not going
to eat me, are you?'

Soon they were both laughing, though there was nothing remotely
funny about their circumstances.

Mark Dawson found out the lad's name was Jamie Begley and that
he had been in a scrapyard up the tracks with his brother when there
had been an accident on the railway. He had got scared with all the
people running about and had hidden in a car and fallen asleep.
When he had woken up he had found the same situation Mark had
discovered when he had come round in his ditch.

Mark remembered falling and banging his head but after that
everything was a blank. He had no idea how long he had been
unconscious but when he had woken up it was dark, the rain had
stopped and there seemed to be no one about. He had twisted his
knee and found it difficult to get out of the ditch, so he had waited
to see if it would improve. His enforced idleness had given him
time to study the odd light that seemed to permeate Blair.

He found the light was exactly the same in his ditch as out, as if
every surface was equally lit. By rights the ditch should have been
in shadow but it wasn't – and yet there was no discernible source of
light. No sun, no moon, no street lighting. It was odd, but nowhere

near as odd as the number of corpses he could see strewn across the tracks and station platforms. It was as he was about to finally force himself out of the ditch, regardless of the pain in his knee, that he saw the boy, the first living soul since he had tumbled into the ditch. He had grabbed him because . . . Why had he grabbed the boy? Because he feared for his safety? Because he needed to talk to someone? He wanted help? He didn't know, and now, sitting with the lad, he didn't care.

'So everyone seems to have been killed? Murdered?' he said.

Jamie nodded, gratefully chomping on a Snickers Mark had found in his pocket but hadn't yet risked sampling. The fall had made him feel sick and he suspected he might be concussed – he knew one of the symptoms was nausea – so he would have to be careful.

'I've seen lots, all of them murdered,' said Jamie. 'There's a hut in the yard, it was full of dead ladies, all nude. And all over this track there are people, old and kids. What's happened to them?'

'I wish I knew. It doesn't make sense.'

They had hauled themselves out of the ditch and were sitting leaning against the embankment, both pondering their next move. Jamie's chocolate bar had only helped to rekindle his appetite and he realized he was hungry. For his part, Mark couldn't decide what to do. Part of him needed to get to the train wreck – the reason he had fallen down the railway cutting in the first place – to see if he could find Karen, but common sense told him she wouldn't be there now, or if she was it was too late. His best chance would be to make his way to the hospital – there must be someone there who knew what had happened. Besides, his knee needed looking at – God knows how long it had been in that filthy water – and the boy needed his hand stitching. From what he had seen of it, the cut was more than just superficial; the longer treatment was delayed the more chance there was of permanent damage.

The boy suddenly grasped Mark's arm, the pressure evidence of his concern.

'Could it be a war?' he said, his eyes wide. 'You know, nuclear attack. Russians.'

Mark immediately shook his head, but his heart raced at the thought. Not so much at the idea of nuclear war, but biological warfare. Everyone in Blair – or the whole country, come to that! – could have been poisoned or driven mad by some bug to which he and Jamie were somehow immune. Yes, that made sense – if

such a word could be used to describe this horror. A nuclear
attack would have meant damage but there was none apparent.
Germ warfare, however, was a possibility: all the more reason to
get to the hospital.

'Look, Jamie, we need to decide what to do, but whatever it is,
we'd better do it together.'

'No way am I going anywhere on me own, don't worry.'

'Right. You've got a bad hand, I've got a busted knee, best bet
is to find a doctor. And where do doctors hang out?'

'Hospital?'

'Give that man an orange!'

'What?'

'Never mind. The hospital's on Regent Street. About half a mile.
Trouble is, we've got to go through the station to get there.'

They looked along the track towards the charnel house that had
been one of BR's finest Victorian twin-platform stations. God alone
knew what would announce itself once they got inside.

Mark found that his knee wasn't as bad as he thought. As long
as he kept his leg stiff and avoided bending it was bearable.
Nonetheless, their progress was slow. They kept to the left-hand
side of the tracks, using the sleepers as stepping stones. Once or
twice Mark missed his footing and Jamie grabbed his arm with his
bad hand, the two of them suppressing their cries of agony for fear
of alerting someone to their presence.

Blair Station was an end-of-the-line station, with a platform on
either side of the two tracks, the exit being via a long ramp on the
right-hand outgoing side. The building featured ornate ironwork
canopies unchanged since being built in the late Nineteenth Century
and had long been a source of pride for the inhabitants of the town.
No longer, however. As they approached, Mark and Jamie could see
that there were at least fifty bodies on the left-hand platform alone.
As many more were strewn across the two tracks, with countless
more heaped along the length of the right platfrom all the way up to
the open iron gates of the exit. It was a veritable hill of corpses.

Bodies became more frequent on the tracks as they neared the
station. Mark stopped at the twisted form of a young girl. She was
face up, her eyes closed – thank God – but her legs were broken,
bone protruding from both shins. She must have been nine or ten
at most. Jamie turned away, but Mark continued to stare at her. He
knew her, he was convinced of it.

He brushed the hair out of her eyes. Her face was bruised over the temple but at least she looked at peace. He checked other bodies. They were all adults, all injured, their wounds consistent with falls or being knocked down. He could find no knife or gunshot wounds. *Trampled*: the word sprang into his mind unbidden. He remembered the scene when he had peered over the embankment wall. People charging up towards the train crash, blind to all but their need . . . *that* was where he had seen the girl before! Her mother had been dragging her on her knees and had let go of her. He looked at her face more closely. The mark on her head wasn't a bruise; it was a footmark: someone had walked on the girl's face!

Why, he didn't know, but Mark walked over to the corpse of a fat middle-aged man, pulled the coat off his back and carefully draped it over the girl's face and body. Poor little thing . . .

Jamie came and tugged at his arm. 'Did you know her?'

Mark wiped tears from his eye. 'Not really, I saw her . . . no, I didn't. It's just . . . unfair.'

Jamie didn't understand what the man was thinking but it didn't matter. His actions had been those of someone who had a heart, and that was the last thing he had expected to find when he had set off from the junkyard. He felt slightly safer.

Mark walked on. Whatever had happened, he just prayed it was confined to this part of Blair. Jamie caught up with him and they wove their way past corpse after corpse until they were able to reach the sloping end of the left platform. The bodies tended to be in clumps like dead sailors lashed to dinghies, people clinging to each other for survival. Or, he thought, was it something worse? He noticed now that several bodies had their hands around the throats of their dead companions, some even reciprocating the action. Surely they couldn't have choked each other to death? That was absurd, obscene . . . but then, what wasn't absurd or obscene about their slowly stumbling their way through an open graveyard?

Mark slowly turned round to examine the corpses around him. Two women, three young boys, a baby girl, three policemen, two teenagers: . . . but age and sex were immaterial: no one had been spared. He stopped his turn and paused. Something else wasn't right.

Unlike Jamie, he hadn't paid much attention to the weather, he was just grateful it had stopped raining, even though he was still soaked. He just assumed it was a dull, cloudy day, and with the knock his head had taken he couldn't be sure that his eyesight wasn't playing him up. But now he noticed something was missing, something so everyday that you never paid it heed but now it had gone, it was noticeable. But what was it? He looked up at the sky. In every direction it was the same grey sheet, so dull and lifeless it seemed to suck the colour out of the world.

'Is everything grey to you?'

Jamie nodded, holding out his undamaged hand. 'Everything. Even me, I look grey.'

Mark nodded. The kid was right. Mark had been wearing blue jeans, a white shirt and a red jacket; now they all seemed to be shades of grey. If he squinted he could discern just a touch of red or blue, like the colour being almost turned down on a TV but not quite all the way. But what about the light? Where was it coming from? And if he could spot where the sun was, he might get a handle on the time: his watch had been smashed during his fall. But there was no sun, in any direction, not even the faintest—

Shadows! He looked down, spun round, waved his arms in the air, but it was true: there were no shadows.

He loped as best his leg would allow back down the platform and on into the open air between the two tracks, mindful of the bodies scattered in his path. Then he stopped and turned full circle. Everything looked the same, as if lit by the same light from every angle. Whichever direction he looked, there were no shadows; *everything* was grey. Underneath the station canopies or out in the open, the level of light was identical. Night or day, light sources cast shadows, however weak, but now there were none.

Mark walked back up the platform.

'What is it?' said Jamie.

He debated whether to tell him but decided it didn't matter. 'There are no shadows.'

The boy looked around. 'Oh yeah, you're right.'

He didn't seem too bothered, but then why should he be? Shadows were intangibles you ignored. Working in advertising with photographers, however, Mark was aware of how crucial lighting was when shooting products. It could take a whole day just to get a table-top shot right. All shadowed areas had to be lit, and the shadows cast by those lights compensated for. It was tricky and the result was wholly artificial, but now he was standing in a world where every angle, every view, seemed lit to eliminate shadows. It was strange and illogical – and unnerving enough to put his fears about biological warfare at the back of his mind. Because it was impossible. Whatever had happened to Blair, it was beyond the realms of reality. So where did that leave him and Jamie?

25

IZOTTA'S NIGHTMARE

Izotta was naked on a bare bed and before her stood several older naked men, all erect, all staring at her body, their lust undeniable. The first man climbed onto the bed, mounted her and began a steady rhythm, his face obscured as he buried his face in her neck. Izotta wrapped her legs around him and squeezed, her brown flesh in sharp contrast to his pumping white buttocks, and humping up to meet his strokes. There was no sound. The man speeded up and she felt him lose co-ordination as he emptied himself into her. Then, without a word of endearment or thanks, he got up and walked away, the next man taking his place, his face also obscured. The sex continued, each man quietly but urgently fucking her, each unloading himself then departing, yet none of them satisfying her – indeed, she wasn't even aroused: she was simply there, a convenient receptacle to be discharged into. And there seemed to be no end in sight as the queue of men seemed constant. She tried to see if she could recognize them but they always seemed to be looking away or down. All she could see were their erections and their bodies, several flabby and covered in grey hair, an indication of their age. As the fifth man entered her, she began to look round the room and noticed it wasn't a normal room. There was the bed she lay on and four grey bare walls, but that was all, except on one side where a wide window looked out on more grey.

The fifth man ejaculated, rose and walked away. She followed his progress as the sixth man climbed onto her; he walked round to the back of the queue and began stroking his still erect penis. Good God . . . she counted the men. Six. There were six men and each of them was intent on servicing her again and again. For the first time she became worried. She'd had multiple partners before, but only when drunk and one of her lovers had brought a friend; she had enjoyed it – two married men for the price of one – but this was . . . odd. She looked over at the window again. There were faces!

Women's faces, and these were more distinct. She recognized them – and saw their fury. They were the wives of men she had bedded over the years. She had always made a point of finding out what her lovers' spouses looked like, often imagining their reaction if they came home and found their moaning husbands buried in her cunt up to the hilt, unable to stop themselves as they spurted inside her. Many a time she had orgasmed with that single image in her mind: a wife watching her husband lose control inside her body. But now they were all here. Mrs Coughlan, Mrs Matthews, Mrs Jordache, Mrs Dixon, Mrs Rankin and Dorothy Dougan. Mrs Dixon was the oldest at fifty-eight, Mrs Rankin the youngest at thirty-two, Mrs Matthews had five children. She knew their faces, their ages, their jobs, their children's names. She had even been in their homes, once without any of the family knowing. (Technically it had been breaking and entering but she had regarded it as checking out the opposition.) Most of them had suspected their husbands were having an affair but none had ever pointed an accusing finger at Izotta, though there was that one delicious time when Mrs Dixon had called on her husband's mobile while he was making love to Izotta and she had insisted he talk to her while she sucked him off. Many a time she had relived that exquisite moment too . . . But now these wives were watching her, their eyes wide with hatred. And then their hands were in sight and in them she saw weapons: bread knives, screwdrivers, a hammer, a poker.

Izotta tried to push the sweating animal on top of her out of the way, desperate to see if there was a door for her to escape through. There wasn't – which meant the women couldn't get in – but the sight of so many cuckolded women out for her blood sent her cold.

The man on top of her finished, rose, and was replaced by the next. It wasn't going to end. Suddenly there was a pounding and she saw the women hammering on the glass. She couldn't understand where she was or how this had happened. She couldn't remember *anything*. And then to her horror the windowpane split left to right, like a crack in ice, then shattered. As glass crashed into the room, the women climbed over the low sill, their shrieking voices now piercing the silence like blades through flesh. Izotta struggled again but had no strength against the weight of the man on top of her. Instead, to her horror, she began to rise to a climax, that familiar warmth in the pit of her stomach beginning its relentless march through her limbs and down into her groin. *No, no, not now, no*, she heard herself screaming. *Must escape, must go*. But her orgasm wasn't to be denied. She started to tremble and sweat, her vagina super-sensitive to the fat member ploughing its length like a piston. And the women came nearer, their weapons raised high, their voices higher, and as Izotta screamed her orgasm, they lunged at her, her dark flesh exposed to their metal and as she came the man on top pushed himself away from her, pulled out and began to ejaculate blood onto her stomach. And then she saw, grinning down at her, the dead face of Gordon Dougan, his teeth broken, his deathly white face shadowed by large bruises, one eye closed, the noise of his pleasure welling up from somewhere inside him like the last rattle of a corpse. And as the dead man spewed onto her and the women hacked at her flesh and face and thighs Izotta's orgasm killed the pain and horror and grey and she felt her flesh dissolving and her senses stretching until, suddenly, all sensation stopped and there was absolutely nothing.

The first thing Izotta saw when she opened her eyes were the shattered windows of the flat, their glass strewn around the room, fragments peppering walls and furniture. Outside the world was grey, the colour so uniform the windows might as well have been painted squares.

Izotta tried to judge her situation but it didn't make sense. She was looking down on the room as if from the top of a step ladder, but there had been no steps in the room. She soon found she had to squint as the light in the room was too bright. So bright, in fact, it made looking around almost painful.

But as she became accustomed to the harsh illumination, she could see the room was wrecked, everything moved out of place apparently by the force of the windows' implosion. Wallpaper had been shredded, the carpet ripped, but that was nothing compared to what had happened to Mr Farmer.

Mr Farmer! Her mind suddenly flashed to her last sight before darkness had claimed her: the man-slug descending on her like a voracious predator. But she found she couldn't remember what had happened after that. She had survived, but that was about all. Mr Farmer, however, plainly hadn't.

His carcass was spread-eagled in the centre of the room, his legs pointing straight at the window, his arms extended at right angles, his huge belly flopping over his sides onto the floor as if someone had let all the air out of him. His face was also suffering from the effects of gravity, the weight of his cheeks and chins pulling his features taut so that he almost looked mongoloid.

Sickening as the sight of the dead man should have been, Izotta wasn't repulsed by it. She had never really been squeamish – too many traffic accident reports and hospital follow-ups had seen to that – but this was different. She didn't *care* what had happened to the fat man, and because she didn't care, she could view his corpse unemotionally – and that cold eye allowed her to appreciate the fact that the man seemed almost to be smiling; as if he had been suffering from terminal indigestion and had at last, however drastically, gained relief from his excess wind.

Then she remembered the fucking and the men – and their wives and their brutal revenge. She didn't know whether she felt guilt or anger, but she was relieved it had only been a dream. She calmed herself: there were more important matters for her to be concerned with now. Like what had happened after Mr Farmer had fallen on her. And how had he died? And why was she in such an odd position?

She looked around, aware for the first time that she couldn't actually feel anything. She was neither hot nor cold, felt no soreness nor fatigue, only pain from the bright light. She couldn't even tell if she was standing, sitting or lying down, so she slowly turned her gaze to the wall behind her, then on downwards to see where her feet were. But she saw something she didn't expect. Something which proved, whether it was in her mind or in her ears, that she still had the power to scream.

Her own body lay by the kitchen door, her sightless eyes staring up at the ceiling, her mouth open in a stilled cry of horror, a large pool of dried blood encircling her head.

26

LAMBERT INSIDE THE DOME

Lambert's first instinct was to slam on the brakes but his hands refused to co-operate and he hit the dangling corpses at twenty miles an hour, his scream blotting out the loud crack as the windscreen crazed. Finally he pulled on the brake and the car slid to a halt, his heart racing, his mind freeze-framed on what he had seen as the blackness of the dome's edge had lifted.

The world had turned grey. It was the normal countryside landscape with trees and hedges and fields and stone walls it had always been, the country lane running ahead of his car, but everything had lost its colour. It was as if he had entered a monochrome movie. And then he had seen the three corpses, hanging from the branch of a large tree that itself overhung the road. Before he could stop he had hit two of the bodies, their feet and lower legs slamming into the car's bonnet, ripping the two video cameras from their mountings, smashing the windscreen and frosting his view of this strange new world.

After he had recovered from his initial shock, he checked the rear-view mirror. The bodies were still there. Two men and a boy of about fifteen, naked, swinging by their necks, hands limp by their sides, faces contorted in agony. One of the men had been eviscerated, his insides a dark hollow. Lambert couldn't see if his insides were on the road and didn't want to know.

He checked his instruments and equipment. Apart from the two cameras, he found everything was still working, but he suspected no one would be receiving the information being transmitted. He clamped his hand on the wheel of the car and began to speak into the small microphone that hung from the band round his head, as much to give him something to do as to help with any subsequent scientific enquiry.

'I'm in the dome. The cameras have gone so I'll tell you what I see and what is happening. First off, everything's grey in here, like the colour's been removed. It's rather odd. I keep wanting to blink, as if I've got fuzzy contact lenses in. As I came through the wall of the dome – which isn't solid despite appearances – I hit three bodies hanging from a tree. Presumably murdered during the madness that took over the place, I can't tell how long they've been hanging there. They broke my windscreen so I'm going to have to punch it out so I can see where I'm going.'

It took him five minutes to get the windscreen out. Had he been mobile he would simply have kicked it out, but he only had his arms, so he had to use his vacuum flask to bang the frame out of place, then push the whole windscreen out onto the bonnet where it stayed.

'God, that was hard work,' he puffed into his mike, wiping sweat from his face. He couldn't help noticing his arms were trembling. 'OK, I'm going to move off now towards town. As yet I can't see anyone else.'

He slipped the car into 'Drive,' twisted the accelerator grip and edged forward.

The lane was winding and every time he approached a bend it was screened by the high hedges on either side of the road. He felt himself holding his breath in anticipation of what might suddenly appear.

'I can't remember being so shit-scared. If I knew what might be coming, I'd be better prepared.' He eyed the revolver on the passenger seat. It was little comfort.

As he negotiated the fourth bend he saw a car parked up against the hedge on the other side of the road. It appeared to be empty. He slowed as he reached it and looked at it through the space where his door had been removed. He suddenly felt very exposed – there was nothing between him and the outside world – so he started to speed up. The car was a Peugeot 206, but he couldn't tell the colour; all he could make out was that it was light, perhaps cream or yellow. It was only as he passed it that he saw the body lying at its rear. It was a young woman.

She was fully clothed and face down in the grass. He debated whether to stop and check if she could be helped, but then he saw the hole in her back where she had been shot, her blood all but concealed by the darkness of her jacket. What was going on?

'I've just passed a car. There's a dead woman lying behind it. She appears to have been shot in the back. I'm not sure if I should continue. My idea about people going mad and order breaking down inside the dome seems all too true. My only worry is what has happened to the killers.'

He found a partial answer as he rounded the next bend. Here there was a tractor all but blocking the road. A man sat in the cab, his head lolling to one side, staring down at Lambert, the inside of the glass behind him plastered with a dark stain that could only be blood. There was also no doubt that the man had shot himself in the mouth, the revolver still in the hand that lay in his lap.

Lambert brought the Escort to a halt. 'Found another dead body. Tractor driver. Looks like he committed suicide inside his cab with a pistol. Blown out the back of his head. I wonder if he had anything to do with the others I've found?'

Lambert decided it still wasn't the right time to get out of the car, so he edged it onto the verge and scraped it past the tractor, his rear offside wing rasping noisily on one of the tractor's large tyres.

Finally past the obstacle – and aware that driving back the same way was not something he would like to do in a hurry – he again stopped the car and surveyed the tractor, his eyes flitting from his side mirror to his rear-view mirror and back. From this side he could see there was also a shotgun propped up inside the cab, perhaps the one used on the girl. He looked around. The tractor had been coming out of a field and up the long rise of the grass he could see a farmhouse.

'I can see a farm. I'm wondering if I should go and take a look there, or carry on to Blair. Or come out . . .'

He decided to travel a bit further. So far all he had seen was confirmation of his theory about insanity run rampant. What he was after were some answers – and a few dead bodies would not provide them.

'I'm going on for a bit. If the road's blocked or I don't find someone alive, I'll come back out. If I can. The instruments tell me the temperature is a steady twenty degrees celsius, humidity is fifteen per cent, no pollen or air pollution worth mentioning, no wind, air pressure's a steady one thousand and twenty millibars.

There is no direct sunlight but the available light's about on a par with a dull summer afternoon, if you exclude the disappearing colours. There are no radiation readings. Truth to tell, Horry, it's extremely average. But that's better than it is outside, isn't it?' He peered up at the slate sky. 'You know what it reminds me of? Those holiday domes: you know, ambient temperature, perfect lighting, all your needs catered for. Except they don't have killers on the loose, do they?' He shut himself up. He was waffling.

Cresting a rise he saw Blair for the first time, its presence shielded until then by the hedges bounding the lane. It was like looking at a photograph. There was no colour, no movement, not even drifting smoke. He looked up at the sky. No clouds. In fact, the sky was so uniform, without any clue to distance or depth, he could believe he was inside a dome. Like the ceiling of a planetarium where pin-pricks of light give an illusion of distance, so the complete absence of defining scale – no sun, no stars, no clouds – meant the sky could be a hundred miles away or literally just beyond his fingertips, yet he knew it reached to about two and half thousand feet at its centre and fell to earth where he had entered the dome. He looked back at Blair, giddy from leaning out of the car and staring upwards at nothing.

He thought he detected a change. Whether it was a movement or . . . yes, there. There *was* something. A light. He couldn't place it exactly, but there was a small white light somewhere in the town – and he knew that was where he should be going . . .

'Blair's still there. I don't know if you're getting any of this, or whether you'll be able to check it later, but it's there all right.' They had strapped a camera to his wheelchair which he was to use if he ever ventured away from the car, but he couldn't use it until he had got into the chair. 'I'll use the camera on the chair when I finally decide to go walkies. The town seems quiet from here. Can't see any fires burning. Very quiet. Dead might be a better word, given what I've seen so far. It's as grey as the whole place. I know I'm in a dome so I can rationalize it, but to people in here, it might just seem like a weird sky. It's possible they won't realize they're trapped unless they've tried to get out. I think I see a light down in the town. Now we know power's been cut off and there are no other lights anywhere, so this I'll have to investigate. Unfortunately.'

He set off again, his heart starting to pound strongly, the rushing in his ears louder than the car's engine. He had never been so scared in his life. In the car he was mobile and he could always use it as a weapon – anyone got in his way and he could run them over – but in his wheelchair he was just a target. Now that his life could well be on the line, he decided that the line he had been giving Horrigan was just that. Sure he was curious and, scared as he was, he was pleased to have come this far, but if it came right down to it, he had every intention of turning the car round and going back the way he had come. *If* he could come out because, after more than twenty-four hours, no one else had and there had to be some people trying to escape.

He had travelled a hundred yards when he saw another body by the roadside on the left. It appeared to be a man in a dark overcoat, sitting on the verge, his head slumped forward. Considering how quiet this country lane would normally be, he seemed to have found a veritable rush hour. He slowed as he reached the figure. He saw now that he wore a cloth cap stained with something light. Birdshit? His trousers were badly frayed, his boots ragged.

'Another body,' Lambert said into his mike. 'Looks like a tramp. Can't see how he died. Might be natural causes. He looks peace—'

Lambert let out a yell as the figure jumped up and thrust his dirty bearded face through his empty windscreen.

'Good morning to you, chief. Any chance of a lift?'

27

MARK AND JAMIE ON THE MOUND

Directly in front of Mark and Jamie was the lift that took goods and disabled passengers up to the foyer of Blair Station. It was jammed open, the metal trellis gate twisted outwards, a dozen bodies crammed into its small space. Even if they pulled all the corpses out, there was no guarantee that it would work, which left only one alternative.

Mark looked across the platform that crossed behind the twin sets of buffers at the tracks' end. That too was covered in tangled corpses, but a path could be picked out without too much difficulty, as could one on the opposite platform for about thirty yards to the base of the slope that led up to the exit and the world outside. It was here the nightmare would really begin. Even in the eerie grey light, he could see the corpses were three and four deep all the way up the slope. The protective barriers on its edge had been smashed or bent and several corpses hung over like broken dolls in a vandalized toy shop. It was their only way out, given their pressing need for medical help, but they were going to have to walk for fifty or a hundred yards over dead bodies, some of whom may even have been people they had known.

'Jamie, that's the only way out,' Mark said, pointing at the hill of cadavers.

Jamie nodded dumbly. He was as anxious as the man to get out of the dead place and he too had sussed that the only way out was over the bodies, but he didn't think he could do it. The only body he had ever seen before now had been his gran's lying in the Co-op funeral home, her old face smooth and sunken like one of those badly made waxwork figures at the waxworks in Blackpool. So unlike the rosy-cheeked, jolly gran he had known that he had never believed the body had *really* been hers. But he had no reason to doubt these bodies were real.

'I'm − I'm scared,' he said, his voice so small it didn't even produce an echo.

'So am I,' admitted Mark. He had never been paternal, and had found children awkward accoutrements his friends tended to bring round and show off, like their new car or their holiday snaps. If they weren't crying or needing changing, they were making too much noise or acting as bored with him as he was with them. After any such visit he and Karen had quickly broken open a bottle of wine and thanked the Lord that, despite Karen's love of children, they hadn't been landed with their friends' spoiled brats. But this kid, he seemed bright and brave and, despite his youth, Mark was glad he was around. Terror was an emotion best shared because then there was a better chance that the right choices would be made, even if it meant depending on a twelve-year-old.

'No point in delaying,' he said. 'Your hand and my knee need help. No one here's going to help, so we've got to make tracks.'

Jamie nodded, holding his hand palm up and trying not to cry, but it hurt so much.

Mark led the way through the grey bodies, carefully judging each step so they could avoid an old woman's hand, a young girl's feet, a pregnant woman's belly, the policeman's twisted leg, the teenagers' open eyes and mouths. There was black blood everywhere, in patches still sticky under his feet, most faces striped with it like camouflage make-up. Everyone seemed to have died violently, either in fighting or by being crushed. The madness that must have swept the place was unimaginable. And it had all started with the train crash and people's understandable fears for others. So how had it devolved into this? What madness had they caught? Caught . . . Again, the idea of biological warfare stamped its foot in the empty space that had become his mind. But the light . . .

Two minutes later they reached the bottom of the rise to the exit gates and paused. There was no easy route; however careful they were, there was no way they could avoid stepping on people.

'How are we going to . . .?' Jamie trailed off, the enormity of their task suddenly horrifyingly apparent.

Mark took a deep breath and tried to convince the both of them.

'They're dead bodies, that's all. When you're dead, you're dead. What matters is that the living live on. If we get out of here we may find other people alive or people who need help and we can help them. We can't do anything for . . .' *Run*, he thought. That's the only way to do it. No careful steps, or searching for delicate toe and hand holds. No trying to avoid people's faces or stomachs or crotches. Just climb them like a rockfall, grabbing and standing on whatever had to be used. And don't stop.

'We're going to climb as fast as we can. No stopping, no worrying, just go for it. Right?'

Jamie nodded. He was scared that if he actually opened his mouth to speak he would vomit and once he had given in to his fears he would never be able to do it – and he wanted out of the station as much as the man.

'Shouldn't take more than a minute, should it?' Mark tried to sound reasonable, as if they were convincing each other about a doctor's injection. 'One minute and it's done. OK?'

Again Jamie could only risk a nod, his stomach a cauldron ready to overflow.

Mark looked for the best place to start. But what was best? The slope was about twenty feet wide and fully fifty yards long, every inch buried in bodies, broken faces, clawed hands and stranded limbs that formed an abandoned human garden. There must have been about – God above – five hundred bodies. There were more people laid out dead in front of him than would die in Blair in the average *year*. He had no choice; if he thought about it any longer he would simply give up, Karen or no Karen, wounds or no wounds.

He launched himself onto the back of a fat man in a suit and as he felt the body slump beneath him he stepped onto the chest of a young girl then onto the body of a man in a dayglo jacket – a lollipop man? – then, feeling himself falling over, he grabbed the shoulder of a middle-aged woman to pull himself further on.

'Come on,' he shouted, the pain in his knee catching his breath. 'It's easy. Just go for it!' He glimpsed Jamie leaping onto a body and he returned his own task.

Three more steps and he had surmounted two teenage girls in punk make-up, their strangely pre-ordained death masks all the more hideous in the greyness. He managed to clamber over the twisted body of a man in a boiler suit, an elderly woman who had lost her wig, and a woman in jogger gear. Then, to his horror, he slipped and fell forward, his face mashing into that of a middle-aged woman, the dust from her heavily powdered skin making him gag. He reached up to push himself off her but his fingers slipped into her mouth and her false upper plate fell out and slid across her cheek to land on the back of a man's head, her dead breath exhaling in his face. He whipped himself back with a shriek, lost his tenuous purchase and rolled over sideways on top of the bodies, suddenly slipping between a man and a woman, the man's staring eyes inches from his own, the smell of sweat and shit and piss and vomit and blood now apparent at such close quarters. His bad right knee made hard contact with someone's skull and he had to pull his left leg up to relieve the pressure, only to feel his other leg slip under a body that moved and dragged him down with it.

He struggled frantically, his screams muffled by the dead mouth of the man, the bloated tongue grazing his own, his screams swallowed by the man's long emptied lungs. He thrashed in desperation, but his legs and hands were pinned by his own body and he could feel a cavity opening beneath him that would soon let him fall through onto the stone platform and allow bodies to fall and crush him in an avalanche of dead flesh.

He stopped moving and concentrated instead on fretting his hand up alongside his chest until he could reach the man's face. He scrabbled his fingers over his features until his fingers slipped into two notches and he was able to push in and force the face away from his own. He sucked in air, the stink now stronger, but it was the breath of life and he relished it. Two more deep breaths, then he pushed the man's head back and only as he heard the neck snap did he see that his fingers were in the man's eye sockets. Mark screamed again, his mind beyond logic, and struggled to free his other arm but found it was trapped up a woman's dress, her cold nylon-clad thighs crushing it as bodies above and beneath her compressed her limbs. Soon the pain in his trapped arm was a match for that in his knee and the red mist that was slowly swamping his greyed vision became almost welcoming.

He felt his nails snag in the nylon as he pulled and pushed against her crotch like a frantic lover. Slowly but surely he found his hand was able to travel further with each stroke until, finally, with a cry of relief, it came free and he was able to shift it between himself and the man pressed against his front and start to create space between the two of them. He pulled his now sticky fingers out of the man's eyes and placed both hands on the man's shoulders and pushed himself upwards. His wounded knee caught on something but he ignored the white pain and continued to struggle like a rugby player in a collapsed scrum. After what seemed like ages of agony, he suddenly slipped free and fell back, his head and body resting on a mattress of bodies, but as he fought for breath, sweat coursing down his face, a hand grabbed his own and began to tug.

At that moment, Mark lost control of his actions. His only thought was that he was on a pile of dead bodies that were now coming to life to destory him. The walking dead, flesh-eating zombies, vampires . . . all the undead creatures he had ever seen in movies and videos shrieked in his memory, promising him fictions about to become bloody fact. He pulled his legs free, twisted round and kicked at the hand holding tight to his wrist, then rolled over up against the far wall of the slope and, kneeling up, batted blindly at the hand still grabbing for him.

He heard shouts and screams and knew they weren't all his, but didn't want to know what unholy dead thing was after him, what broken mouth could make such terrible squeals of agony. The hand touched his thigh and he punched at it with his fists and was rewarded with more shrill screams of pain. Good, good, they felt, they knew pain, he had a defence, but he needed to be standing and for that he would have to pull himself up the wall.

So, risking having his back to his enemy – he had no option if he was to get upright – he clawed his way up, his fingers scrabbling at the mortar between the bricks, his nails soon ragged and torn, until he was upright and flat against the wall, his face hot against cold brick. Now all he had to do was turn round and confront the creatures. Ignoring the pain that stabbed at his knee like a fork into meat, he edged himself round, hands flat against the brick, pressing himself away from the screaming thing that was trying to get to him.

He saw movement, a figure kneeling, its hands reaching up to him. He swung his right leg along the wall, ready to kick at its head and send it tumbling down the mound.

'*No!*' it shouted, hurling itself at his left leg and clinging to it. Mark lost his balance and fell over, his bad knee bent back to its limit, his head filled with pain. Weeping and desperate, he pushed himself away from the creature wrapped around his ankles, frantic to straighten out his damaged knee. A hand suddenly punched into the bloody joint and he shrieked in agony and kicked out with his other leg but missed and the thing grabbed at the waist of his jeans and hauled itself closer to him.

Mark interlocked his fingers into a single fist and raised his hands to rabbit punch the thing that was squirming its way up his body. But just as he was about to bring it crashing down on the back of its head, it looked up at him.

'Please don't hurt me no more,' said Jamie, his face streaked with tears. 'Please don't hurt me no more. I was only trying to help you up . . .' He fell forward onto Mark's chest and sobbed quietly. He had reached his limit. He couldn't face anything more.

Mark stared at him wide-eyed, his breathing ragged, adrenalin like electricity making him jerk. *It was the boy*. His only ally and he was about to club him to death. Oh Jesus . . .

They hugged each other for minutes, both crying with horror and relief, their position atop the corpses forgotten.

Eventually they recovered sufficiently to ease themselves apart and slowly edge their way over the corpses, their backs to the wall. Whenever one of them slipped, the other would grab for him and steady him until they could continue. They didn't care now what they stood on: all was dead meat; they might as well have been walking on a butcher's counter.

It was a slow process but after five muscle-straining minutes, they reached the top of the slope, only to find that the foyer was similarly covered in bodies. But there was also a broken window in the wall they were leaning against that afforded an exit onto the station concourse.

Jamie was first through, surprised at being grateful that there was the body of a man draped over the lip of the window which protected him from the shards of safety glass that edged the four-feet-square frame. Slipping down onto the concrete outside, he leaned back and helped Mark negotiate the frame, making sure that the man stood on his good leg first.

Once outside, they leaned against the station's wall. Jamie peered back through the window. He found it hard to believe they had actually climbed over all those bodies, but that moment when he had tried to help Mark up out of the hole had been the worst. After that, dead bodies just became dead bodies. It's the living who cause pain and terror, not the dead. He looked across the concourse. The world was as grey out here as back in the station.

The road was jammed with cars in both directions, bodies littering the pavement and car bonnets. Some were even upright, crushed between bumpers, unable to escape, like cops on eternal traffic duty. It was bizarre. Too bizarre, in fact, to take seriously. Here he had walked over people's faces, felt noses break under his trainers, stood in people's mouths, stomped on women's tits, used heads as steps, and all to get out into a grey world full of yet more dead people. He wondered again about his parents but found he was numb to their fate; the last couple of years he had pretty much had to fend for himself so why should it be any different now?

'What now?' he asked Mark. His hand was throbbing fit to bust and all he could think of was plunging it into a bucket of iced water for a week.

Mark clasped his shoulder. 'We'd better make for the hospital. Thanks for what you did. Helping me. Sorry I . . . well, sorry.'

Jamie nodded. 'I'm hungry,' was all he could think to say.

Mark shook his head. Kids. All this *and* he's hungry. Then he realized he was hungry too. He wondered if he should feel guilty about it but decided it didn't much matter. Who was to judge him?

The journey to the hospital would have been simple under normal circumstances. All they had to do was follow Campbell Road to the junction with Withern Street, then turn west and a third of a mile would find them outside Blair General – but there was nothing normal left in Blair.

Their first problem was the traffic. It was jammed nose to tail the full width of the street as far as they could see, as if every motorist in Blair had decided to catch a train. It wasn't so much a road as a car park. Untangling it – if ever that eventuality occurred – would take days, especially with most of the cars abandoned or with dead drivers at the wheel. They found the easiest way was simply to walk *over* the cars. It was hard on his knee but the cars had spilled over onto the municipal gardens and the slick slope of the grass would have been even more hazardous.

So their progress was slow, every step demanding their full attention because of the rain that remained on the metal and chrome. The cars were obviously of many different colours but in the light that suffused Blair they were a universal grey, which added to the illusion that they had been abandoned for an age. There were bodies on the ground between the cars, in many cases propped up and unable to fall, so close were the cars parked. And there were bodies in the cars, usually in the back seats, as if their drivers had killed them, then run off to meet their own fate. Mark couldn't help being reminded of stories in the newspapers of murdered families: three daughters and a father gassed in a car; children with their throats slashed, a dead adult nearby. And yet, every time Mark stared in through a window, he hoped there might be movement, someone who hadn't died, but it was hopeless. He finally gave up: twice he had nearly slipped between the cars and it wasn't worth the risk.

He paused on top of an empty Volvo estate and looked back at Jamie. The boy was two cars behind, his height making it harder for him to surmount windscreens. He had stopped on the bonnet of a Scirocco, hands on hips, to catch his breath. He looked as dead as any of the bodies about them, all colour drained from his skin and clothes. Mark looked up at the sky, then swivelled around but could see no change in the dull panoply that covered the town, and still no discernible light source.

They had covered about half the length of the jam, the only sound the denting of metal panels and the occasional curse as a knee or hand took too much strain. Mark waved Jamie over, then carefully lay down on the car roof. Jamie quickly clambered over the remaining cars and squatted down on the Volvo's bonnet, ignoring the dead gaze of a woman in the Peugeot 306 next to him.

'There'll be a café up there,' said Mark pointing over his shoulder to a row of shops ahead. 'We'll get something there.'

'Good. I'm starved.'

Mark suddenly sat up. 'Can you hear *anything*?' he said.

The boy shook his head.

'Not even birds or a dog or equipment or anything?'

Jamie nodded. Mark was right. All was dead silence. Everything had died; people, animals, birds, machinery. The whole town was dead. Mark and he might be the only ones left. He wondered if he could have started it with the train crash; if he had set something loose which had infected everyone.

'What's causing it?' he asked.

Mark shook his head. 'No idea.'

'Could something bad have set it all off?'

'Like what?'

'Well, like the . . . the train crash. Could that have made everybody crazy?'

'It did.'

Jamie's heart missed a beat.

'Everything did go crazy. That's why I fell down the embankment. I was trying to get to the crash. My wife was – might have been – in it. I felt . . . possessed. I just had to get there. Everyone else seemed to feel that way too. That's why they've all killed each other, desperate to get to the crash.' *Or*, the thought occurred to him, *desperate to escape. But escape what*?

'So whoever . . . whatever caused the crash could be to blame?'

'Whoever?' Why a whoever? Mark wondered. What had the kid seen? 'No, I think there's more to it than that. There's a lot of people here but not everyone. Must be thousands who didn't come to the station. Where are they? Have they got out of town? Are they inside hiding? Or are they all . . .'

'Dead.' Jamie finished for him. He wanted to confess, to tell his new friend that it was he who had caused the crash, that people had died because of his stupid actions, but something held him back – and it wasn't just that Mark's wife had been there. There was something else nagging at the back of his mind that told him he wasn't ultimately responsible for what he had done. Yes, he had started up the crane to get his own back on Wayne but someone had *told* him to do it. Had *made* him do it. The fat man. That fat man he had seen that morning . . . or was it yesterday morning? And where had he seen him? In a block of flats, but which one?

Mark saw the boy deep in thought and sought to lift his spirits. 'Jamie, we're going to get out of this. Just don't give up.'

'I wasn't.'

'Oh well, so much for the pep talk.'

'What?'

'Nothing. Let's get on.'

Time meant very little now. With no watch and no sunlight, they had no template by which to judge the time of day or its passage. All they knew was that it took too long to climb over the cars. There must have been a hundred of them jammed nose to tail, all so many useless hunks of metal now. Or oversize coffins.

Every once in a while Mark would call a halt on top of a Ford or Citroën or Fiat and cock an ear, convinced he'd heard some sound, a cry for help or a whimper of pain. But, if he had, it never repeated itself. He and Jamie were truly alone and as soon as he had checked if Karen was alive, then they would head out of town. On an impulse he lay down on the top of a Nissan Cherry, reached down through the open driver's door and turned the ignition key. Nothing. He tried the next car and the one after that. None of them so much as turned over. He switched on lights, indicators, windscreen wipers, but again there was no reaction. Even the cars had died.

Finally the traffic became more spaced out – a pile-up had blocked the road. Mark and Jamie dismounted and wove their way between the cars until they found a cafeteria, sandwiched between a shoe shop and a building society, all containing a scattering of dead customers. They stood outside the smashed glass door and read the hand-painted menu on the inside.

'Bet everything's off,' said Mark.

Jamie laughed. 'Or cold.'

They stepped through the shattered glass door panel and looked around. It was a dump, deserted except for a couple slumped over a table halfway down the double rows of fixed tables and benches. One of them, a woman, had a knife protruding from the back of her neck. Already inured to such sights, Mark walked over to the counter and looked at the pies in the hot cabinet. *Dave's Plaice* was just a glorified chip shop, a supposition supported by the man in a white jacket bent over the large frier, his head submerged in oil. Presumably it had been hot when he had been put in it.

Jamie heaved himself up and stared at the poor sod.

'Chips off, then,' he said.

'Looks like he's had his,' said Mark – and again they both laughed. Then Mark stopped. 'Should we be laughing?'

'No,' said Jamie. He felt guilty about it too, but it did help him to cope.

'Pies'll be OK,' said Mark. He reached round and pulled out a couple of chunky meat-and-potato pies from the glass cabinet. They were cold. He broke one open and sniffed the contents – no smell – and the greyness of the insides wasn't any guide either as the light in the shop, as outside, tainted everything.

He took a bite. It had no taste at all, completely bland, but its consistency was right, even to the piece of vein he picked from between his teeth. He nodded to Jamie and he tucked in with gusto, demolishing the pie almost immediately. He then sat up on the counter and picked out another and greedily ate that too.

Mark finished his and took out a cheese-and-onion pie and ate that; there was no difference in taste.

Jamie leaned down to the shelf below the counter and brought up a can of Coke, pulled the tab and swigged. It was flat and tasteless but it helped the pies go down. He passed it to Mark and he took three hearty swigs and burped. Mark then noticed a telephone under the counter, presumably for the 'Takaway Orders' advertised over the frier. He picked it up but wasn't surprised to find it was as dead as everything else. Cursing, he moved over to the table by the door and they both sat down, Jamie with his back to the window, Mark looking outside as they scoffed their third and fourth pies.

Jamie could feel himself filling up – it was a really weird sensation – but his hunger would not be denied.

'What about your family?' asked Mark, finishing a Fanta. His deep hunger made him wonder just how long he had lain in that ditch. He normally wasn't much of an eater and a missed meal rarely bothered him, but he was *empty* and all the shit he had been through had done nothing to dampen his appetite.

Jamie knew he should care but he honestly didn't. 'Wayne, my brother, can go stuff himself. Mum . . . she drinks. Dad too. If they're alive they'll be drinking themselves stupid. If they're dead, then there's not . . .'

He realized what he was saying and fell silent. Maybe he had been knocked about once too often to care any more. Besides, this stranger had shown him more consideration in the last couple of hours than his entire family had over the last couple of years.

'Sure you don't want to go look for them?'

'No. Not on me own, anyway.'

'Well, tell you what. After we've checked the hospital, we could go find your parents. Where do they live?'

'Finlay Road, on the Catchmount.'

'Right. The hospital's only fifteen minutes from here. We'll soon – *fucking hell!*'

Jamie looked up from his pie. Mark was staring bug-eyed past him at the café window. Jamie spun round.

There was a middle-aged man in a pinstripe suit staring back at him, eyes wide, mouth quivering and drooling. He had a shotgun. He lowered the barrel towards them and pulled the trigger – and their world exploded with more noise and colour than they had seen since the greyness had descended.

28

IZOTTA'S NIGHTMARE CONTINUES

'*I'm dead! I'm dead! I'm dead!*' was all Izotta's mind could tell her. Over and over she repeated the information, its true meaning soon lost because of its impossibility and incomprehensibility. And yet, even as she continued her mantra – *I'm dead, I'm dead. I'm dead* – she realized she wasn't frightened.

'That's right,' said a voice.

Izotta's mind stopped screaming and she stook stock. She couldn't see anyone else, yet she had distinctly heard the voice. But then what did it matter? She was *dead*.

'You can't see me,' said the man's voice. 'You can see all but you cannot see yourself.'

'What?'

'How can the dead see themselves, except as corpses?'

Izotta looked down at the two bodies in the room, her own and that of Mr Farmer. Had he killed her?

'You killed yourself,' said the voice. 'By being where you shouldn't have been, you became a part of it. But what's done is done. I'm here with you and you're here with me. We'll make a fine team.'

'What is happening?' She could feel herself weakening, wanting to listen rather than question.

'You have said it yourself, and that you have said it proves the veracity of it: you are dead yet your spirit lives on. As does mine. It isn't exactly as I expected but it's still wonderful, isn't it?'

'Wonderful?'

'So few enjoy this existence. So few. Because it takes so many to provide it.'

She didn't understand. She looked around, but all she could see was glaring brightness and the two dead bodies.

'We are the light,' said Mr Farmer. His voice was calm and authoritative and Izotta felt herself relaxing as he continued to speak, the nightmare that he evoked strangely comforting in the purity of its purpose.

'Our people have been here all through mankind's time, plaguing him, dealing out misery. It is our sustenance. We don't choose to be this way, we simply are – just as you couldn't choose your sex or the colour of your skin – and I, for one, am pleased to be what I am, and proud that what I do I do so well. It is a skill we are born with. Some humans have an aptitude for art or languages; we have a facility for spreading evil. We touch a person, see their thoughts, make a suggestion, let it fester. Sometimes it might only produce a nightmare or irrational prejudice; others may turn in on themselves, their minds consumed by *self*-hatred, mutilating, starving or abusing themselves. The seed grows but fails to see the light and so they wallow in their misery, their minds poisoned compost where little evil buds can sprout and grow to taint their fragile minds. And there are so, so many of these failures: girls with eating disorders; adults who believe they were molested as children; compulsives who repeat mindless tasks over and over; youngsters who use drugs even though they know the havoc they wreak; those of masochistic sexual appetites. And in the worst cases, those whose minds fracture and who begin listening to another voice telling them what to do. Many a schizophrenic has been created because one of us touched them and they didn't understand. They hear voices and they vent their confusion on those around them. They babble and burble on, eccentrics to the indulgent, madmen to those with sense. They can become violent, slashing at themselves and striking out at others. They may need medication to dull the barbs that have been implanted; or even hospitalization where the wild weeds wrecking their sanity can be confined within walls. And then there are those who can cope with the new evil in their minds; who nurture it, treasure it and, when the time is ripe, act on it: *these* are my successes . . .

'The men and women and children who do the unspeakable because they *enjoy* it. The seed may have taken months, even years to come to fruition, while in others it can be almost instantaneous, like pulling the trigger on a gun. I have been in Blair for thirty-two years and I have touched minds virtually every day of that time. Many have only acted out petty indulgences – adultery, shoplifting, dangerous driving, hitting their children, using foul language, indulging in perverse masturbatory fantasies; some have even enacted those fantasies in reality and paid the penalty – or found a like mind. For some the seed *improves* their lives: it makes them more assertive or enhances their sexual urges. But if there is evil under the stone and my probing releases it, then the true self is revealed, not some alien spore that takes over the personality. I cannot *make* men evil; there are those who are innately evil and it is the degree to which they wish to control it that dictates how they act. The fight that goes too far, the parent who executes his family, the man who becomes obsessed with a woman . . . In some cases they destroy the object of their desires, in others they kill themselves as proof of their dedication. Look at all these lost souls here – and look at the simple catalysts that fermented such an atmosphere of terror and a need for so many to exorcize their demons on their neighbours. Take a boy and the knowledge I gleaned about his hated brother's workplace and its potential for destruction. And a disaffected soldier, a trained killer waiting for the right order: I let him know what he could do and he killed and killed, as you saw before our . . . mating. To kill and maim so many, and to traumatize so many more, it all added to the growing discontent and panic of the population until my seed ran rampant last night, like a windborne plague spreading from one infected heart to the next as easily as colds are passed by sneezing; a cancer determined on growth regardless of the cost to its host.'

'But why do it? Why ruin so many lives?' Izotta was struggling to find her own voice.

'It is what I do,' said the other voice. 'I plant the seed, I watch it grow, I enjoy the fruits of my labours. *I*. And as long as I enjoy it – much as you enjoyed sex – I will continue to do it. I know you, I am you now, and you have wrecked many a man over the years with your desire for adulterous sex. As long as the man on top of you belonged to another woman, that was the satisfaction. I know your mind better than you do now. I have touched you, tasted you. I know of the father who left your mother when she became pregnant because he wouldn't leave his wife – and the poison your mother told you about marriage and men. And how you couldn't resent his colour because it came out in you. And how you couldn't resent his sexuality because you wanted it, but you could detest his status. You may have thought it lack of commitment, but the fact that *every* man you sought was married must have told you something. The risk of discovery may have heightened your passion – forbidden fruit tastes sweeter – but how would you have felt if your liaison had been discovered? After all, you would lose nothing, but he and his wife and family would lose all, and you would simply move on to the next husband. Don't deny it; see it for what it is – and *relish* it. You have never attempted to form a stable relationship with a single man. Instead you have used your body to infect men with lust, to lead them astray. You spread *your* evil uncaring of the consequences, but revelling in them nonetheless. But there is a simple explanation for this, Izotta.'

'What?'

'You are one of us.'

29

MARK AND JAMIE HOSPITALIZED

Jamie felt the heat from the shotgun as Mark slammed him onto his back, his bad hand banging against the wall beneath the imploding café window. His scream of pain was lost amidst the bellowed panic of Mark and the boom from the gun and the sound of glass dancing across the tables and chairs behind them. Then there was a dreadful silence.

Jamie opened his screwed-up eyes and found himself looking into the terrified face of the cringeing Mark who was pressing him to the floor. It was clear he was expecting to be blasted in the back by the man with the gun, but after long drawn out seconds Mark craned his head round and peered up through the shattered window. The man must have gone because he immediately knelt back off Jamie, letting the two of them breathe.

Mark could see the businessman had walked into the middle of the road and was looking around in a daze, as if unsure what to do next. Mark tried to judge whether he would be able to rush him before he decided to finish the job, or whether he and Jamie should try and sneak out the back of the café. The choice was obvious but even as he edged away from the window, the man looked up the street and shook his head as if something was approaching which even the power of his shotgun wouldn't be able to deal with.

Mark stood up and crept over the splinters of glass to the doorway, wagging his hand at Jamie to follow. Jamie rose and got behind Mark and peered out round his waist.

'What's he doing?' he whispered, his voice hoarse. The smell of gunsmoke was strong and he didn't like it.

'He's seen something . . . hey, you realize what this means?'

'He might try again?'

'No. It means there's someone else alive in Blair!'

'He acted real friendly, Mark.'

'Yeah, but he's on his own. Maybe he's just scared. Seeing us took him by surprise.'

'Yeah, and maybe the loon wanted to kill us.'

There was that possibility, thought Mark. But where there's a will . . .

'I'm going to try to talk to him. He might know what's . . .'

Mark's voice trailed off as he watched the man fall to his knees and start wailing. His voice was high and shrill, like that of a hysterical girl.

'The light, the light!' he cried. 'He promised! He promised everything would be dark.'

Then he took the shotgun, put the barrel into his mouth and pulled the trigger. His body fell back onto the road, most of his head splashed across a travel agent's window twenty feet away.

Mark didn't know what to do or how to react. A minute ago he had nearly blown the two of them apart. Only reflexes he used on the squash court had got him across the table to pull Jamie out of the madman's sights. And now the lunatic had blown his own head off. The only other person they had seen alive in the bloody town and he was dead.

Jamie pushed past Mark and walked into the street. By the time Mark realized the danger the boy might have been putting himself in, he was already staring down at the hole on top of the man's shoulders.

Mark limped over to him, the pain in his knee more intense since his acrobatics, and grabbed his shoulder.

'Kiddo, I don't think being out here is such a good idea. What if there are others?'

Jamie looked down the deserted street with its shopfronts, abandoned cars, bodies and second and third-storey windows looking down blank and empty. Or were they staring down, hiding other murderous eyes?

Jamie nodded. 'What did he mean about the light?'

Mark looked up the street. *Good God* . . .

Somewhere in the distance there *was* a light. Bright and up in the air, too dazzling to reveal its source. The rest of Blair was still grey and flat, but the light was white and vibrant. And inviting.

'Where's that?' Mark asked.

'Near where I live. The Catchmount estate. High enough to be one of the blocks of flats. What is it?'

'A searchlight? Bloody strong, whatever it is.'

'Are we going to see what it is?'

'After the hospital. It's near your house, you say? But whatever it is, *he* sure didn't like it.'

Jamie looked down. The man still had a face, but behind it was just a mess like spilled strawberry jam, and a great swash of black blood that had found its way to a drain. Maybe they didn't need to find out what the light meant.

'Hospital,' reminded Mark, forcing his eyes from the light, so pretty in all this grey . . . 'Your hand, my knee, my wife – then we'll try and see what's what.'

They started to walk away from the man towards the hospital but after a dozen steps Mark edged them onto the pavement where they hugged the fronts of the shops.

'There may be others like him,' he said. 'Armed. They could be up there.' He pointed to the office windows above them.

Jamie pointed to the windows on the opposite side of the street. 'What about those?'

He had a point. Mark looked back at the dead man. His shotgun. He ran over and prised it from the man's fingers, broke open the barrel and ejected the two spent cartridges. He frisked the man and found a shape in his lefthand jacket pocket. Reaching in he pulled open a box of shotgun cartridges, eleven red casings in all. He slipped two into the barrels, closed the gun and felt its weight. He had been clay pigeon shooting a couple of times in the past with clients and knew the rudiments of handling a firearm. It still surprised him how heavy they were, but that was not a problem if it served its purpose.

He looked down at the businessman. The shotgun would serve as a weapon of defence, of course, but *his* solution was also another use for it. If he found the madness was everywhere and he couldn't find Karen, what would be the point of carrying on?

He looked up the street. It looked like an ordinary shopping day with too much traffic. The shoppers had mostly vanished, though there were bodies here and there, and in shop windows they could also see corpses. But what if, in one of those shops, hiding, was another madman with a gun?

They began dodging back and forth across the street, using cars as cover. It was slow and nerve-wracking, to say nothing of the agony it caused his knee every time he had to bend for cover beside a car, but it was also necessary. It was to be fifteen minutes of slow, sweaty progress in the grey before they caught sight of the hospital.

Blair Hospital was a three-storey Victorian redbrick affair with a wide frontage that concealed a ground-floor corridor linking wards that ran back to the jumble of outbuildings and temporary accommodation that passed for a modern caring health service in Blair. Mark had been into Casualty once when Stan had sliced his finger while cutting some layouts and the place had seemed stuck in some Fifties time warp. Dull, drab, mysterious: it would be right at home with the way the town was now.

The memory of Stan made him wonder about the other people he knew. He could try and kid himself but he knew the odds were that most if not all of them would be dead by now. Whether they had become victims or gone mad like the businessman, he just hoped it had been swift. And then he realized what he was thinking and he started finding it hard to breathe. He could only hope Karen had been spared both fates.

The Casualty Department was easy to spot. It was surrounded by ambulances and police cars, all jammed together as if a child had got bored with its Corgi toys and had shovelled them into a corner. Again there were more bodies. A few were scattered across the lawn and flower-beds that ran between the hospital and the road, not a few of them wearing nightclothes: these had obviously been patients trying to escape the hospital.

He started to run, weaving his way between the cars on the entrance driveway that ran in a crescent the width of the building, the looming dark bricks coming closer with every painful step. He found it impossible to get in through Casualty, so he skirted the traffic and made for the main entrance about fifty yards further along in the centre of the building. Here there were more bodies and vehicles but there was room to squeeze through.

He paused at the entrance, aware that whatever madness the people around him had been running from – nearly all the bodies were pointing away from the building as if knocked down by a blast – it might still be lurking inside. He felt Jamie by his side, the boy taking his hand. He was trembling.

'If there are any docs, we'll get them to look at your hand.'

'And your knee,' the boy added.

Mark squeezed his good hand and led the way.

Jamie had never liked hospitals – they always meant pain – and this looked even more frightening than it normally did. As the building swallowed them up he felt a cold chill pass over him and he started to sweat. People *died* in hospitals. People went in who never came out. Show me any other building where that happens, he thought. Nowhere, that's where. Everyone he knew who was dead, whether it was of cancer or heart attack or in an accident, had died in hospital. Yes, they cured people but they also failed – and one time they would fail with him.

The entrance was as grey as the rest of the world and actually less gloomy than he remembered – that weird light again. There were nurses and patients strewn about, most stained with blood. All glass had been smashed and the benches were lying higgledy-piggledy, some on top of bodies.

Mark paused at a window marked Reception. He didn't know what day it was or when the madness had happened, but if Karen had been admitted there would be paperwork. Even with the advent of computers he knew they had to keep their clerks busy. He walked into the office and looked around. He hadn't a clue what he was looking for but on the wall he found a plan of the hospital. The usual 'ologies' – Gynaecology, neurology, pathology, urology – were spelt out in black blocks with arrows pointing at colour-coded buildings. But scrawled in biro were two phrases – Shooting Victims and Train Crash – with crude arrows pointing at Ward numbers 5, 6 and 7.

'Do you know anything about a shooting?' asked Mark.

'Yeah, that guy we—'

'No, something bigger. Lots of people dead, maybe?'

James looked around the reception area. He wanted more bodies?

Mark ignored him, dashed out of the office and across the waiting area, careful to avoid stepping on any of the bodies, and followed the arrows along the main corridor that ran the length of the building to wards 5, 6 and 7. They were the last three wards on the west of the building – as far away from the Casualty Department as possible, which seemed stupid but who was he to argue with the NHS?

Soon his run had reduced to a lope, then a slow steady walk. The corridor was a good twenty feet tall and almost as wide and, apart from the odd body and a couple of trolleys, surprisingly empty. The walls were covered in murals of country scenes and seascapes now all rendered grey and bland. Their footsteps echoed down its length and more than once Mark pulled them up to listen for other sounds, convinced the echo was in actuality someone else's footfalls.

Jamie was more nervous inside the empty building than he had been outside with the corpses. There was something spooky about the long high bare corridor and the way their footsteps seemed to echo somewhere else in the building. The grey light changed the silly pictures on the wall into black and white daubings, what life they might have had from colour rather than realism washed away as effectively as if they had been splashed with grey paint.

Every so often there was a turn-off to a department or ward, and at each of these turnings they would pause and wait as if expecting traffic to come zooming across. But all they ever saw behind the scratched plastic flap doors were more empty corridors or the occasional prostrate body, some in white or light blue uniforms, others in dressing gowns or pyjamas. Most were adults: the children's wards, he knew, were at the other end of the hospital.

They reached an abandoned electric cart with a train of trolleys piled high with used metal food trays. Mark tried the starter, the lights, but nothing worked. He glanced up at the ceiling. The neon lights were out, yet the tube-like corridor was as well lit as anywhere else in Blair. Didn't hospitals have emergency generators that kicked in if power was lost? Mind you, everything seemed to have died. And everyone . . .

They walked on until they reached a toilet.

'I need a pee,' said Jamie.

Mark did as well, so they carefully pushed open the door and looked into the Gents. There were two stalls, one open, the other jammed shut, sprawled naked legs jutting under the door, blood fleecing one hairy ankle.

'You go first,' said Mark, nodding at the empty stall. 'I'll keep guard.'

Jamie entered the stall and tried to shut the door, but Mark stopped him. 'Best keep it open. I'll be at the door.'

Jamie backed into the stall and skimmied down his trousers, his bowels grumbling.

Mark propped open the door to the corridor and took a deep breath. Either he had a cold or there was little or no smell, but both urinals were blocked, water overflowing onto the floor.

He leant the gun against the wall and stretched. His knee still hurt but as long as he kept the leg stiff it was manageable. He could see a sign ahead for Ward 5. That's where they would look first.

A couple of minutes later Jamie tugged his elbow. 'No paper.'

'Least of our worries, really,' smiled Mark. The idea of not being able to wipe his backside bothered him but, in the context of the disaster that had overtaken Blair and its inhabitants, it was patently absurd. But, he reminded himself, it was also an everyday problem. If he was concerned about his personal comfort or hygiene, then he still had some grip on reality, even if reality had lost its grip on his town.

Jamie took Mark's place while the man took his turn on the toilet.

Two minutes later they edged their way out into the corridor and on towards Ward 5. At the transparent scuffed doors, Mark paused. He knew there were two wards, 5A and 5B, one on top of the other, joined by a bed-size lift and a flight of stairs and, overhead, another corridor connecting the B wards. If these two wards proved empty they would use the upstairs corridor to check out 6 and 7.

'Stay close,' he said, holding the the shotgun in front of him. They pushed open the doors, stepped over the body of an old woman and walked through to the ward.

It was almost empty, only a couple of the dozen or so beds in sight occupied. There were a pair of private rooms on both sides of the passageway, two beyond the supply room and sister's office on the left, the others beyond the empty kitchen on their immediate right and a small, empty waiting room next to it. Mark decided that, if admissions had been made, there would have to be a record of it in the sister's office. He pushed open the door, sliding the body of a nurse across the floor as he did so. There had been mayhem in the room and the sight made him want to vomit, but instead he focused his concern on the boy and told Jamie to stay outside.

Inside the bodies of two nurses lay on their backs across a table, their throats slit, blood pooled blackly about their heads like mourning bonnets. Their skirts had been ripped off and their underwear cut open, their thighs, stomachs and genitals slashed. One had the stand from a desklamp embedded in her vagina. On the floor in front of them lay a naked man, his face bloody, a broken medical bottle jabbed into the back of his neck. The rest of the room had been wrecked, cabinets on the floor, windows smashed, papers and charts over every surface.

He soon gave up looking for a patients' list and instead returned to the hallway and led Jamie into the ward, the shotgun cocked, and checked the names on all the beds. All four private rooms proved empty, three of them obviously unoccupied. As for the ward itself, it seemed to be a general surgical ward, many of the patients having been admitted several days before. Their beds had been slept in but were now deserted. The three patients they did find seemed to have died without violence, perhaps of shock or lack of care. At the bottom right of the ward one bed was shielded from the rest of the room by a floral-patterned curtain that ran round a curtain track hanging from the high ceiling.

No end of nightmare images invaded Mark's mind as to what might lie behind the curtain. More violated corpses? All the patients piled onto the single bed? Another armed man unarmed with sanity?

Jamie was equally reluctant to pull aside the curtain. He had caught a glimpse of what Mark had hidden from him in the sister's office and while he had become surprisingly tolerant of the horrors they were encountering, he saw no reason to hunt them out.

'Shall we leave it?' he suggested.

Mark wanted to agree, but he knew if he didn't look and he didn't find Karen elsewhere he would be haunted by the notion that she might have been behind the curtain; that she might have been there injured, pleading quietly for help and he had chickened out, had deserted her. He shook his head. *Damn.* He reached for the edge of the curtain at the corner and gripped it with a shaking hand. As he counted down silently, he mouthed the numbers to Jamie so he would know when he was going to do it.

Five, four, three – his hand began to spasm, terror forcing his muscles to disobey so he lost his grip. He concentrated, forced his fingers to curl – *two* – then realized that anyone inside would be able to detect the shaking of the curtain, see his exposed fingers, might even now be preparing to slice them off – *one*!

He pulled aside the curtain, the zing of the metal hooks filling the empty ward. Then he stepped forward, raised the shotgun, tensed his finger on the triggers and stared into the newly revealed secret, the curtain fanning back and forth, its hooks continuing to tinkle gently above him.

The bed was empty and unmade, the bedside cabinet bare. He glanced down at the floor: nothing hiding there.

He and Jamie let out their held breaths simultaneously, nervous smiles threatening to crease their lips but not quite succeeding. Mark wiped a shaking hand over his face, felt his cold sweat, then turned and lowered the shotgun until the barrel touched the floor.

'Fuck,' was all he could say as he sat back on the bed and tried to keep calm.

Jamie stayed outside the curtain, nervously scanning the other beds, anxious to get out of the claustrophobic room. If anyone came after them, they had nowhere to run, they would be trapped. 'Mark, can we go on? I don't like being in here.'

Mark nodded. He needed another piss. He led the way back up the ward, making sure to skirt the sister's office and on to the wide flight of stairs that led up to Ward 5B.

The stairs turned back on themselves halfway up and here they found another dead nurse, though there was no blood. She may have fallen downstairs. Mark couldn't help noticing she was pretty.

Ward 5B was much the same as 5A, except the sister's office was empty and there were only two bodies in the whole ward. And no curtained-off bed. Surprised by its seeming emptiness, he double-checked the side rooms, and found a white-coated doctor stuffed under one of the beds. Whether he had been butchered and dumped or attacked as he hid he couldn't tell, but the needle in his neck had hit the spot, a near perfect semi-circular scar of dark blood on the wall evidence of the cause of his death.

The sister's office did yield a list of admissions this time, but none of them was for a Karen Dawson. They left the ward, pushed through the self-closing plastic flap doors and entered the upstairs corridor.

As wide as the one below, it was only ten feet high and less threatening for that. It was also competely deserted in both directions. Now the absence of death was as chilling as the presence of corpses. Why was it empty? Did those patients and staff fleeing in panic from whatever overwhelmed them know something about this corridor that made them avoid it?

Ward 6B was closed, a sign explaining that it was being redecorated. Mark decided to try Ward 7B then come back downstairs and try 7A and 6A.

Ward 7B was twenty yards further along the corridor. It was only as they approached the plastic doors that Mark realized there were no lights on in the corridor *and* no windows. Downstairs there had been high ventilation windows that would have let in some light but here they might as well have been underground. And yet the grey, colour-destroying light was as uniform here as anywhere else. Odd as it was it did offer the advantage of no shadows: they could see the length of the corridor and check that no one else was with them.

Pushing through the doors of Ward 7B, whatever hopes they had both entertained that somehow the chaos had lessened at this end of the hospital were soon dashed (For Jamie now was as anxious as Mark to find his wife because that would increase the number of survivors by fifty per cent.)

Apparently a geriatric ward, there were maybe a dozen bodies of old people sprawled across the passage between the private rooms. None of them had been cut as there was little blood, but what faces and limbs were visible were purpled and bruised, almost as if they had been skittles knocked down and run over by a giant bowling ball. It reminded Mark of the station: a mad scramble to escape something so terrible it forced ordinary decent people to forget their humanity and trample over neighbours and friends.

Stepping over them, Mark dodged into the sister's office and found the admissions list pinned under the body of a fat male nurse, his eyes staring at Mark's hand as he pulled the clipboard from under his chest. There had been three new admissions, all marked 'E. Cas.' Emergency Casualties? The third name was KAREN DAWSON. Her assigned bed was 10. *Yes!*

But even as joy coursed through him like the rush of a drug, a dread clamped itself on his heart and he looked down at the dead nurse, then back past the staring Jamie at the dead people in the passage. How many corpses had he and the boy seen in the last few hours? A thousand, two thousand, more? And how many people had they found alive? One. And he had been insane. He stumbled out of the office and on into the ward, his heart pounding.

All the beds had been occupied but now most were empty and those that contained bodies carried no evidence of violence. The old women could have died of heart attacks or strokes or simply neglect.

He suddenly wondered if some of them might have died because the drugs they depended on hadn't arrived. Two were plugged into monitors that sat silent, as dead as their users. He knew there were machines that fed painkillers according to the patients' need and, staring at one old woman on his left and the look of agony on her sunken face, he guessed the medicine had stopped flowing and she and others would have died in unendurable agony. Oh God . . .

Bed 10 wasn't empty. But even as he took in this information, he realized the body slumped facing away from him on the bed couldn't be anything other than dead. There was a large pair of scissors embedded in its back, only the handles visible. He caught his breath when he also saw that it was a woman, the bare legs drooping onto the floor, the arms flat alongside the body. She looked as big as Karen and though he didn't recognize the dressing gown, he presumed the hospital would have provided it.

He couldn't bring himself to see if it was Karen. Jamie saw his reluctance and wondered why the man didn't just reach over and see if it was his wife. That was what they were here for after all.

Jamie picked up the chart at the end of the bed and handed it to Mark. He took it but didn't read it. If it was Karen, what did it matter what had been wrong with her, what her pulse had read?

'Jamie,' Mark said, feeling behind him for the next bed to sit on. 'Could you see what colour her hair is?'

'What?'

'Don't argue!' he snapped. 'I'm sorry. My wife had red hair. Just look.'

Jamie edged round the bed, wary of the curtain drawn across the space between bed 10 and bed 12, just as in Ward 5A. The woman's head was covered by her rucked-up dressing gown.

'Can't see.'

'What do you fucking mean? Sorry. Oh fuck . . .' Mark stood up, walked to the body, grabbed the collar of the dressing gown and tugged it down.

Thin black hair. It wasn't Karen. He whooped with delight but the obscenity of his joy at discovering a murdered woman cut him short. What had happened to the world . . . So where was she? He looked past Jamie at the curtain that shielded the next bed. What did that conceal?

He walked round, pushed Jamie out of the way in frustration and, tensing himself, grabbed the curtain. Again his hand shook and again his terrorized mind conjured up murderous phantoms on the other side of the curtain. Gritting his teeth and hawking in deep breaths he readied his grip but, at the last moment, he pulled up the shotgun and pointed it at waist height, ready to deal with any threat. He pulled too hard at the curtain and its hooks ripped from the track above and it fell half open.

The bed was empty. He looked around the ward. All the corpses were of old women. They had nowhere else to go. He looked at the end of the ward beyond bed 12. There were two white-painted wooden doors. One said SLUICE, the other said TOILET.

Jamie also looked at the doors. The claustrophobia he had felt in the other wards was not alleviated.

'Jamie, I want you to do me a favour,' said Mark as he walked round the bed and moved towards the SLUICE door on the right.

'You've seen cop shows on TV where one of the cops kicks open the door and the other one points his gun at anyone inside?'

'Yes.'

'I want you to undo the doorhandle and push the door in, then stand back so I get a clean sight of the room.'

Jamie was reluctant to agree, but there was a look in Mark's eye that he knew brooked no argument. He walked to the door and, pressing himself against the wall, slowly reached for the handle. Sure he had hold of it, he looked to Mark for instructions. Mark raised the shotgun, cocked both hammers, and nodded.

Jamie slowly edged down the handle until it was almost vertical, then he pushed and felt the door move inwards. He let go and flattened himself against the wall as if expecting an explosion.

Mark blinked away sweat as the door swung slowly open, his mind a jangling landscape of alarms and lights. He didn't know what he was going to see but he was tensed for the worst.

The door was halfway open when it stopped. Looking down he saw a leg. Another body. It looked female. He waited a few moments, then started to move the twelve feet to the door, his finger ready to let the gun deal with whatever might attack them.

He reached the door and pushed at it with his free hand. It wouldn't budge; the body must have been jammed. He looked at Jamie. Should he ask the boy to slip through the gap?

'Jamie . . . can you take a look?'

'Don't want to,' he said truthfully. He was nearly crying.

'I know, I know, but it's . . .'

The boy's bottom lip was trembling and he could see a trickle
of urine puddling on his right shoe. Poor little sod. What had he
got him into?

Mark lowered the gun and placed his hand on the boy's shoulder.
'I'm sorry, Jamie. I'll look, you just keep—'

Suddenly there was a crash and something blurred into his vision
to the left. Mark tried swinging round but the shotgun hit the jamb
of the door and as he tried to pry it free both barrels discharged,
blasting a circular hole in the tiled wall inside the sluice room. As
the boom echoed round the ward and Jamie screamed, someone
charged into Mark knocking him onto the floor.

There was a flurry of hot breath, spit and a flashing blade that
slashed across his face, failing at first to find flesh. But Mark then
felt a hot pain in his left ear. He screamed, lashing out with his
foot, connecting with soft flesh. Blood splashed across his face.
His own. He shouted in horror and pain, grabbed at hair, tugged it
one way then the other, then heaved the naked attacker over onto
the floor beside him. He pushed himself away, feeling at the scalpel
still skewered through his ear like a nail in a piece of two-by-four.
The shock of the injury muddled his thoughts and before he could
respond, the naked woman – he saw her breasts before he saw her
face – had lunged at his ankles, forcing him to crash back against
Jamie, who screamed in pain as his bad hand was pinned against
the wall.

Mark had the wind knocked out of him and his vision began to
blur. He grabbed at the woman, felt a large swinging breast, dug
his fingers in around the nipple and tugged fiercely. A squeal of
pain encouraged him to continue his assault. He grabbed at the hair
whipping frenziedly in front of him, pulled the woman's head back
and raised his fist to punch as hard as he could into the harridan's
face. As soon as his knuckles made solid contact with her nose, the
woman slumped to the floor unconscious.

The first thing Mark noticed as he tried to drag breath into his
lungs was that his attacker was totally naked, her bare arms above
her head, her legs splayed obscenely wide.

Then he saw that it was Karen, her face and breasts smeared in
dried blood, a new flow dribbling from her cut lip and nose, his
own blood dropping onto her ankles. His shock was so great that
he reached up and pulled the scalpel out through his ear without
thinking. The pain and the sickening gush of blood that plopped

onto his wife's legs from the punctured ear combined to make him scream aloud and as the realization that he might just have killed his own wife sank in, his screaming increased.

Sanity became a distant memory as he fell to his knees and pawed at his wife like an uncomprehending puppy worrying at a dead companion. Jamie sank to his knees too, staring at the tableau before him, and slowly buried his head in his hands and wept for the mother he had forgotten and now realized he truly never would see again.

30

WHEN HARRY MET LAMBERT

His name was Harry. He couldn't remember his surname. Couldn't remember much, come to that. The cider, he said. Lambert had been reluctant to let him in the car but couldn't really refuse. However, he did make sure to hide his revolver before opening the door and letting the scruffy man inside.

The first thing he noticed was that Harry should have stunk to high heaven but in fact gave off no odour. He surmised this was probably another aspect of the dome. To confirm this he felt down the front of his own trousers while Harry struggled to make sense of his seatbelt. Feeling inside his nappy, Lambert found dampness and, pulling his finger out, sniffed at the urine he knew should be there. He smelled nothing. Determined to be as scientific as possible, he then licked his finger. Again, nothing. He could neither smell nor taste his own urine. He poked another finger into his ear and licked at the bitter wax, except it wasn't bitter; it had no taste. So, he concluded, not only had this event conspired to drain colour from their surroundings, but had also removed smell and taste. And, looking at Harry, he was grateful for that small mercy in a world that seemingly offered no mercy at all.

'Right, all set, chief,' said Harry pointing through the windscreen, unconcerned that the glass was missing. 'Let's go.'

'Where do you want to go?'

'Anywhere, chief. Good place, anywhere. There's lots of them and they're all different.'

'Haven't you seen anything odd? Like the sky? Seen any . . . accidents?'

'Grey days, grey days. All look the same to me, chief.' He turned to look at Lambert and for the first time he noticed the man's cataracts.

'Oh, I'm sorry. How bad is your eyesight?'

'You I see, the future I don't.' He cracked a broken smile.

Oh God, he speaks in riddles.

He put the car in 'drive' and set off, but then slowed and stopped. He needed to know if Harry knew anything before they went any further.

'You in any rush, Harry?'

'Nope, chief. You?'

'No. My name's Wesley, by the way. Wesley Lambert.'

'Harry. Just Harry. My wife kept my other name.'

'You divorced?'

'Maybe. Left her years ago. She must have cut the knot by now.'

'You been on the road long, then?'

'Twenty years, chief.'

'That's a long time. Must have seen some things in that time.'

'Seen things, done things. Been seen, been done. Same thing.'

'Seen anything odd lately?'

'What's odd, chief?'

'Blair. You been there?'

'I've been everywhere that's anywhere to be,' he sang. 'Blair? Bleagh. Drummed me out of the station after just one night. Bastards. Wasn't hurting no one. I don't bother people, they don't bother me. Just lay me head, grab food where I can. Dogies, too. You ain't got one?'

'Cigarette? No. Sorry. Got food, drink.'

'Drink. Proper drink, chief?'

'Pardon? No, sorry. Just soup.'

'Soup? Sooooop. Poop, soup. Poop.'

'How long had you been sat there?'

'Since I was dropped, chief.'

'Dropped? You had a lift?'

'Yes.'

Lambert was getting infuriated by how unforthcoming Harry was being. Either he was unstable or in shock but, either way, it wouldn't pay to pressure him, so the game would have to continue.

'Were you going to Blair or leaving?'

'Leaving, leaving, leaving. They threw me out of the station, then they all went mad. Lots of them, running and shouting. Near ran me over with their feet. I got out, got out of there sharpish, chief. Woman knocked me down. In her car. She was upset. Gave me a lift to hospital but when we got there it was all . . . mad. She wouldn't let me out. Kept on driving, faster and faster. Crazy. I told her. You're crazy, crazy, crazy, crazy. She stopped. Made me get out. Had a knitting needle. Sharp. Poked at my face. Wife used to knit. Jumpers for kiddies we'd never have . . . Kiddies. Saw a couple of them run over by a lorry. Driver didn't care.'

'Where did you see that? In Blair?'

'No! Leeds. Nineteen eighty-eight. June third. Court. Gave evidence, chief. He went to jail. Good, I said. Good, they said. Then they let me go, not so much as a by-your-leave. Done my duty, now bog off. Nineteen eighty-eight, June third.'

He fell silent. Lambert didn't know what to do next.

'Did she drop you there? Where I picked you up?'

Harry looked back through the rear window. His beard was flecked with blood, his teeth almost black, his face creased like a charcoal drawing of a characterful face.

'Back there, before the others came, chief.'

'Others?'

'Oh, bad boys, bad boys. They got a lift from her too. I tried to say no, they shouldn't, but one of them punched me. Hurt. Been punched before. I can take it. Secret's here,' he said, pointing at his forehead. 'See it coming, take steps. Be prepared. Look.'

He pulled open his thick coat and showed a dirty shirt and cardigan buttoned wrongly. There was a dark patch in the middle. Lambert touched it tentatively. It was wet.

'They stabbed you!' he said in amazement.

'Punch, chief. Punch.'

'Stabbed. That's a wound Harry. Doesn't it hurt?'

'Punches don't hurt, chief. If you're prepared.'

'But it's a *knife* wound. It could be deep.'

'Punches don't go deep. Secret, you see. Punches don't hurt.'

There was no point arguing.

'Punches wouldn't hurt you none either, chief,' Harry added, nodding at Lambert's legs.

'Not there, no,' he agreed.

'Were they taken or did you give them away?'

'What?'

'Your legs.'

'How could I give them away?'

'Easy, chief. I gave my eyes away. Got fed up with what I was seeing. Wished them away. They're going. Slow but sure. You sure you not got a drink?'

'No. How old was this woman?'

'Girlie, girlie, girlie. Too young. The boys thought she was fine. Fit, they said. Three of them.'

'Two men and a boy.'

'Boy? Two men? Could have been, chief, could have been. Boy punched me. Been punched before. Have to know how take them. The secret's here.'

It seemed fairly obvious that the girl was the one he had seen dead and the three the men he had seen hanging. Maybe the farmer had exacted revenge, or maybe killed them all. What was happening in this place?

'What do you think Blair's like now?'

For the first time Harry fell silent, his hands toying lightly with the blood on his cardigan. It was several moments before Lambert realized the man was crying. He rested his hand on his shoulder and leaned forward to peer up into his face. Harry avoided his gaze like a frightened child.

'Bad place. Never been so bad. The darkness. Could taste it, smell it. Bad, chief, bad.'

'Would you go back there?'

'Back?'

'To Blair.'

'Dead.'

'What?'

'Lots of dead people. Lots. Bad.'

'So you won't—'

'I'll go, I'll go. Go now. Go.'

Lambert took the man's gibbering as a yes, slipped the car back into 'drive' and set off towards Blair. All seemed to be going well until they passed another car that had been driving out of Blair, this one a Hyundai Pony rammed into a tree, the nude driver splayed across the bonnet like a cut of meat. Lambert slowed to look at the wreck.

'Seen this before, Harry?' he asked.

Harry was quiet. 'Yes. Saw.'

Lambert stopped, letting the engine idle. There was only the driver, his head slashed by glass, blood in rills along the length of the bonnet. Both arms were above his head, but one hand was missing. Lambert thought back to the car crash that had crippled him – where he too had gone through the windscreen – and he shivered. The poor sod's hand must have caught on something in the car – the wheel, maybe – and his momentum was such that it was ripped off. But at least he was out of it.

'Saw,' said Harry again.

Lambert nodded. He and the girl must have passed the crash.

'Saw,' he said again.

Lambert turned to him. 'Yes, Harry, you saw it. I bet you saw some other . . .' His voice trailed off.

Harry was holding up a saw. A small hacksaw, to be precise, the one-piece curved metal handle and blade holder containing a thin ragged blade flecked with what looked like blood and flesh.

'What?' was all Lambert could say as he watched Harry reach inside his sodden cardigan and pull out what looked like a piece of meat, but as he pulled out more it became clear it was much more than that. It was meat with function, a purpose: it was a human hand. Harry *had* been punched; it was the dead driver's hand that had caused the blood. For once, oaths failed Lambert.

'Saw?' said Harry. 'Meat for later. Shame to waste it.'

Lambert couldn't stop himself. He vomited into Harry's lap, and over the saw and amputated hand.

He managed to control himself after three retches and the two men just stared at each other, Harry with the saw in one hand, the hand in the other, his lap pooled with vomit, while Lambert gripped the wheel with both hands, his knuckles white in the grey light, his heart threatening to drum its way out of the confines of his chest. He had hidden the revolver on the floor on the right of his seat and there was no way he could reach for it, pick it up, cock it, aim and fire before Harry would have hacked into the side of his head for more 'meat for later'.

What the hell could he do? He glanced from Harry's eyes to the saw and back. One blow and he'd have his eye out.

'Why?' he asked eventually.

'Why?' repeated Harry, his eyes dead and unfocused.

'Why did you cut off his hand?'

'Eat.'

'Have you ever done it before?'

Harry looked puzzled.

'Think, Harry. Have you ever done something like that before?'
He needed time to think himself. Perhaps he could accelerate
quickly and throw him off balance – he noticed that the man
hadn't succeeded in doing up his seatbelt – then jam on the breaks
and have him hit . . . hit what? There was no windscreen for him to
crack his head on. And hitting the dashboard would probably only
damage his teeth and make him angry.

'Yes. I have, chief.' Harry sounded proud.

He began to fish in his left coat pocket, then Lambert spotted
that he hadn't locked his door. There was just a chance.

As Harry's attention was distracted by his struggle to get his
next gift of horror out of his pocket, Lambert leaned across him
and pulled on the door handle. Then, using his hand against the
man's neck and bracing his other hand on the steering wheel, he
pushed at the man with all his might.

Caught off guard, Harry toppled over easily. As he fell out with
a cry of surprise, he dropped the hacksaw and whatever he had
suceeded in removing from his pocket. Without waiting to see how
the man had fared on landing, Lambert pulled himself back, dropped
into 'drive' and twisted the throttle – and found renewed faith in the
Lord as the car began to speed up. Looking in his mirror he saw
Harry staggering to his feet. It was only as the man disappeared
from sight round a bend that Lambert saw what he had dropped
onto the seat next to him.

At first he couldn't tell what it was, as it was caked in dark
blood, evidently some hours old. But then, just as he passed a
junction, he realized it was a baby's foot. Involuntarily he shied
away from it, forgetting he hadn't got a door, and suddenly found
himself slipping into space, but as he wrenched himself back on the
steering wheel, the car responded accordingly and before he could
correct his mistake the car had started to spin. As the back wheel
hit the verge the car began to roll. Lambert screamed as he saw the
grey world turn upside down once, twice, then, as everything came
to a thudding halt, he felt a weight crash into his chest, the breath
left his body and a warm redness swamped his senses. Then all was
dead silence.

31

MARK AND KAREN RE-UNITED

Jamie's hand felt better, it was true, but the torture he had gone through having it cleaned and dressed had been almost too much to bear, not least because it had been done by the madwoman who had nearly sliced off Mark's ear.

After Mark had knocked her out, and both he and Jamie had got over their shock – and Mark had managed to staunch the blood flowing from his ear – they had lifted her onto a bed and tucked the sheets in as tight as they could to make sure that when she regained consciousness, she wouldn't be able to go berserk again.

It was a tense half-hour before the woman had woken up and, as Mark had predicted, she had thrashed and fought to escape. But Mark had knelt over her, staring into her face and repeating over and over again that it was Mark, her husband and everything was going to be all right and that he loved her. His words didn't seem to have any effect until she had exhausted herself and had to lie still and look up at him. And then something wonderful had happened.

She had at first looked puzzled, then frightened and then, slowly, she had begun to understand where she was and who Mark was. It was as if her mind had been a darkened room and lights were being switched on one by one until everything was bright and clear. Then she began to cry and they had hugged and kissed as best they could and Mark too had cried. Then he had fetched a discarded dressing gown to cover her nakedness as he settled her in a chair.

Her voice had been hoarse and her speech unsteady, as if she wasn't sure if she was fully awake, but her story was clear enough, and it made Jamie squirm because everything that had happened to her was his fault.

'I caught the train. It was busier than usual. A lot of schoolkids. I thought the journey was going to be a pain because they were very noisy . . . I was reading a book. Catherine Cookson, I think . . . there was a bang. I was facing back to Blair so the seat took the impact but there was an old man opposite me and he went flying. I remember his arm slapping my face and dazing me. I looked down at him and saw his neck looked . . . then there was another bang and I was thrown forward and the carriage rolled over and I hit my head on a rack and that was it. I remember a smell like smoke and thinking, "Oh no, it's going to catch fire," then I . . . it's blank. Next thing I was . . . was in an ambulance – I could hear the siren and there was banging on the side which was odd and then the hospital was just people running around and screaming in pain. A doctor saw me, checked my head, said I had concussion and I passed out again. I kept waking up and falling asleep. I woke up in X-ray and then in a corridor on a trolley. I remember telling a nurse to ring you but she wasn't listening. The place was so noisy – not the way you think hospitals should be. Then they stripped me, washed me, put me to bed and I fell asleep. I wanted to ring you, Mark, but they said they'd contact you. I trusted them . . . well, you do. Things calmed down after that and it went quiet. I think I heard the nurses talking about another emergency – a shooting, but no one was brought up here. Full, I suppose. It was dark when I finally woke up. There was shouting and screaming somewhere and I remember thinking, "You don't shout in a hospital". I tried to get out of bed but I was too wobbly. I called for a nurse but no one came. And then there was more screaming and some bangs. It was terrible.'

She started to sob and Mark hugged her, ignoring the pain in his ear as he pressed her head to his shoulder. Eventually, she pulled back and wiped her eyes with the heel of her palms. 'Sorry, sorry,' she said.

'It's all right,' insisted Mark quietly.

Jamie shifted uncomfortably on the bed behind her. He was glad he couldn't see her eyes because he feared that, like all the older women in his life – his mum, his aunts, his teacher, his social worker – she would be able to read him like a book.

Karen continued: 'A lot of the old women in here began to cry

– something was wrong, we could tell, but the staff couldn't or wouldn't tell us. And then someone ran in shouting we had to get out, there were murderers about. Murderers! It was such an odd way of putting it. I tried to get up – I wanted to go, *to see*, that was the odd thing. You know me, if there's just a creak in the house you have to sort it out, but last night, when someone had said there were *killers* roaming the hospital, I wanted to see them, meet them . . . *join them*.' She paused, caught her breath.

'I don't know what time it was but it was dark when a gang of people broke into the ward. They started hitting the old people who were trying to get out. My curtain was drawn and I couldn't see but I could hear. It was awful . . . Suddenly two people came up to my bed, a man I'd never seen and a woman. She looked like a patient, had a nightgown on. The man pulled the covers off the bed and ripped my nightdress off. I could see he was going to rape me. There wasn't anything in his eyes . . . he was insane, mad. But the woman was worse. She had this smile on her face; she was going to watch. That's what got to me; *she was going to watch*. The man had a big pair of scissors and he waved them in my face. He didn't speak. No one spoke, it was . . . mad. And I didn't say anything either. I could have shouted or screamed but I just lay there and, well, watched; watched while he set about raping me. Almost as if . . .'

'Yes?'

She took a deep breath. 'As if I *wanted* him to. Not that I wanted to be raped but I wanted there to be rape, like *I* was watching, just like the woman, only it was me who . . . People were screaming and those being attacked shouted for help, but the others just did what they were going to do.

'The man started to strip – he was taking everything off, not just his trousers. I was petrified and, well, excited, but something kept telling me this wasn't normal – if rape's normal. Do you know what I mean? He was very methodical: shirt first, then his vest, then his shoes and socks – and all the time the woman watched, like . . . like a mother watching her son get ready for bed. It was as he bent down to take his shoes off that I grabbed him round the back of the neck and pulled him down so his head hit the edge of the bed. The woman didn't do anything, just watched, this odd smile on her face. The man stayed down a long time, then shot up and stood, all wobbly. He turned round away from me, his trousers round his ankles and, because he still had the scissors in his hand he was finding it difficult to get his trousers off. Then the woman grabbed me and held me down . . .' She started sobbing again and Mark said she didn't need to continue but she pushed him away.

'I've got to tell you, get it out. Got to! The woman was holding me down. I remember she'd been eating garlic. She kept saying hurry. "Hurry, hurry, hurry." Suddenly she stopped and her eyes opened wide and she tried to reach behind her, then she let out this little noise, and fell on the bed beside me. He'd stabbed her with the scissors. Just because she'd told him to hurry up!

'He wasn't moving, just staring, so I sat up and head butted him in the stomach and he fell down and banged the back of his head on the radiator.' She pointed at the black stain that ran down to the floor.

'He dropped dead,' she said without emotion.

'You did what you had to do,' said Mark, stroking her shaking hand.

'I know that! I'm not stupid!' she shouted. 'I'm sorry, but it was him or me. Anyway, I sat there for a long time trying to understand what was happening, then I heard more shouting and screaming – and I ran into the toilet, but it doesn't have a window you can get out of and there's no lock, so I came back out, got hold of the man and dragged him into the toilet and propped him against the door so no one could get in.'

Mark saw her avoiding looking at the toilet door. 'Did anyone try?'

'Yes. Several times. I knew if anyone did get in I wouldn't stand a chance so, whenever the door was pushed or someone outside made a noise, I pressed my back against his body and pushed back. No one got in; they all gave up quickly and went away. I don't know how long I was in there and at some point I fell asleep. I could hear some people moaning. I guessed it was some of the patients dying but I couldn't help them. Listening to their pain and suffering . . . I tried to fight it but . . . When I woke up it was all grey, yet there were no lights and the window was painted out. I looked through his trousers pockets and found a scalpel. Then I heard a noise out here and realized I had to get out. I thought I might be able to outrun whoever was here but when I came out and saw the shotgun I didn't have any choice. I decided to kill you. And I would have. I was going for your eyes.'

'And you didn't know it was me?'

'*Obviously*!'

Mark could tell she was still very tense – who wasn't! – so he decided to give her something to do. He introduced her to Jamie, who suddenly seemed very shy, but was persuaded to show her his hand.

'Could you do anything for him? And my knee and ear and your face while we're at it?'

She started to shake again. 'I'm sorry, sorry – I really wanted to kill you, but I had to survive.'

'There's nothing wrong with wanting to survive, love. It's what Jamie and me have been doing for the last few hours. I don't know what's been happening but all we've got left is survival. Once we're fixed up, we'll decide what to do next.'

'Leave,' said Jamie.

'What?' said Mark.

'Leave,' repeated the boy. 'I know you said we'd go looking for my parents but I know they'll be dead. We'd be better leaving town, see what's happened anywhere else.'

'But there must be other people,' said Karen.

'They're all dead.'

'We found two alive – and they both wanted to kill us!' said Jamie. 'Sorry . . . We need to find a place with few people. The country, outside town.'

He was talking sense.

'You sure? About not looking for—'

'They won't be looking for me . . .'

It was such a sad thing to say, especially after all the grief they had gone through looking for his wife. Mark hugged the boy to him, ignoring the strange look Karen gave him. He had never been affectionate with children before, especially those on the brink of adolescence; 'natural criminals,' he used to call them.

'I need a wash,' was all Karen could offer.

'We all do. Let's take it in turns,' said Mark. 'Strip wash using a sink, then look after our cuts, then get out of here and out of town.'

Jamie nodded enthusiastically. Hearing Mark's wife's story had churned up his insides.

Karen took hold of Mark's arm and squeezed too hard, but the sight of her bruised face distressed him so much that the pain was irrelevant.

'Do you know what's happened?' she asked as they walked to the sluice room.

Mark shook his head. They forced the door open, dragged the nurse's body out of the way and helped Karen wash. He could see that shock was slowly taking its toll; her story had come out in a rush and it was as if she now had time to reflect on the last terrifying hours and realize what she had done: survive a rape attempt, kill a man, see murder at close hand and hide from maniacs – only to then try and kill her own husband! He was amazed she was still sane – although he did have to help her remove her dressing gown because she was trying to soap her neck through the collar.

When she was finished, he stripped, carefully peeling his jeans over the gash in his knee, then washed all over, neither of them bothered that a twelve-year-old boy was squatting in the corner while they went about their ablutions. Washed, he encouraged Jamie to follow suit – and decided the cajoling required wasn't so much shyness on the boy's part as an ingrained reluctance to wash.

Unable to find Karen's own clothes, they found a skirt and blouse in a bedside cabinet. Unfortunately there was no underwear, but they found that the dead woman on her bed took the same size shoes. Jamie put back on his own clothes, filthy though they were, while Mark took a pair of corduroy trousers from a dead doctor, cutting off the leg just above his knee.

They then made their way to the sister's office, Mark explaining what Karen should expect as they walked up the silent ward. Even so, the sight of the piled-up bodies around the entrance to the ward was more sickening than he remembered. Perhaps it was the chance of finding someone still alive, especially Karen, that had altered his sensibilities – where's there's hope, there's life. Or perhaps now, he had simply come to his senses.

The grey light helped them to find the bottled wound cleansing solutions and dressings they needed and after much teeth-gritting and wincing, their wounds were sterilized, dried and dressed by Karen. Naturally, they hurt even more, but at least the danger of infection had been reduced and, aware that they really had no idea how long their journey would last, they grabbed a shoulder bag and stuffed it with any recognizable medicine, together with antiseptic solutions, sticking plaster and bandages.

They left the ward, walked down the stairs and made their way along the main ground floor corridor in silence, Mark hugging Karen to him as the full horror of the events of the night before hit home. Jamie trailed behind them, distracted by the occasional glimpse of a bright light high up in the thin windows that lined the upper wall of the corridor. For some reason he found himself smiling, even though he knew he shouldn't be. He felt funny, but didn't want to mention it to the other two. It was . . . *private*.

When they emerged from the hallway and Karen saw for the first time the metal-grey sky, the bleached-out colours and even more corpses, she stumbled, then fell, Mark only just managing to grab her in time.

'I'm sorry, I should have told you what to expect.'

'What caused all this?' was all she could say.

Mark still didn't have an answer. He knew he should be reassuring but how could he be? He walked her to a low parapet at the side of the steps and sat her down. They had to be logical about their next move. *Logical*? He caught the laugh before it could worry his companions. He walked out onto the tarmac and looked around.

Nothing had changed except, to his left, back the way they had . . . of course, the light. It was bright enough to reflect off a third-floor window of a bank across the street. Perhaps it was the sun making a belated appearance but no, the sun never shone from that direction, whatever the time of day. There was something unnerving about the light, something wrong – if anything in this world gone mad could merit such a description. He knew he had promised the boy they would look for his parents, but Jamie seemed to have changed his mind – and he wasn't going to argue with him.

He looked along the drive to an abandoned ambulance. A radio. They had tried telephones without any response; maybe a radio would be more effective.

He walked up to the Renault ambulance, leaned over the empty driver's seat and unhooked the telephone-style receiver. Dead. He flicked the switch on the handle but it made no difference, then toggled the buttons on the panel. Of course: the battery was dead, it wouldn't work. So what communication wasn't powered by electricity or car battery? Aha. Mobile telephones.

It took five minutes of gruesome work, sifting through the pockets of better-dressed corpses before he found a Vodaphone. Flicking it open, he again drew a blank. On an impulse he checked half a dozen wristwatches, a couple of pocket calculators, and even an electronic diary he found in an unlocked briefcase. Everything was dead. Even windable watches had stopped, all of them locked to 1:11. Disappointed, he picked his way back along the drive to Karen and Jamie.

'Telephones and radios don't work. All electrical stuff is dead. Watches have stopped as well.'

'Pulse,' said Karen staring at the sky to the west.

'What?' said Mark.

'Remember I did that science fiction paperback cover, about life after World War Three? The rose growing out of a hand grenade? I read it to get an idea what it was about. One thing I remember was that when nuclear weapons detonate they send out an electromagnetic pulse that knocks out anything electronic. In the book the Chinese won because their first bombs were planted at strategic locations in the US and when they went off they took out America's ability to respond. The Americans had no electronics. Telephones, computers, radios, TV, missile commands didn't work. Pulse.'

Mark stared at her. For someone who had almost fainted five minutes ago, she seemed remarkably lucid. Then again, she always had been the one who took charge. Initially there might be shock, like in their recent car crash, but then she would sort things out. If only she could this time . . .

Jamie spoke up, his gaze fixed on the light reflected on the office window across the street. 'But nothing's been blown up.'

Karen looked around. 'Say bombs hit Manchester.'

'Karen!' said Mark, eyeing the boy.

She ignored him. 'Imagine they dropped nuclear weapons on Manchester. Remember when we lived in Didsbury and you worked out we'd get hit by four bombs. One for the airport, one for Woodford, one for Trafford Park, one for the city centre? Say that's what's happened and we missed the blast here in Blair. There wouldn't be any damage this far out, but the pulse would affect everywhere. God knows what would have been thrown up into the sky but the nuclear winter is caused by dust in the atmosphere.' She pointed at the sky. 'Looks dusty to me. No one'd come into the town because they'd have their own problems, and everyone here would panic. Wouldn't you?'

'But not everyone would disappear, would they?'

She pointed at the nearest body. 'They haven't.'

Mark was worried. She was too calm, too logical. He looked into her eyes and she stared back defiantly. He thought of saying something but decided to leave it. It was her way of dealing with the shock. If she could think it through, ascribe logical explanations, she could handle it. He remembered a time they had been mugged in Manchester. Some wild-eyed toe rag had pulled a knife and taken his wallet. Karen had spent half an hour explaining that the boy had been desperate for drug money and that it would have been pointless resisting because he didn't care what he did to get the money – why else hold them up in Piccadilly Gardens at lunchtime? By the time she had finished working out her shock she'd made a good case for adopting the lad!

He turned his attentions to Jamie. 'You OK?'

But Jamie wasn't listening. Ever since they had come out of the hospital into the the open he had been hearing another voice. That light was talking to him, telling him everything would be all right, that all he had to do was come home.

Mark followed the boy's gaze. The light. He knew it was near the boy's home but he'd said he didn't want to go there.

'Jamie, you ready to go now? If we follow the road we'll be out of town in a few minutes then up onto the moors. Should be safer.'

'No,' he said quietly.

'No what?'

'I don't want to leave.'

'But you must. You said you didn't want to go back for—'

'I am.'

'For your parents?'

'Fuck them,' he said vehemently. 'Fuck them all. I'm going back for it.'

'It?' What was he taking about. 'What it?'

'That.' He nodded at the bright reflection on the grey building.

'The light?' said Mark.

Jamie nodded. The light was warmth, colour. It was a friend.

'But it's just a light. We don't know what it is. We'd be better leaving.'

Jamie shook his head slowly. The light needed him.

Karen stood by Mark and looked down at Jamie. 'Mark's right,' she said. 'We'd best just leave. There might be people . . .'

'Don't need people. Just need the light.' Why couldn't the man understand. Wasn't it obvious? Didn't the light make everything clear like light was supposed to do?

'And we'll find it but not here, not in Blair, not this light.'

Mark put his hands on Jamie's shoulders and stooped down until his eyes were level with the boy's. 'Jamie, we decided we'd leave. That we'd get Karen then go. There's nothing here now—'

'The light. the light's here.'

'It's just a *light*. We don't know what it is.'

'It's good.'

'How do you know that? How do you know it's good?'

Jamie shrugged. It just was. Couldn't the man see that?

'Snap out of it, kid.'

Jamie suddenly punched Mark in the stomach. No one was stopping him going, no way. 'Don't call me kid. I'll do what I want.'

As Mark doubled over, Jamie pushed his hands off and stepped round him. Karen caught the boy's elbow. 'You ungrateful little brat. After all—'

Jamie kicked at her shins and as she stepped back to avoid the blow she let go his arm.

'*You fuck off too, lady!*'

The anger in his eyes was startling. Karen tried to placate him. 'Look, we're only trying to do what's best.'

'For who? Not for me. You're not my fucking parents! I want to go. I have to go . . .'

He started walking across the drive to the lawn, his eyes fixed on the reflected light. It needed him. He needed it.

Mark hobbled after him; the punch hadn't hurt but it had knocked the wind out of him. 'Jamie, if we stick together we—'

The boy spun round, fists raised. 'You and her can do what you like. Grown-ups always do. Me, I'm going where I *know* it's safe; where I'm *really* wanted.' He glanced back at the light. 'I'm going.'

'Jamie, it's for your own protection.' Mark grabbed at him but he squirmed loose and ran. He had covered almost the full width of the lawn and was on top of the small wall that fronted the pavement when he stopped and turned round. He was crying.

'I've got to go. You don't want me. Not if you knew what I'd done.' Why did he have to choose? Why couldn't they all go to the light?

Karen had joined Mark. 'Done what?' she shouted. 'There's nothing you could have done that—'

'You! I done you!'

'What?' said Mark and Karen together.

Jamie was sobbing, his chest heaving. 'The train crash. It was me! I done it. I drove a crane onto the line. The trains hit it.'

Mark and Karen were stunned.

'Come on, Jamie. This isn't funny. If you want to—'

'*I did it*!' he screamed. 'I killed all those people and I nearly killed you. I'm as bad as any of them who did this! You're better off without a killer.'

Mark tried running towards the boy, anger and compassion jostling for dominance, but his knee hurt and before he could reach him, Jamie had turned and jumped onto the pavement and darted away, his sobs as loud as his footsteps. Mark came to a sliding halt on the wet lawn and stepped onto the wall.

The light was brighter here, almost too bright, like an early morning sun catching his eyes if the bedroom curtains were open. Through the glare he could see Jamie weaving in and out of the bodies and cars, and could hear him shouting.

'*I'm coming, I'm coming!*' was all the boy could say. And all he could think.

Mark was about to step down after him when he heard Karen.

'Let him go, Mark. You did your best.'

He turned to look at her. Had Jamie been telling the truth? Had he really been responsible for nearly killing Karen – and killing others? If he was, then fuck the little bastard, but something told him that even if he had been responsible he hadn't been to blame. With all the madness in Blair, it took no stretch of the imagination to believe darker forces were at work – and to work on a twelve-year-old's mind would be far easier than the minds of the maddened adults who had slaughtered those about him.

He looked back at Jamie but the boy had gone. He stared at the light. It was a cold sharp light; it offered no warmth, no promise of help, so why was the boy running to it? And why had he shouted that he was coming? He rejoined Karen and hugged her.

'Did you believe him?' he asked.

'Yes.'

'What if I'd brought him back?'

'Be grateful you didn't,' she said.

'It mightn't have been his fault. All this has to have an explanation.'

Karen pulled away, fighting back her own tears. 'I had to *kill* someone because he caused the accident that put me here. I'd be in Manchester now if . . .'

She realized what she was saying: she might have been in Manchester – assuming there still was a Manchester – but Mark and those at DCA would be here, in all this. *DCA!* 'What about Stan and Nick and the others?'

Mark shook his head. 'Let's just leave while we can.'

They set off in the opposite direction to Jamie, their progress slow but steady, Karen carrying a Tesco bag filled with their medical requisitions, Mark carrying the shotgun, broken over his arm for safety. There were fewer bodies on the drive and as they reached the street, they could see the road leading out of town was almost empty.

'How far do you think this lasts?' she asked.

'No idea. If you're right about your pulse . . .'

'If I'm right about my pulse, love, we'll be dead of radiation sickness inside a day.'

Mark looked at the grey horizon framed by the houses on either side of the street. 'Do you think we should stay, then? Near the hospital?'

Karen looked back at the floating star in the middle of the town; it was icy and harsh like the light in a refrigerator illuminating food well past its sell-by date. She hugged herself. 'Whatever's out there can't be as bad as that.'

Mark didn't ask whether she meant the light or the town but he suspected which it was – and agreed. They carried on walking.

It was as they were passing a nurses' home a hundred yards on from the hospital that Mark spotted something mechanical that would still be working and would speed their escape from Blair.

'Fancy a bike ride?' he said.

32

LAMBERT TRAPPED

Silence was the first thing Lambert noticed. Not the pain, though that was obvious, nor the fact that he was lying on the wrong side of the car, but the silence. The engine had stopped running, but there were also no other sounds, not even birds singing. He cocked an ear but there wasn't even a rustle of the leaves in the trees that loomed over him. He hadn't noticed that before. It was worrying. Next he took stock of his position.

All the instruments he could see which had previously been giving digital readouts in red, green and orange were now dead, and the microphone had been ripped off his head. He was lying in the passenger seat, the car more or less upright, but the back end had been crushed and he was covered in splinters of sharp glass. He checked himself over.

There was blood on his chin and he felt a cut on his bottom lip and a small gash on the side of his face. There was also an eggsize lump on his right temple. Both his hands seemed all right, though his right thumb hurt as if he had been hit with a hammer, and he couldn't feel any pain in his chest or arms. His legs, of course, were a different matter. Hauling himself up by the base of the passenger door window he looked down at his useless limbs. The left leg seemed okay, draped in the passenger footwell, but the right was trapped under the steering column which had been forced down by the impact, pinning the ankle. Fuck.

He looked around the car. The baby's foot had gone, thank Christ, but so had the revolver. He pulled himself up to check the back seat. What equipment there had been was either missing or broken. His vacuum flask had disappeared but, how useful, his nappies were still present. Fumbling under them and a broken Geiger counter he found his Tupperware box of sandwiches. Well, at least he wouldn't starve. Then the enormity of his situation struck home. No one was going to come and rescue him; unless he could get free, he would die. Forget getting to Blair to find answers: all he wanted to do now was drive back to the edge of the dome and out into the world – if he could. He couldn't believe that he had ever told Horrigan that he didn't care if he made it or not. Now that he could see death as a virtual certainty rather than some vague threat, life took on a whole new value, as sexless and unambulatory as it might be.

He began to thrash, panic dictating his actions, but soon he regained his senses. Twenty years disabled had taught him that struggling was the least productive thing to do. Instead he checked both his legs for cuts and blood: without sensation he could be bleeding to death and not know it. Neither leg seemed bloody and the dampness he found at the top of his thigh, instead of the arterial blood he feared, turned out to be shit. That he was sitting in a pool of excrement was the least of his worries. What mattered now was how to get out, how to get the car working or, failing that, how to get into his wheelchair. Except, he realized, looking across at the driver's side of the car, there was no longer a wheelchair attached to the car. In fact, there was no frame either. It was as he looked through all the windows in an attempt to locate the missing wheelchair that he saw a figure approaching from behind the car.

The lane rose up an incline, hedges eight feet high on either side and, framed against the grey sky between the hedges and the black tarmac of the road, was a tall black figure waving his hand at the heavens. Except that, as a longer look showed, the hand being waved didn't belong to the figure: it was Harry and he was folding aloft the hacked-off hand he had shown Lambert.

Sudden pain creased Lambert's neck and he had to relax, Harry disappearing from sight as Lambert lowered his head. Trying to raise his head hurt even more and he realized he was in danger of serious injury – but the alternative was not seeing where the madman was and to have to then wait like a sitting duck for him to find him – and then what would Harry do to the man who had thrown him out of his car? Lambert craned his head round until he could see the reflection in the driver's mirror. Harry was still there, cursing someone or something, stamping his feet and occasionally pausing to berate the skies but always resuming his journey towards the Escort and its beleaguered occupant.

Gun. Lambert needed the gun! Where the hell was it? He felt underneath the seats, in the footwells, as far as he could over the back seat but he couldn't find it. He checked the mirror again. Harry was a hundred yards away the other side of the junction, a black figure of death set in grey. Lambert hadn't a chance. He sat up and heaved on the steering wheel to try and free his leg, but it was useless. He had no leverage and even if he found some, he hadn't the lower body muscles to pull his leg out. He might as well have been nailed into the car. All that was left was the hope that he could find a weapon to hit the man with as he tried getting at him. But again there was little to hand.

Most of the electrical equipment, though it possessed weight, was sufficiently fragile that any further impact would probably disassemble it rather than Harry. This meant the only solid items that remained were the vacuum flask – but its outer casing was plastic and he hadn't found it anyway – and a pair of rubber field glasses, which would just bounce off the bastard! He picked them up nonetheless and tried them. No, they were useless. Then he raised them to his eyes and focused on the reflection of Harry in the driver's wing mirror. He almost wished he hadn't.

The man might have failing eyesight, but he had plainly seen the car and was making a slow but steady beeline for it. There was nothing Lambert could do but keep the binoculars trained on him in the mirror and watch every agonizing step as the burbling lunatic came ever closer. Every so often he would pull at his leg or pound at the steering wheel, almost screaming in frustration, as if the wheel would have miraculously moved that vital half an inch for him to free himself but, of course, it never had.

Harry was only seconds away from the junction when he stopped, his head tilted as if he could hear something. Lambert held his breath but couldn't hear anything himself. But, after all, the man was mad: he might well be listening to voices in his head. He took another faltering step, then stopped again to turn and peer into the distance, but what was there for him to see, except black and white landscape and grey sky? Lambert lowered the binoculars, wiped the sweat from his eyes, then resumed his watch. Harry hadn't moved. Something was holding his attention, but what? He wished he could see over the hill. Maybe it was help on its way, but then again it was

more likely to be other lunatics. Oh God, now there was a thought
. . . But then he noticed something odd. A tree had disappeared.

There had been a tree to the right of Harry on the other side of
the hedge in the field. It had gone. Had he imagined it or . . . The
hedge suddenly vanished! Or at least a clump that had strayed onto
the verge. One second it was there and then it was gone as if painted
out. It was clear this was what was fascinating Harry. So much so
that he took a step towards the place where the hedge had vanished.
What was it? Mist? Low cloud? Lambert didn't know and neither
did Harry, which explained his next action: he threw the hand at
the grey. And it too disappeared.

Lambert nearly dropped his binoculars. OK, OK, it's just a heavy
mist. Fog. The hand went into it. It happens. How many times had he
seen dense fog with a definite edge, say on a motorway? Well, not
that many times, but he had seen morning mist in fields lying like
pools of liquid. They'd had an edge, they would consume. Harry,
however, wasn't satisfied. He took another step towards the grey
wall and this time used his own hand. Bad move.

He reached forward. The angle precluded Lambert from seeing
how far he penetrated, but he saw the result when the man pulled his
hand back and looked at the resulting stump. But he didn't scream or
cry out as Lambert expected; instead he just stared at where his arm
suddenly ended. There was no blood spurting from a severed artery
or dripping onto the road that Lambert could see, just nothing. Harry
clearly didn't know what to do but like the madman he patently was,
he turned back to the greyness and took a step towards it, only to
suddenly jerk back.

He spun round, both hands reaching for his face – except he didn't
have a face. Lambert could see *into* his head. His face and eyes and
mouth and nose had vanished, leaving some of his skull visible but,
on his forehead, where he must have been leaning slightly forward,
even the bone had disappeared and his brain was visible, grey in the
greyness. Suddenly the man slumped to his knees then fell forward,
his face hitting the ground with a resounding crack, the remains of
his head rupturing and sending dark liquid slooshing across the
road. Then Lambert watched as the man's body was consumed by
the advancing grey wall. First his feet, then his calves, thighs and
buttocks. Everything was eaten up slowly but surely, as effectively
as a drawing being erased: the last thing to disappear was the arm
without its hand.

The greyness was soon within feet of the junction – and wasn't slowing. Lambert tugged and heaved on the steering wheel but it wouldn't even turn, let alone lift. His frantic mind had already guessed that the grey was the wall of the dome advancing inward to consume everything in its path – which would explain how Roswiay and Warforn Peck had both been so easily and effectively reduced to nothingness. And another ten minutes and Lambert and his stricken car would, like them, become history.

33

MARK AND KAREN LEAVE BLAIR

Time meant little. There was no sun, no street lighting, no watches to gauge the time of day. Nothing to mark the passage of time except the regular pain in Mark's knee as he struggled to pedal the mountain bike up the long hill out of Blair. As he pushed down with his left leg his right leg was carried up by the pedal and the wound forced open as his leg crooked at right angles. Blood could be seen staining the pad and twice he had to stop and rest it. He probably would have been better walking but the impression of speed afforded by wheeled transport was vital if they were to feel they were making any progress.

They had left the last house behind some ten minutes ago. Whilst it helped alleviate their anxiety that someone might be watching them from behind drawn curtains, weapon to hand, now they were out on the open road with fields on either side they felt even more exposed. The greyness rendered their vision monochrome. Up ahead the sky seemed to reach to the very ground, the lack of colour ensuring that distance meant nothing. The grey could have been the horizon or it could have been a sheet of cloud dropped in front of them, shrouding the hills they knew lay ahead in mist. As they stopped for the third time for Mark to rest his knee, he took stock of what they had brought with them.

They had plenty of medical supplies, though precious few pain-killers. He had chewed several aspirin but they made little difference. They had sterilizing solutions and dressings but that was it. No food – they hadn't been able to find any in the hospital – and whilst Mark had remembered to bring the shotgun, he had lost most of the cartridges. They had probably fallen out when he was fighting with Karen. There were two in the gun and just two left in his pocket. It was not a great comfort. Their clothing was light but the temperature seemed comfortable enough, and there was no wind and no rain to chill them.

He laid his bike down and hopped to the verge, then settled himself down keeping his damaged leg as straight as possible, wincing with every movement.

'What if it's like this all over?' he said to break the silence.

'All over?'

'Everywhere. Forget your pulse or whatever we think it is. Just assume whatever this is has happened everywhere at the same time in the same way. Where are we going?'

'To hell.'

'Why do you say that?' Mark was surprised at Karen's comment.

'What do you think hell is?' she said sitting beside him.

'Boiling oil, eternal damnation, pain,' he offered.

'Hell is no hope,' she said, holding his hand. 'You know I had a boyfriend who died of cancer. Paul. I've never talked to you about the end. Too private. Something not to be shared.'

Mark nodded.

'He had cancer of the pancreas. Inoperable. He died within months. Horrible. I was with him when . . .'

'I know.'

'One night he told me he'd discovered what hell was. He said it was being somewhere you didn't want to be and knowing you couldn't get away. Whether it was a job or a marriage or a house or, in his case, an illness, hell was not being able to escape.'

Mark looked up and down the road. One way lay grey, the other more grey and a beacon of white light. He thought of a lighthouse, but realized a lighthouse was supposed to act as a warning, to save lives. Somehow he thought this light was doing the opposite. They were right to run from it, but where to? Hell was as good a word as any to describe where they were.

He put his arm around Karen and hugged her, she wincing at the pain in her ribs but enduring it. She rested her head on his shoulder, breathing deeply.

'Hell?' he said. 'Hell wouldn't have you in it.' He felt her shake.

'That's pathetic,' she chuckled.

'I thought it sounded quite romantic.'

'"Hell wouldn't have you in it"? It's so maudlin. It's like that time you bought me that heart-shaped teapot with "Darjeeling for my Darling" on the card.'

'Hey, I'm sorry I'm no Romeo but I do my best.'

'But you know I don't drink tea!'

'But it was such a good pun.'

'What about "Here's some Maxwell House for my spouse"?'

'Or "Cadbury's Choc-o-late for my best mate"?'

They both started to giggle.

'Where does this road go to?' he asked, changing the subject.

'I think it's Wigthorpe.'

'Famous for its Thorpes.'

They laughed again. Mark hugged her tighter and kissed her. He could feel himself growing erect and was appalled at the thought. He broke free. It had always amazed him in horror movies how the hero and heroine managed to have a shag despite the presence of danger. Now he understood, but he had no intention of imitating them. Karen tutted at his move away but didn't belabour the point.

They mounted their bicycles – his a mountain bike, hers a ladies' racer – and wobbled off up the narrow road.

They had been cycling for ten minutes when Mark called a halt, foolishly putting his bad leg down first and letting out a yell.

'What is it? Your knee too bad?'

'No,' he said. 'Look at that.' He pointed up the road. They had finally reached the top of the slow rise out of Blair. Ahead the grey wall of the sky came down across the landscape.

'What? I don't see anything.'

'Precisely,' he said, lowering his bike to the road, crossing to the opposite, higher verge and hauling himself up against the hawthorn hedge that bounded the fields beyond.

He looked again at the greyness. About a hundred yards ahead the road dipped away so that all they could see was the view over the crest of a hill to solid grey – a view of the sky, like looking out to sea from the top of a cliff – but it wasn't right. There were trees dotted liberally about the fields on either side but none poked above the horizon. He peered over the hedge and saw the same sudden drop in the landscape repeated, but there was no hedge or fence to stop cattle or sheep straying over the edge. He looked back

down the road. Blair was hidden round a couple of bends but there
was a silver in the gloom, presumably the light Jamie had been so
entranced by. He wondered if it was growing.

Stepping off the verge he urged Karen to stay with the bicycles
which, of course, she refused to do, so they slowly walked together
along the road. On the left the high verge and hedge conspired to
form a natural wall some fifteen feet high. On the right a wide
ditch fell away from the road, an abandoned car halfway along,
but it was the road ahead that held Mark's attention. He couldn't
believe the road would fall away so precipitously. Even if it did,
then he should be able to see the landscape beyond. After all, up
until a few minutes ago he could still see Blair to their rear as plain
as the greylight would let him.

He had covered half the distance to the drop when he suddenly
halted and stared at the end of the road. Just beyond the car facing
him that had slid into the ditch at an angle of forty-five degrees,
there was a turning on the right, give-way lines spanning its width.
Except that the lines abruptly disappeared, as did the road. He knew
there were bad cambers on some of the back roads in the area,
but none that would remove a carriageway from sight at such a
short distance. And then, as he watched, one of the give-way lines
disappeared, just as if the road had rolled out of sight.

The next line began shortening. The grey was *consuming*
it. It wasn't a horizon, it was a *wall* – and it was moving
towards them.

'Oh God, no,' he said, pointing at the side road. 'Look at the
lines on that lane. Watch!'

Seconds passed and the rest of the foot-long line disappeared.
Karen saw what happened and gasped.

'It's a mist,' she tried to explain. 'Fog.'

'It might be but . . .' He walked towards it.

'Mark! Don't!'

He looked at her. 'I'm not stupid, but we've got to see – it's
where we want to go.'

He stepped over to the high verge and picked up a small rock, then
walked another ten yards until he was just in front of the abandoned
car and threw the rock at the grey wall. The rock sailed through it.
At least it wasn't solid.

He found a three-feet-long branch on the edge of the ditch.
Picking it up, he advanced on the wall, carefully judging the

distance. He stopped just in front of it, and ran his gaze to the left and right and then upwards. It gave him vertigo. It was if his senses had lied to him and he was standing on the edge of a giant abyss of grey that fell away in front of him to unimaginable depths. He felt nauseous and quickly looked back down at his feet.

Stepping towards the grey, he poked at it with the stick. No resistance, no vibration. He prodded half the length of the branch out of sight. The greyness gave off no temperature, no smell. If it had been a mist he would surely have felt cooler standing this close to it. He looked to his right down the road. Oh God. The grey wall sliced down the middle of the road as effectively as the Berlin Wall had sliced through its mother city.

He pulled back the stick. Except there wasn't any stick to pull back. The yard of branch had been cut in half. And 'cut' was the most appropriate word. It had been severed as effectively as if it had been sawn off. He stared at it, mesmerized. He could see the edge had been planed smooth, could see the rings inside the wood. Tentatively, he touched it. It wasn't warm, wasn't wet. He sniffed it. Nothing. He looked back at the wall, suddenly seeing a tidal wave of acid towering above him for hundreds of feet, a malevolent obstruction that was consuming everything as it slowly advanced on him and Karen and the countryside and Blair. Unable to believe his own conclusions, he poked the stick into the grey again, keeping an eye on a knot six inches from his hand. He pulled it out in a second and another six inches had vanished.

Suddenly he found it difficult to breathe and, dropping the piece of wood, he staggered back, his hands fluttering as if they wanted to draw some imaginary curtain on the nightmare in front of him. All he could see in front, above, to the side, was grey death, slowly, unstoppably stalking him and Karen and anyone or anything in its path. Whatever it was, it wasn't biological warfare, it wasn't nuclear attack. His mind reeled from the inexplicableness of it, his mouth salivating wildly as his teeth chattered his terror. Shock consumed him and he started to reel, unable to control the spastic movements in his shaking legs. He heard Karen's concerned cry but it was so distant it might as well have been on the other side of the wall.

His knee gave out and he fell sideways, tripping on a tuft of grass and thudding into the side of the crashed car's rear, his head whipping forward and thumping metal, leaving him with a view of the bottom of the ditch. Puzzled by his new situation he looked

to his right and saw greyness reflected in the car's rear window.
There was no escaping it.

Reaching behind him, he grabbed the side of the car with
fumbling fingers and forced himself upright, then rolled over so
that he was leaning back against the car's rear door pillar, Karen
standing in front of him, her face creased with fear.

'*Got to get back*! *Back to Blair*!' he said.

He fumbled along the side of the car – he could see the front
offside of the car was almost on the road and would afford an
easier exit from the ditch. Karen leaned over to help him but he
waved her away; as like as not he'd pull her into the ditch with
him. It would be safer to use the car as a prop, get to its front and
pull himself up out of the ditch. He continued to crab the length of
the car, but as he reached the bonnet of the Escort, he felt a jab in
his back – and heard a voice.

'Turn round slowly. Then get me out of here or I'll shoot you!'

34

IZOTTA BEGINS TO SEE

'*One of us*? *One of us*?' Mr Farmer's accusation hammered in Izotta's mind – or what passed for her mind now.

It was all so impossible. She couldn't be dead, this couldn't be happening. What about her job, her flat, her holiday to Tunisia, the Marks & Spencer bill to be paid, the brie in the fridge, the ladder in her tights, that broken fingernail, her period due in three days, the cracked toilet seat, the new distributor for her Capri, her mother's sixty-fifth birthday . . .

'Forget them, girl,' said Mr Farmer. 'All that is behind you now. Irrelevant. A history that will recede. Trivia obscures so much potential, you see. Over the years I have learned to remove that clutter, to enjoy only that which my mind needs. Removing physical pleasures and daily concerns opens up so much fertile territory. But don't worry, you're beginning to lose your wasteful emotions – and worry will go with them.'

Mr Farmer was right. Izotta could no longer conjure up horror and terror at her insane circumstances. Even the knowledge that she was dead had simply become a fact, as relevant to her as the name of any victim in one of her newspaper reports. *Izotta Kominski, 36, reporter with the Blair Advertiser, was found dead today. Someone tell her, please.*

Humour? No, just bitterness that her end should come so soon. But even that twinge of her humanity seemed a lie, as if she was faking it; reminding herself that she had been human and trying to prove it. But it didn't last long; her mind was being systematically cleaned out by Mr Farmer: he was gathering up all remnants and

reminders of her previous life and dumping them like unfashion-
able clothing sent to a jumble sale. He might claim they were
one but he was in charge and soon he would be in complete
control – and what would be left if there was no body and no
emotion?

'Fret not, girl,' he said. 'For what you have lost, you have also
gained. See.'

Izotta looked down. The floor had become transparent and she
was looking into the flat below.

There were more bodies there, a family of four. She could also
see broken furniture, smashed crockery, every detail as clear as a
photograph – and the colours were so vivid, in stark contrast to
the grey world outside. A green carpet, light blue walls, blood.
She looked to her left, through Mr Farmer's bedroom and across
the landing and into the flat of an old woman, whom she could
see slumped over her kitchen table, a half-bottle of Lamb's Navy
Rum and a jar of pink pills scattered in front of her. She could
read the headline on the evening newspaper that lay in front of her.
TRAIN CRASH HORROR: 30 DEAD. And then beyond that the
woman's bedroom and a yellowed old man, his eyes staring at the
ceiling, a crumpled pillow by his head still bearing the impression
of his face.

Izotta tried to close her eyes but she had no eyes to close. Her
vision was unblinking and perfect. She looked in every direction
but everything had become sheer; solid objects mere memories as
bodies floated in mid-air where they had died, some bloody and torn,
others broken and limp. Soon the entire fabric of the block of flats
had disappeared and all that was left were bodies floating in space,
and the unbelievable light that was as revealing as a searchlight,
and as unnatural as sun at midnight, but Izotta was becoming used
to its power. Then, below, at the base of what had been the tower
block, she saw a pit of whitest light.

She looked back at her own body and that of Mr Farmer, both
floating as if held by invisible wires, just two more corpses stacked
into the sky with the other dead occupants of the building. What had
Mr Farmer gained from this? He was as dead as she. And what was
going to happen to them both?

She heard laughter, felt laughter, her vision rippling with pinks.

'We are so, so lucky,' he said. 'And the pleasure hasn't even
started yet.'

'Pleasure? From what?'
'From all the people.'
'What people? Everyone is dead.'
'Are they?'

35

OUT ON A LIMB

'I believe this is what is called a Mexican stand-off,' said Lambert, his revolver pointed squarely at the face of the young man looking down into the car.

The man was joined by an older woman, attractive despite her scruffiness. She was holding a shotgun and pointing it over the man's shoulder at Lambert.

'You related?' said Lambert.

'Married,' said Karen, her gaze steady.

'Well, tell your husband that unless he gets me out of this, I'll shoot him. You, too.'

'No, you won't,' she said.

Mark, surrounded by guns, was understandably nervous. 'Why can't you get out?'

Lambert nodded at his trapped leg. 'I'm paraplegic. Can't feel anything below the waist, so I can't get myself out.'

'So why the gun?'

Lambert looked at the revolver. Why indeed? After a frantic search when he had heard voices coming up the hill, he had discovered he was sitting on the damn thing and was glad to have found some protection; if another Harry came by he wanted to be sure he could stop him. Glancing in the mirror at the advancing wall of grey – barely twenty yards away now – it would also have another use: suicide.

He lowered the gun to his lap. 'You've seen the wall?'

Mark looked at the grey that cut them off from the rest of the world. 'Yes. It's moving.'

'I don't know what it is, but it'll eat this car and me in it if you don't get me out.'

'Shit. Karen, we've got to help.'

Karen was still pointing the shotgun at Lambert. 'What if he's mad? The last person you met with a gun tried to shoot you. And he's already threatened us.'

'Wouldn't you?' He kept staring at the gun on the man's lap. 'Where did you come from? One of the farms?'

'No. Outside.'

'Outside what?'

'You don't understand, do you? No radios, TV? Thought not. Look, we're a bit pressed for time here, but what's happened has only happened to Blair. The town is covered by a dome. I came through it from the outside where there are an awful lot of people trying to sort this thing out. Now as far as I can tell, that wall is shrinking inwards and it won't stop.'

'You sure?'

'Yes. Our only option is to outrun it.'

Karen finally lowered the gun. 'A dome, you say? Circular? Wall coming in all the way round?'

'Yes.'

'So where are we going to run to?'

Lambert looked at the wall through the rear window. It had crossed the side road. He reckoned it gained about two yards a minute, which meant less than ten minutes before it reached the back end of the car. 'I don't know, but I'm not giving up yet. Are you?'

Both Karen and Mark looked at the wall.

'No,' said Mark, reaching in and trying to prise up the steering wheel to free Lambert's foot, but a minute of sweaty heaving produced no result.

'Bastard's stuck tight. I don't see how . . . Need something to cut the wheel.'

Lambert remembered Harry's weapon. 'There's a saw!'

'Where?'

'I don't know. I haven't seen it in the car. A hacksaw. It might have fallen out. Look for it.'

The wall had covered another yard.

Karen and Mark looked around the car, Mark kneeling down to look under it, then working his way back along the ditch towards the grey. Karen leaned the shotgun against the bonnet then crossed the road. There was debris on the other side, including a metal frame and, buried in the hedge, a folded wheelchair. She only hoped it would still be usable.

Mark was within five yards of the wall, its looming presence as unnerving as a tall building teetering in a gale, when he saw a dull glint on the other side of the road – barely two feet from the wall's edge. He walked at an angle towards it, and peered closer. It was a hacksaw, dirty and ragged, but a saw nonetheless.

'Found it!' he shouted. But even as he watched, the wall crept another three inches, its edge as sharp and well-defined as a laser's. He leant down to grab the blade, but then, realizing the wall was mere seconds from his head, he panicked and jerked back, dragging the saw back with his foot. Then, kicking it down the road, he limped after it.

Lambert wiped the sweat from his face. He had checked the gun for the first time. It was fully loaded. At least he wouldn't feel the wall bite into him.

Mark leaned into the door, hacksaw in hand. He studied the steering wheel and determined that, if he could slice through a section near the spoke facing him, he should be able to push or pull the curved rim far enough to slip the man's foot out. He looked back at the wall. It was so damn *close* . . .

'Karen,' he shouted. 'Keep an eye on the wall. Let me know how close it is.'

'Right.'

He started to saw at the wheel rim.

'My name's Mark,' he said between breaths. 'Mark Dawson. I work in advertising. This shit just happened. My wife was in the hospital. I went looking for her and found her and we were trying to get out of town.'

'How bad is it?'

'Like a fucking war. Bodies everywhere. Hundreds. Seems to have been mass panic. We've only found two other people alive. Plus you.'

'Where are they?'

'One shot himself, the other left us.'

'My name's Wesley Lambert. I sort of predicted this would happen—'

Mark stopped sawing. 'So why didn't—'

'No one believed me and by the time they were ready to act –
they *were* going to evacuate the whole town – it got cut off.'

'Are you the only one here?'

'Yes.'

'Why?' He continued to saw at the plastic. 'Why don't they send
in the army?'

'You don't want to know.'

'Twelve yards!' shouted Karen.

'I have a right to know.' He stopped sawing. He had managed
to get through the plastic and padding but the metal of the wheel
was proving almost impossible.

'Don't let your wife know, then.'

'What?'

'Blair will disappear. I suspect the curved wall will meet itself in
the middle and the dome will dissipate and the town and everyone
and everything in it will vanish.'

'Hey, break it gently why don't you!'

'Eleven yards! It's getting close, Mark. Hurry up!'

'You asked,' said Lambert. 'So just fucking hurry, like the
wife says.'

Mark pressed home the blade. And it snapped.

Both men stared at one another, neither able to speak.

'Ten yards!'

Mark dropped the hacksaw and heaved on the steering wheel. It
wouldn't budge.

'Fucking thing! What now?' asked Mark.

'You and the missus better run. I've got my own solution.'
He picked up the gun and tapped his own forehead. Mark batted
it away.

'No! There must be something else.'

'Nine yards! Come on, come on!'

Mark stood up, wiping sweat from his brow. 'Saw's broken.
Can't shift it.'

Karen pulled him aside and thrust her head into the car and
surveyed the scene. 'Men!'

She picked up the hacksaw. The blade had snapped at one end.
She turned it over, undid the small butterfly bolt that held the blade
in place and took the blade out of the haft.

Three strokes at the wheel and she stopped, her face contorted in
pain. She opened her hand to reveal dark blood streaking her palm.

'Look, love, leave it,' said Lambert. 'Save yourself. You did your best. Me, I was the one who crashed.'

'Shut up.'

Mark leaned in. 'We've got five minutes at most. What are we going to do?'

Karen turned and, to Mark's surprise, cut a small hole in his right trouser leg then, before he could protest, she ripped around his leg until she could pull the corduroy free from below his knee. Mark stood puzzled in his makeshift shorts, while Karen continued to hack and rip at the cloth until she had a strip two feet long by three inches wide which she then wrapped around one end of the blade.

'Mark, get the medical stuff. Pads, sterilizing solution.'

'What?'

'*Do it*!'

She looked at the wall. Seven yards at most. But it was so close and so wide and high that it felt like the sky was about to fall on them. She knew that if she was to stare at its oppressive presence for any length of time she would become mesmerized and unable to do anything, so she tore her gaze away and focused on the trapped man.

'Are you really paraplegic? No feeling at all?'

'Twenty years. Another car crash. Nothing.'

She pulled his trouser leg up to expose his white ankle. The wheel had dug into his sock just above the bridge of the foot so that it was caught at an angle that precluded movement in any direction. She heaved again on the wheel; it might as well have been set in concrete.

Mark knelt behind her, carrier bag ready.

'The wound-cleansing solution. Bottle,' she ordered.

Mark fumbled in the bag and pulled out a pint-size brown bottle. Karen undid the seal, unscrewed the top then poured it over the hacksaw and Lambert's ankle.

Mark stood up. 'Oh God, no.'

'Check the wall, Mark.'

Karen and Lambert stared at each other, both aware of what was about to happen.

'You are, of course, a fully qualified doctor?' he said.

'No, but I do have a degree in graphic design.'

'Well, at least it'll be tastefully done.'

Both paused a moment until Lambert gave a slow nod and

scrunched up his fists. He might have known it wasn't going to hurt, but he could see what this stranger was going to do to his leg.

Karen pulled the sock down as far as she could, then pushed down with the blade and caught skin. Then rupturing the epidermis, she began to saw into the front of his ankle at an angle of forty-five degrees, aiming for the heel. Blood flowed copiously, soon covering her hands and the blade and masking her task. She gritted her teeth and fought back the urge to throw up.

'Four yards!' shouted Mark.

'Mark, pour that stuff on my hands.'

Mark leaned in, and immediately leaned out again and threw up onto the road.

'*Men*!'

Lambert touched her shoulder. 'Give it to me,' he said. Sick as he felt, there was no pain and, for the present, practicality overruled his emotional reactions.

She reached onto the road, clasped the bottle by the neck and passed it over to Lambert. He slooshed it over the wound and the woman's hands, the extent of the damage immediately revealed. She had already penetrated an inch into his flesh, and the cord that ran from his shin bone to his foot had been parted like twine to reveal bone. The grey light served to disguise the scarlet of the blood but did nothing to hide the flesh and sinew inside his leg.

Karen grunted as she leant down on the blade and began rasping it across his ankle bone. She didn't know how far she would have to go, but she was going to do as much as she could in the time available before trying to pull him free. She refused to acknowledge the fact that she might have to amputate his entire foot.

'Three yards!' Mark coughed hoarsely.

'Mark! Get the wheelchair from the hedge. If we get him out we need him mobile.'

Mark was grateful for something to do other than count down to their doom. The wheelchair was directly opposite the car so there was still time to get it out before the wall reached it.

Lambert looked out of the back window. Solid grey. Less than two minutes and it would reach the car boot. He wondered if there might be a chemical reaction with the petrol. He turned the gun over in his hand. Two minutes and he would force the woman to stop and leave him. She had done all she could and didn't deserve to throw her life away on him. After all, stupid idiot that he was, he was the only one of the three who had chosen to be here.

He heard a clatter as Mark pulled the wheelchair from the hedge and dragged it across the road to the car.

Mark checked the advancing greyness. 'Oh God, two yards max! Hurry, Karen!'

'He's one impatient little sod at times,' she muttered under her breath.

'But he means well,' said Lambert, provoking a sick grin from Karen. She wiped one of her hands over her face, smearing herself with blood.

Mark poked his head into the car, fighting his urge to vomit. He could see the logic of Karen's surgery but he could never have brought himself to have suggested it. He never had been one for blood. Death, he realized with bitterness, he could handle, but wounds to the living . . .

'Got one minute,' he said. 'Let's see if it'll move.'

Karen wanted to shout at him – it was so typical of Mark to step in and take charge when all the dirty work had been done – but now was not the time. She dropped the blade on the sodden seat, took the bottle from Lambert and poured more over the wound, temporarily revealing how much of his ankle she had severed.

'You, grab your knee and push. Understand? *Push*. Mark, you lift the steering wheel if you can.'

Karen took hold of the foot around its top, her thumbs edging into the V-shaped wound, and together they pushed and tugged. But to no avail.

The wall continued its relentless advance, ready to consume them in seconds.

'Again,' urged Karen.

And again all three manipulated Lambert's dead leg until, with a jolt, the steering wheel rim slipped into the wound.

Mark panicked. 'What fucking good's that!'

Karen elbowed him in the ribs. 'Shut up! You, push your thigh towards the seat.'

Lambert did as instructed and as Karen held his foot in one hand, she pushed at his ankle with the other. At first nothing happened – the wheel might as well have been welded to his foot – but then there was a slow movement and, suddenly, the leg slid free, and blood that had been temporarily halted by the pressure of the wheel splattered all three of them.

'Right. Mark,' said Karen. 'Pull him out.'

Spitting the blood out of her mouth, Karen stepped back from the car, dizzy from the effort, and took a moment to orientate herself. She saw the wheelchair, only inches from the wall which was about to touch the rear of the Escort. For one bizarre moment she was tempted to run headlong into it, like a spurned lover into the mist desperate to end all the worry and torment, but sense prevailed. She grabbed the wheelchair and pushed it alongside the car, glad to see it hadn't been damaged in the crash.

Mark was pulling Lambert out by his legs, his hands wrapped around the man's calves, both his wrists swamped in blood. Niceties were forgotten in the rush and Lambert fell onto his back, cracking his head on the base of the car's door frame. Dazed, he allowed himself to be manipulated upright and flopped in the wheelchair, his legs bundled onto the steps. Then, releasing the chair's brake and finding the motor didn't work, his two saviours pushed him up the road.

'Mark, you take the wheelchair, I'll take the bikes. Put the first aid stuff on his lap.'

Two minutes later they were a hundred yards further down the road, Karen padding Lambert's wounded foot with high compression bandages in an attempt to staunch the flow of blood, as he and Mark looked at the Ford Escort as it finally disappeared.

'I forgot the gun,' was all Lambert could say.

'A dome, you said,' said Karen.

'Yes.'

'Circular?'

Lambert nodded. For the first time he could remember he thanked God for the numbness in his legs. What it would have felt like had he been normal . . . As it was he was feeling light-headed – whether that was shock from what he had seen being done, or the physical trauma and blood loss of the amateur surgery itself, he didn't know – he just hoped he didn't pass out.

'Here, hold this pad in place while I strap it on. So, if that wall is moving in on all sides, all we can do is go back into town?'

'Yes. And while we're being logical, the dead centre of that circle would be the last place to be consumed.'

'And then?'

'Then we die. But at least . . .' *At least what*? He shut up.

Mark spoke up. 'And you've no idea what it is or how to stop it?'

'No. Sorry. It's happened a couple of times before, I think, and it's triggered by, well, badness.'

Karen finished running the roll of sticking plaster around the bandaged joint, pleased that she had taken the St John's Ambulance course at evening classes. She stood up, her back cracking, her grey face still stained with blood. The streaks of darkness on her face reminded Lambert of the soldiers he had left on the other side of the wall.

'Badness?' she said.

'Bad weather, bad vibes, bad feelings,' he tried to explain. 'Before this came to a head, you must have been aware that the town was in a bad way.'

'Yes,' both Karen and Mark agreed.

'It has something to do with that, which means we haven't a clue how to stop it. You can't cure a problem unless you know how the cause works.'

'Do you know where the centre of the dome is?' said Mark.

'We checked it on a map. Road called Steel Avenue. Looked like a council estate with tower blocks.'

Karen and Mark looked at each other. '*The light*!'

36

JAMIE'S WITLESS WALK

Jamie's mind was filled with light. A warm, welcoming invitation to a brighter future. Peace and tranquility, love and laughter; it was like the circus coming to town, his best holiday ever at Butlins, a Super Nintendo with *Street Fighter II*, a pair of Air Jordans and a CD Walkman all rolled into one big Christmas present. It was all he ever wanted, all he'd ever needed and it was just a few minutes away across town, calling to him.

He didn't see the bodies, the crashed cars, the smashed windows or the fire damage. Mark and Karen and the man with the shotgun were like shadows swept away by advancing summer sunlight. Gone as soon as they were noticed and just as insignificant. No, all Jamie saw now was life like it used to be before his parents stopped caring and Wayne found drugs; life as he'd always dreamed it would be when he was hiding from the shouting under his covers or shivering in the block's basement as the gangs roamed the streets at night. Life like it was for the people he saw on TV.

The light was brighter now, bouncing off windows and chrome and flaring around the deserted streets like those mirrored balls on *Come Dancing* on the telly. He remembered his parents taking him to the Tower Ballroom in Blackpool where he'd sat hypnotized as hundreds of couples dolled up for the evening had swirled and skirled around the polished wooden floors, little pricks of light like diamonds showering their every step. It was magical, like heaven. And today it was even better.

Then, suddenly, he lost sight of the light and he caught his footing on a kerbstone. A street had intervened and a taller building was obscuring the light's source. Jamie stopped, unsure of where he was, his mind fuzzy with vague promises and recent experiences, a jumble of thoughts that overrode his current perceptions. He felt as if he had set out across an empty street and suddenly a horn had sounded, making him jump and stand still in panic at the same time. But there were no cars to threaten him, and no drivers to sound their horns. So why was he so scared and lonely? And how had he—

He saw movement. *People*! There were people walking in the street up ahead. Who? Where had they come from? He raised his hand to wave, then remembered a shotgun blast, a man killing himself and blood over a picture of Paris. And he remembered Mark and Mark's wife. Where were they? He darted to his right into the shelter of a doorway and pressed himself against the door, his heart racing. He had left them, hadn't he. But why? *Why*?

He edged forward and peeked round the corner of the shop window, the array of expensive watches and rings on display now so much worthless metal, all watches stopped at 1:11. He saw more than one person but, thankfully, they seemed to be walking away from him. As he watched, others appeared from doors and alleys, all slowly turning up the street and heading for the centre of town. They walked in a straight line, but whenever there was an obstruction, like a car or more bodies, they would take a detour, hardly reducing their pace, their heads held up, staring into the sky. Then he remembered the light. Could that be it . . .?

He watched an elderly couple walk past less than ten feet from him, both bearing the same glazed expression, the same slack-jawed, rubbery-limbed gait, like . . . like Shaggy in a Scooby Doo cartoon when the bad guy's got him in his power. Like Bugs Bunny when he's been zapped by the witch and he's heading for the stew pan. Like . . . *victims*.

Then directly opposite him, the door of the Blair Building Society opened and four people walked out, all women. They were dressed identically and he guessed they were staff, but where had they been and why were they walking up the street like they were zonked on dope? He thought of shouting but didn't have the nerve. The unnatural silence in the town was undisturbed by the people walking its streets and he had no desire to become the focus for any sound.

He leaned back against the door, his legs shaking, confusion fogging his mind. He had wanted so much to find others alive after all the death, but now he saw them he couldn't approach them. They were as frightening in their way as the corpses, their minds seemingly just as dead. The way they followed the light *the way he had been following the light* . . . What was wrong with him? They hadn't got guns – they were *girls*! Just get out there, Jamie, and ask for help.

He leaned into the street again and saw yet more people walking past. No one looked his way. No one looked anywhere except ahead. They were like zombies in a movie but without their cannibalistic appetites. Then, suddenly, a naked Asian man turned the corner twenty feet from him.

He looked straight at Jamie and the boy's heart missed a beat. So terrified was he by the man's appearance that he found his legs wouldn't work. The man walked closer, Jamie pissed himself and started begging to be left alone, but his mouth was dry and all that came out were strangled gasps. The man continued to walk straight for him. He was tall, well over six feet, and muscled. He had the physique of a boxer or wrestler and hands that would crush Jamie's head as easily as if it had been an egg. Too late, Jamie tried to run but instead of dodging round the man, his stupid legs carried him into him and he bounced off, falling at his feet. But the man didn't flinch, even though Jamie had elbowed him in the balls. Instead, he just stepped round him and walked on without a second glance.

Jamie lay on the pavement and watched the man walk away, his heart racing faster than he could ever remember. Then the door of the jewellers he had been standing in opened inwards and three men stepped out, all dressed in suits. *Suits*! The man with the shotgun!

Jamie crabbed away from them, ignoring the pain in his damaged hand, an image of the pain to come from the three men if they caught him far more persuasive.

They continued to walk towards him, each grey and blank faced, their purpose impossible to read. Jamie decided not to wait to find out. He got to his feet and, as the men reached him, he bolted up the street.

He had passed several people – including the Asian giant – before he slowed and tried to make a rational decision as to his destination. He wanted to avoid people because he couldn't trust them. For all he knew it was all some plot to throw him off his guard so that all of a sudden they could tear him limb from limb. He had to hide, to keep out of their way. These bastards were dangerous: if they were real survivors like him or Mark or Karen why weren't they shouting at him, or talking to each other, instead of just walking on like their brains were switched off?

He stopped in the middle of the street, aware of his exposed position, but resolved to make a rational choice. It might be his only chance to . . . He caught sight of a light. *The* light, up there, on a window, and bouncing down windows the length of Smithfield Street. Such a pretty light, such a good light. Why did he have to run? All he had to do was head for the light and everything would be safe. Why worry?

Yes, why worry? said a voice.

Yes, why worry? agreed Jamie.

He turned and began to shamble along, his gait a match for others on the road, a dulled raggle-taggle army of programmed humanity, and he just another of the herd, mesmerized by a light, a light that spoke to him and to all the others.

He walked on, time an alien concept, his mind fixed, eyes soon only seeing a grey tunnel with a pinprick of light at its end that promised an everness of bliss. The light would give him all because the light *loved* him. He was coming, and the small voice in his head thanked him and promised him his heart's desires in return.

Occasionally there would be a stab of pain somewhere near him and a black speck would float in front of the small circle of light. But the voice would be there to reassure him, telling him to ignore everything but the light and he was happy to agree. For the light *was* happiness.

Yes, said the voice. *Come to the light and be happy*.

So Jamie continued to walk towards it, oblivious of the growing crowds around him and ignoring the pain that scratched at his mind every so often. The light was all he needed, and he would not be distracted.

37

BACK TO BLAIR

The journey back to Blair was slow but uneventful. They soon abandoned one of the bikes, Mark pushing Lambert while Karen cycled alongside. As they travelled, wary eyes on the dome's wall behind them in case it speeded its rape of the countryside, Karen and Mark took turns telling their stories so that Lambert could get some understanding of what had happened. As an outsider privy to information about similar events, they both hoped the stranger would suddenly shout *Eureka!* and point to an exit but, of course, he didn't.

For his part Lambert listened with increasing dread as events in the dome were spelt out. He had imagined what might have been happening, but to have his worst fears confirmed as the three of them strolled along a quiet country lane was horribly surreal. He had got used to the strange monochrome light – it reminded him of bleak winter days – but then, every so often, they would come across a body or a car. He could tell from Mark's and Karen's stories that they had learned from their short but brutish experience, so neither of them bothered to check for life. He, however, insisted on looking at some of the bodies. He checked three: a teenage girl naked but for her bra who had obviously been raped, then strangled; a middle-aged woman in a housecoat who had severe head wounds; and a man in his twenties, probably a student, with blood on his clothes but no obvious cuts, who was lying against a garden wall, his hands by his side, his face contorted in agony.

'Looks like a heart attack, but in someone so young . . . I need to see some more.'

Karen and Mark wanted to protest but the man seemed to be formulating some theory and, as it might lead to an escape plan, they wheeled him into the small car park of a pub with the appallingly ill-judged name The Jolly Butcher's Arms.

Here there were five bodies: three men, a five-year-old girl and an elderly woman. The child had been beaten to death with a walking stick by the old woman who had then had her throat slashed. Of the three men, one had lost a hand and had plainly bled to death, but again the other two showed no real signs of violence.

'Strip them,' said Lambert.

'What? We don't have time for—'

'We've time to find out more. It's all we *do* have time for.'

So Mark and Karen stripped the two men, both of whom were aged about twenty, one black, one white. As instructed, they held up their arms, parted their legs, and rolled them over, Lambert nodding sagely until he told them to stop.

'Again it looks like heart attacks,' he said. 'That's three young men, all engaged in violence, all of whom just keel over from cardiac arrest, or possibly a brain haemorrhage – it's difficult to tell in this light if there's a blue cast round their lips. Extreme violence, an outpouring of the deepest darkest desires, then the plug is pulled and bang! They die. As if they had overdosed on adrenalin; too much excitement and their hearts or minds just packed in.'

'That would explain why there are so many bodies and no one else alive,' said Mark. 'There must come a point where whatever's got hold of them proves too much and they die. Maybe there is justice after all . . .'

Lambert shook his head. 'This isn't justice. Every one of us is capable of something bad: you, me, everyone. Most of us keep it under control. You must have known people who when they've got a drink in them change and become violent; or people who on their own are as meek and mild as pie, but when they're in a crowd, like at a football match, or on holiday with the lads in Majorca, end up in all sorts of bother. Doesn't mean they deserve to die, just that they've been got at.'

Karen sighed, remembering her own desires during the attempted rape on her and her violence towards her attacker. Did she deserve to die for that?

'Shouldn't we be moving on?' said Mark, looking over his shoulder at the wall that was following them like some sentient storm, anxious to consume them should they fail to keep up their pace.

Lambert waved them onward, Karen leaving her bike and walking with Mark behind the wheelchair.

Finally they reached the outskirts of the town proper, with its blank houses, grey gardens and vacant shops on either side: normal things suddenly rendered supernatural. Lambert remembered movies where heroes had tramped through deserted Londons and LAs and had been impressed by the eeriness the scenes created, but to actually be in it; to be wheeled past dead children and broken adults, crashed motorbikes and looted shops, to see the debris of violence cast about like so much litter brought home the hell that was Blair. He wondered how many people had succumbed to madness, or to madmen – and how many more had cowered away, muttering silent prayers while their gods looked elsewhere.

As they edged round an ice cream van on its side, dead children jumbled inside its burned cabin, he reflected bitterly on his argument with Horrigan when he had claimed that he was willing to give up his life for one glimpse of what had happened in the town. If only his tongue had been as paralyzed as his legs . . .

By the time they reached the grounds of Blair General Hospital, Lambert was explaining what he thought would be happening outside the dome.

'I suspect they'll send in some troops eventually, despite what Horrigan told me. He'll be overruled by panicking politicians and stupid military men. They'll only use volunteers but there are plenty. They'll probably send in small squads at first, six or ten men, at regular points around the perimeter. I also think they'll try parachuting some in, or abseil some down from helicopters. What will happen to them once they're inside I don't know. I don't even know if the wall had started moving when I came through, but even if they do get in, there's nothing they can do.'

Mark stared up at the grey, his ears swamped with silence. 'You mean there are helicopters up there, above the grey?'

'Squadrons. Plus planes. They may have been slow to deal with it but I would say that right now Blair is the most important place in the world.'

'Well,' said Mark sarcastically. 'That's a comfort.'

'Isn't there anywhere we can go? What about underground?' asked Karen.

Lambert offered no hope. 'Seismic surveys suggest the dome is ovoid, like two woks rim to rim. So it will be as deep at the centre as it is tall, and there's nothing in Blair that goes that deep: over two thousand feet. Sorry.'

They stopped opposite the hospital entrance. This was the first location where there was a multitude of bodies; they had already passed corpses and abandoned vehicles but here they could see sixty-odd bodies scattered across the hospital lawn. With Blair home to forty thousand people, Lambert finally began to grasp the enormity of the event: major earthquakes don't cause as many casualties; civil wars, as vicious as only they can be, rarely claim so many victims in a year. Yet here, in a small Northern town, thousands were soon to be destroyed – in a country where three people dying in a car crash can make national news.

'God, it's unbelievable,' said Lambert trying to control the bile he felt rising.

'Not all of them will be victims,' said Mark. 'Some might have had heart attacks like you said, but I've also seen bodies where they obviously committed suicide. Whether it was to escape this or they realized what they'd done . . . The guy who tried to shoot me and Jamie, he killed himself.'

'This Jamie, where did he head off to?'

Mark pointed at the light. It was still a reflection on a window but now there was also a glow above some buildings.

'It's growing,' said Karen.

'What's powering it?' said Lambert to himself.

'No idea. Nothing works. Look at your watch.'

Lambert nodded and held it up. It showed 5:52.

'When did you enter?'

'About quarter past two,' said Lambert.

'But nothing works here,' said Karen. 'Cars, phones, radios, clocks. So why's yours still going?'

'Hey, that's a point,' said Mark. 'Your car. Did you drive it to where we found you?'

'Yes,' said Lambert, frowning in thought. 'Now why did the car and my watch work while everything else has stopped? Unless it's because it was working as it came in. Nothing that was sent in could get a message out but that doesn't mean it wasn't working.'

'So if the car wasn't wrecked we could have driven out?' said Mark, but then he remembered how the wall ate the car.

Lambert changed the subject and stared at the light.

'This Jamie. He ran to that light, you say? Maybe there are others who went to it.'

'Even if there are, it's just a matter of time,' said Karen. 'How fast do you think the wall'll take to get here?'

'There's plenty of time, don't—'

'Don't patronize me!' she exploded. 'We deserve to be told the truth! If my time's limited, I want to know. You listening, Mark?'

'Yes, boss,' he said quickly.

'You?'

Lambert blushed his apology, impressed by the woman's fortitude. He twisted in his chair and calculated how far they had come and how far away the light and the centre of the dome was.

'At two yards a minute, from where we were to the light must be about three-quarters of a mile, a mile at most. Take the lower figure. Ten hours. Assuming it doesn't speed up.'

'Naturally,' said Mark. He leaned down on the back of Lambert's wheelchair and rubbed his eyes with his knuckles.

Karen kneeled down and checked Lambert's dressing. 'Still bleeding but not a lot. We could do with dry dressing it.' She nodded to the hospital on her left.

'Ten hours,' was all Lambert said. Karen shrugged and stood up.

'So?'

'We check out the light,' said Lambert, then his face froze open-mouthed.

'What?' said a frightened Karen, whirling round to see what had taken the man by surprise.

People. People *alive*. Living people walking from the hospital entrance and from the west side of the building. A dozen, fifteen at least, all shambling along as if dazed, their arms limp by their sides, their eyes fixed on the source of the light.

'You d-don't think they're . . .' stuttered Mark.

'I wouldn't finish that if I were you, Mark,' said Lambert. 'I had you down as being more intelligent.'

The three of them watched the procession build up. Soon there were fifty walkers, all ambling slowly across the lawn and down the drive towards the road where, already, the leading figures had turned to face the light and were walking in line in its direction down the street. And beyond them, they could see others leaving buildings and side streets to join the shambling crowd. It was an exodus, except, if Lambert was right, there was no promised land at the end. But then again, where did they think they were going? What was compelling so many survivors to forsake the shelter of their hideaways and venture onto streets that only the day before had run with madness and blood?

'Mark, go check them out,' said Lambert.

'H-hey, I'm not—'

'I can't do it. Unless you want to send your wife . . .'

'Do it, Mark,' ordered Karen. 'We have to know.'

Mark gave her a look, but she gave him a graver one back and he reluctantly limped to the lowest point of the wall. Hauling himself onto its wide parapet, he set off across the lawn, picking his way between the corpses towards a group of five women all dressed in bedclothes who were walking slowly towards him.

He stopped and looked back at Lambert and Karen but beyond them the grey wall rose up to fill his vison like a tidal wave. He remembered films he had watched of real tsunamis and tornadoes, raging floods and forest fires – images of nature at its most vehement and implacable – and yet, as violent as they were, they were nothing compared to the skywide grey slab that seemed to be falling towards them. He could sense its crushing force bearing down on him. It made him want to fall to his knees and whimper. Already it had obliterated the tallest tree they had passed on their way back into town and soon it would reach the first houses.

He turned to the women. They were only feet away and the first thing he noticed was how strongly the light reflected in their eyes, almost as they were lit from within. The first two – both middle-aged, their faces slack, postures slumped, flesh and clothing both dirty grey – walked past him. He stood in front of the third – a young Asian girl with long tousled black hair – and she paused, then side-stepped him and walked on.

He grabbed the fourth by the arm, frustration and anger growing in him. After all, apart from Jamie, Karen and Lambert, these were the first living people he had seen in what seemed an age. She was tall and thin, probably in her fifties, the grey light lending her skin a deathly tone but, he realized, her skin was warm. He pulled her round so that she was looking straight at him, but even here he could see a light dancing in her eyes.

'Listen to me, listen,' he urged. 'What's your name? Where are you going? Talk to me. Please.'

She stopped, like a machine that had run down and was awaiting new instructions. She was a nurse, her uniform torn so that her bib hung down below her waist. There were bruise marks on her chin and neck. For an awful moment Mark thought she was actually dead and he was holding an animated corpse, but he forced himself to feel for a pulse – and found one. He grabbed her other wrist and shook her violently, but it had no effect. He let go and stepped away – and she set off again, as if programmed to do one thing and one thing only. He loped back down the lawn to the other two and reported.

Lambert frowned. 'How fast was her pulse?'

'What?'

'Her pulse. Fast or slow?'

'Slow, I suppose.' He counted it out in his mind. 'Slow. Less than once a second.'

'And she looked like she was hypnotized?'

Mark nodded as he watched a girl walk along the road, soon lost amid a crowd of other sad automatons.

'They're heading for the light,' said Karen.

'That's pretty obvious,' said Mark.

'No, it's not,' said Lambert. 'Nothing's obvious when you don't know what's happening.'

Karen stuck her tongue out at Mark. Lambert smiled up at her. He liked women with balls. He imagined she gave Mark a tough time normally – and he probably loved it. But enough psychoanalyzing, he thought, what were they to do?

More people came into view from houses opposite the hospital and from offices.

'They're alive,' Lambert began thinking out aloud. 'They survived the madness. Now they're all walking towards that light; a light that's dead centre of the dome. I think there's a connection, don't you?'

Mark let out a long sigh. 'So you want us to go to the light too?'

'Yes. You can always stay put if you want. Four hours should see the wall here. Choice is yours.'

Mark was annoyed. Lambert had assumed charge and was now ordering them about, dictating where they should go. True, he didn't have a plan of his own or any other suggestions and what the guy said made sense, not least because it gave them longer before the wall arrived, but all the same . . .

Karen squeezed his arm and pecked him on the cheek – Mother Hen even unto the end of the world, Mark thought, and loved her all the more for it – then she turned to Lambert.

'My husband never was much of a team player.'

'Neither was I,' confessed Lambert, then realized with dismay they were speaking of each other in the past tense. 'Let's go. I'll wheel myself if you want, Mark.'

The jolt as Mark began pushing the wheelchair was answer enough. Lambert knew that what they were doing was the only logical alternative but he was also aware that it was probably a waste of time. Roswiay and Warforn Peck had both disappeared without trace and there had been no evidence at their centres to suggest they'd actually had a centre. What he expected to find when they reached the source of the light he didn't know and, for all his brave claims to Horrigan of this thirst for knowledge, he would be quite prepared now to live in blissful ignorance of the causes and effects of the Blair catastrophe if it meant he could simply live.

Mark remembered as a child being taken by his father to football matches at Manchester United – a sport he had lost interest in after run-ins with rival supporters on two consecutive Saturdays in the late Seventies. He still had a scar from the bottle on the crown of his head. His lasting impressions from that time – rather than the terror from later years of dodging anyone wearing rival colours – were of a lot of noise and the smell of sweat and Bovril and a lot of pushing and shoving before, during and after the match. The sight he remembered most prior to any match had been the streams of people heading in one direction, oblivious of traffic or roads and pavements. Ten, twenty thousand people swarming towards a single destination. And here, now, in the very centre of Blair, it looked the same, but felt very different.

Whilst a trip to those early football matches was exciting – tense with expectation and noisy with rival supporters trying to out-shout and out-insult each other – here there was dead silence, broken only by the soft tread of feet on tarmac and the occasional crunch of glass or *ching* of metal as debris was disturbed. No birdsong, no machinery, no distant dog barks or car horns. Mark had seen

Blair at its busiest and noisiest over the past months, but even on a Saturday afternoon in December or on the sunniest day at the height of the tourist season, he had never seen the town centre so busy. The only saving grace was that so many people had survived the initial insanity, but even so, the streams of people in the many streets, the slowly moving crowd in the square outside the town hall, the steadily emptying houses, shops and offices, the thousands of grey souls all shuffling in the one direction like faithful penitents to a religious festival was unnerving. But it was the quiet that was the most unsettling: it was the January sales in silence; a victory party without voice; Christmas without celebration.

As they moved along with the crowds, Mark counted off the familiar stores in High Street, their multi-coloured logos and displays now plain and uninviting.

Woolworths, Boots, Eye Express, Co-op Travel, Bentalls, Fads, Granada TV Rental, Burger King. So many everyday names now so out of place, their customers gone never to return, their owners and operators derelict of duty or dead. Some had been looted, others bore signs of arson but the heavy rain must have kept the fires from spreading. Yet the streets thronged with people, a slow grey crowd bereft of argument, chatter and laughter. It reminded Mark of funerals for the famous where people would line the street to pay their last respects, heads bowed and conversations stilled. Here the heads too were low, the talk equally non-existent, but who was the funeral for? Themselves? Or the dead that littered their path?

Mark tugged on Karen's arm and steered Lambert into the shelter of an Argos doorway. All three watched as the dull tide slowly drifted by until Mark spoke up.

'How can so many have survived and Karen and I not have seen or met them?'

'I've been thinking about that,' said Lambert. 'Imagine you're at home, there's a noise in the street, you look out, someone's being beaten by a gang of yobs. What do you do?'

'I'd go to help.'

Karen laughed. 'You wouldn't – and I wouldn't let you. We'd call the police.'

'What if the phone was dead?' said Lambert.

'I'd have to—'

'No, you wouldn't!' insisted Karen.

'She'd stop you,' said Lambert. 'Quite right, too. Like it or not, getting your own head kicked in doesn't solve the problem. Now, imagine *hundreds* of people seeing hell outside their front doors, finding no one at the end of the phone, and seeing those who did go out being attacked themselves. You'd close the curtains and hide, weapon to hand, praying the screaming and the banging didn't come to your front door. And then, imagine that when daylight came, it wasn't daylight but this sick grey and, outside, dead bodies, chaos – and no power, no telephone, and no radio or TV to tell you what'd happened. Just like you said, you'd assume a nuclear attack, war, anything your fractured mind could imagine. And with families hiding together, hysterical kids, terrified wives . . . you'd *stay* in hiding. For how long? I don't know, but for all we do know the survivors could have been sitting there staring into space, waiting for the call. Hell of a thought, isn't it? Thousands of the poor bastards just sitting, mute, waiting . . .'

They looked out in silence at the passing crowd, every single member walking in the same direction.

'And I'll tell you something else,' said Lambert, pointing at a corpse in the gutter, a young woman dressed in a summer frock, her head a bloody pulp. 'You've got your dead, and there are these people, the "living" for want of a better word. But where are all the animals? The birds? Insects? It's summer, there should be bees and wasps and flies. Cats, dogs, pigeons, where are they?'

Karen shrugged. 'It's that old question: where do birds go to die? When was the last time you saw a dead bird that wasn't run over in the road?'

'It's more than that,' said Mark, reluctantly being drawn into the speculation. 'With all these dead bodies you'd expect it to be fly heaven. Some of these must have been here a day. Even dogs would be interested.'

'Must you?' said Karen.

'Lot of dogs fled before the dome came down,' said Lambert. 'Maybe the flies did too. Or maybe it's the temperature – it's not that warm. Add it to the list.'

'Long list,' said Mark.

'Speaking of fly heaven,' said Karen. 'Last year Elsa's daughter Faith – she's a friend of mine – came home from Sunday school in tears. It took us ages to pry her from her kitten. Seems the old fart of a priest had said that because animals have no souls they wouldn't go to heaven. And when she asked what he meant, he'd explained it to her: when her cat Jasper died, he wouldn't go to cat heaven, and he wouldn't be waiting for her in her heaven when she died either. Understanding man, Father O'Keefe.'

'Your point?' asked Mark.

'Work it out for yourself,' sighed Lambert. 'Then add it to the list too.'

It had taken them an hour to negotiate their way through the streets to where they were standing, and the source of the light was still obscured from them by other buildings. All they could see was a bright, wide shaft of light that reached up into the sky, lighting up windows on all sides and sparking the otherwise lifeless eyes of the people who stumbled about them oblivious to their presence. Every so often Mark or Karen had grabbed someone in an attempt to get their attention but they were enraptured by the light; like moths, their flight would brook no interruption. It had been these pedestrians, together with the corpses and vehicles, that had conspired to hamper their progress. Lambert kept apologizing for his wheelchair and Mark kept telling him to shut up.

'You realize there could be people here we know? From the agency, our neighbours?' said Karen.

Mark nodded. Of course he had thought about it. From the moment he had seen the crowds emptying from their hideaways he had prayed his friends had made it – whatever was wrong with these people he knew they were still alive and where there was life there was hope.

Suddenly Karen darted away from them and wormed her way through the crowd until she had grabbed a young woman, but as Karen's shoulders slumped, Mark could see that it wasn't whom she thought it was. Dejected, she made her way back, people moving out of her way as effectively as if she were some pop star with a troop of bodyguards. He hugged her to him when she regained the shelter of the doorway. She was trembling. As she buried her head in his shoulder she began apologizing for being so stupid but he told her to hush up. He'd lost count of how many times he thought he'd seen people he recognized, only to realize everyone looked the same. And what would he have done if, say, he *had* spotted Stan? Nothing, that's what; he'd just have stood there impotent as his friend idled in front of him, braindead, emotionless, aware only of the need to tramp on towards that damn light.

He recalled a favourite uncle from his childhood, Uncle Frank.

He'd had a stroke so severe he wasn't able to speak or walk and he spent two years being cared for by Mark's aunt until he succumbed to another stroke. Mark remembered as an innocent seven-year-old trying for hours to get Uncle Frank to talk to him and getting blank stares in return. It was an experience he didn't want to repeat with anyone else he had known before they had lost their lucidity. So he had inured himself to recognition – and Karen's bitter reaction was positive proof of their need for neutrality.

Karen pulled away, wiped her face, then began to fuss with Lambert's ankle. Although it had stopped bleeding, they all knew it would need serious attention soon, otherwise it might prove impossible to reattach his foot. However, as he reminded Karen, he was more concerned about remaining attached to his whole body than his foot. Nine hours wouldn't make much difference.

They moved on, and as they passed a Mothercare with a special offer on Pampers, Lambert made a joke.

'And here's me without my wallet.'

'Oh no, I forgot,' said Karen. 'Why didn't you say?'

Mark was puzzled.

'What Karen means, Mark, is that paraplegics are incontinent, and I am indeed, as we speak, sitting in my own poo.'

'I'll *have* to change you,' said Karen.

'You will not! Can you smell anything?'

'No,' said Karen, testing the air. 'Smells and tastes have gone, like the colour.'

'Unless you get up *real* close,' said Mark with a shiver, remembering his close encounter at the station with the pile of bodies.

'And I can't feel anything, so let's leave it,' insisted Lambert.

Mark stared askance at the man.

'For God's sake, we've all done it when we were kids. It doesn't bother me and it isn't bothering you.'

'Still . . .' mumbled Mark.

'Still what? OK, let's stop for a pit change, shall we? We've got plenty of time. Nine hours by my reckoning. What's a quarter of an hour to change my nappy?'

'Don't get so het up,' said Mark.

'Het up?' shouted Lambert. 'I'll give you het up! I came into this godforsaken place because I honestly thought it was better to see truth and die than wobble on pretending to live. Now I realize I was talking utter bollocks! Living is what counts and I want to live.

I presume you two do too – and so do all these poor bastards – and, like it or not, we're the only hope they have. Hell of a responsibility, I know, but there it is. And in case you haven't noticed, we haven't a fucking clue what we're doing so, for now, I'm quite happy to sit in my own shit if it gives us that extra few minutes to see what's what. OK?'

Mark nodded, suitably admonished and, he had to admit, more scared than he had ever been in his life. Because Lambert had said it straight out: everyone was going to die and the only people who could save them were a failed advertising creative director, a woman who earned a living drawing cuddly hedgehogs and a cripple with a death wish.

38

JAMIE'S ALARM CALL

Someone jostled Jamie, and pain splashed into the mire that was his mind, its impact rippling through his senses . . . and he turned to glare at them.

It was a black girl in her teens, short straight hair framing a blank face: the first person he had noticed in an age. Who was she? Where were they? He tried to speak to her, to warn her about his hand, but no words would come and he felt for his throat. Why couldn't he speak?

Why do you need a voice? All you need is the light, a voice in his head said. *Don't worry. Just follow the light. The light is all. Follow the light.*

Yes, said Jamie in his mind, *yes, the light. The light* is *all I need.* He turned back towards it but people blocked his view and all he could see was a bright aura above them all, and it wasn't enough.

He eased his way between two old men but his hand caught on one of their hips and his bandage snagged on something and ripped off the scab that was forming in his palm. He shrieked in pain and swore at the man, but it was still in his mind. He had to turn and bend down in order to pull his hand free. It had caught on the zipper of the man's trouser pocket. *Who has zips on their fucking pockets*? he could hear himself shouting, but the quiet of the crowd was u. disturbed by his voice. Carefully he unhooked the zip fastener, then adjusted the bandage so that it covered the weeping wound in his palm. The pain was unbelievable.

Forget the pain, the voice said.

Can't. Hurts.

Pain doesn't matter, not any more. No pain, no fear, no worry. Just the light, just the light.

The light? Jamie thought about the light; its beauty and brightness, the cleanest light he had ever seen, like the one given off by an angel he had seen in a book at school so long ago.

Yes, yes, encouraged the voice. *Now come to the light with the others and share in its wonder. Let it wash away all your fears and pains.*

Yes, agreed Jamie. The light *is* all that matters.

He turned to face it and even though he still couldn't see it he knew it was there and so did everyone around him. The light was all. And he was ready.

The crowd moved on, the ground rough. He knew they were near now. Underfoot was slippery mud and grass, trodden by hundreds of feet before him, with hundreds still to follow. The crowd was spreading out. Soon he would be able to see the light for himself and everything would be all right.

He moved to his left, a middle-aged woman in some kind of uniform blocking his path. He tried to squeeze between her and a man on crutches, but his foot caught on the man's plaster cast and all three of them fell over each other, the woman landing right on his hand. Their tumble had a cumulative effect and soon a dozen others were sprawled in the mud, but none of them seemed concerned, instead they picked themselves up and continued their journey towards the light. All, that is, except a twelve-year-old boy.

Jamie lay on the ground, all but unconscious with shock, his face ground into the mud, his right arm stretched out ahead of him, the hand palm up but pinned to the ground. As he struggled in the dimness between awake and away, his whole mind focused on the searing pain at the end of his arm. It felt as if a spike had been driven into it. Then, as he looked through tear-filled eyes, he saw to his horror that was exactly what had happened for, protruding from the open gash in his palm, was a woman's shoe, the four-inch heel embedded in his flesh. Looking up he could see the middle-aged woman hobbling away on one high heel, her other foot bare, already dirty from the mud. He couldn't believe what he saw. There was a woman's shoe *stuck* in his hand. The fat bitch had fucking *nailed* his hand to the ground!

Jamie screamed and, for a while, he couldn't hear it, only a quiet insistent voice telling him to hush and think of the light, and how it would heal his pain.

But it wasn't that kind of heal that was worrying him. The woman had ground her *heel* into his fucking *hand*! And then he heard his scream, like a train approaching from far away getting closer and closer until, finally, it roared from his mouth, shattering the silence. A long scream of pain and then, suddenly, he stopped it. He shifted himself forward, grabbed the shoe and pulled the heel out of his hand. It didn't increase the pain doing it, but that which remained was still unbelievable and so strong it shut up the voice in the head. He staggered to his feet, bumping into people all around him, then wove his way through the crowd until he could find space enough, and light enough, to see the damage.

It was a low broken wall and, scaling it, he found himself head and shoulders above the rest of the milling crowd – and saw the light for the first time in all its resplendent glory. He was immediately in awe of it. It was a tower block that had become a huge fat neon tube sprouting from the ground, its light hard and white and all the more beautiful for its power to disperse the grey that had overtaken the town. And there were streams of people two and three deep walking towards it from all directions, like animals to Noah's Ark, their heads raised and creased with beatific smiles as the light of hope bathed their faces, warmed their flesh and cheered their hearts.

Never could he have imagined how beautiful it was and how right the voice had been in its promises. He held up his tortured hand towards it, convinced it would heal him, but the ache in his hand wouldn't be denied and the longer he tried to bathe it in the light from the tower in front of him the more it hurt, and the more it hurt the more he saw that the light was just a light, a beacon to attract the many people about him. He lowered his hand, new pain rushing the length of his arm and causing him to gasp. Dragging his eyes down to his hand he saw black blood dripping onto the wall. Blood. *His* blood. And his pain.

Come to the light and all will be better, urged the voice. *Come to the light.*

Fuck you! Jamie's mind screamed, and the small voice was silenced. Yes. Now I know, now I really see. He pushed his index finger into the hole in his hand, felt the electric shock of agony jab at his hand and reverberate in his mind like a ball bouncing about a pin table. Yes, I can feel it, you fucker, and

I know who you are! I know what you want, you fat fucker! *I know you*!

He looked back at the light. It was only a light, just like a hypnotist's watch is only a watch. He had nearly succumbed but now he knew who was behind it and what it meant. You fat fucking bastard! *You* made me crash those trains, *you* made me a killer, and now *you're* trying to kill all these people. He spat at the light, uncaring that his phlegm carried only as far as a man walking in front of him. He even recognized the block where the light came from now. It was where that fat cunt had touched him, had given him money and the idea for getting back at his brother. That fat fucker had turned him into a killer and now he was going to pay. But how? He looked about him.

Thousands of mindless zombies were arriving to line up in queues to enter the tower. But what for? He didn't know but he knew it was wrong. He thought back to the friends he had deserted, Mark and his wife. He wondered where they were, if they had escaped or if they too had, literally, seen the light, and were here, lost among the lost. He knew he couldn't help anyone else but those two he might. He had to find them, to warn them.

He looked about him, an island of sanity in a sea of grey morons content to listen to the voice in their head bidding them to embrace their doom. He would be about as much use to them as a match in a fogbank. He didn't even know which direction to walk. He began crying again, this time not with pain but with frustration. He couldn't do *anything*.

39

MARK, KAREN AND LAMBERT SEE THE LIGHT

Jubilee Road was a narrow street jammed with an ashen tide of people, their dull march pulling Mark, Karen and Lambert with them. If they harboured thoughts of leaving the crowd, they knew they no longer had a choice. Like a river at full tide coursing through a narrow strait, they had no alternative but to let the flow take them. There was no urgency, just a relentless momentum designed to bring one and all to the light.

On one side of the road rose the metal fencing surrounding Chanters Mill, on the right the long terrace of workers' cottages, the two producing a passage twenty-five feet across and almost a hundred yards long leading to the Catchmount Estate which they could see was the source of the blinding light, but which was still shielded from full view by the school building at the top end of the road. Letting the crowd carry them, they slowly approached the end of the road, aware that they would soon see for themselves the attractant for all the hapless souls about them.

Ahead Mark and Karen saw the crowd spreading out into an open area that used to be a grass field but was now clearly a waiting area for the inhabitants of the town. And then, blinding them with its brilliance, they saw the light. It was stunning and, for a few astonished moments, the three of them stopped in their tracks and stared, the spreading crowd working its way around them.

The housing estate had been made up of rows of maisonettes surrounding a large open area with four twelve-storey tower blocks at one end, the nearest of which had been transformed into a tower of light. Its basic shape was still there – one hundred and twenty feet high by fifty feet square – but its windows and balconies had disappeared. All that was left was a rectangular block of blinding white light, so harsh it would surely have blinded them had they looked at it long enough. It would have been easy to believe the greyness that had embraced the town had been caused by this monstrous light sucking all colour out of its immediate vicinity. The way the perfect white shape stood out against the grey with such unnatural geometry reminded Lambert of the equally abhorrent nature of the black semi-circle of the dome squatting in a green Pennine valley. That purity of line and form – even if both were impure in purpose – confirmed his opinion that the two were inextricably linked and they were indeed staring at the engine that drove the collapse of the dome. But if this was the engine, what was its fuel? The answer, unfortunately, seemed to be standing around them.

'What is it? What's powering it?' said Mark.

'They are,' said Karen, covering her eyes with her hands and trying to blink away the rectangular flares imprinted on her retinas.

'They?' said Mark.

'The people. They're all going into it. They must be what's driving it.'

'Rubbish,' said Mark.

'Not rubbish,' said Lambert, turning his wheelchair away so he didn't have the light in his eyes. Even so, he could feel it on his back; not so much heat, more a physical presence, as if something was pressing against his skin. 'It seems very logical. Did you see the people going into it at the bottom? Something is causing all this and here we are, standing in front of a great light that's drawing in every survivor. But if that block is the same size as those next to it, there's no way this many people can get into it.'

'Meaning?' said Mark, his head starting to throb.

Lambert took a deep breath. 'Meaning it's *consuming* them. They're all being drawn here like zombies; there must be a reason. That thing wants them. Why, I don't know, but I bet you don't see anyone coming out. And remember, when this happened before, nobody survived and there were no bodies.'

'Oh God,' said Mark. In front of him he could see perhaps five thousand people in queues three and four deep snaking in all directions to the tower, all aiming to enter it at its base.

'We've got to do something,' said Karen, grasping Mark's shoulder hard enough to make him wince.

'Can't argue with that, love,' said Lambert. 'But just what do you suggest?'

40

IZOTTA SEES THE LIGHT

Izotta looked down at the pit beneath her and saw, as Mr Farmer had said, the people walking to it. But even as she took comfort from seeing so many survivors, she saw them then for what they truly were.

Fuel.

There were streams of walkers, all stumbling forward as if sleepwalking, their eyes fixed on the light ahead bathing their features with an iridescent glow that bleached out clothing colours, facial expressions, skin tones, individuality. As they reached the pit each would pause, look down, then amble over the edge. At that last moment some saw the truth of their fate and their screams would tumble into the abyss with them. She followed one line of victims back from the tower and saw it disappear behind another block of flats. There were eight queues, all shuffling towards the light, their translucent blank faces showing that they believed they were to be redeemed. The bliss of ignorance. *Thousands* of people, all those left alive in Blair after the chaos. So many were there she wondered if there might even be outsiders but she had no way of telling.

'We've got to stop them!' her mind suddenly raged, a last welling of spirit. 'Got to save them!'

'No, we haven't. Mustn't,' said Mr Farmer. 'They belong to us now. They are our food. Stop fighting the inevitable, Izotta. Enjoy the spectacle, feel the energy, anticipate the future – for that is what we are, the future. They are merely the here and now – and that will not last long. But for us . . .'

Their hybrid existence may have been rapidly voiding itself of emotion, but even in her numbed state Izotta could still recognize greed, perhaps even lust – but then again, if she wasn't sure what that fiery emotion felt like, she truly was lost.

Mr Farmer spoke again. 'Izotta, let me tell you about us. There have been many of us through history, though we rarely meet. Our paths never seem to cross; some instinct keeps us apart. Though we are aware of one another and our special talents, we remain solitary creatures, each with our own territory. Some of our fathers were of the same breed but there are those amongst us, myself included, who develop our skills spontaneously, our talent seemingly appearing from nowhere but plainly the result of some race memory. As a result, many of us are failures, unable to fathom our abilities and we idle along, angry, often unstable and psychotic. Some of us even fail to cope on this level; the result of this is almost always death by decapitation, a gunshot to the temple, a head-first dive from a high point . . . it's as if we cannot trust our minds to cease their work unless they are physically destroyed. I know this because I have weathered my own crisis and I am grateful for the renewed clarity surviving the urge for self-destruction has brought. Overcome the need to obliterate your existence and you are able to exploit it in others. Some are far more successful and cunning, using their ability to gain positions of power where they can disseminate disaster under the auspices of leadership. How many dictators have been of our breed I do not know, but there must have been many. That vital spark that drives a man to be so ruthless that he stops at nothing to secure power; who is to say he is not one of us, or that there are those of us who have the trust of such men, who literally have their ear, and so are able to help design their cruel policies? But I have no such ambitions. In my own small way I have helped destroy many a life through the years, and I have remained here in Blair, biding my time, because I felt I was special. I'll never match some of those who lived in Germany or Russia or who live now in the Middle East, sowing their seeds so spectacularly, but I knew there was more to all this than simple destruction. Starting wars, murdering innocent people, spreading terror is all well and good but, as you have seen, here in Blair something altogether different is happening. Something new. It has occurred before, on four occasions to my knowledge, twice in Britain, once in France and once in Mexico, but not on this magnificent scale. These thousands, half the town, remained

immune, because they were clean and decent enough that even if
there were stirrings of lust or discontent their love of family or fear
for their own safety or the need to protect those about them overrode
their deeper desires. And now the end is in sight; the evil ones have
expended themselves, wrecking all they could until overtaken by
the need for self-destruction, leaving innocent survivors, their pure
souls and empty minds like infants waiting a lead. Now we are to
provide that lead, a guiding light. All these hapless innocents are
to be ours and as we consume them so shall we grow until . . .'

'No! Not we. *You* . . .' But her spirit was a like a spark in a
hurricane, doomed to be snuffed out.

'Can't you feel it, racing through you like liquid silk, shining
and smooth, reaming out your very essence, letting loose your
earthly shackles and helping you to take flight? Opening up regions
of thought and sight you thought closed and beyond
imagining? Nothing you have ever experienced is as exhilarating
as this, is it? And it can only get better.'

'Why? What is going to happen?'

'*I don't know!* That is part of the joy. The anticipation. Give up
your notions of good, stop making excuses; be what you want to
be, what you really *are*. Be like me. *Like us*. Our union wasn't
planned, but now you can share in the wonder that is us. Together
we will experience pleasures so pure and infinite it will make
your crude orgasms seem as the touch of a single grain of sand
in a desert. At last all are gathered. There are dissenters, those
who have not entirely surrendered because they were asleep or
unconscious at the moment when our terror consumed the town.
There is even an outsider – an invader with some knowledge of
what has happened – but he has no power, nor do the others. They
are of no importance, not with these thousands poised to sacrifice
themselves. So let it start.

'Let the end begin.'

41

THE TOWER

'Mark, climb up on the wheelchair,' said Lambert, frustrated by his waist-height view. 'See if you can see anything that might help us.'

Mark didn't understand. Karen pushed him towards Lambert.

'All we can see is people,' she said. 'Higher up you might spot something else.'

Feeling foolish, Mark lifted his good leg onto the arm of the wheelchair and, letting Karen and Lambert hold his thighs and bottom, they heaved him up until he was balanced on the wheelchair arms, a good two feet above the tallest member of the crowd.

Shielding his eyes against the laser-intense light from the tower a hundred yards in front of them, he slowly scanned the crowd surrounding them in all directions. It was like being in the middle of a pitch invasion after a major soccer victory where the number of fans so swamps the players that the footballers can no longer be seen. He, Karen and Lambert were, of course, the team. He couldn't see anything untoward, just hundreds of zombified townsfolk, all facing the light, their eyes apparently immune from the whiteness. And still they came from all directions until they pooled in the open area around the base of the tower.

He braved a glance at the tower but could only stand the glare for a second, but even that photoflash image showed him that the base of the tower, the walls and doors, had disappeared and people were just walking straight into it. But how could they all fit? It still held the dimensions of the tower blocks around it.

He turned back to look up Jubilee Street. It was jammed with people, but he could see at the road's top end that the crowd was thinning, and that could only mean one thing: nearly everyone was here. No wonder the grey wall was moving faster if the people were powering it.

'How long before it gets here?' asked Lambert.

Mark shrugged. 'Well, it should have been another five hours but judging by the fact that it's already eaten that church spire we passed it looks to be speeding up. Could be two hours, maybe less.'

'But that's not fair,' said Karen. 'It could at least keep up a steady pace!'

Mark and Lambert looked at her and she suddenly burst out laughing and apologized. Mark swung round to look eastwards.

The grey was everywhere; buildings he had recognized only minutes before were now dissolved by its relentless advance. It was like being in a huge photographic studio with grey backdrops on all sides concealing the bare walls behind.

'There's one consolation,' he said.

'What?' said Karen.

'We won't have to get the central heating fixed now.'

Karen followed his gaze and realized their flat must have been overtaken by the grey, but it didn't bother her. Perhaps it was because she had never developed any affection or sense of belonging for the place; or, more likely, it simply didn't count in the scale of things any more.

Mark listened for any sound, for words or screams, but the world was silent. Just a sea of grey people washing around their little island of sanity as they headed for—

Suddenly there was a shout. *A shout?*

'What was that?' said Lambert, tugging on Mark's leg hard enough to make him wobble. The sound seemed so alien it couldn't be true.

Mark managed to prevent himself falling and saved his curse in case the voice came—

'*Mark!*' the voice shouted.

Jesus . . . He turned round, mute faces at his feet in every direction, but then, fifty yards to his left, his head only just above the crowd, he saw a boy waving.

'Jamie!' he shouted.

'It's you!' shouted the boy, waving his bloody hand, the pain irrelevant now that he had seen an aware human being.

'Stay there!' shouted Mark. He realized the boy would get lost if he tried to cross the crowd.

Mark edged himself down, the pain in his knee like a hot knife prising off his knee cap, but his discovery was more than compensation. 'It's Jamie! The boy! He must have . . . well, I don't know but we're going to find out.'

He grabbed the wheelchair handles and began pushing Lambert through the crowd, uncaring of whom they bumped into, but as no one objected, or even reacted, what did it matter? All that mattered was that, in a world of cold dead faces, he had seen a young friend's grin.

A minute of bustling and they had reached him. The boy was standing on a three-feet-high wall, his face sheened by tears of joy.

Jamie held out his arms, his fingers curling and uncurling, desperate for a hug, but the knowledge that he had caused the crash that had hospitalized Karen stopped him from closing the gap to them.

To his surprise – and evident delight – Karen walked straight up to him, grabbed him by the waist and hugged him to her, letting the boy blub his relief and apologies into her neck, his arms tighter round her than they had been round his mother in many a year.

Both Mark and Lambert were touched by the boy's distress and Karen's forgiveness. In the midst of a field bereft of a single spark of emotion, the two of them gave off a glow of humanity enough to warm the coldest of hearts – except no one here seemed to have been left a heart by the evil that was sucking their town dry.

'How's your hand?' said Karen.

Jamie held it out. 'It's OK.'

It wasn't, and Karen immediately grabbed the first-aid bag from the back of the wheelchair and began to fuss over the boy's wound. As she doused it in sterilizing solution and dabbed away the dirt, the boy winced an explanation.

'I'm sorry I ran out on you. It was the light. It spoke to me. I could hear it, promising me so much . . . It was great. Amazing. Like Christmas times a hundred. Promising me mum and dad and Wayne like they used to be . . . but it was all lies. He just wanted me for himself.'

'He?' said Lambert. 'For himself?'

Jamie was puzzled by the questions. He'd never wondered about the sex of the voice. It was a bit like the way he thought of God; even though no one had ever seen Him, everyone just accepted that He was a man.

'Yes,' he nodded, gritting his teeth against the stinging in his hand. 'The voice who spoke to me was a man.'

'Did you know his voice? Was it young or old?'

Jamie considered this. 'It wasn't that old, but it was a man. I think I'd heard it somewhere before. He'd spoken to me before.' His mind was fuzzy, the pain distracting.

Lambert wheeled himself up to the boy. Their eyes were almost on a level with each other. 'Jamie, my name's Wesley Lambert. I'm a sort of scientist. I was stupid enough to come into town from outside. I'm not going to lie to you because I think you know how bad things are.' He waved an arm around his head. 'All that grey is actually a wall that goes all the way around town and it's getting closer and soon it's going to meet, over there at that light. What happens then I don't know but if you think you heard his voice somewhere else it might just help us.'

Jamie's response to Lambert's honesty was typical for a twelve-year-old boy – and refreshing for that very reason: 'Why are you in a wheelchair?'

''Cos I'm a lazy bugger! Conned these two into pushing me around all the time.'

Jamie smiled. 'I did hear his voice before but I can't . . .'

'Recently?' said Mark. 'After all this started or before?'

Jamie concentrated. He had stopped listening to the voice because he knew he couldn't trust him, but why? Because he had shown he couldn't be trusted before . . .

'The train crash!' he blurted out. 'He told me to do it.'

Karen knelt down and gripped his forearms. 'The voice that brought you here also told you to cause the train crash?'

Jamie thought about it. 'Yes. Well, no, not exactly. I met this man, fat man, and he talked to me and gave me some money for food. But he . . . he touched me . . .'

'What? Where?' she asked.

Jamie stared at her. 'No, not like *that*. Up here.' He tapped her forehead. 'He got in there and told me to crash Wayne's crane at the junkyard. He moves the cars around with it. I sneaked in, started it up and crashed it through a fence, just like he told me to. *Made* me do. But then I sort of woke up and saw the trains . . . your train crash . . . and the screams and the bangs . . . and then the people. Wayne blaming me . . . but it wasn't me it was the man, that fat man. He made me do it.' He dissolved into tears again and Karen hugged her to him.

Lambert prised them apart and turned Jamie's streaked face to look at him.

'Where did you meet the fat man? Where did you talk to him?' Lambert had guessed at the answer, but Jamie's shaking finger pointing sideways to the blinding tower of light confirmed it.

'He lived in there, when it was a proper block. Cyprus House, I think it was. The fat man lived there.'

He looked along his finger at the light, then shied away blinking. 'It's him, isn't it? He's doing it?'

Lambert sat back and rubbed his face. 'Yes, I would think so.'

'A fat man is doing *this*?' asked Mark.

'Someone or something is benefiting from all this. If Jamie says the voice he heard was the fat man who made him cause the train crash, I for one am prepared to believe the one in charge of all this is the same fat man who used to live in that block of flats.'

'But a man? All *this*?' said Karen, her eyes dancing from blank faces to slumped shoulders to the shuffling feet that threatened to crush them.

'You know I told you this had happened a couple of times before? One thing that had never fitted in was part of the story told by the boy Euan who escaped from Roswiay. He said it was his fault. It was dismissed at the time – and by me – as the natural reaction of a lad running away from his family and finding out they had died: the guilt of survival. But he told the doctor who found him that *he* had wished it on the town, saying he hated everyone because they all spoke to him when he didn't want them to. Told him all their secrets, let them into their bedrooms and showed them what they did. It was that phrase "spoke to him when he didn't want them to" that always struck me.'

'Maybe there were some weirdoes in his town who let him in on . . .'

'No, he said *everyone* spoke to him. He was quite specific about that. He claimed he could actually hear what they were thinking and what they really wanted to do and that when they knew he knew, they did it. Again the doctor who treated him dismissed it as a paranoid delusion, but what if it wasn't? What if he really could read their minds and listen to their thoughts? Take Jamie's fat man: if the boy's telling the truth, the man told him what to do. Now, what if it was Euan who told them what to do but didn't realize he was doing it? What if their delusions were actually his? What if he started the destruction of Roswiay? And what if Jamie's fat man is doing the same?'

'It's a bit far-fetched. That one man could . . .' Karen looked at the people around her and the grey that covered them and realized that nothing was far-fetched any more.

Mark spoke up. 'Even if it is true, what good is it to us? Best I can tell, that block of flats isn't a block of flats any more. We can't even look at it.'

'We need some sunglasses,' said Lambert.

'No problem,' said Jamie. 'There's a chemist's over there in the precinct. They've got loads of sunglasses.'

The boy had run off before they could stop him.

'Be careful,' shouted Karen, shocked by how loud her voice was in the midst of a crowd.

'It might help,' said Mark.

Jamie weaved his way through the crowd without much trouble. He was thin and wiry and the crowd, though dense, wasn't packed too closely away from the tower – and although he couldn't see which way he was going, the light was to his back and the precinct was in a direct line from it.

He reached Allum's Pharmacy and found the door off its hinges, the windows smashed, the inside of the small shop wrecked. There were also some bodies, but they might as well have been cardboard cut-outs for all the heed he paid them. He had become immune to the death about him and was now concentrating solely on whatever it took for him and his friends to survive. He did wonder how the man in the wheelchair could have gotten into Blair while they couldn't get out, but for once he was willing to trust the judgement of adults – and it came as a relief.

He found the sunglasses stand on its side by the remains of the baby food shelves and, grabbing a floral plastic bag from the floor, he shovelled as many spectacles as he could into it. He wondered if there was anything else he could liberate but time was of the essence and his anxiety wouldn't let him think clearly. He had what he had come for, now he had to go back.

He spotted the others stood on the wall and he made a beeline for them, grateful that the crowd around him blotted out the bright light. What such a short time ago had been his friend now seemed such a hard taskmaster. He only hoped they would have a way out of this mess. After all, the guy in the wheelchair was a scientist; if anyone should have an answer it would be him, surely?

Lambert continued to drum his fingers. He didn't know what to do. 'How far is the grey wall now?' he asked.

'Difficult to say,' said Karen.

'Can you get me up on the wall so I can see for myself?'

Two minutes of sweating struggles later and Karen and Mark were propping Lambert up by his shoulders as he looked around the town.

'Not long,' he said finally. 'I think I saw the bloody thing moving over there along a terrace. It's definitely accelerating. And there aren't many more people to come.'

All three looked about them; no one paid them any heed.

'How many people here, do you reckon?' said Karen.

'If it's the same on all sides of the tower,' said Lambert, 'perhaps ten thousand.'

'Which means . . .' said Mark.

'Three-quarters of the town is already dead. And this lot haven't much longer.' He tried to look back at the tower but it was like having needles stuck into his eyes and he had to look away. 'OK, sit me down.'

They gently lowered him to the top of the wall and he sat down, his legs dangling over the edge like those of a badly made Guy Fawkes dummy.

Another minute passed, then Jamie returned, his carrier bag held aloft, his face beaming in triumph.

'Sunglasses! Got all I could!'

He held open the bag and three hands delved inside and pulled out a motley collection of sunglasses in a variety of styles – everything from aviator Reactolite Rapides and trendy Polaroids to Mickey Mouse frames, Dame Edna Everage-style ornately framed women's spectacles and single-piece ski jobs.

Lambert slipped on a pair and tried to stare at the tower. He might as well have been staring at the sun. Seeing him wincing, Mark handed him a couple more.

'Try several at once,' he said, doing the same himself.

Mark was the first to be able to view the tower. He had four pairs on, the combined tints of the lenses sufficient to render him blind when looking at his companions but, looking at the tower, the brightest day was revealed. He could see the skeletal structure of the tower rising before them, the glow brightest midway up and at its very base. Around it people were walking in orderly lines, the colour of their flesh and clothing suddenly brought back to life at the moment they vanished into the light.

Karen used a roll of sticking plaster from their improvised first-aid kit to hold together the disparate arms of the three or four sunglasses each of them had to wear in order to view the tower. Soon they were all able to see for themselves the same scene, but it did nothing to help them to a solution: all they had now was a better view of doomsday.

'I hate to say it, folks,' said Lambert, pointing at the light. 'But the safest place is at the centre, and that's the centre. We've got to get nearer the middle.'

Jamie shook his head. 'Can I just stay here? I don't want to . . .'

'Sorry, kid,' said Lambert. 'It's all for one and one for all. We have to stick together, whatever happens.'

Jamie looked at the people who surrounded them and gave a vague nod. Whatever might happen, he would rather be with people who talked and laughed and hugged than with the dead robots traipsing past them.

After they got Lambert down off the wall, Karen and Jamie took one handle each of Lambert's wheelchair as Mark led the way towards the light.

Izotta could feel the presence of strangers, and Mr Farmer's irritation at their existence, but she couldn't see what harm they could do. Like a hair in a glass of milk they were plainly alien, but of little threat. But Mr Farmer's agitation rippled through her, helping to rekindle her independence. Perhaps there was hope after all . . . Her vision suddenly tinted a vivid lilac.

'No hope!' screamed Mr Farmer, suddenly aware of possible mutiny. 'There is too little time for them to do *anything*. The pain they will endure as they see the truth unfold will simply be the garnish on our repast. Fret not, Izotta, they will not spoil our fun.'

But she could still sense his annoyance – and why would

he be annoyed if there wasn't a possibility that things might
go awry?

Mr Farmer turned his focus on Izotta.

'Loyalty is vital in any relationship. Much as it would pain me
to dispense with you, believe me when I say you are not vital to
the success of this event. I am keen to share the rewards of our
venture, but I do not need you. Continue to hope for failure and
I shall consign you to the pit with the rest and there you will find
torture beyond imagining.'

Cowed, Izotta signaled her compliance and slowly the purple
lifted.

They had covered about half the distance to the base of the tower
and had found that the intensity of the light remained constant,
four lenses sufficient to save their sight. Around them the people
were more tightly packed as they – what? Waited? Yes, they were
waiting, *queueing* to . . . to what?

Jamie was sitting on top of Mark's shoulders but he could see
nothing beyond people crowding to get into the base of the tower.
Its entire ground floor had disappeared and the tower seemed to float
in mid-air. People entered abreast on all four sides and disappeared
through a curtain of light. But what was on the other side?

Lambert called a halt and asked Jamie to see how far away the
grey wall was. Jamie told them what he saw. They were shocked
to realize it had covered half the length of Jubilee Street and was
barely three hundred yards away.

'How high is the sky?' asked Mark.

Looking up, Jamie found he couldn't judge the distance but
Lambert did the calculation for him.

'The top of the dome is half the radius. Like a football sinking
into water. It must be about five hundred feet at the top.'

Mark felt a pain in his chest and had to lower Jamie to the ground.
He thought he was having a heart attack but knew that was nonsense.
A panic attack was all it was; it would pass, but how could he stop
the pounding of his heart or the hot pain in his bowels. Death was
close enough to touch and then . . .

Lambert tugged his hand. He knew how the man felt and took
bitter comfort in the fact that he wasn't alone in his terror. In the
past he had always found pressure exhilarating; adrenalin helped
him to come to solutions that otherwise he might have fumbled with

for ages. But there he had elements to play with – facts to mould and form – while here he just had the inevitable. He remembered Horrigan's comment from so, so long ago about knowing the make of the truck that runs you over not making any difference. As ever, the bearded sod was right on the nail. He only wished he could be outside to hear him say 'I told you so'.

Suddenly there was a cry, thin and reedy and somehow odd. Then another, then two more, then a succession of heavy thuds.

'What is it? What is it?' he asked, his view restricted by shoulders and chests.

'Paratroopers!' whooped Mark. 'There's bloody paratroo . . . Oh God, no.'

'What? What?'

'Their parachutes aren't opening. Too low to work. They're just falling . . . oh God.'

He and Karen and Jamie watched in horror as ten men fell out of the grey above them, each desperately tugging at the parachute ripcords on their chests, their legs kicking, their cries of terror as sharp in the stillness as smashing glass at dawn. In each case the pack barely had time to open before they disappeared into the crowd at full velocity. And then, just as suddenly as the men had appeared they were gone, the sky grey and empty.

Karen started to shake, the horror of the men's deaths starting to overwhelm her. Lambert grabbed her hand and squeezed. 'You'll have to check if any of them survived.'

'Survived?' said Mark. 'Are you kidding?'

'It's possible. If they landed on the crowd, it could have helped cushion their fall.'

Mark wanted to protest but he knew Lambert was right. How many times had he read stories of people surviving falls from aeroplanes only to have their descent safely checked by snow or trees or soft ground?

'Jamie, you stay here with Wes. That way, if you stand on his wheelchair we can find you again. Karen, we'll try to find these poor bastards. Bring the medical stuff.'

Karen slipped the bag off the wheelchair and followed him through the unconcerned crowd. Not a single face had turned to look at the men who had fallen amongst them, not one step had faltered.

Lambert shouted after them: 'Be as quick as you can.'

Mark didn't bother to reply.

Progress was slow, the crowd was tightly packed and soon Mark's frustration gave way to action as he started to shoulder people aside, and elbow others in the stomach. As ever, no one minded.

After a couple of minutes they found their first paratrooper. He had landed on three people and all four were prone on the ground, the crowd streaming round them. All four were dead. They soon found a couple more soldiers, the scene the same, broken bodies stopped in their tracks by the crushing impact of a couple of hundred pounds of man and equipment landing at over a hundred miles an hour.

Scouting around they found another three, two of whom had landed on each other like a precision freefall team. In most cases, legs were bent at odd angles, necks twisted, eyes open, blood leaking from mouths. Not surprisingly, terror creased their faces, though not those of their victims.

'Look, the poor fuckers are dead,' said Mark, fighting back tears. 'All of them. Let's get back to Lambert.'

Karen agreed. It wasn't the injuries that were making her feel squeamish but the irrefutable evidence of the fragility of the human body and, as she looked up, the imminence of their own death as the grey sky fell in on them.

Mark stood up from the seventh dead paratrooper – a blond six-footer no more then twenty-five years of age, his strapping frame twisted like broken scaffolding.

'Lambert, they're all dead. We're coming back!'

'OK.'

Their voices were shockingly loud in the silence and Mark chose not to shout again. He looked toward the tower and, squinting against the glare through his sunglasses, saw Jamie waving. Pushing Karen in front of him he made for the boy, but then there was a cry, like a dog yelping in pain. Mark stopped and looked around. Blank faces, bright in the light from the tower, swarmed by them, ignorant of his presence.

'Did you hear—'

It came again, somewhere to their right.

Mark grabbed Karen's hand and pulled her through the crowd, its members like a never-ending succession of closing doors that had to be pushed open if they were to make any progress. They heard the sound again and, homing in on it, found a black paratrooper lying cruciform over several dead Blairians.

Mark knelt down to him and pushed the sunglasses up onto the top of his head. The man's startled eyes showed pain and puzzlement in equal proportions.

'Legs,' he said, a small trickle of blood running down his chin. 'Legs, can't feel them.'

'OK, OK, I'll check,' said Mark.

One was splayed straight out and Mark pushed at the foot. There was no response from the man. His other leg was bent underneath him and Mark could see it was badly broken – and if he couldn't feel that then his back must be broken.

'Legs look all right, mate,' he said. 'Must be shock. Knocked the wind out of your sails.'

'Say that again,' he said, his face showing the struggle to concentrate. 'What happened?'

'Long story. Why are you here?'

'Dome. Everyone scared about it. They decided to send us in. Dropped in four squads.'

'Four. And you're just one squad.'

'Yes. Why, aren't they here?'

'Haven't seen them.' Mark didn't dare contemplate where they might be if they had parachuted into the grey outside the area they were in.

'What about me mates?'

'Some might have made it but . . . same as you, parachutes didn't open.'

The man didn't react to the news. Too much to take in.

'Any troops on the ground?' Mark didn't want to know but he had to ask.

'Yes. Couple of hundred, spread round the perimeter. Any of them turned up?'

Karen tried to keep her voice steady. 'No, not yet. Give them time.'

'Time's what we haven't got.'

'What do you mean?'

'There's a light coming out the top of the dome. Afraid it's a bomb or something. Sent us in to neutralize it.'

Mark fought back bitter laughter. '"Neutralize it?"' He looked back at the tower. Neutralize that? How?

'A light?' said Karen, lifting the man's head and easing off his helmet, its strap snapped by the impact.

'Out of the top. They don't know what it is. Sent us in.'

'What height did you jump from?' asked Karen.

The soldier tried to shift his head to look at her but he couldn't. Instead his eyes swivelled to look up into her face. She gave him her best motherly smile.

'Jumped at five thousand, opened chutes at a thousand but as soon as we hit the dome at two and half thousand feet we were here, in a second. Must have blacked out.'

Poor bastards. 'What were you going to do?'

The soldier fumbled his hand around until it alighted on a black strap over his camouflage jacket. 'Anything we could. Shoot it. Dismantle it. Explosives.'

Explosives? Maybe that would help.

'Have you got them?'

'What?' the man's eyes suddenly went out of focus and he started to blink rapidly.

'Hey, soldier, hey, come on, don't give up.'

The man struggled to stare at Mark and, for a while, he regained his control, but then he started to cough, blood dribbling from his mouth. Mark realized for the first time that he could actually see the colour red because of the illumination provided by the tower.

'What were they going to do if you didn't . . . succeed?'

'Time limit. Twelve hours. After that they were going to try shooting.'

'Shooting what? Missiles? Are they mad?'

'No. Desperate. Happened before. Never this big. Never a light. Like a laser shooting up. Keeps growing. Weird. Weird . . .' He dissolved into another coughing fit.

Karen leaned over to Mark's ear. 'He's dying. Let him be.'

Mark was going to protest but what help could the man be to him now?

There was a shout from Lambert, muffled by the people in between them but clear enough. Mark stood up, spotted Jamie perched on the wheelchair and waved but as he didn't know what to say he stayed silent.

When he looked back down, Karen was kneeling by the man's head. She was stroking his forehead with the beret she had slipped from his shoulder epaulet as the man jerked and coughed blood in tiny fountains into the air and over his face. His big hand held Karen's in a crushing grip but she hid the pain. And then he died, right there before their eyes. A perfectly healthy, fantastically fit giant of a man just coughed his life away and expired on Mark's wife's lap. Karen gently slid his head down her lap and laid it to rest against the bosom of a middle-aged woman he had killed when he had crash landed.

Mark helped Karen to her feet, but the man's hand still gripped her. Mark eased his fingers between the man's and, one by one, uncurled them from her hand. As he was about to let the hand fall, he noticed the man's watch. It was a complicated timepiece with lots of dials and, as expected, it had stopped, but it also had a day and date facility.

'What day is it?' asked Mark.

'God knows . . . it was Wednesday yesterday, wasn't it? Yes. So this is sometime on Thursday, not that it matters.'

'Thursday the eighteenth?'

'Yes.'

'So why does his watch say Sunday the twenty-first?'

Karen stared at the watch. She didn't bother to say it had been damaged in the fall. Instead she retraced their steps to the group of three paratroopers and checked their watches. Two of them confirmed the date, the third didn't have a calendar. She came back.

'We've been in all this for a day but four days have gone past outside. No wonder they're keen to send people in. Let's get back.'

Lambert took their news surprisingly calmly.

'Interesting? Is that all you can say?' shouted Karen.

'Calm down,' said Mark.

'Calm down? Look at us. This. *That*! What's the point of calming down? Even the poor bastards they sent in die.'

'Present company excluded,' said Lambert.

'Oh, very funny,' said Karen.

'Love, will you calm—'

Karen shoved her husband aside and leaned down into Lambert's face. 'You're the expert, so start expertising a way out for us.'

'I have.'

Wind taken out of her sails, Karen visibly deflated and stepped back.

'You have?' said Mark.

'Yes. And no.'

Karen bristled, but Lambert held up his hand.

'We've got about an hour before the top of the dome reaches the top of the tower. Your paratrooper said the light was visible outside. That's not happened before, which leads me to believe it's the sheer size of this event that makes it so dangerous. It's not just a matter of a town as big as Blair disappearing compared to villages like Roswiay or Warforn Peck. Or that we will die – a fact I'm as reluctant as you to accept – but that the light is escaping. If we continue the analogy that the light is the engine and these people the fuel that drives it, then if the light is breaking out of the dome like a chick hatching from an egg, what is going to happen once the light is visible outside? If what attracts these . . . these *zombies* is the light, what happens if that light is visible for hundreds of miles? What if it could be seen in Manchester and Sheffield and Derby and Stoke and Leeds? Would the same thing happen? Would the dome get bigger still? A dome the size of the north of England? The UK? What would stop it?'

No one spoke. Even Jamie appreciated what the man was saying. He was standing behind the wheelchair, his hands gripping tight on the handles, his heart racing. Although his greatest terror was reserved for himself and the idea that he might be dead in less time than it took to watch *Gladiators*, he could also appreciate the scale of the horror Lambert was describing. He remembered again his holiday in Blackpool – probably the best week of his entire life when all his family were happy and they had money to spend – and the night on the South Pier when they all watched the laser spinning on top of the Tower. He remembered the hundreds of people staring up at the same fantastic display, each transfixed by the thin green lights coursing out over the Irish Sea. It wasn't a big step to imagine that same enthralled crowd staring at this tower shining out over the countryside and invading everyone's minds with thoughts of . . . well, they had seen the violence and the corpses and all this.

Mark squeezed Karen's hand. 'Lambert, you said you had an answer.'

'I exaggerated but I think I know where we should go.' He nodded towards the tower of light that was obscured from him by the crowd that continued to mill past.

'*In* there?' asked Jamie.

'In *there*?' repeated Mark.

'Logic dictates.'

'Logic?' sneered Karen. Then, her shoulders slumping, she indicated Lambert should continue. 'Sorry.'

'The sky's falling, the walls are closing in, this is the engine, they are the fuel. Where are they going?'

'A boiler?' said Jamie.

Mark laughed, then shut up.

'A boiler?' said Lambert. 'Quite possibly. And where there's a boiler, there should be a . . .?'

'Boilerman?' said Jamie.

Lambert nodded. 'Jamie's fat man told him what to do, to crash that crane. That's his tower block. It may be coincidence, but until we find out what's in there we'll not know.'

'So we follow the crowds?' said Karen.

He nodded. 'And it's probably a one-way street.'

'*Flying men, flying men!*'

Izotta felt Mr Farmer's shock and then his amusement as the parachutists plummeted to earth.

'See how futile they really are?'

'Who?'

'Humans. They think by sending in soldiers they can stop the inevitable. So futile.'

'Yes,' she agreed. All hope was lost. She had little of herself left now. Like a child torn from its parents when very young, she only had the vaguest notion of what being human used to be like. The warmth, the feeling, the bonding, all were gone. All she could do now was watch, her only emotion the sparks that rippled through her sight when Mr Farmer reacted to something. It didn't matter, for what was the point of caring without a goal? Parents care for children because they represent the future; lovers care for each other because without each other they would be lost, but what had she to care for or about now? Nothing. Suddenly yellow waves burst over her senses.

'Well done, Izotta. You have grasped the essence of our existence. Without care or physical boundary we are free to watch.'

'Why?'

'Why watch?'

'Yes. It's no use to us. All this death has done nothing except cause our own deaths. Is that what you wanted?'

There was a long pause. She could see from the ochre cast of their view that he was as puzzled as she. So long had he been immersed in his own smug satisfaction at achieving his heady goal that he hadn't actually questioned its purpose. Then the yellow disappeared, the whiteness returned.

'All this death is a goal in itself.'

'But it will be over soon. What then?'

'Soon? Oh no, not soon. This is only the start: it is but the spark that sets the fire that consumes the forest that covers a continent.'

'This will continue?'

'Indubitably.'

'And us?'

Again the golden light of doubt. But why should there be doubt? This was all of his making, his work. Why should he not know . . . But hadn't he said he didn't know its ultimate purpose and that was its joy?

'You are worried,' she said.

Suddenly she felt his anger: a purple sheen covered her vision, rippled with deepest blue. Why anger?

The purple became harsher, electric. He raged, words and thoughts mere baggage as deepest, deep-set emotion pummelled her into submission. But even as she acknowledged his dominance and dominion he fanned the last lambent flame that flickered deep within her burned conscience and she resolved to make one last effort to spoil everything. For whatever creature Mr Farmer had been and had become, Izotta had been human and she hadn't wanted to lose that state, however weak and pitiful it might now seem.

Lambert, Mark, Karen and Jamie were huddled together in a protective knot twenty paces from the base of the tower, people jammed shoulder to shoulder in all directions making their progress slow and tiring, like wading through deep water or walking against a strong wind. It was unnerving to be so close to so many people who ignored you. So many eyes not seeing, so many mouths unspeaking. It was as if God had decided the leaseholds on His cemeteries were up and the tenants were having to seek new accommodation.

Lambert was doubly frustrated because he couldn't see anything but people's backs, the light from the tower like a moon hidden by clouds. Even were he to be in a position to see, he was still confined to his wheelchair.

'What are we going to do when we get to the tower?' asked Mark.

Lambert didn't know and he was becoming increasingly concerned that should they reach it, the pressure of the crowd would leave them with no choice. Whatever they found there – a door, stairs – they would simply move with the crowd and even if they found an answer to their problem they would be powerless to act on it. Like being trapped in three solid lanes of traffic on a motorway and spotting your exit but being unable to make the lane changes to use it, they would be carried along. Aware of this possibility, he turned to look up at Mark.

'We shouldn't all go. There might come a point where we won't be able to turn back. We need a plan.'

'Now he tells us,' said Mark, struggling simply to hold his ground, never mind retrace his steps.

'I'm best suited to judge what we find, so we need to find a way to let me go ahead while you wait. We need rope.'

'No problem. Got some here.'

'Very funny, Mark. Where could we get—'

Karen pushed in front of Mark. 'Bandages. Got lots of them. Could tie them together. Might give us a few feet.'

'Excellent,' said Lambert. 'Let's try it.'

They huddled together as a group, Mark and Karen with their backs to the advancing crowd, Jamie on Lambert's lap. Karen took out all the bandages from her carrier bag, then unravelled them and, pooling them on Jamie's lap, they began to knot them together.

They had nine bandages, each of which unrolled to six feet in length. Allowing a foot for each knot, they had forty-five feet of bandage. Not a lot.

'So what now?' said Mark.

'Tie it round my chest so if the worse comes to the worst you can pull me back.'

'Do you think it'll hold?'

'Ever seen a bandage break? It'll stretch but it won't snap, but it's the knots where we might have a problem. Still, it's all we've got.'

'We could still try and find some rope. A washing line?'

Lambert nudged Jamie's bottom and the boy stood up on the arms of the chair and looked over the crowd.

'The grey's at the end of Jubilee Street now. The mill's gone completely.'

'No more houses?'

'No, just lots of people, everywhere it's people.'

'No choice.'

'I should go,' said Mark, taking a deep breath. 'I'm the fittest, despite my knee.'

'And Jamie's the lightest, come to that,' said Lambert tugging on the knotted bandages. 'But I'm better qualified to see what's there. I predicted this, remember.'

'But—'

'But time's running out, Mark. I go now or we all die soon. Comprenez? Right, wheel me as far as you can, then I'll take over.'

They looped the bandage under his chest, pulled it tight, then trailed it behind the chair, Karen keeping hold of the end and Jamie's hand at the same time. They were about fifty feet from where the crowd disappeared into the light. There was no sound. Mark could see the tower now only as a wall of light, the exact converse of the wall of grey they were running from.

'Right,' said Lambert, fear drying his voice. 'Go back to Karen and wait. When I've entered the light, keep tight hold and I'll see if I can get back. If you feel a tug, keep pulling. If I can't wheel the chair, I'll tip it backwards so you can drag me.'

'What about the people?'

'Can't be helped. I'll use my arms, see if I can shove them out of the way and avoid being trampled.'

'Look, it *would* be better if I went,' said Mark.

'Do you want to? Do you really want to go in there, Mark?'

They locked gazes, their true expressions masked by their sunglasses, but both could see the fear etched in the grim set of their mouths and their worried frowns.

'No,' said Mark simply, his heart racing as he forced himself to speak the truth. Never mind his duty to Karen or that he wouldn't know what he was looking for even if he saw it; he simply didn't want to die. 'Good luck.'

'Thank you. And don't feel guilty, Mark. I just have less to lose than the rest of you.' He tapped his thigh. 'Only half a man to lose.'

'But it's a good half.'

'Oh, shut up.'

Lambert began wheeling towards the light, his chair soon lost from sight as the crowd jostled around him.

Mark pushed his way back through the crowd following the bandage, bright white in the light from the tower, the people around him just so much foliage to be brushed aside.

He reached Karen and, taking the bandage, wrapped it round his wrist. Then he turned and, hugging Karen and Jamie to him, slowly walked back towards the light. He counted his paces until he reached fifteen and stopped. Judging by the brightness in front of them, Lambert would have entered the light. He pulled on the bandage to check its tautness and suddenly it sprang back to him and flopped on the floor where the crowd trampled on it.

Frantically he started to reel it in until it came free of someone's foot and jumped up and slapped him in the chest. One of the knots had worked free. Lambert was gone.

Even before Mark was lost in the crowd, Lambert realized he had made a serious mistake. Despite flipping on the brake and bracing his arms against the tyres, the wheelchair still moved forward. He tried to bat at the people around him but no one responded; they simply continued to shuffle the chair towards the light. Lambert had no choice but to unspool the bandage on his lap, aware that this was his last lifeline and that it was pathetic. Noble as his intentions might be, his actions were just plain stupid and not for the first time he wondered about the impulse that had got him into this situation.

He remembered an Edgar Allan Poe story called 'The Imp of the Perverse' about a man who committed a perfect murder but couldn't help telling someone about it. His relationship with Blair and the dome had been the same all along: something had made him equate the growing crisis in the town with Roswiay and Warform Peck; had made him call a meeting; had conned them into thinking he would spill the beans if they didn't let him tag along; had made him persuade Horrigan that he had to enter the dome; and had made him suggest this most stupid of all actions. Why had he done it? Why?

He wondered about rocking the chair and tipping it over so that he could crawl back to safety, but knew that the second he hit the floor he would be trampled on. So, heart pounding, he made one last attempt to check his momentum. He strained his arm and neck muscles until he felt his face reddening with the effort but eventually he had to let go with an explosive gasp.

Soon the bandage was stretched taut and he thought for one moment it might hold but then the knot around his waist suddenly sprang loose and the bandage whipped over his shoulder into the throng behind him. There was no escape.

The light was bright, but his sunglasses and the people about him helped dim it enough so that he was able to discern a point somewhere ahead where the light actually started, like an open door or window. It was ten yards away but there was nothing he could do as, wheels locked, he was pushed forward step by shuffling step by his silent companions. He tried to see their faces, but all were looking ahead and he was on a level with their waists. His heart was racing, his respiration so fast it made him light-headed. He lashed out at those nearest to him – a teenage boy in football gear and a young woman in a shop uniform – punching at their sides as hard as he could, but it had no effect. Whatever was about to happen, they were dead already; only he would experience it fully aware. He wanted to yell, to give vent to his horror and his anger at his death, but there was some small spark in him that refused him the luxury. Whether he was punishing himself for his arrogance and stupidity in getting himself into Blair in the first place, or whether he still retained that detached element scientists develop as they study things that would upset lay people, he didn't know. And then, with five yards, maybe fifteen seconds to go, the fear left him.

Like a head cold that had vanished overnight, he felt an unnatural confidence grip him. Having recognized his inevitable demise his brain was allowing him the luxury of curiosity. Soon he might have an answer, see the truth, *understand*. And, after all, what else was there to life but understanding? All the good friends, good love, and good times were just so many memories to be wiped in a milli-second as death beckoned; but to understand the 'why' of death, that might have value. As a result he could feel himself craning forward to get a better look, cursing the people in front of him. He had to see, he had to *see* . . . And then, suddenly, there it was.

A pit, as large as the base of the tower of light. Wide and open like the smoking caldera of a volcano and, like the sacrifices of savages in old movies, the citizens of Blair were walking straight over the edge.

Lambert watched an elderly man as he approached the edge. His eyes had been raised up to the blinding light above, but as he reached the rim of the pit he lowered his gaze and looked down, smiled, then walked over the edge, content to fall. He watched several other people and they all acted similarly, taking pleasure in the drop.

He was soon on the lip himself, but just before his wheelchair began to tip forward, he grabbed the leg of the woman on his right and hauled himself out of his seat, letting the chair fall to his left where it was scuffed along and quickly fell into the pit. As expected, he found himself being trampled, but he ignored the pain and hugged the leg of the woman as he tried to halt her progress. Occasionally feet would stand on his legs and although he didn't feel their pressure, there would be a sudden jerk and he and the woman would stop, only for her to move again when his legs came free.

As he finally reached the edge, he peered over and found that the light, though bright, wasn't as blinding as the tower above. He only had a few seconds to take in the details and then, as the girl took her last step on terra firma, he let go of her leg, grabbed the lip of the hole and hauled himself over the edge into the abyss.

Mr Farmer was preoccupied. For some reason Izotta couldn't understand, he was focusing on one of the intruders. She could see that the man was a cripple and that he was barely managing to cling to the edge of the pit, so why was Mr Farmer so concerned about this one piece of flotsam in a sea of people? The level of his concern was evidenced by the fact that, as she wondered about it, she was overwhelmed by the colour of his reproach. Turning her attention to the crowd she saw the others who hadn't submitted to Mr Farmer's will. They stood out like daisies in a field of dirt, but they too represented no threat. Those walking towards the pit would either drag them with them or, at worst, leave them high and dry, lone witnesses to the grey about to overwhelm them all.

Overwhelm them all? Did that include her and Mr Farmer? He had avoided answering that question as if he didn't know the answer. All he wanted was for the process to continue without interruption, for the pit to consume all so that the light could grow and breach its confines and shine out in the wider world and act as a magnet for a bigger audience.

'Leave it,' said Mr Farmer, his anger deepest purple.

'I only want to know.'

'It is not our place to know. Only to serve.'

'Serve who?'

The purple darkened until it was indigo and Izotta stilled her mind. It was clear Mr Farmer's anger masked a deeper fear, but what was there to be frightened of? She felt his attentions return to the cripple, a broken bearded man one twitch away from the final fall to oblivion. What threat could he possibly pose?

Lambert continued to stare into the hole before him. There had been a ledge six feet beneath the rim, barely two feet wide, and Lambert had landed on it on his right arm. There had been a terrible snapping sound and he had felt a pain worse than any he could imagine as he collapsed onto his front, his screams lost to the dirt in his mouth. After an age of tearing, rivening pain, he had forced himself to take stock of his surroundings, aware that pain was an irrelevance this close to death.

The pit was deep and sheer, offering no handholds for any who might change their minds. Most people fell down its side feet first; others cartwheeled or rolled, all lost to gravity. But all that proved was that the sides sloped and possibly that the pit had a bottom where the sides met, but what was there?

He pushed himself as far back as his good arm would allow from the edge, the pain making him sweat and bite his lip until he tasted blood. People kept catching on his legs and threatening to take him with them to oblivion. He looked into the hole for a long time, almost mesmerized, his mind daring whatever hid in the infinite blackness to show itself, but it might as well have been a coal hole or the nozzle to a giant petrol tank: fuel fell into it and was used to drive it on; its purpose was clear, only its workings were incomprehensible. He could see the damage to his right arm and felt the excruciating pain, but he gritted his teeth as he worked his way onto his back, his cries of agony lost to the pit. Finally rolling over, his arm on fire, he looked up.

The tower block rose above him, its steel frame now neon tubes criss-crossing his vision like a luminous Meccano set, the floors of the building invisible. And there, to his astonishment, some distance above him, he could see a man. A lone figure, floating in air, his eyes trained on his own. A fat man, hovering like a blimp (for a brief second he found himself looking for the tether that must be holding the bloated figure in space, like the advertising balloons he sometimes saw floating above petrol stations). Then, as he began to wonder why the man was there and Jamie's fat man came to mind, the figure began coming closer, descending on him, his arms outspread and, as he drew nearer, Lambert was able to see his face, and see the wide eyes, red with hatred, and the mouth open in a scream, teeth glinting in the light that surrounded him. The man came steadily closer, haloed by light like a demented angel. Their eyes locked and Lambert felt the man enter his mind, probing and delving into his memories. The man was intent on raping him. Lambert tried to scream as the man came within a dozen feet of him, his size all but blotting out the light from the tower. If he was simply to fall on Lambert he would crush him, but that was the least of his worries as images flashed through his mind of himself lying broken on the edge of the pit, people stepping over him as he stared up terrified and immobilized at a phantom above him. Lambert could see *himself*; could see his terror through the other man's eyes and it was at that instant he knew the fat man was in him.

Suddenly he saw, knew, believed and hated the fat man for what he was telling him. He knew why he had felt compelled to study previous appearances of the dome; why he had insisted on coming into it; and why he had so foolishly wheeled himself to the very edge of this pit. He wasn't a seeker after truth, or some lame excuse for a scientist with a death wish. No, now he saw the truth of it, why the military men and bureaucrats had listened so favourably to his insane theories, understood why he had been allowed to join the group at the dome, and why Horrigan had let him go into it – and why the fat man hated him so.

The power was within some even though they didn't know it. The fat man, Mr Farmer he called himself, had prepared the way for the person who would take charge of the next stage of the evil's sprouting. Except Lambert didn't want anything to do with it and the fat man was outraged. He had sacrificed his own existence for the dome and its future and here the future was refusing to take its rightful place. Mr Farmer tried to explain to his reluctant host what was expected of him, for with his invasion of the man's mind, the jigsaw was complete and finally they could both see the truth of it all.

'You will survive this,' the voice said in Lambert's head, its strength such that the pain in his shattered arm became that of a hangnail. 'When the pit has consumed all the dome will disappear, the light will remain and you will be found. For a while the light will pose no threat, and it will simply become an anomaly in the world. Weeks, months, perhaps even years will pass as it understands the world about it but then, one night, it will strike and such terror will be unleashed, such unholy murderous misery that what has happened here will seem a mere pinprick to the festering wound that will grow in the world. And *you* will be its agent and focus. *You* will spread the seed of calm before the storm; *you* will propagate complacency. As the only survivor you will talk to and touch the world's leading experts and you will pass on a story of hope that will ensure that they do nothing to destroy the light. Despite all that has happened they will be persuaded that it is all over and there is nothing to fear from the light.'

Lambert tried to protest but he was powerless against the fat man. For his part the fat man continued to babble his lecture, aware that time was short.

'Like a child leaving its parents, the light is feeble and defenceless in the outside world – it has never left the security of the dome before – and it will need protecting; someone who can persuade the world to leave it alone and let it mature until it is ready to strike.'

'I won't.'

'But you will. You have the words and the experience to tell them what they need to know and you will have my talent for infecting thought. As you talk to them, so you will touch them and they will see the wisdom of your words. Others will speak publicly about the light, but they will be *your* words, *your* ideas. And as they talk and touch others, so the contentment will spread like a warm blanket – and once enough people are convinced that the light poses no threat, restrictions on its study will be lifted and it will become a monument, a natural phenomenon to be used as a backdrop for snapshots. And then when it is fully grown, aware of its power, ready to feast, it will strike and a whirlwind of terror will be unleashed.

'Remember the Flood? Noah and his Ark? God's displeasure? The Tower of Babel? Sodom and Gomorrah? Blair will be seen as just another of God's retributions. A sign that if man doesn't mend his ways, God will take a hand in his turning. And the light will be seen as God's work; a monument to his intervention, a stigmata on the earth to be revered and visited like some medieval shrine. Not all will believe, but enough in positions of power will and the light will finally rule over all. And you will be its emissary, its messenger. A John the Baptist to its Jesus Christ.'

'No.'

'Yes. You have no choice.'

And before Lambert could disagree again, the fat man's eyes opened wide, his mouth formed a huge O and he suddenly crashed down onto Lambert. Even as Lambert heard his ribs break and felt his nose mash into his face and realized he was to die, he experienced a deeper pain as the man poured into his mind with the heat and coring power of molten metal, the liquid intensity rushing through his thoughts in an unstoppable wave, washing all conscience and regret away.

Mr Farmer became Lambert.

At the moment the bearded man's mind absorbed Mr Farmer, Izotta was overwhelmed with a greyness. They had been as one and now he had gone and she was completely alone. Below her the people continued to walk to the pit and around her the tower blazed out, but now she was alone with her thoughts and, she knew, her death.

She looked down at the bearded man. He was lying on his back, his arms and legs splayed out like an X, his mouth slowly opening and closing like a fish gasping for breath on a pondside. She could neither feel nor see Mr Farmer, their bodies long since taken by the light. She was going to die and, whilst moments before she would have welcomed it as a blessed release, now she saw it for what it was and, despite what she had become, at least she still existed – and she wanted to continue to exist. Better this than nothing. But even as she wished it, the light around her began to dim. She knew that Mr Farmer had taken over the mind of the bearded man and the only reason he would do that is if the man was going to survive. She had felt his fear and his desire for survival. Perhaps she could do the same, but who? All these dead minds . . . There were only a man, woman and child left who were sentient. But even as she considered her choices, her mind wound down further, her thoughts like muted echoes in a darkening hall.

She needed the weakest mind, one open to her signal, and she needed it now. The man and woman she didn't know, but she knew the boy would not only have a less sophisticated outlook, but that Mr Farmer had already used him. He might still be open to invasion. She stared down at the small figure in the crowd, focusing her mind on the boy, calling out to him.

'Boy! Boy! Here, look! Up here, boy!'

Jamie was really frightened, but Mark and Karen seemed frozen with fear, unable to do anything except hug each other, both of them near tears, and witter on about how much they loved each other. He wanted to run, to punch his way through the morons who were streaming past them, but he didn't have the nerve. The only alive people in the world now were Mark and Karen and useless as they had become he didn't want to leave them.

Then he heard a voice. A woman's voice, pleading but kind. He looked around. It wasn't Karen, so who?

'Up here!' it said. 'Up here!

Up where? He looked up at the grey sky, then across to the white tower, but all his shaded eyes could see was a block of light, almost blinding in its intensity despite his multiple sunglasses.

'Up here!' insisted the woman's voice. '*Look at me*!'

He continued to stare, ignoring the jostling passers-by. He couldn't see anything.

'Take off your glasses,' she urged.

What? *The light . . .*

'Take off your glasses. *See me, see me*!'

Unsure of his own actions, Jamie pulled off his taped-together glasses and looked directly into the light.

She saw his eyes.

There was an explosion at the back of his head. It felt as if his skull was hollow and something had broken through at the top of his spine and was flooding up into his mind. He covered his eyes and screamed.

Mark and Karen turned to him and grabbed him as he fell, both asking what was wrong. Karen fought to prise the glasses from his fingers so she could cover his eyes again, but his grip was rigid.

There was a river of flame in Jamie's head and it was growing, the inside of his head a crucible being filled with liquid heat. He began to shake, memories flitting across his mind like survivors from a shipwreck, only to be drowned by the incoming rush of Izotta's own mind. He tried to speak but couldn't remember words. His eyes were fixed ahead, but even though he was staring at the blinding light, Karen could see his pupils were wide open. But Jamie couldn't see it any more; he couldn't see *anything*, couldn't hear, speak, feel. Images of his life, of his childhood friends and toys, his family, his home, school, were one by one dashed against the rocks of a stronger psyche. Izotta's childhood became his, her family his own, his flesh darkened, he became a girl, he had no brother, no dad, he . . . a single word floated through the torrent that poured into his mind, like a last message in a bottle: the word *sorry*. And then it was over.

Mark shook the boy as his eyes closed and he went limp. Karen couldn't understand what had happened. Perhaps it was a convulsion and he was epileptic, but why hadn't he told them? Karen felt his pulse, checked his respiration.

'He's dead!' she shouted, and started to pummel at his chest.

No! Mark rubbed the boy's hand, panic preventing him from sensible action.

Karen kneeled down over the boy, opened his mouth and began resuscitation. Blowing air into his lungs, counting three, then depressing his chest.

'His heart,' she said. 'Punch his heart.'

In a daze Mark did as his wife ordered.

After a minute of frantic action Karen was out of breath, her side cramped from crouching, and she knew it was futile to continue. Whatever the cause, the boy had died. She sat back as Mark continued to thump the boy's fragile chest.

'Leave it,' she said. 'He's gone. Don't know—'

'No!' shouted Mark, thumping all the harder. 'Can't have. Mustn't! He's only a kid. After all we've—'

Karen grabbed his wrist and prevented any further blows, the tension in his arm causing both their arms to shake. Mark looked at her in despair; for all the pain and horror he felt now the boy might as well have been their son.

Karen let go and sat back, her elbows stabbing viciously at the knees of people shuffling by them, ignorant of the drama at their feet.

Suddenly the boy coughed, threw his head back and let out a huge sigh as if he had been holding his breath all along. Then he sat bolt upright, his head unsteady on his shoulders, his face frozen in a squint as he first looked at Karen then swung round to peer at Mark. He croaked a word which neither of them caught.

Karen leaned in to his mouth and held his brow, feeling cold perspiration.

'What? What did you say?'

There was another gasp, then he spoke again:

'Sorry.'

Mark was as near to madness as he had ever been in his life. There had been times in the past when he had seriously considered just giving up and staying in his bed and letting the world drift by, regardless of the consequences. Like his first week at university when everything went wrong and he messed up his first essay and missed lectures and his only friend was bloody Annie Nightingale on Radio One; or the time he thought he'd got a girl pregnant at nineteen; or the time he was made redundant on his 25th birthday, a month after buying his first house. Desperate days. But he had overcome those crises and had been left, or so he thought, the stronger for the experience. Nietzsche said some fascist crap about it, but this was different; this was important.

When Lambert had disappeared and the bandage snapped it was like the parting of the umbilical cord that had kept Karen and himself attached to hope. Lambert knew something of what was going on and so had been their totem. Now he had gone, the grey was coming, everyone was dying and they had minutes to live. So he had hugged Karen to him and felt her warmth and burbled his inadequacies into her ear, aware from her trembling that she was equally terrified and that she was looking to him for an answer. For so long he had let her take the lead, or at least sought her approval for his actions, that he didn't want the responsibility. Even his venturing into agency ownership was only attempted after she had sat with him night after night and persuaded him that his idea was a good one. Without her, he would still have been slaving away in The Marketing Practice in Altrincham, up to his ears in price tags and product descriptions for that damn supermarket chain. Karen had given him the nerve and been his crutch, but now they were both adrift with no logic to cling to, in an alien world slowly swallowing itself. In minutes they would be dead . . . or would it be something else?

Then Jamie had had his fit and both had been sure the boy was dead. True, he seemed all right now, a bit disorientated but otherwise fine. Perhaps, Mark reflected bitterly as they huddled together, he would have been better out of it. So they hugged and held and hoped, for that was all that seemed to be left, but then Mark noticed something. The crowd was thinning. He pulled away from Karen and looked around. No, the crowd wasn't thinning, it was *parting*.

They were standing in a bare patch of ground twenty feet across, the people walking to the tower turning as if reaching a rock in a stream and sidling around the perimeter until they could join together again. Anxious for anything that might signify a change, Mark pulled away from Karen's hands and walked towards the crowd. But as he reached them they didn't react, so why the circle?

He called Karen and Jamie over to him and they walked across. The crowd edged away as they approached, the circle moving with them like a spotlight. His mind racing, Mark told Jamie to walk back while he and Karen stayed together.

Soon he and Karen were in the grip of the crowd again while Jamie was standing on his own in the circle.

'What's happening?' asked Karen.

'Buggered if I know,' said Mark.

Jamie didn't speak.

Mr Farmer gleefully savaged the mind of the scientist, taking great joy in shredding his existence. He knew that in the time left he wouldn't be able to subjugate him entirely but such was the ferocity of his onslaught that the man simply wouldn't be able to recover from the intrusion before he had to surrender totally – and by then they would be out in the world. He wormed his way through the man's body, feeling the dead legs, the broken arm, relishing the return to corporeal existence. Exhilarating though his afterlife existence had been, he had come to regret the loss of human pleasures. Moribund though they might be, eating and watching others' reactions to his presence were distinctly human traits. Now he might be able to experience them again. Although he had never known the true purpose of his existence, now that he had seen the future and tricked his way onto the next stage, all he had to do was wait for the end – and then the new beginning.

As for the Izotta woman, she would . . . where was she? Even inside Lambert he should be able to sense her above him. He looked through the man's eyes, through the light. She . . .

Where was she?

*   *   *

Izotta stared at the man and woman. Weak as she was, she had barely been able to keep the boy alive after she had clumsily switched off his basic functions. She had learned little from him – her attack had been so swift it had burned his mind away like acid. She didn't even know the names of these two. Were they his parents? She tried to remember his memories but it was no use; besides, she was using most of her concentration co-ordinating the boy's movements.

She became aware that the two were staring at her, at the boy. Then she noticed the empty area all three of them occupied. What did it mean? Whatever it was they suspected he was the cause. But what was it? She tried to speak but all that came out was a guttural bark.

Karen leaned into Jamie. The boy was blank-eyed as if sleep-walking but now he was trying to speak again. She knelt down and looked him in the face.

'What is it, Jamie? Do you know something?'

The boy nodded. Izotta wanted to let them know but how could she explain? And there was so little time.

'I . . . I . . . all right,' she managed. She needed time to think and the woman was distracting her.

Karen stood up, the back of her hand feeling the boy's cheek. He was cold.

'He needs help,' she said, turning to Mark.

Mark simply stared back. The grey was well within the boundaries of the field between the tower blocks now.

'He's not the only one.'

Karen looked over at the grey, then scanned the horizon. Except the horizon was now the walls of a room. There were enclosed arenas in the USA bigger than the space they had left to them. It truly was over.

Suddenly Karen's knees gave way and she fell down sobbing, her hands knitting in her lap, all her resolve drained. She was used to responding in crises because there were choices; she simply did what seemed best but here there were no alternatives: just a clock counting down and oblivion edging towards them.

Izotta wanted to help, but couldn't think. After all, her continued existence was an accident; it hadn't the purpose that Mr Farmer's had. She didn't know what to do.

*   *   *

There was something wrong, Mr Farmer could sense it. The Izotta woman had left the tower but hadn't died. What he had done, combining with the survivor, was fraught with enough risks without there being the added complication of Izotta. For all he knew she might survive the end and live on into the outside world, and then what? She was no longer an ally; she might interfere and if she did, all this might come to nought. Having glimpsed the coming glory, Mr Farmer wanted his share. He deserved it; after all, had he not paved the way for it? So he began to probe, to use his undiminished powers to seek out the woman, to see what she had—

The boy. *His boy.* He was outraged that she was using his own instrument against him. Whilst he could sense her weakness and confusion, she might strengthen and, once settled back into the rhythm of human existence, she might find a way to survive. He had to stop her. It was his mistake that she had gone over with him; it was his job to finish her, but how? He was a cripple lying on the very edge of the pit, there was little time left. He needed to marshal an attack but he couldn't even see her; he simply knew that somewhere over the rim she stood like a stain on a blueprint, destined to spoil the final product.

He tried to move the Lambert body but the legs wouldn't respond. He tried to use the arms but one was broken and although pain meant little, its strength had been drained. So be it. Besides, once outside, it would mean little; he might be confined to a wheelchair but there might be the chance that he could transfer again to a more mobile body. But even if he couldn't, why worry? Hadn't his greatest pleasure always been to observe? And here hadn't he captured a custom-made vehicle in which he would be able to do just that: to sit and watch and plant those seeds . . .

Izotta? Izotta? he asked. He knew she heard him but she refused to answer. He could ignore her, let her die with the rest, but he didn't know how much of his abilities she had absorbed. After all, she had done exactly as he had, latched onto a human mind and sucked it dry in order to survive. If there was a chance that the boy's body could survive afterwards she had to be dispensed with.

He considered his options. He had no control over the speed of the grey's approach; he couldn't move from his ledge; he hadn't the time to try and command the dead souls hurling themselves into the pit; more to the point, he wouldn't want to: they were fuel, after all. So what tools did he have?

He had his mind. He could invade hers again, razors at the ready, but to do that he had to see her for the eyes were indeed the gateways of the soul. He needed eyes, he needed eyes. And then he had the answer.

The grey had been created to cull the human population of the town. Animals, birds and insects were not included. Base instinct had led most animals to flee the town hours before it was finally encapsulated by the dome and those that remained died, huddled in dark corners, whimpering as their simple minds were overwhelmed by the evil afflicting their surroundings. But not all life forms had the intelligence to understand something was about to happen. Those things that crawled in the earth were able to live on oblivious of what was happening above them, their world too small and fragmented to be worried by any calamity greater than their unceasing fight for survival. And it was here Mr Farmer was able to find a new ally. He had his tool and it had a thousand eyes and a million legs.

Mark was suddenly scared of Jamie. Since his fit he hadn't been able to speak and now the crowd were avoiding him and, try as he might, he couldn't catch the boy's eye. He seemed to have trouble focusing, almost as if he had brain damage. Maybe that was it but even if it was, why was he reluctant to go to him? He grabbed Karen when she made to go back to the boy.

'Leave him.'

Karen was shocked. 'What? Leave him? He's only a boy.'

She shook free of his hand and put her arms around the boy's shoulder.

Mark edged away from the crowd but came no nearer to the boy than he could help. There was something . . .

Izotta was grateful for the woman's concern. She felt very lonely in her new body, like a child armed only with a small torch in the corner of a strange darkened room, unable to see what else might be in with her. The woman's worry warmed her and she let herself bathe in the humanity of her gesture. It had been so long since she had been held by another who was concerned for her. She remembered her lovers and her recurring nightmare of disfigurement and how in her dream every one of them came to her front door, took one look at her scarred face and walked away without a word. She had known what it had meant then and she knew now. Loneliness was as ugly a feeling as fear or hate, and just as insoluble, otherwise one wouldn't be lonely or fearful or full of hatred in the first place.

'What are we going to do?' said Mark.

Karen shook her head. She was resigning herself to their fate and simply wanted it over. She hugged the boy all the tighter and wished Mark would hug her too. But Mark was facing away from them, looking towards the base of the tower.

With the walls coming in, Mark realized Lambert had been right in saying the source of the light was the only place to go. Perhaps he had survived in some way. After all, he had no idea what was there. For all he knew it might be the door into another dimension; there was enough weird shit about to make even the most outlandish episode of *The Twilight Zone* look like factual reporting. He looked at the grey. They were in something little bigger than Manchester's Nynex Arena now. Christ, it was moving so *fast*. They had only two options: wait and die or run to the light and see. He knew there was no debate.

So he walked over to Karen, who held her arm out for him to hug her, but instead he grabbed her hand and pulled her upright.

'We're going into the light. There's no choice.'

'But it's—'

'It's what? *We don't fucking know*! But we do know what *that* does.'

He nodded at the grey barely a hundred yards away. 'No choice, love, we've got to.'

Karen was about to nod her reluctant agreement when she felt a punch in her chest and she was sent reeling. As she landed on her backside she looked up at Jamie. The boy was stock still, as if electrocuted, his fists tensed, his eyes staring ahead. Oh God, another fit.

Suddenly Mark gave out a cry and scooped Karen up under her armpits and dragged her across the clearing until they were with the crowd.

Only then did she see that the ground where she had been lying was moving. At first it was like a ripple on still water, but it didn't grow; instead the dirt slowly shifted and rose, as if something was trying to get out from under the damp earth. And then it did.

Izotta heard Mr Farmer's voice. He was with her, *in* her. Her vision turned purple, then indigo, then a blue so dark that all colour and light were blotted out. His words were blurred together into an incoherent scream of hatred, but even in the shrieking she knew the message: death. He had devised a way to kill her and now was the time.

She wondered if she might muster the strength of will to flit to another body, perhaps that of the woman, but even as she thought it her being was wracked with numbing pain. She fell to her knees, her limbs limp, her mind a cauldron of seething negative energy and as the blackness lifted and she was allowed to see, she saw what was coming up out of the ground. Hundreds and hundreds of insects.

Centipedes, spiders, millipedes, cockroaches, beetles, lice, flies, fleas, grubs, maggots, worms: every conceivable form of insect and multi-legged creation she had ever seen, all of them crawling and scrambling over each other in their desperate eagerness to get to her.

'*Oh no, no, no, please, no!*' she heard herself screaming over the cacophony in her head.

Mr Farmer watched with satisfaction. He had planned to take her mind but, now he had an army at his command, he decided to take her body as well and eradicate the problem forever.

In a flash the insects were on her, racing for her face, her arms and legs unable to react. Some ran up the inside of the boy's trouser legs, others took advantage of his hunched position to scuttle up to the knees then jump straight onto his T-shirt, barely six inches from his shrieking mouth. Izotta managed to fling up an arm to protect herself, but it was too late. They were in the boy's hair and nose and eyes. Hundreds of insects, their feet and feelers and mouths skittering over his/her face, mandibles pinching and biting at his/her flesh.

She opened the boy's mouth to scream again and three of the loathsome things crawled inside. She shut it immediately, only to feel herself biting two of the insects in half, their bisected bodies wriggling and writhing in her mouth, scratching at her tongue and gums, their hard shells and myriad feet screaking across the enamel of her teeth. Then she felt something long and slimy slither up her left nostril, butting its body against her septum again and again in its attempts to squeeze through the narrow passage into the boy's sinuses. Something was buzzing loud, then louder, in her right ear. She reached up to bat at it but her hand was suddenly stung in half a dozen places and she felt the living river of ants run up the inside of her sleeve.

Karen screamed as she watched the boy swatting desperately at his face but finding he could feel no skin at all, just the writhing segmented forms of insects with hundreds of scratching, scuttling legs. Now they had reached the boy's crotch and Izotta could feel their frenzied panic as they strove to worm their way into and over his genitals as yet more ran up both legs to meet them. Karen wanted to run and help but couldn't bring herself to move closer; she was frozen with fear, like a non-swimmer watching a drowning man from a promenade.

Mark was also rooted to the spot, aghast at what was happening. In a matter of seconds the boy had been overrun and was almost indistinguishable now under the assault. He knew it was useless to intervene, that the insects would only attack him but he—

He grabbed Karen by the wrist and jerked her away, but she was dead weight. He grabbed her face and forced her to look at him. '*They might come for us next!*'

Karen stared back at the horror before her but even in the depths of terror reason prevailed. Her guilt at not trying to help was more than tempered by the obvious fact that neither of them could have done anything. There wasn't an inch of the boy's body that wasn't covered in insects.

Izotta fell silent, catatonic with terror, unable to move or respond as she felt more insects wriggling under the boy's T-shirt, snaking over his chest and rummaging in his armpits. She tried to spit the insects out of her mouth, but a dozen more ferreted their way in. She felt one multi-legged abomination crawl over her tongue, nudge the back of her mouth then make its determined way down her throat, every leg digging into the sides of her pharynx as it scrabbled for purchase.

Suddenly the sensation of swallowing a live centipede overcame all other horrors and she started to vomit. She opened her mouth to be sick only to be slammed onto her back by the swarm of insects that rushed for her open mouth and fought their way into her gullet.

As her final breath was stolen she saw through the legs and feelers on her face the eyes of the woman, her face ashen with shock. She tried to think herself into the woman's thoughts but all she could feel was a white wall: horror had distanced the woman from reality. *Oh, God help me*, Izotta heard herself begging, only to hear laughter in reply.

Die, bitch, die, said the voice.

And then the boy – and Izotta – died: her last memory choking to death on live things; her last sight a spider walking across an eye she couldn't close; her last thoughts of lovers who would not be thinking of her as *they* died.

Mark and Karen watched as the boy twitched several times, then lay still on his back, his stomach thrust up into the air, his legs splayed out, hands clawed at the side of his head as if trying to dig their way in.

The insects then scuttled away like a receding tide, back into the hole they had come from, none of them paying the terrified couple any heed.

Mr Farmer was exultant. From his initial sighting of a humble millipede that had crawled onto one of Lambert's dead legs, he had found a way to deal with the upstart Izotta woman. Now all he had to do was wait for the grey to fold in on itself and he would live on.

Mark caught his breath, his bladder loosening. The poor boy, the poor boy. Why him, why did he have to die like that, after all this . . .

Yes, why did *he* die, he managed to reason. Why not all three of them? Why just the boy? There was nowhere to run, the insects could have attacked them without any problems. He looked at the grey and saw that the top of the tower was within striking distance of the dome's roof. Hadn't Lambert said that when they met it would be over?

'Got to go to the light, Karen. Come on.'

Karen resisted his tug.

'Come on, there's no time!'

Again she refused to move.

'What? *What is it*?' Mark sounded like a frightened child.

Karen looked at him, her face oddly blank. *Oh God, no, don't say she's lost her mind too*. She pulled her hand free and walked away back into the crowd.

Mark was frantic. 'Karen! Karen! What are you doing? The wall's that way. The only—'

But she was gone. He was riven with indecision, but ultimately his loyalty to his wife overrode his desperation to escape and he ran after her, amazed at his devotion.

Shoving his way through the crowd he found her, the crowd proving more of a problem for her. Then he saw her bend down. Christ, she could get trampled!

He barged two elderly women out of his way and reached for Karen just as she stood up, turned round from the dead paratrooper's body at her feet, and pointed a machine gun at his stomach.

Mr Farmer relaxed. Soon it would be over. Or rather it would really begin: the feast after the aperitif. Shame he was riding a cripple but he'd see what happened on the other side. The power at his disposal now that he had usurped the scientist could well astound even him. He tried again to move but it was useless, so he lay back and stared up at the light, his creation. A beautiful monument to evil. Only minutes now . . .

Mark stumbled backwards, the gun at his stomach. He had tried to reason with Karen but her eyes saw no logic. He wondered if she meant to kill them both to save them from whatever horror was at the end, but she wouldn't respond to him. And as he fumbled his way backwards through the crowd, he could feel the light on his back and knew they were getting nearer to the centre.

'Karen, please, let me—'

She wouldn't be reasoned with. So many times he had let her take control and been grateful of it but now . . .

Mr Farmer *wallowed* in smug self-satisfaction. All his life he had been unaware of the true purpose of his powers and now he knew the truth and was going to play an even greater part. It was the least he deserved for his dedication. So many wonders would be there on the other side, and so much pain to be inflicted. *Soon, soon.*

But then he felt something. The smallest pinprick of opposition, but from where? The Izotta woman had been destroyed, Lambert had been reamed out, only those other two remained and they were no . . . *the woman.*

The woman had resolve, determination. *Decisiveness.* But how, when neither had the faintest inkling of what . . . She was coming, forcing her husband to obey her. He liked her spirit but . . . she had a weapon. So what? A gun, pathetic little bullets, gunpowder, loud bangs . . . but there was something more . . . her mind. It was still

her own but . . . but her spirit had been . . . augmented. Added to. *Entered.*
  No!

Mark tripped, fell, and found Karen kicking at his leg, urging him to get up. He grabbed at legs that were walking by and hauled himself up. He was near to tears, more terrified by his wife's loss of mind than by the imminent loss of life for both of them.

For her part Karen watched her husband rise, satisfied that he was still with her. She knew what she was going to do but didn't know why. She felt like a highly trained soldier carrying out orders without question. Fire into the hills, never mind who's there. Shoot out those windows, don't worry who may be sheltering behind them. See that man lying on the ground? Blow his brains out, never mind that you know him. She wanted to question, but every time she tried there was an agonizing pain in her temple and she didn't want the pain. She would obey instead.

Fury. Mr Farmer was awash with it. It torrented through him like a raging flood. He had to act, he could no longer lie and wait. Time was on his side but he had to be certain. He began to draw in his thoughts, retracting his control on Lambert's mind and instead focusing his energies on the dead nerves that reached below the man's waist. His mind spun itself around the broken spinal column, bridging gaps between thousands of nerve endings, forging electrical and chemical links between long-dead cells. Like an abandoned spur of a railway network, Mr Farmer created links between the man's main system and the long-disused nerve trunking. Even as he felt his power draining, he strove to make the final connections and fire the myriad impulses that would bring long-dead muscle to spasming life. The pain was unbelievable, beyond colour, but it had to be done: it was the only way he could be sure to save himself. And then the wreckage that had been Lambert's legs began to move again.

Mark turned away from his wife and walked on. The light was bearing down on them like a giant sunlamp, bleaching out all but the brightest colours on the people around them. And then they were there at the base and he stopped.

People bumped into him but he braced himself against their

pressure. Looking to his side he saw that there were fewer now and that they continued to walk until they fell into a giant hole that stretched out under the tower of light. So this was it. The boiler. The engine. *Oh God* . . . He felt his legs weaken and then his bad knee gave way and he dropped, his full weight slamming down onto it. Something ripped at the base of his thigh, and everything was ignored as his mind focused on the shattering pain in his ruptured knee. He squealed like an animal, babbling his agony through clamped eyes and clenched teeth. At that moment he would have traded death for release from that pain but as he opened his eyes, and shock fired messages of denial to his mind, he again saw the pit and regained his bearings. He had never believed pain could be willed away, but what confronted him as near as dammit did it. As Lambert had found out, pain didn't matter this close to death.

Mark looked up. The grey was descending the tower with visible momentum. There couldn't be more than two minutes left. He looked over his shoulder. Karen was standing looking into the pit, the gun pointing to his right. He wondered if he could rush her but knew his body wouldn't respond.

He looked to the right. Nothing. Just the pit and the people and . . .

There was a hand, its fingers scratching for purchase. Someone was climbing out of—

Lambert!

His head appeared over the rim, his other arm pulling him up as he squirmed awkwardly onto solid ground.

Mark tried to move to him but his legs were still rubber. 'Lambert! Lambert!' was all he could say.

Lambert, his face blank, ignored him, and instead slowly pushed himself upright onto his knees.

Mark sensed Karen walking towards the man. Good. She could help him.

Lambert looked up at her, his expression unchanging.

Mark saw his wife looking down at the man, the gun pointing at his head.

Karen saw the man but saw him for what he really was and knew what she must do.

Mr Farmer saw the woman, searched for her eyes but she still wore the sunglasses behind which he knew an enemy lurked. There was little time.

Mark saw Lambert rise to his full height. His mind told him it was a miracle that the man's legs could support him, but he also noticed that the man hadn't pushed himself up. Indeed, he seemed to *float*. Then he saw the arm that Lambert had used to pull himself out of the pit. It was broken, bone protruding through the upper arm, white shards glinting. There was no way he could have used it.

Karen followed Lambert's rise with the barrel of the machine gun, all the time keeping it pointed at his face.

Lambert tried to speak, to form words.

Must talk to her, thought Mr Farmer. *Delay would be enough. Let her share this. Offer her dreams.*

Karen heard the voice, saw a vision of the world outside. Daylight, greenery, children, peace, love. It was wonderful.

It works, it works.

Mark could see Lambert hovering fully three inches off the ground. Maybe it was something to do with the light. He tried to stand himself but his knee felt like hot lava and wouldn't co-operate.

That's it, that's it, said Mr Farmer. *Come on, you gullible bitch, watch and feel. And wait. Just seconds, just a few more seconds.*

Karen saw a wide green field, a beautiful naked blond boy, perhaps ten years old. He was lying in the sun, his body lightly tanned, while all around other children played, equally naked and equally unconcerned about their nudity. They were simply joyful to be out in the sun, feeling its natural warmth on their youthful flesh, their lives ahead of them. Karen wanted to be with them, to be young again, to find that innocence she knew she'd had once as a child, when there wasn't violence and ugliness, just plain childhood simplicity. That brief moment, that month, that summer, when sensuality is found but sexuality is still at bay, and shared wonder at naked differences isn't tainted by erectile tissue or bodily fluids. Karen stared at the vision before her, delighting in its purity.

Mark shouted at her. Whatever she was staring at, he could tell it wasn't Lambert.

Karen heard a voice somewhere over the hill, looking at her, but it didn't matter. Why rush? There was nothing to be ashamed of and nothing else to do, just enjoy sun on skin.

Seconds only and then it will all be mine.

Mark looked up. *Oh God, no . . .* the grey was descending like a lift, dimming the light of the tower, darkening the pit. It was only six floors away. Everywhere the light was diminishing and the grey crowding in, probably already swallowing stragglers behind them. *Karen*! *Karen*!

Watch it, woman, watch your pre-pubescent dream.

The boy sat up, his golden hair glistening. He shook his mane. God, he was beautiful, his eyes brightest blue, the lips thick and sensual, his body hairless.

Watch, watch, watch, said Mr Farmer.

'Karen!' shouted Mark, beginning to crawl towards her as best he could, his shattered knee scraping in the dirt, making every inch a searing torture.

The boy smiled.

Watch, watch, watch, urged Mr Farmer.

'Watch,' said another, quieter voice to Karen.

The boy opened his mouth.

'Watch,' said the woman's voice, weak and reedy but audible. 'Watch.'

The boy opened his mouth wide and suddenly a penis pushed through between his teeth from inside his mouth. Fat and bloated, it stretched the boy's mouth, its glans purple-shiny, veins like cords running its length. It pushed on and out of the boy's mouth at Karen and then the hole in its top flared open and it began to spurt.

'Watch,' said the woman.

No! screamed Mr Farmer

The penis jerked back then ejaculated blood, a long thick arc of deepest gut red onto Karen's front.

She screamed and pulled the trigger on the gun.

Mr Farmer screamed.

The woman screamed.

And nothing happened.

Mark saw Karen pull the trigger, saw it fail to respond and somehow found the energy to crawl the final few feet to her side, his rapidly swelling knee forcing him to keep his leg straight.

She was screaming and clicking the trigger but nothing was happening. Lambert stared at her, his expression unchanging, his thin legs dangling beneath him like twisted shirt tails as he continued to hover above the ground.

The grey above was four floors away, its oppressive presence smothering the light.

Suddenly Mark couldn't see. Then, remembering the sunglasses, he batted them off his face and stretched as far as his leg and pain would allow and just clicked the safety catch on the machine gun as Lambert swung at him with his good arm.

The gun chattered into life, Karen falling backwards with the recoil.

No! Mr Farmer managed before the bullets ripped into him. Too late, he realized he was too deeply locked into the physical body of the cripple and he had neither the time nor the power to extricate himself.

The bullets scythed into Lambert's stomach. Then, as Karen fell, the spray ran up his chest and into his face, the impact at point blank range exploding his head. His body crashed instantly to its knees, then fell back into the pit.

Karen's finger wouldn't loosen on the trigger and Mark had to fall beside her as the gun continued to fire into the air until the last cartridge was spent. Karen began to shriek and shake, the smoking gun dropping beside her as they both stared helplessly up at the grey roof twenty feet above them. Too late, too late.

The golden boy had died and with him the dream, and the grey sunny world was washed red and black. Karen could feel herself falling, the need to remain sane removed. All was ugly, all was unnecessary: better oblivion than a world where innocence was inevitably spoiled.

Then there was a hand. A coffee-coloured female hand. And a voice. 'Don't go. There's no need. Stay. Live. It's over. He's gone. And with him the threat. He took it with him. He should have died and the cripple should have lived but he took the cripple and now they're both dead and the light can't live on. It's over.' The voice began fading. 'Sorry for every . . .'

42

A NEW LIGHT

Karen opened her eyes. Sunshine! Blue sky. Clouds. She prayed the dream wouldn't turn sour again. To see such beauty and then—

A face came into sight, blotting out the sky. She wanted to scream but a hand covered her mouth.

'It's all right, darling, it's all right. It's me, Mark. It's over. Look, it's gone!'

She felt an arm behind her back, felt herself rising, and then she saw the truth of it. The grey *had* gone and with it the light and the pit. Instead there was a wide blue sky so huge it made her want to cry. There was beauty, there was wonder after all. She hugged the man, cried into his shoulder, thanked him, what for she didn't know but she had to thank someone for their salvation.

Mark hugged the love of his life and let himself go. The dome had vanished so fast it had barely registered but now he could see the sky and feel a breeze on his sweaty face. The perspiration was soon joined by copious tears. They were alive. *Alive*!

As her husband hugged her, his shaking tremoring through her, Karen looked around and saw the devastation and the ambling, shambling figures, their faces creased with fear and puzzlement. Some were weeping, others shouting their confusion or cursing the inexplicableness of their sudden awakening, but most were simply standing in tight knots, touching each other in disbelief, unsure of what had happened, or indeed was happening.

Mark controlled his sobbing and, taking a deep breath, gritted his teeth against the pain in his ragged knee and helped Karen to her feet. She saw the machine gun and kicked it away in disgust remembering what she had done.

'It wasn't Lambert, was it?'

Mark shook his head. 'I don't know who it was but it wasn't him, no.'

They both scanned the remains of Blair. It had been levelled. Nothing remained, just broken bricks and earth with nothing higher than a couple of feet off the ground, worse than the images they had seen of Hiroshima after the Bomb. Where the pit had been there was a circle of white ash or sand, but no tower block, no evidence it had ever existed.

Mark hobbled away from the circle with Karen and made a rough count of the survivors. Probably no more than a thousand. He wished it could have been more but they had been fighting blind. One of them came up to him, a middle-aged man in a red dressing gown, his garb and thinning white hair and beard making him look like an emaciated Father Christmas.

'What happened? What's all this?'

'What do you remember?' said Mark, patting the man's shoulder.

'Screams in the night. Hiding in my bed. Falling asleep. Then . . . here.' He looked around.

Mark pointed at the others. Girls and boys, mechanics, mothers, grocers, teenagers, salesmen, housewives, postmen, waitresses, shop assistants, artists . . . all as lost and frightened as the youngest child and the frailest pensioner among them. 'I'd start getting people together. Someone will be coming. Help those who can't help themselves.'

The man eventually nodded, pleased to have something to do. Mark guessed he was a teacher or a doctor.

'What about us?' said Karen, hugging Mark to her, both of them still trembling.

Mark hopped on his good leg as he wiped blood from her face, appalled that it was there, but oddly pleased he could see the red of it.

'Honest answer?'

'Yes.'

Mark lowered himself to the ground, careful to keep his damaged leg straight. After Lambert had fallen into the pit, the light had flared for a second, then had been extinguished, followed by an outrushing of air like a giant vacuum cleaner was sucking up the town's air

– and then total stillness. Light had slowly filtered through the swirling dust until the sky had revealed itself in all its powder blue beauty. Mark had lain on his back staring up at it for a long time, unsure if he was alive or dead. Finally assured that he was indeed alive by the stabbing in his knee, he had sat up and looked around him. His first concern had been for Karen but the sight that had confronted him had stopped him short. And it was then that he realized that if he or Karen ever owned up to playing a part in what had happened, they would be doomed to become suspects or specimens for the rest of their lives – and having stared death in the face for so long and smelled its stale breath what he wanted more than ever was the security of his wife's arms and a calm haven away from all the world's ills. For whatever the fat man's role, it had been the innate evil of human beings that had kick-started the engine that had consumed Blair. He chose his words carefully for he knew that he was doing wrong, that there was more at stake than his peace of mind, but he didn't care. And perhaps that was the darkness that lurked within him. If it was, then so be it; he could – and would – live with it.

He held Karen's hands tight and looked into her eyes. 'We don't say anything. We just become part of the crowd.'

She was surprised. 'What? What about Lambert? Jamie?'

'What about them? I know it sounds cruel . . . No one here will remember this but what if we say we do? What do you think will happen to us?'

'Happen? But it's over.'

'This is over but out there—' he nodded to the west '—it's only beginning. Think of how many have died; what's been destroyed. I mean, just think over the last few . . . *look* at it all. It's the worst disaster Britain's ever had. And only us two were awake while it happened. Imagine the shit that'll come down on us! The questions, the enquiries, the bloody media. Think of how many people must be related to all these who died; what are they going to think of us surviving? And all the time we didn't have a clue what was really happening anyway – yet we killed someone who came in here from outside to help. Explain that.'

'I killed Lambert.'

'I let go the safety, love. We both did it. And we know it was right, otherwise we wouldn't be standing here now. And neither would all these poor fuckers.'

'But *why* did we kill him? He was . . .' She remembered a voice, a vision of a naked boy, ugliness intruding . . .

'He wasn't Lambert, not then, that was the point. Someone or something had him. That's what we killed and that's what controlled the dome and the light.'

'But what if all this happens again? We have to—'

Mark shook his head. 'We have to *live*, that's all. We have to live. We don't know what happened. A fat man, a tower of light, the pit . . . Christ, even the corpses have gone. It's like there was nothing ever here. You and I killed a man, true, but where is he? And *why* did we kill him? I don't know, it was just right. It had to be done. Now try explaining that to his colleagues or his friends or the police. Let's just leave it, love, please. Let's join the others and let the authorities do the rest.'

Mark felt guilty about everything he was saying but also knew it to be true. For once he appreciated the trauma rape victims must suffer reliving their ordeal in court, except in court there was an accused while here there was nothing: no logic, no sense. They would have a hard enough time simply coming to terms with events without being in the public eye as witnesses. He knew it was heartless – but he knew it was also the only way either of them had of getting on with their lives after coming so close to losing them. They were as much innocent victims as every other survivor and deserved an equal chance of returning to normality.

Karen wanted to protest but a small voice told her to agree. So she took a deep breath and nodded, glad to let Mark make a decision for a change.

They walked across the open ground to a small knot of bewildered children huddling for mutual protection. When they saw Karen with her arms open all four of them rushed over to her and hugged her, tears mingling with smiles on every face.

Mark looked back across the town. God, it was *all* gone. In the distance he could see hills but in every direction was just a wasteland of grey nothing. Then he saw a flash, and then another. *God, what now?*

Helicopters! It was choppers – three, four of them! He scanned the horizon. Two more! Help was coming. It was over.

AFTERSHOCK

It was a Monday morning. Mark was reading the *Daily Telegraph* while he supped his orange juice and munched his way through a bacon sandwich. The room had recently been decorated and, despite the frying, still smelled of fresh paint. But he didn't mind. It was a normal smell, just like the orange juice was a normal taste, the bacon a normal meal. Karen came into the kitchen dressed in a tight blue jumper and jeans – but there was nothing normal about her voluptuous figure, however.

Mark dropped his paper and put his hand around her waist, pecked her on the cheek, then buried his face in her bosom. She ran her fingers through his hair and hugged him. Finally he let go and she sat down opposite him. She glanced down at the newspaper where she saw, ringed in red, an article. She picked it up and read it before Mark could stop her.

It was a story on attempted child abductions in Leicester. Over the previous week there had been nine bids by a couple of women to kidnap young children, none of which had been successful. She turned the paper over and found another red ring, this time a story about a series of attacks on domestic pets. Cats, rabbits and dogs had been shot with an air rifle and had then had their throats cut. The police and the RSPCA were baffled. There had been more than a dozen attacks all within a mile of each other in the last month. In a suburb of Leicester.

Karen tutted and handed back the paper. 'Why do you bother? You know the government will be monitoring all this stuff now.'

'Yes, but you can never be too sure.'

'Besides, that paper's a week old.'

'Is it my fault the weather's been lousy?'

He folded up the paper and dumped it in the swingbin, pleased to see Karen smile.

'So, what are you going to do today?' he asked.

'"Henry Hamster".'

'Still?'

'Hey, it's not as easy as you think. You try constructing an adventure for a rodent which includes fifty words beginning with "H", most of which have to be illustrated.'

'Will you include "humping"?'

'No,' she said, flicking soapsuds at him from the sink. 'But I could include "hospital".'

'In this weather?'

She looked out of the window at the sea. It was still rough. Not impossible to navigate, but unless it was an emergency not worth the risk.

'And you?' she said.

'Final chapter. Had an idea last night.'

'Surprised you had the energy left to think.'

'It was our wedding anniversary.'

'And don't my nipples know it.'

He gave her a silly grin, then explained. 'I've decided there'll be a secret passage from the diamond mine to the sheriff's office.'

'Oh, how convenient. You'll have to establish it—'

'— earlier on. Yes, I know.'

He got up, popped his morning pill, drained his orange juice, then put his plate and glass in the sink, squeezed Karen's rump and walked through to the brick-built storeroom. This was his study – Karen's was on the second floor, above the lounge and below the bedroom. He settled in front of his Amstrad, careful of his dodgy knee, and slotted in the disk of his third paperback original, *Guns Without Glory*.

Mark had given up advertising and had been living off Karen's earnings for the last eighteen months as he tried to establish himself as a writer. He had given himself two years to make it and he seemed to be on the brink of succeeding. He would never be rich in his chosen genre but he would survive, especially as escapism had come back into vogue after the national trauma caused by the inexplicable loss of Blair and all but eleven hundred of its inhabitants. Mark wrote Westerns, not because he was a particular fan, nor because they were lucrative, but because they were mythological and dealt with simple good and simple evil and had nothing whatsoever to do with the present day or reality: two things both of them had made a determined effort to avoid since escaping from Blair. After several months of keeping out of the glare of the media and under-going intensive counselling and therapy – some of it with the prescribed drugs they both continued to use – they had settled on Amsey Island off the North Wales coast.

Amsey had been home to a lighthouse that had last been used in 1968. It was half a mile out to sea, accessible only at high tide in good weather and a perfect – if oddly shaped – place to get away from the world. There were also no neighbours (whatever had caused the disaster at Blair, the presence of a population had, literally, helped to fuel it). On Amsey, there was just Karen, himself, their two dogs, several thousand seagulls and the occasional heart-pounding nightmare. It was as safe as it got – Karen losing herself in the innocent worlds of her children's books, he in a Wild West that never was – but he still checked on the outside world via newspapers to be sure.

And, medication notwithstanding and mindful of a certain Hitchcock movie, he kept a wary eye on the seagulls outside his window too.